CW01085732

Some families are haunt
haunted by their pasts. Som
are.

Joe Peterson is haunted by all three.

His parents' return from their mission, combined with a family reunion, forces Joe's kin to deal with his new life: out of the Mormon Church, out of the closet, and living with his lover Kabe. When a decades-old murder of a child lands on Joe's desk, digging into it dredges up long buried truths and festering secrets about folks Joe thought he knew – including Kabe. Joe and Kabe must lay the ghosts of the past and bring closure to a family scarred by loss to move forward in their life together.

MLR PRESS AUTHORS

Featuring a roll call of some of the best writers of gay erotica and mysteries today!

Derek Adams	Z. Allora	Maura Anderson
Simone Anderson	Victor J. Banis	Laura Baumbach
Helen Beattie	Ally Blue	J.P. Bowie
Barry Brennessel	Nowell Briscoe	Jade Buchanan
James Buchanan	TA Chase	Charlie Cochrane
Karenna Colcroft	Michael G. Cornelius	Jamie Craig
Ethan Day	Diana DeRicci	Vivien Dean
Taylor V. Donovan	S.J. Frost	Kimberly Gardner
Kaje Harper	Alex Ironrod	DC Juris
Jambrea Jo Jones	AC Katt	Thomas Kearnes
Sasha Keegan	Kiernan Kelly	K-lee Klein
Geoffrey Knight	Christopher Koehler	Matthew Lang
J.L. Langley	Vincent Lardo	Cameron Lawton
Anna Lee	Elizabeth Lister	Clare London
William Maltese	Z.A. Maxfield	Timothy McGivney
Tere Michaels	AKM Miles	Robert Moore
Reiko Morgan	Jet Mykles	William Neale
N.J. Nielsen	Cherie Noel	Gregory L. Norris
Willa Okati	Erica Pike	Neil S. Plakcy
Rick R. Reed	A.M. Riley	AJ Rose
Rob Rosen	George Seaton	Riley Shane
Jardonn Smith	DH Starr	Richard Stevenson
Christopher Stone	Liz Strange	Marshall Thornton
Lex Valentine	Haley Walsh	Mia Watts
Lynley Wayne	Missy Welsh	Ryal Woods
Stevie Woods	Lance Zarimba	Mark Zubro

Check out titles, both available and forthcoming, at
www.mlrpress.com

LAYING GHOSTS

A Deputy Joe Novel

JAMES BUCHANAN

mlrpress
www.mlrpress.com

Published by
MLR Press, LLC
3052 Gaines Waterport Rd.
Albion, NY 14411

Visit ManLoveRomance Press, LLC on the Internet:
www.mlrpress.com

Cover Art by Winterheart Designs
Editing by Kris Jacen

Print format ISBN#978-1-60820-778-7
ebook format also available

Issued 2013

The insistent ring of my cell phone made me pull it off my hip and glance at the face. I knew that name, and, honest, seeing it... well it was like a sunrise after a rain. I hit accept as I got up from my desk and ducked back into the break room. "Joe's Pizza." Hadn't clocked back in from lunch yet, so I could take a personal call, and it's not like I was all that busy right then anyhow.

Of course, I'da taken this call even if I'd been in the presence of Heavenly Father himself.

A lot of static cut across Kabe's words. "Holy shit, dude, same suck-ass joke as always." I didn't care about the tease. I didn't care that I could hardly hear him. That voice was the best darn thing to hit my ears in what felt like a million years. "You're such a dork." He might have razzed me, but I could suss out the slow, deep current of warmth under what he said.

I hadn't seen Kabe in over a week. "Guilty as charged."

I wondered if he could tell how big my grin was just by my tone. Lord I'd missed him, more than I really wanted to admit. I'd gotten used to the warmth and the smell of his body next to mine at night. I'd roll over and the absence of him would wake me up. Just coming home to an empty house, hearing my boots echo...I don't know, it dropped my heart more than I ever thought possible.

"It's been kinda, ah, quiet around without you." Never, ever thought I'd have a life like this, with someone, and I liked it more than I believed possible.

"Hey, I haven't even had time to jack-off," he laughed, "so don't tell me who's missed who."

Trust Kabe to take the conversation down to the lowest point in the stream. "So how much longer until the forestry service cuts you loose?" Mother bear, Ranger Nadia Slokum, prodded Kabe into applying for a fire crew back in February. My boy'd gone and landed himself a job—he finished up his EMT certification in early spring, got his fire-fighter's 'red card' by completing a few weekend courses and passing the final exam: hauling fifty pounds of gear through three miles of wilderness in less than forty-five minutes. His probation officer, being on board with the whole idea, gave him a letter saying that he could travel outside the county, and the state, so long as he was working a fire and checked in by phone when he was able.

"Dork." He repeated the barb, but added a laugh. "We're in Milford." Milford? That put him about an hour and a half away. "Stopped to gas up the truck and get something to drink."

"You're on your way home?" His training, plus being an experienced rock junkie and back-country camper, qualified Kabe for a minimum wage job digging fire breaks, clearing dead wood, back-cutting brush and risking his life to fight wilderness blazes. Up until now he'd logged a lot of blisters, pulled muscles and about a dozen hornet stings. Then his crew got called out for the first real fire of the season up in Great Basin National Park. He got tapped and he went: brave, gung-ho and ready for action.

"Yep. They declared hundred percent containment at about two in the morning." He sounded downright exhausted. "Started cutting crews loose just before dawn."

"Well." All of a sudden I got excited, and not just south of the border. "I'll see you when I get off work then." Boy, I sounded like a kid who found out they canceled school for the rest of the year.

"We got to put shit away in Cedar, but, yeah, our bed tonight." Oh, Lord, that sounded like one sweet promise. "Got to run." He huffed it out like he didn't much want to get off the phone either. "See you."

"Hold you to it, boy." My way of saying, *I've missed you more than I can really put into words.* "Drive safe up the mountain."

"You got it," Kabe answered before clicking off. We never actually said good-bye. That's what folks said when you didn't expect to see the other again. As first responders, nobody ever wanted to jinx nothing.

The news, though, put a bit of bounce in my step as I headed back to my desk. Made everything just a little more bearable knowing Kabe'd be home before sundown. I sat down in front of the computer. A dozen old folders were stacked in front of me and I entered the data from the open one into the national databases. Although I was back at work, Doc Snow had me on light duty. He didn't want me chasing after deadbeats on foot or jumping off walls. I understood that he needed to make sure my knee was stable after my accident, but still, my Lord, this duty equaled boring. I did get that it had to be done. Clear old cases. Link some crimes to others out there.

Still, it made me feel like a secretary not an officer.

"Hey, Peterson." The new Watch Commander came up behind me. "How are you doing on the cold cases?"

That was one of the main reasons I needed Kabe around to make things more bearable. I rolled my neck a couple of times before answering. "I'm almost caught up on what we have." I'd like to say I rose above my situation, but I really couldn't. Diamond had resigned, her kid needed twenty-four-seven home care after release from the hospital and she had to step up. I'd lost a year of pay and a rank over my relationship with Kabe. Before that, I'd been a sergeant, and the Watch Commander; all of it got pulled from me when I'd consented to my boss' discipline for messing with a guy on probation—legally in custody. But that meant they needed someone to fill my slot and I got Diamond's job.

Lt. Jared Lowell, formerly of Orem PD, took a cut in pay, and gained a lot better hours, to take my job. "Okay, what year are you back to?" While it was my own damn fault that gave him the opportunity, it didn't mean I had to like the man for it.

Even if I felt sore, I wouldn't change the turn my life took when I met Kabe.

And while Lt. Lowell didn't hit the top of my list of favorite people, I knew better than to piss in my own back yard. I made an effort to play nice. "Once I get these in," I thought a moment, "we'll have everything from about eighty-two on in all the national databases." Not like we had thousands of cold cases. Most of what I'd been reviewing were old burglaries, assaults and property crimes where the statute of limitations had run out long ago. We had a few murders, where the officers *knew* who did it, but just couldn't *prove* it. Then there were the nameless ones: the Johns and Janes buried by the county under the last name Doe who died alone in the forest or along the highway. Someone out there loved them, though, and deserved to know what happened to their kin. "Already cleared half a dozen or so cases with dental/tattoo hits and the like." Most, so far had been through the missing persons clearing houses. I suspected that the *likely matches* I'd gotten back would resolve a lot more in time. Then there were the few felons serving time that popped on DNA hits.

Mostly, though, this duty gave me a lot of time with my own thoughts. I'd be playing hunt-n-peck on the keyboard and my mind would drift off to imagining what Kabe was up to. Cooked up a lot of ways to have fun with him, you know, like we tended. This past week rubbed really raw, me missing him more than usual. I couldn't wait to see him, wrap him up in bed and forget the rest of the world existed. Well, except for tomorrow, 'cause my folks were coming home after two years in Russia serving the Church and I had to go get them from the airport.

But before and after...yeah, a lot of nekkid consumed my dreams.

Lowell's voice called me back to the here and now. "Only to eighty-two?" He settled his weight on the edge of the desk I'd been assigned to. Thick arms folded across a barrel chest, he stared down at me from beneath bushy white brows. Even his red-tinged, but grayed out, mustache seemed to twitch with irritation.

I'd pulled every old file outta the storage cabinets in our current building. "Well, that's all I've found files for." Honestly, there were a lot more boxes in evidence storage than I had files to match...most of them pressed up against the very back walls in dingy brown boxes. And look, I knew I needed to get to those, but the farther back you went, the cases meandered from slightly frostbitten cold-case to down right freezer burned. Twenty-five years ago meant locked in permafrost.

"The department goes back longer than that," Lowell reminded me.

"Yeah." I almost managed to not sound snotty with my response.

"There's got to be older files."

I knew he was right, but I protested all the same. "That's more than thirty years ago." I wanted to be out on patrol, making a difference, doing what I did best. This duty made me feel like some clerk. I hadn't spent my life training for data entry.

"And if we can clear them though the Fed's combined indexing systems," he let a heavy pause settle down between us before he finished his thought, "it's out of the unsolved and into the solved files."

"Well, I'm having trouble with some of the older stuff because we have the old style info on it and not the new format. And a lot of it is backlogged at the OME's office." The Office of the Medical Examiner for the state, where new cases took six to nine months to process. Ice cold cases, yeah, they got shelved towards when there was a bit of time when nothing much else was happening. Like maybe when Hell froze over. "It'll be a while before anyone can enter final details on those."

"Okay, but the department has existed more than thirty years." He repeated it with a little more aggravation than the first time he said it.

I tried not to let my own issues mess with trying to live with my new boss. "Yeah, and?" Cain't say I was too successful.

Again, Lowell insisted, "Where are those records?"

"They ain't here." I huffed and pushed back from the computer. "I ain't found them yet."

"Well." He stood, tapped the desk and leaned over me. "Find them."

I couldn't quite let it be. "Why? Thirty plus years...everybody's dead or long gone." I wasn't like this normally. But this was not *doing*. This was just *waiting*. Cooling my heels while someone else decided if I could go back to working at what I loved. It drove me nuts.

"Because your purpose right now," he glared, "deputy on disability Joe Peterson, is to enter all of our cold case files into the databases." He rapped a meaty set of knuckles near my keyboard. "I will drag this department, kicking and screaming, if I have to, into the twenty-first century. Where do you think old files might be?"

"Ah." I backed down a little, sorta. "Okay, up until, maybe twelve years ago, the sheriff had the old offices and county jail had cells in the new county courthouse." I probably sounded as bored as I was. "That was built in the early eighties. Maybe at the old cells in the courthouse. I think some stuff was moved into storage there along with a lot of the old county records."

"You got a phone, deputy, get on it." He ordered as he started to walk away.

There's protesting and then there's banging your head against brick walls. This argument, for me, headed towards the latter. "Yessir," I muttered, not quite giving up my attitude even if I abandoned the fight. Took me five or six different times striking out with folks who had no more clue than I did before I really thought about it. Picked up the phone one last time and dialed the maintenance office over at the county building. If anyone would know what lurked in the musty, dusty corners of the courthouse, it'd be the janitors.

Had a nice long talk with the head maintenance guy. Took a bit of cajoling to convince him why my boss' *do now* should become his problem. I finally got him to ask around his crew while I waited on hold. When he came back on the line, I got a definite *maybe* on whether they knew where those files were. It equaled better than a sharp stick in the eye.

By then it was time for me to clock out. I'd never been much of a clock watcher before I got injured. But, honest, this current assignment couldn't hardly get more boring. A few cases I reviewed caught my attention, got me lost in the reading of them, trying to think 'em through. Besides being few and far between, they tended to be solved when I entered the right data in the right place. That gave me a momentary thrill. A few others, well, I could see likely as clear as the officers handling them had as to who done it...those though, they just needed the technology to catch up to the evidence. Waiting a few more months for the old blood and other fluids to run through the DNA wringer weren't going to make 'em any colder.

The rest of the lot seemed only slightly more interesting than watching grass grow.

I shut down the computer, stacked the files on the edge of my desk, before I headed over to where Lt. Lowell sat filling out some sorta paperwork. I knew he saw me. I'd come up on him just so he could see me. He didn't, however, seem to be in any rush to acknowledge that I existed, much less waited on him. Shuffled my feet a bit, picked at a bit of lint that somehow attached itself to my sleeve and basically fussed, without really fussing, while he seemed bent on ignoring me. I'da never done that to one of my men...make 'em wait without even the courtesy of asking for a moment. And I know that what I worked on didn't rate too much on the scale of urgency, still a little courtesy never hurt.

Probably payback for my bit of lip earlier.

Finally, he scribbled his name on the bottom of the paper and grunted out a, "Yes," as he stacked it with the other sheets in his out-box.

Took a couple deep, but not obvious, breaths before I figured I could say anything without coming off all bitter and put out. "Talked to some folks at the courthouse, they think they might have some old boxes and such belonging to us." The lieutenant nodded like he listened, so I figured I'd just rush it on out. "They ain't sure, but someone seemed to recall coming across them."

"Okay." That came with him starting to write on the next form. "Head over there and see what you can find."

I didn't even rate a look. I guess neither of us was too keen on the other. Still, he outranked me and I had to explain myself. "The head maintenance guy's going to meet me day after tomorrow." When I saw his lip tighten up, I cut Lowell off. "He's got guys out sick. It's his schedule not mine. I'm going to come in part of my day off to go take care of this." Figured reminding him that I usually wasn't a thorn in folks' sides might not hurt right then. Wouldn't quite make up for some of my attitude from earlier.

"You're off tomorrow and the next day?"

"Yessir." Reminded him about that too. "It's the end of my work week. My folks are coming home from overseas. I got to go pick 'em up in Salt Lake." Just for good measure, I threw in an excuse. "Since I'm not on patrol it's not like I'm leaving y'all hanging."

"Don't have to explain." He grunted. "You're finished with your shift. I don't expect you to live here." What little of his attention I'd had up 'till then pretty much evaporated. Felt it like a slow fizzle of heat being wicked off my chest. Guess that meant I was dismissed, so I didn't even bother to say good-bye as I headed out.

CHAPTER 2

Took me about fifteen minutes to drive on home. I knew what I wanted to see at the end of my drive. Heavenly Father understood what I needed, granted me one of those small miracles in life, 'cause there it was: a beat up Toyota mini-pickup pulled up in the gravel we called a drive. Well, not the truck itself, but what it represented. My boy had come home, to our home, what we shared together.

This long, hard day might yet have a silver lining. I wanted to wrap myself around Kabe, throw us on the bed and not come up for air for hours.

Opened my front door and smelled smoke. After about two breaths of panic, I realized I didn't hear the smoke detector screeching. When I stepped on inside, I figured where the smell came from. This big ol' pack sat right next to the door and Kabe's boots rested maybe two steps beyond it.

It all reeked of cinders.

Kabe himself, well, he sprawled dead-to-the-world on the couch. Hadn't even changed out of his filthy t-shirt and cargo pants. Likely, he just stumbled in, tripped out of his boots and passed out. Hard work he was doing these days on a fire crew.

Thought of a hundred scenarios of how I'd show him how much I'd missed him around the moment he stepped through the door. And not a one of them was gonna happen with him out cold.

I knew what this kinda duty was like. Not the firefighting, but the *we're in disaster mode, everyone on deck* long hauls. The life of a first-responder. I didn't ever have to explain to him why I missed a special night. He never had to explain to me why, in the middle of getting it on, I had to un-cuff him and let him run because of the number flashing on his phone. Honestly, that he and I shared that now made each and every moment we spent together just that much more, I don't know, intense.

Trying to be fairly quiet, I headed on upstairs, got changed into a set of sweats and sneakers, and snagged a blanket out of the back of the closet. Came back down and tossed the cover over Kabe. He didn't even twitch. Then I pulled out the deposition transcript I'd gotten in the mail that afternoon, sat down at the kitchen table and started reading through it. My day already smelled like yesterday's news, almost getting into it with my new lieutenant, figured I might as well keep on with the misery.

What a mess with that whole accident and all, the one that bummed up my knee. Icy roads and a kid running from me, and what he'd witnessed his so-called friends do to one of their own. It trashed my patrol vehicle and put me out of commission for close on three months. Broken hand, surgery to reattach the ligaments in the back of my knee and a heck of a lot of physical therapy to get me to the point where I could go back to my job. And while I was back, for the moment, it weren't necessarily a given that I would get to stay.

We'd had an election the past year, the elected taking office in January. Some of the supervisors that didn't like me were out and new ones were in. I, or my lawyers, didn't have a read on the new crop yet. Could be worse. Could be better. It'd take a while to find out which.

So right now, I had my attorneys for my injuries as they related to my accident on the job, another set for what was all winding through the civil courts because of the highway pile up and a third group for butting heads with the County Board of Supervisors. Who, when this all started, weren't so keen on keeping me on as a deputy. Hadn't wanted to fuss with it that much, but my boss, Sheriff Simple, brought the lawyer whose name was first of the seven on the door to my house to talk me into getting representation.

Good thing too, 'cause I'd lost count of the number of lawsuits, insurance companies and litigants all up in it at the four month point. There was a herd of lawyers for everyone involved. Taken three days to get through their questioning of me on just the accident and now I had to go back through my testimony— all nice and bound up in a book as thick as an unabridged dictionary— to make sure it was all right. If this was all just the preliminaries, well, I didn't even want to think on what trial would be like.

After about the first hundred pages, I decided to take a break. Figured some air would clear my head, and since I was dressed for it, I went for a light run. By the time I got back, Kabe'd managed to move some; he'd rolled slightly farther into the couch. Had to chuckle at that as I headed into the kitchen to fix up something for dinner. Went simple with canned tomato soup and a grilled cheese sandwich. About the time I slid the sandwich onto the plate, I heard Kabe stumble into the kitchen. Turned around to see my boy rubbing his eyes while leaning against the back of a kitchen chair.

"Hey, good looking." Even with the pattern of the couch cushions etched into his face, days without a shower and bleary eyed, Kabe had to be the best looking guy on the planet. "Been a while." I could feel this all out loopy grin tearing my face up.

I got a big ol' yawn in response, one that almost dropped his chin to his chest. "What time is it?" He kinda breathed the words out at the tail end.

Didn't bother to check the clock since I could figure by the way the sun just barely caught the southwest corner of the big front window what the hands of the clock said. "Getting 'round about five."

He barely waited for me to spit it out before hitting me with, "Is that food?" He sniffed the air like a bloodhound tracking scent.

"No, it's just a picture of food." I teased a bit before I offered up the plate. "All yours."

I swear a vacuum cleaner wouldn't have sucked that sandwich down as fast. Two, maybe three, bites and it disappeared. The mug of soup went down just as quick. Once he'd inhaled it all, he huffed out, "Fucking A, that was good."

"I bet." On any long term call-out, including fire-lines, you were lucky if you got some sorta mystery meat sandwich a couple of times a day. Most times wilderness fighters made do with surplus army rations or tuna eaten straight out of the can; since, you know, the thankful neighbors couldn't just pull up sixty miles from nowhere and drag a pot of soup outta the trunk. "Hot food is in short supply on a fire line." I took the mug back. "Showers are few and far between too."

"Fuck yeah." He didn't sound quite as beaten down as a few moments ago.

"Plenty of hot water." I pointed towards the bath. "Knock yourself out."

While he showered, I fixed myself another sandwich. Chewed on my food as I read through a few more pages of my deposition. I sounded like an idiot with the *ums* and *uhhs*. 'Course the attorneys all did too. About the time I started to get bored again, I realized Kabe had been in the shower a pretty long time. He tended to follow the get in, get clean, get out pattern.

I poked my head in the door to the bathroom. I could see Kabe's form propped up in the corner of the tub surround. When I swept away the shower curtain, I found him sound asleep, so far still standing, his shoulder kinda wedged in the corner. I had to laugh...quietly though. "Hey, boy." Reached in and slapped his cheek. "Trying to drown yourself?"

Jerking back to somewhere resembling consciousness, Kabe mumbled, "Huh?" He blinked and kinda looked around a little confused. "What?"

Figured it wasn't worth messing with him. "You're dead on your feet." I reached in and turned off the water. "Here." Then I handed him a towel. "Head on upstairs."

Like he still hadn't quite puzzled through how I'd just appeared, at least to him, in the bath, Kabe hesitantly started to dry himself off. "You going to come up?"

"In a bit."

I got a lopsided grin off of him. "I'm naked." That made two of us with the same idea. "Been a while." He came in close, reached up, and pulled my face down into a kiss. Just before our lips met, he whispered, "Missed you."

"Missed you too." I mumbled as I kissed him long and hard. Didn't hardly come up for air for five minutes maybe.

When we finally figured we needed to breathe, he pulled back and brushed my chin with his thumb. "So meet me upstairs?" Another yawn came up while he asked it.

I matched Kabe's grin as he backed out of the bathroom. "If you insist." While he headed up, I collected his clothes off the floor and outta his pack and tossed them all in the wash. If I left them lying around, well they might just be ripe enough to get up and walk out the door. Then I dropped the dishes in the sink with some water. That equaled clean enough by my book, at least with my boy waiting upstairs for me. Took the stairs two at a time, pulling my shirt off as I went. I came up into the bedroom to one of those almost perfect sights.

Kabe had thrown the covers back. He lay across the bed, all sprawled out with one leg kinda cocked to the side. His long dick rested against his thigh and his nuts just peeked out from between his legs. Sexy. Waiting. His head turned towards the door, eyes shut like he dreamed of what would happen next. Probably did dream too, since his mouth hung open just a bit and soft snores slipped past lips I'd been waiting to kiss for a week.

Well, heck. I probably could have rousted him and Kabe'd been game. Having worked shifts similar to his last week, he needed the sleep more than I needed to get off. Got myself a pair of PJ bottoms, changed and slipped into bed next to him. I pulled the covers up then wrapped my arms around him. Early or not, this, this was what I needed too.

Just him.

Home.

With me.

We had plenty of time for everything else.

CHAPTER 3

Kabe thundered down the stairs tugging a white t-shirt over his head. A running man, sketched in rainbow scribbles, and the slogan *be yourself* graced the front. That probably would go over the heads of most folks around here. His jeans sat a little lower than they ought, but, for once, didn't look painted on. He vaulted over the back of the couch and landed with his butt in the seat. As he reached for his hiking shoes, Kabe asked, "Where you going?"

"Huh?" I pushed away from the breakfast island and hooked my thumbs in my back pockets.

Grinning, Kabe shook his head and pointed at me. "You're pretty dressed up for just heading to the gas station."

I looked down at what I had on, plain white, western-cut shirt, dark blue jeans and my nice boots; I guessed he was right. "Oh, yeah," I shrugged and rubbed my hand over the close cropped beard I'd grown while on disability, "folks get in about half past three today." My department's rules on facial hair stated it had to be neat and less than a half an inch in length, so I kept it up.

Kabe smacked his forehead with the butt of his palm. "That's right, you told me." He grabbed his phone off the coffee table and checked the face. "But it's barely ten."

"Yeah, well," I started ticking off all I had to do that morning, "Jen Cummings is gonna drop off my folks car at their place. Lacy's stopping on her way in to pick up things from the big market in Cedar, but there's a few things mom's gonna want from the little place here." Their cupboards were all empty, even to the point of not having stores put by for end times. I'd fix that next time I went down to the superstore in Cedar City.

Heaved up a sigh and kept going, "Gotta do the walk through with the real estate gal and make sure everything's squared away in their house from the vacation rental these past two years." We'd been lucky and their house hadn't sat empty much. It weren't on the lake or anything special location wise. But, it was one of what they called the *pioneer heritage houses*...built back in the 1800's and I guess that had draw. "I'm gonna get the keys back for all of it before I head on into Salt Lake to pick up my folks. You know, so I can be their pack mule for them."

"Okay." Kabe stood up, shoved his phone into his pocket, finished stomping into his shoes and came over towards me. "Let's go." He leaned in to hook his thumbs in with mine.

I had a lot of work to do and I knew he might look all rested, but he had to be bone weary. "You don't have to come with me." Wilderness fire crew work meant eighteen hour days and sleeping on the ground under your truck. After a week of that, I bet he needed a month to get back to feeling at all human.

"Yeah," he grinned up at me with one of his soul shattering smiles, "I think I kinda do."

"Why?"

Pulling his thumb outta my left pocket, he ran his hand up my arm. A little squeeze at my bicep punctuated his next statement, "Because you're going to have to tell your parents." That dropped a rock on my head. "About you and about me. And if I don't go with you, you'll chicken out."

I tried to push him off—with my words, not my hands. "You're on something...it don't have to be right then." Otherwise, I kinda liked having him pressed up against me like this.

"Yeah it does." Kabe thumped his index finger against my chest. "'Cause if you don't tell them, they're going to come home, run into the next door neighbor who's going to be all up in their face with, 'Oh my God, how are you handling your son being GAYYYYY!'"

"It ain't gonna happen like that." I might have been protesting, but in my heart, I knew he was likely right.

He snorted. "If you're lucky it'll happen like that because the other option is that asshole, Pete Sampris, is going to take his uptight ass over to their place and have a counseling session as their fucking bishop about it all." Both of us shuddered at that thought. "So whose mouth do you want them hearing it from?"

Just the mention of Pete's name was enough to tie my stomach in knots. "Get in the truck."

"See, you can be reasoned with." He laughed, disentangling himself from me. "Although, I don't know why you didn't write them and tell them what they were coming home to." As he walked over to where his light jacket hung on the wall, he asked, "Are you sure one of your brothers or sisters hasn't?"

I watched him slide his arms into the military cut jacket and thought on it a bit. I was fair certain none of them had spilled the beans. I'd have gotten a rare telephone call from Russia if someone had. The rest of my family, they'd all kinda found out in a roundabout way. Most of them used one of those big social sites to connect. I'd finally linked Kabe up as a friend and later he went in and changed my details to being in a relationship. That, added to him posting all these photos of us, together, on his page spelled it out. Probably took on about a month before someone finally put two and two together and Lacy picked up the phone to ask me what was going on.

I huffed out a breath and started towards the door. "No, I know Lacy hasn't." Tina might be the oldest among us, but Lacy's word was law in our tribe. "She told me that she and Tina talked it over and decided it was my piece to say." My guess is that Lacy played down whatever argument they'd had. "Sam just wouldn't, you know." I kept talking as we headed out to the truck. "Tucker and James, well, Tucker's still working overseas with that defense contractor so I doubt he'd say much." As I walked over to my truck, I could hear Kabe lock up our place behind me. Strange how now it was *our place*. Used to be *my place* and I couldn't even remember when that shift in my thinking started.

"I don't know." I stopped and waited for him to catch up. "Maybe their wives might be the type to gut punch like that. I got the sense offa Lacy, last time we talked, that she's kinda muzzled the rest of the family." Most folks had better sense than to get her crosswise. "See, you're not supposed to tell folks on a mission bad news, not unless it's like they need to come home 'cause someone's dying or something." I used the keys I fished out of my pocket to point at my chest. "I ain't dead."

Kabe yanked open the door on his side of the truck, stepped up on the running board and glared at me over the top of the cab. "No, you're just excommunicated."

What could I say to that? We dropped the conversation then, riding in silence for the short drive to the little market. Didn't take long to get what we needed there for my mom's fridge, plus some sandwiches for our lunch on the road. Then it was back in the truck for a short hop to my folk's place.

Pulled up in front of the stone and brick house I grew up in. Jen'd been by and left my folks' Taurus over by the detached garage. I snagged the keys off the front tire and tucked them in my pocket. Then I jogged over to catch up to Kabe on the front porch. Mrs. Adams drove up about then.

The walk through wasn't much, just made sure stuff still worked and nothing had been stolen. Not like my folks filled their place with gewgaws anyhow. They'd never been ones for collecting. Momma said it just made for more things to dust. After that, Kabe and I hauled in a few bins of photos, jewelry and other things I'd been storing for them while they were away. There was a lot more in the storage shed out back. I'd bring it in for them tomorrow, a little at a time.

While I took the box of guns and other valuables to their bedroom, Kabe rummaged through the photos that went on the mantel and started setting them out. When I came back out, Kabe stood, staring at one of the frames. "Hey, Joe?"

"Yeah?" I grabbed up a container of handmade quilts. "What?"

Kabe flipped the frame around so I could see. "This is your family, right?"

Set the bin back down on top of another. "Yep." A faded photo confronted me, one of those professional things where everyone's smile seemed to be held just a little too long. My mom and dad sat with the three older boys standing behind them.

Lacy stood on the right of my mom, Tina knelt at her knee and another girl, a toddler in one of those Raggedy Anne dresses, perched on her lap.

"Ah, three boys, three girls?" Kabe raised his eyebrows and kinda scrunched up his nose. "Is there something you're not telling me, dude?"

"Huh?" Took me a moment to process that he was teasing me about being the little girl. "Oh, sheesh, boy." I shoved his shoulder with the flat of my hand. "That was taken before I was born." Taking the frame from him, I pointed out the people in the picture. "My folks." I don't know who told my dad that his tie went with his coat, but both were straight out of the seventies. Flowered dresses on the gals and loud stripes covered the boys' shirts, all with lapels so wide they looked like wings. "This is Samuel, Tucker, James. The oldest girl is Christina, then Alice," I realized I'd probably never used anything but their nicknames, "You know, Tina and Lacy, and the little one with pigtails is my sister Rosalie."

The funny look hadn't vanished off his face. "I didn't know you had three sisters. I mean, you've kinda talked about the rest of them. What, she piss everyone off or something?"

"Naw." It was one of those things my family didn't talk about much. Upset my mom too much if we did. "She, ah, drown in Panguitch Lake when she was seven...a few months after I was born."

"Shit," Kabe hissed, "that sucks, dude."

"Yeah." I shrugged. "It was like living with this ghost around me all the time growing up." I set the picture up on the mantel with the others. "You knew this presence hovered at the edge of everyone's thoughts, but nobody wanted to admit it."

Lacy called my cell about then, just touching base, and cut my discussion with Kabe short. She and her middle girl, June, expected to hit town in about another hour. They'd straighten up, put out the rest of the family photos, and get the house ready for the folks. The remainder of my family, those that were coming in, would start showing up in about a week. Lacy figured that my folks needed some downtime to get settled before the army descended for the family reunion to celebrate their return.

Like I said, Lacy called the shots.

After I buttoned up the house and tucked the spare key up above the door for Lacy, we headed out. We drove my folks' car as my truck couldn't seat four. A few miles down the road, Kabe broke the silence in the car. "So did I tell you what happened while I was in Great Basin?"

My tease was half-hearted. "You fought a fire?" I was a little distracted by the dread of what was going to happen at the end of this drive.

"Dork." He shot me a glare. "No. For a while I was working a line and we hooked up with the smoke-jumpers from the BLM." Most of the wilderness fire fighting around here was done through the forestry service, but the Bureau of Land Management, since they owned half the acreage in the west, had their own crews. "Got to talking and well, their captain's going to talk with my captain about maybe me doing a little cross-training with them."

Knew that Kabe had done a lot of base jumping in the past. "Jump off a tower?"

"No." He grinned. "Out of a plane. Their newest guys haven't done it enough yet so they had to work regular fire crew duty. That's how I met the rest of the BLM crew."

"Oh," I muttered. "You're crazy, you know that, right?"

He just rolled his eyes and didn't answer that. Kabe and I didn't talk a whole lot more on the drive up to Salt Lake. Mostly, he punched buttons on the radio looking for something other than the re-broadcast conservative talk radio, country or the not quite pop offered to listeners where we lived. Theoretically, there were a handful of stations that served our area. Half only got reception in certain towns and all, except the public access one, were owned by the same big company.

I missed my truck's V-8 on that long stretch of interstate. Still, it gave me a lot of time to run through about a thousand ways of how to tell them what I was. I almost spooked myself out of the whole thing with some of the scenarios I cooked up. But I knew Kabe was right. If I didn't tell them, someone else would. That'd devastate them.

Not like hearing it out of my own mouth weren't likely to anyways. The church held a hard line on the whole gay issue. I'd heard some wards, on the west coast, were more open. I didn't live there and neither did my folks. This weren't going to be easy on any of us. Sometimes, though, you got to do what ain't easy because it's the right thing to do.

Me telling them was the right thing to do.

Still, every mile under the tires seemed to shrink the passenger compartment another inch. Felt like the weight of what I had to say pressed my lungs against my ribcage. Maybe I should have just wrote them. Wouldn't have been the nicest way to let the cat out of the bag, but at least then I'd not have to witness them deal with the announcement. Harder on them. Easier on me.

No.

No matter how bad it was going to be, telling them in person had to be done.

Managed to get to the airport without a whole lot of traffic and parked in short term. When I walked around the car, Kabe reached out and squeezed my shoulder. I was glad he'd come. I needed him there, 'cause I weren't sure I could get through the rest of the day without him by my side.

"It'll be okay." He squeezed again.

"I don't know." I blew out a big ol' breath filled up with worry. "Don't know as it'll be okay, but it'll be done." Couldn't stand in the parking lot forever. It'd just delay the inevitable. I swallowed hard and started walking. Kabe kept pace right with me.

We shouldered through the crowds in baggage claim, scanning for my folks' flight numbers on the displays above the carousels. Took me a bit before I caught sight of my folks. Actually, what I caught sight of first was my mom's ol' pink coat. She'd had it, or one just like it, as long as I could recall. In the two years it'd been since I'd seen them last, a little more age had settled down on her shoulders. Still, Momma's hair held a bit of straw color and she always looked put together like a proper lady. My dad was there with her. All cowboy old: lean and angular as if the sun tanned him down to worn saddle leather. A set of battered suitcases sat at their feet. We'd timed things just about right.

I called out, "Mom, Dad!" as I jogged towards them. They turned and I got smiles. "Hey, you look great." I missed them something awful. Little quiet things, like sitting down to dinner after church in their kitchen or Saturday afternoons watching college ball with Pa. Or even the glares he'd give me when I recycled that worn joke and actually called him Pa to his face... the older amongst us christened him that based on some ol' TV show.

Kinda was glad they hadn't been around to see all the fire rain down on me this year, but I was sure happy to have 'em back.

"Really?" My dad grabbed my forearm with one hand, kinda pulled me close and patted my shoulder with the other. My family, they ain't big huggers. He stepped back and palmed his face. "I think I look like I've been traveling for the better part of a week."

"Okay, yeah, you're a little haggard." I conceded as I leaned down to press my cheek against my mom's face. "How you doing, Mom?"

"Tired." She smiled as I pulled away. "Ready to be home." Kinda sweeping her gaze around the baggage area like she tried to get her bearings, she added, "Hardly remember what my house looks like."

"Soon enough you'll be home," I reassured her. Then I looked to my dad and pointed at the bags surrounding them. "Is this everything?"

"Yep." He nodded. "That's about it."

Realized my momma stared at me. "What?"

"When did you start growing," she kinda touched my face around my chin, "that?"

Sorta self conscious, I scratched at the short blond growth on my face. "This winter. Thought I'd give my face a break from shaving." When she gave me a dubious look, I changed the subject. "Let's get those suitcases to the car and get y'all home."

"Here, Joe," Kabe stepped up and grabbed up one of the larger bags by the handle. "I'll get this one and one of the carry-ons. Think you can handle the rest?"

Before I could answer, Pa asked, "Who is this young man?" He kinda looked Kabe up and down a bit. "Don't look like a skycap to me."

The butterflies I'd been carrying around in my stomach for most of the day started fighting to get out. "Sorry, my manners." It felt like they might just succeed. "Mom, Dad this here's my..." Ice dropped into my gut and I suddenly found myself at a loss for how to describe what Kabe was to me. Sifted through a few things in my head and settled on the most plain of them all. "My friend, Kabe Varghese. He's Sandy and Taylor Harding's grandnephew; living out here now. Kabe I'd like you to meet my folks, Elisabeth— Liz— and Walt."

I got a funny look. "What'd you say his name was?"

Kabe jumped in, "Kabe, like Gabe with a K." He was pretty used to folks having a little trouble at first.

"Pleased to meet you, Kabe." My dad held out his hand and Kabe took his shake. "Unusual name there."

"Yeah. My *dadaji*— grandfather— was from India so we kept the name thing going as part of our heritage."

Before we could get more into the who Kabe was and why I'd brought him along, I dumped a bag, with a shoulder strap, into his arms. "Here, grab that." Then I loaded myself up and started walking...fast. "Just follow us. We're parked in the lot."

"What the hell is in here, dead bodies?" Kabe hissed as he caught up with me. "These bags weigh a ton."

"Watch your mouth." I looked over my shoulder. My folks were, maybe, ten paces behind us. "Two years worth of stuff, that's what's in there."

Kabe also cast a glance back and dropped his volume a notch, "You going to tell them now?"

Knew what he fished for and no-way, no-how would I have the discussion right then. "Not in the middle of baggage claim, no."

"Okay," he glared at me, "when?"

I stepped out through the automatic doors and headed for the parking area. "We got close on four hours between here and home and probably dinner along the way."

He caught up to me at the parking lot entrance. "Do not leave it for the last fifteen minutes, dude." My folks hadn't made it across to the structure yet. Still, Kabe kept his voice at just above a whisper. "Just, so you know, been around for a few coming outs...not so good if you wait to have, like, the 'Mom, I love you, I'm gay and I've got to board the troop transport to the Middle East right now,' conversation."

I propped one of the bags up against the wall next to the elevator. "We will talk before that." Mumbled that out as I fished in my pocket for the car keys and hit the up button. I wasn't sure when we'd talk, but I had four hours to figure out some way to bring it up. I mean, I guess I could just blurt it out. That'd equal harsh.

Kabe rolled his eyes like he didn't think I had the stones to keep my promise. "I'll hold you to it..."

That's when my dad walked up. "What are you boys talking about?"

"Traffic." I sidestepped the question and earned a glare outta Kabe. "Wondering whether we're going to hit it on the way outta Dodge."

"Oh," was all I got. We rode up to our floor in silence. While I got the bags squared away in the trunk, my folks settled into the back seat of the car. Kabe and I piled in and we headed out.

Traffic out of town weren't that great...hit the beginning of rush hour. Don't know why they called it *rush* hour, 'cause nobody rushed nowhere on the interstate at that time of day. Kabe managed to keep my folks entertained by asking them about their mission in Russia and bringing them up to date on some of the less explosive happenings up our way. So far, they hadn't asked why I'd brought Kabe along. Maybe they just figured I'd wanted company on the long drive into Salt Lake. Plus, my folks seemed tired—content to let Kabe ask them questions but not really up to a big conversation.

It was getting on past seven when we pulled off the interstate to have dinner in Beaver. Another hour of road still sat between us and home. We decided to eat at the only real café in town: complete with dining room tables, grandma décor and waitresses that called you *honey*. Didn't take long to get our seats and order up.

Figured this was about the best time to get the deed done, but each time I tried to start moving the conversation to what I needed to tell them we'd veer off onto something else. Then the food came and that stopped any talking for a bit. Finally, we all had a few bites and weren't starving no more. I chewed on a handful of fries and tried to think of how to tell them.

Pa moved his mashed potatoes around on his plate, like he was thinking too. Then he looked up and kinda heaved up a breath. "So, Kabe, when did you move into the area?" My dad weren't the most sociable man on the planet. Not that he tried to be rude, but Pa never said much, even to family.

"This summer." Kabe answered before he shoved a forkful of grilled fish into his mouth. I swear my parents looked at him like he suddenly grew two heads when he ordered that...and asked that they leave off the rice and add more vegetables.

"Really." My mom held her own much better in the conversation game. "Where'd you grow up?"

He managed to swallow before answering, "San Francisco Bay area."

I knew I should jump in and take the reins, but my heart

just kinda seized up in my chest and my jaw locked. Felt like my whole body wanted to jump up and run.

Like nobody even noticed my quiet panic, my mom commented, "Quite a difference between there and Pangutich."

"Yeah," Kabe acknowledged, "it's a lot quieter."

"What do you do?" That was my dad's question.

"Job wise?" Kabe shot me a sour look like he realized I was letting them delay things. He didn't seem pleased. "Right now I'm on a Forestry Service fire crew." Still, he kept his tone nice enough...weren't my folks that irritated him. "Worked the ski resort this winter. Taught rock climbing before that."

"Oh." Momma smiled bright. "So that's how you and Joe met?" I guess she felt as though she'd just made the connection between this young stranger and her son. "Rock climbing?"

I choked down a bite of my chicken fried steak— what Kabe called a heart attack on a plate— and finally managed to find my voice and my balls. "Sorta, Mom." Tried to steer that bit of conversation away from the cliff it could well go off of. I'd have to get down this mountain tonight, but better to do it slow and steady then jumping into a free fall. "Actually, we met 'cause there was a fall out in the back-forty of the Harding ranch. Turned out the guy actually pushed his wife off a cliff. Kabe helped with that recovery and we sorta hit it off from there." Felt like a wolf circling a bear. I knew I needed to jump in and get this thing done, but I also knew I wasn't going to come away without getting torn up myself. "We've been doing a lot of stuff together since then, have a lot in common." Just had to work myself there, inch by inch.

"So, you live out at the Harding Ranch?"

"No." Kabe launched another paint peeling glare in my general direction. "I did for a bit, but I'm living in Panguitch now."

Pa seemed to mull that over before asking, "Whose house are you renting?" Houses didn't go on the market much in Panguich. Folks tended to own 'em and rent 'em out since most places round here sat with the *for sale* signs in their yards for years on end.

My mom gave a little laugh. "Maybe he's been taking care of our place, Walt, while we were gone."

"No." Kabe hadn't left off his staring at me. "I'm living with Joe."

"Ahh, yeah, he's staying with me." Kinda picked at my fries as I said that. Nervous energy and all.

"But you don't have a room for a renter." My mom chided me as she cut her chicken into precise little portions. "Well, I guess that room you used for storage had bunk-beds in it when you moved in...you gave those to Lotti Hall for her girls, right?" Without waiting for my answer, she smiled up at Kabe. "I hope Joe ain't charging you much for that. As I recall, a twin-sized mattress and a nightstand were all that fit in there."

It was my turn to stare at Kabe. "No." Figured my expression looked all helpless. "That's still the pantry." This weren't how I wanted this discussion to go. Kabe shot me a look back like he wanted to know what I was waiting on.

Momma shook her head. "You don't make him pay to sleep on the couch?"

All through this, Pa seemed to catch wind that something was up between Kabe and I. He shifted his eyes, looking at us in turn, his mouth tightening up like he tried to puzzle through our thoughts. Finally, he rocked back in his chair and crossed his arms over his chest. "Why are you boys trading glares back and forth?"

I swallowed. Then swallowed again. "Mom, Dad, he lives with me." This might equal the worst place to cross the stream, but at least we'd all be on the other side in a few minutes. Almost whispered out, "He sleeps in my room." Didn't try and whisper, it was just all the volume I could manage with my brain screaming *no* and my heart trying to beat its way out of my chest.

Momma, bless her heart, seemed confused. "Where do you sleep then?"

I could tell by the shock crawling over my dad's face that he sussed up exactly what I meant. My shoulders sagged and I dropped my gaze to the plate in front of me. "In my room."

Momma ran her napkin through her hands, like she was frustrated with me. "You got rid of that big ol' bed of yours?"

I couldn't tell them this way, but there was no way not too. Like a rappel, once you've stepped off the lip of the cliff there's only one direction to go. I reached out for the only belay I had, "I cain't do this Kabe."

"You do it or Pete'll do it for you." He hissed back.

"Pete will do what?" Now Momma sounded annoyed.

That's when Pa dropped the front legs of his chair, hard, on the wood floor. Made us all jump an inch. "Come out straight and tell me why you look like you've just swallowed a porcupine."

"I'm…I'm," the word lodged like a pine cone in my throat. "Ah heck, Kabe's my boyfriend."

My mom's scowl made me feel all of five again. "That's not a funny joke, Joseph."

"It ain't no joke." I couldn't look up at them. I kept stabbing the food on my plate, chopping it into smaller and smaller little chunks. "I wanted you to hear it from me before, well before we get home and you catch wind of the gossip."

"What, exactly, are you trying to say?" Pa's growl froze my gut.

Took every inch of will I had to get the next few words between my teeth. "Dad, I'm gay."

A little strangled sound passed my mom's lips. My dad's face went hard. "What'd you say?"

"I'm gay."

"Who all knows?" Momma hissed out the question like it could bite her.

I rubbed my temples with the thumb and middle finger of one hand. "Everyone." Kabe hadn't said nothing, but he moved his leg up against mine...using the touch to let me know he was there for me.

My dad had covered his eyes with the palms of his hands, bracing himself by his elbows on the table. "So let me see if I've got this right." He looked between his fingers and sucked on his cheek. "My son is a homosexual who's chosen to act on it and live in sin with another man. Does that about sum it up?" While Momma made me feel like a little child, disappointing my dad could scare me back to before I was born. All I managed was a nod. He thought a moment more and then growled out, "What does the Ward have to say about this?"

Felt like I was gonna puke right there in the middle of the restaurant. "I'm out." A nervous laugh threatened to bubble up with the bile when I realized I was really out now.

My mom hadn't done more than sit there, all pale, and shake. Guess she'd just let my dad take lead in this interrogation. "What do you mean?"

"They held a Bishops' Court." I hadn't fought it. No reason to. Once the church decides to convene one, the decision is already written in stone. "They excommunicated me."

"Good Lord, Joe." Pa's face went all slack as his hands dropped on the table. "And you waited 'till now to tell us?"

"What, you think dropping that bomb in a letter would have made it better?" I dredged up some grit or maybe it was just defensive sarcasm, "'Hey, your house is fine, everyone misses you and by the way, I've shacked up with a guy, been excommunicated, suspended from my job and tore up my knee in a car accident... hope your Christmas was better than mine.'"

"You were in an accident?" Of course my mom would focus on that. Heck of a lot easier for all of us.

Did break the tension in my chest a little. "Yeah, Mom." I huffed out some of the worry I'd been holding in. "I'm fine now." Took a moment to reassure her. "Wasn't nothing big."

Kabe rolled his eyes. "Having all the ligaments torn off the back of your knee...that's not nothing." Out of all everything, he chose now to jump in.

"Put a sock in it," I snapped at him. There were a lot bigger fish to fry right then. "I'm fine. I'm back to work."

My dad launched us right back into the first subject. "What did you do to him?"

"Excuse me?" One of Kabe's signature shoulder rolls accompanied his almost sneer as he jerked back. "Do? To? Him?" Took him maybe a full minute to get those three words out. Most times Kabe let nastiness roll off his back. With Pa coming at him direct though...Kabe'd fight back.

I couldn't let that happen. Kicked Kabe under the table and snapped, "Dad." It was my turn to growl. "Nobody did nothing to me, least of all Kabe."

That's when my mom stood up. "I don't think..." She reached for her coat. "I think it's time to go." Her attempt at a forced smile hardly worked. "Joseph, get the check." She waited for my dad to stand. "We'll be at the car. It's time to go home."

As they walked away, I thought I might just dissolve into a puddle of Joe ooze. Kabe reached over and rubbed my back with the knuckles of one hand. I might have said something to him, but the waitress came up behind us.

"Are we done?" She burbled. "How was everything?" Both Kabe and I kinda turned towards her and I guess she caught our moods offa our faces. "Right." Her smile faded away. "I'll get the check."

CHAPTER 4

The last hour of our ride home felt more like six. You could taste the stale, tinny tension in the car. And nobody said a darn thing. All of us just sat there in dark, stony silence with nothing to keep us company but our own thoughts. I wondered if my folks' minds roiled around as much as mine. Figured they probably prayed— deep and hard —searched their souls for what this all meant. For them and me and our whole family. The Word of God, it's where my kin always looked for answers.

All the things I'd imagined hadn't lived up to the absolute mess I'd made of telling my parents. Went down both better and worse than I'd ever anticipated. Frankly, I was surprised my dad hadn't dropped dead from a heart attack right there at dinner. Still felt like I might puke at any moment from all the pent up stress of the day.

At least the butterflies flew the coop hours ago. Now my gut just bubbled with the acid of the shame my parents would be suffering through. I'd spent years of my life coming to terms with myself and Heavenly Father. But here I'd gone and dumped them off in the edge of a cliff without a rope or nothing.

I'd never wanted to do this to them. That's why, up until I met Kabe, I'd kept it all a secret...something they just didn't need to know. Expected them to go to their graves never having known that about me. And maybe, if Kabe and me hadn't been indiscreet, joking around where someone could overhear, well, then I might have been able to ease them into the same understanding I'd come to. Introduce them to Kabe, let them get used to him being around—

I stopped myself. No sense letting my thoughts go down through that round of what ifs.

One thing kept me sane. Out of the corner of my eye, I'd catch a glimpse of Kabe's face. He leaned against the passenger door, half turned toward me. Every so often, the lights of an oncoming car lit up his eyes. The only way I survived that ride was the little flashes of sympathy I caught off him. He didn't say nothing. What could he say, with my parents all of a foot behind us? Still, I knew he was there and I knew he watched me. That was enough right then.

After that eternity, we turned off the road into my folks' drive. My dad barely waited until I shifted the car into park before jumping out. He jogged over to help my mom as I switched off the ignition. Kabe reached over then and patted my leg. "The hardest part's over."

I snorted out a laugh. Wasn't a pleasant one. "Not by half." The night might have been over, but now I had to spend the rest of my life dealing with the fall out. Heaved up a sigh as I unbuckled. "Help me get the bags."

"Okay." Kabe scrambled out of the car and met me at the trunk. I loaded us both up with bags. "Ready?" His smile flashed, backlit by the low glow of the trunk light.

"No." I almost swallowed the word. "But we're already rappelling down the mountain." A cold breath of spring mountain air filled my lungs. "Cain't stop now, even if I wanted to."

I guess either Lacy or June must have seen us pull up, because the front door popped open. "Dad! Mom!" Lacy stepped out onto the porch. Her wheat colored hair was pulled back off an angular face. "Welcome home!" She beamed as she jammed her bony fists into the patch pockets on her sweater jacket. It might be spring, but that didn't mean nights weren't chilly up here at about sixty-five hundred feet above sea level. "How was Russia?" Plus, I swear, a half-starved coyote carried more meat on its bones than my sister ever had.

My mom stepped onto the low rise. "Different." A soul weary voice answered my sister. Momma leaned in to hug Lacy. "Very beautiful and a little bit sad." As they stepped apart, my mom rubbed her eyes. "I think I'm..." Then she glanced back at me. I couldn't quite catch a read on her face with the light coming from behind her. "I think I need to lie down some." I might not have seen it, but I could likely tell you that she must've looked pained. She patted a quilted bag with little Russian dolls on it that someone probably made her and that probably held her dog eared copies of the standard scriptures: The Bible and Book of Mormon. "Think on some things." She'd be looking to God's word to help her work through her thoughts that night.

Lacy pushed open the door to let Momma through. "June just made up the bed." She kinda leaned into where the warm lights of the living room threw angular shadows across her cheeks. "June, sweetie," she called out, "come help your gran'ma."

June's muffled reply came from somewhere in the house. I caught the voice but not the words as I followed my dad towards the door. I could hear Kabe crunching through the gravel behind me. My dad just jammed his hands in his hunting coat and stared at his feet as he walked.

Pa didn't say nothing until he was right up on the porch. Then he stopped and glared—at Lacy. "You knew about your brother?" He glanced back at me, his face all set hard. "About him and that boy?"

Lacy sighed like she didn't no more want to discuss this with him than I'd wanted to tell them earlier. "Yeah, Dad, I did."

Almost felt as if the rest of the world couldn't hardly breathe with how heavy everything got between them with her answer. Pa shifted, got more tense even than before. "And you didn't say nothing?"

I hated to put her in that position. We'd all gotten sorta bound together in this conspiracy of silence. I mean Lacy was the one who squashed any of our tribe talking, but it was my fault she'd had to.

I'd never wanted to do this to any of them. I wished there was a way that I could unwind this tangle and save them all the hurt. I accepted the consequences of what I did and I'd never give up what I had with Kabe, but still. It's one thing to know that the dirty looks, the threats and the folks that just didn't want nothing to do with you no more were all because of choices you'd made. I could hold my head up and stare 'em down knowing that.

But my family'd all be getting that, and then some, from things they had no control over. People'd speculate that, maybe, my folks coddled me too much. Rumors would flow about my hand-me-down bike, when I was little kid, being more purple than blue. Whispers of what sin was in our house that *caused* this in me. Stupid things. Hurtful things. A thousand little bullets of hate dredged up by a small town.

I could handle what came my way, but I couldn't protect them from it all.

Lacy's sigh pulled my attention back to her. She wasn't one to back down, even from our dad. "It wasn't my piece to say, Dad."

"But you knew." He huffed and shoved his hands in his back pockets. "Do the rest of them know?"

"Yeah." She nodded. "We all know."

Looking over his shoulder at me and then back at my sister, my dad heaved up a hard breath. "And you thought this way was better?"

"I knew it would be hard, no matter what." Her voice was sad, but not apologetic. "We all thought it would be more honest if you heard it from Joe." She rubbed her hands together. "Then it's not gossip."

Pa just tightened up his mouth. As he walked on past her, he muttered, "This ain't good, it ain't honest."

Once he was through the door, I managed to breathe. "Hey, Lacy."

"Hey, Joey." She reached out and swatted my nose with her fingers. "How you doing?" She was one of the few folks that I let call me Joey anymore. Sometimes, well, it felt like Lacy was as much my mom as Momma. She'd taken care of me most of my childhood, 'cause my mom suffered through a lot of blue periods after Rose's death. Probably wasn't the easiest thing for Lacy to have to deal with, you know, being all of nine years older than me.

I managed to smile some for her. "I've been better."

"It didn't go well?" Her voice held a boat load of sympathy I wasn't sure I deserved.

I dropped the bag I carried, held my hand out, open, and sorta gestured at where my dad had gone. Finally, I found my voice, "On a scale of one to five? This equaled a train derailment."

"Really?" She sounded more understanding than surprised.

"Freight train." I rolled my eyes. "No dead bodies, but really messy."

"I don't know how you can say the stony, silent treatment is messy. Cold. Brutal. Not messy." Kabe let go the bags he dragged and leaned against the porch post. "All in all though, I've seen worse coming outs."

I laughed—one of those un-amused sorts of laughs. "Worse?" What could be worse than this evening?

"Yeah," he snorted, "your dad didn't stand up from the table and announce to the whole restaurant that he no longer had a son. Your mom didn't start screaming that you'd killed both your parents. No fist fights. No blood." He punched my arm. "That leaves some hope."

Lacy's eyes went wide. "People do that?"

"Hell, you know." He shrugged and pushed away from the pole. "I've heard of parents threatening to kill guys who came out."

"That's awful." Crossing her arms over her chest, Lacy shuddered.

"Happens." He shook his head and smiled. "Not everyone believes in unconditional love."

"Shame." Lacy mimicked his moves. Then she held out her hand. "By the way I'm Lacy."

He shook her hand. "Kabe." When they let go, he tucked his hand in his front pocket. "I figured you had to be Lacy." He knocked my arm with his elbow. "I'll get the rest of the stuff." We'd just pulled out the biggest bags first, left the carry-on stuff for a second trip. Those bags were darn heavy to drag over uneven ground.

"Sorry." I apologized as Kabe headed over to the car. "I should have introduced y'all." Lord, I'd completely misplaced my manners. "My mind's just kinda—"

Lacy cut in. "Distracted." The word got a counterpoint of the car trunk slamming a few feet away.

She always kinda knew my mind. "Yeah." Of course, right then a half blind rabbit could have known how frayed I was.

Rubbing her hands over her upper arms, she asked the question all women of my acquaintance seemed to think was a cure all. "You hungry, have y'all eaten?" Like food fixed everything. "I can fix up some sandwiches or something."

I did not really want to go inside right then. "Had dinner in Beaver." Even if'n I'd been starving, I'd have come up with an excuse. I gave up a rueful grin and added, "That's when I told the folks."

"Oh, my Lord." She covered her mouth with one hand and just stared, wide eyed, for a moment. "You had to spend an hour in the car with them, with Dad, after that?"

"Yep." We all grew up with the man, knew his moods. He never got mad. He just became disappointed, gave you the silent treatment. Momma, well she was Molly Mormon through and through—she followed her husband's will.

Kabe'd brought the rest of the bags up to the porch at that point. "Happy, happy, joy, joy there." He teased as he sidled in behind Lacy, opened the door just wide enough that he could move them inside the house.

Lacy swatted his shoulder. "June and I can get those in the house." Still she moved over a bit so he could finish. I passed over the two bigger ones we'd brought up first.

That last task done I handed over the keys to the Taurus. "Okay, well it's late." I dug my truck keys out of my pocket. "We ought to be getting."

"Night, Joey." She smiled. "I envy you."

If she weren't my sister, I'da wondered what she'd been smoking. "Envy me?"

"Yeah, you get to go home." Lacy jerked her thumb over her shoulder. "I have to go back in there and deal with the cold shoulder and accusations of hiding things." After a sigh, and another little smile she whispered, like it might be naughty, "It may be time for a bubble bath, a romance novel and early bed."

"Night, Lacy." I stepped in and gave her a quick hug. "You'll do fine."

She put her hand up against my face. Stepping away, she reassured me, "So will you, Joey. So will you." Lacy went back in the house at that, shutting the door on us and the night. The chill of the air dropped a notch or two just with the fading of that light. Right then I didn't know whether that door would ever be open to me again. I didn't think my parents would be ones to cut me off complete, but honestly, I didn't know for sure. The next few hours, days would be a silent, personal war of prayer and pondering and feelings and what was more important: scripture or family.

Not much I could do to help them on that. I turned and tugged on Kabe's sleeve. "Come on, boy, let's go home."

As we trudged toward my truck, Kabe slung his arm over my shoulder and leaned in kinda close, "It'll be okay." His voice was low and reassuring. "Your family loves you. You've always told me that." A few more steps, with me not responding, Kabe took his knuckles and goosed my side. "Hey, your sis is right, at least we don't have stay here tonight."

I set my hand on the side of his head and pushed him away. Not hard. Not mean. Like I was funning some. After all, Kabe just tried to lighten my spirits. I didn't think he could manage right then, but I gave him points for the effort. When he caught my hand in his and sorta wrassled my grip, it brought us eye to eye. There, reflected in the stars in his gaze was all heaven wheeling around us. No matter what happened today or tomorrow or the next, what I had with him was good and right. It had to be.

CHAPTER 5

Kabe nuzzled my chin and the whiskers that grew there. "I don't care what your mom says, I like it." He snuggled up against my side, his skin warm against mine under the sheets.

"Actually," I pointed out, "she didn't say one way or t'other."

"Okay, yeah, dude. She didn't *say* a damn thing...her body language screamed it."

"It's kinda a shock." I'd actually started the beard because, after the accident, it just hurt too much to stand at the mirror and shave. "I never had nothing like it before." It was a look I'd always liked. Enough of my inner life didn't comport with church views so I'd felt constrained not to try it, maintain my outward appearance in line with expectations. "Most LDS men keep clean shaven." Weren't a rule or nothing, but the church discouraged men from growing facial hair; read too much as rebellion and counter culture to sit easy on most Mormon minds.

He settled his head into the crook of my shoulder and used his finger to tease the whiskers on my chin. "So why'd you grow it?"

Sent little shocks down my neck, him playing like that. "Well, I ain't in the church no more, so why keep to that standard?" I sighed; this wearied, hassled sound that wormed its way out of my chest. "My biggest secret is out and it's a heck of a lot more massive than this fur."

Like he tried to distract me from my darker thoughts, Kabe purred, "It's sexy as fucking hell."

Couldn't help but grin. "If you say so." Rolled my head to kiss his forehead.

"I know so." He cupped my chin with both hands and then ran them back along my jaw. "Want me to show you how fucking sexy?"

"Show me?" I drawled out the question.

He tipped his head up to brush my lips with his. "Ride you like the roughshod mountain man you are." Came out as a hot whisper.

"You're going to ride me?" Just the suggestion tented up the boxers I'd gone to bed in.

All wicked, he grinned and got up on his knees, the sheet sliding off his back. "Giddy-up." Kabe threw his leg over my hips. His hand landed up near my shoulder as he straddled me. As he wiggled his pelvis down against mine, his hard dick slid right into place next to my stiff prick. 'Course there was two layers of fabric between us and that just wouldn't do.

Hooked my finger into the elastic of his sexy little briefs. "Saddle up, boy." I don't think he didn't own nothing that had more than a couple square inches of coverage over his ass. Not that I minded all that much. I used that grip to wiggle the shorts off his tight rear end...I swear he had divots where his various femoral muscles met the gluteus maximus. If he sat down in a chair too fast he'd bounce himself right out of the seat.

Kabe rocked forward, lifting his hips off mine, leaning in to kiss me. I met his lips, all warm and needful. Guessing mine felt just the same. Kabe dug his hands under my t-shirt. Sent sparks shooting under my skin as he ran his fingers through the fur on my belly and up on my chest. Me, I worked that scrap of fabric off his butt. The elastic hung up on his hard prick. I just kept pulling, tugging his meat back and down with the pressure. He groaned a little, ran his teeth across my bottom lip. Lord, I loved that feeling. Him all worked up like that.

Then his dick popped free, felt it as the fabric slipped away, heard the little smack of skin on skin. Kabe reached back with one hand. Kinda got in my way some, but with three hands and him twisting and turning, me almost getting a knee in my balls, we somehow managed to get him bare-assed nekkid.

With all that, I never broke that kiss. I was desperate to have him. It was like I hadn't seen him in ages. I tasted his mouth, forced my tongue between his lips. Figured heaven felt something close to this and if it didn't, I weren't sure I ever wanted to go.

Since he was all undone, I figured I might want to join that party, especially if I wanted to be ridden. Kept sucking on his lower lip, running my mouth over his, as I forced my boxers down. Kabe caught on to what I was about and helped some. Least when he wasn't trying to touch everything else. Every time his fingers slipped over my dick, I hissed. I wanted him bad. Couldn't believe it'd only been eight days or so of him not being here. Felt like forever. When I finally managed to kick off my boxers, I grabbed his butt and gave it a good hard squeeze. Pulled him into my body. The weight of him, on top of me, felt right, natural and just pure wonderful.

Having our dicks sandwiched together didn't hurt none either. We rocked that way for a bit, just rubbing. It worked heat up into my bones. I wanted him. I'd missed him. Found myself mumbling it in his ear, "I missed you."

"Ditto," came out with a long, drawn out groan.

"I want you." I didn't sound any more in control than he had.

Felt Kabe shift, heard his hand smack the nightstand. He reached across my body and yanked on the drawer. After a bit of fumbling and cursing, I guess he found what he wanted. He reared back, got up on his knees. Figured I'd take that moment to get my t-shirt on off. Then I ran my hands up his thighs. Kabe grinned down at me. He upended the little bottle over one hand and squeezed out lube onto his fingers. He offered up a smirk before reaching behind himself and pushing the lube into his butt.

Watched while he got himself all good and slicked up. He licked his upper lip and I mimicked his move. Tasted anticipation in the sheen of sweat on my skin. All the while, I rubbed his thighs. That warm skin sliding under mine sent shivers up my arms. "I'm waiting." I growled it out. I could have played with that long fine dick of his, but this was Kabe's show. I planned to just relax and take it all in.

"I'm ready." He purred back as he snapped the lid shut on the little bottle and tossed it on the sheets. He took a deep breath and smiled big. Then he grabbed my dick with his slicked up hand. I shuddered as he touched my aching prick. Thought I might have even hissed a bit. Didn't much care, 'cause there he was rubbing my head against his tight hole. He started rocking back, little by little taking me in. What I wanted to do was just grab hold of his middle and slam my dick on up inside. Held myself back, like I said, it was his show.

When my head popped on through into the inferno of his body, I thought I might just lose it then and there. I didn't, but I couldn't believe how intense it felt. As good as the first time we'd messed with each other out in the middle of nowhere in the back of my truck and me all desperate for him. I don't think I'd ever stop being desperate for him.

Kabe let me go and leaned forward a bit. Then he started rocking, driving his ass down on my cock. There's times I'd rammed him hard, 'cause I knew he could take it, but I'd never done him this hard. It made me throw my head back and just groan. Like a pile driver in reverse. Slamming down, impaling his ass on my dick. Good Lord, he was intense. I squeezed my eyes shut and just road the waves of heat and chills streaming through me, twisting my nerves all sideways.

"Oh, fuck." Kabe hissed it out like his teeth were clenched hard. "Fucking shit."

Managed to open my eyes and really drink him in. Few things could look so fine: his dick bouncing between his belly and mine. Balls mashing up under him every time he slammed on down. Little drops of sweat ran along the edge of his ear and between his pecs. And that hot velvet caress of the inside of his body. He was a wild man, jamming himself on my prick, harder than I'd have done it to him. At least to start off. Get me going and I could break concrete with my jackhammer.

I grabbed at his arms and he sorta fought me a bit. Then he laced both sets of his fingers into mine. His weight came forward, pushing my elbows back into the mattress. It gave him purchase, using the strength of my forearms and his so that he could move even harder and faster. I could feel his palms shaking against mine.

Pushed my feet up so my knees were bent behind him and spread out just a little. He came forward onto my hands even more, put more weight on his knees. I added my thrusts to his rocking. I swear you could have heard the smack of our skin meeting a mile down the road. Mingled all hot and heavy with his filthy whispers and my grunts. I couldn't take it like this no more. I used my grip on his hands to yank him down on my chest. Then I rolled us over, almost off the bed.

My dick popped out of his hole, but I'd remedy that shortly. Got myself up on my knees, caught up one of his own over my elbow and forced his leg back. That opened him all up for me. I leaned over and slammed back into his ass.

Kabe arched his back and yelled out, "Fuck yeah!"

Pinned one of his hands under mine. He reached down with the other and started pumping his dick. I loved watching him jack himself off. His face went through a thousand little expressions from pain to pleasure to things I just couldn't put a name on. I started to slow down some, so I could watch him more.

"No." Kabe's eyes looked wild. "Hard, fuck me hard."

"Okay." If that's the way he wanted it, I'd give it to him. I pounded him like my life might end if I stopped. So hot. So soft and tight all at the same time. His ass just took everything I was giving out.

I slammed him so hard that each time I nailed him deep Kabe grunted out, "Fuck." That nasty word of his drove its fingers into my spine and yanked all the sense outta my head. I dropped my head down and my mouth came up against the arm he used to stroke himself with.

Didn't even think on it, just opened up and closed my teeth down hard on his flesh.

Kabe yelled and started jerking. The flavor of bitter copper seeped into my mouth. His blood. Put my mouth over the wound and sucked. I could taste him cumming, I swear it. Changed the flavor of his hot blood oozing over my tongue. Mixed all wild with the salt sweat off his skin.

With all that jumbling up my brain and the wild fire ripping through my dick and balls, I lost it. Felt the heat drive on through my cock like a landslide pulling all my senses along with it and leaving me a broken, twisted mess at the bottom. I shook my head and got some of my sense back. Looked down to see my own cum welling around the crown of my dick where it just barely penetrated Kabe's hole. I don't think I'd ever seen anything quite that hot. Hot 'cause it was us together and nothing between us.

I sat up, twisted a bit and flopped back onto the bed. Both of us just lay there panting; our hips and shoulders meeting and making it feel like neither of us could breathe without the other. I could feel the loopy grin cutting cross my face.

Kabe laughed. "Wow."

"I rate a wow?" I sounded like a drunk with my words all slurred. Still kinda reeled although a little image flipped past and reminded me of something. "I bit you." I said it more to make it real to myself than anything else. "We ought to get that fixed up."

Kabe rolled over and threw his arm across my chest. He kinda nuzzled into my armpit, working his mouth around the skin. I shuddered with the way it set my nerves off, pulling all the chills from having just shot my wad a moment earlier up into my chest. "In a moment," he mumbled. "I just want to be boneless for a bit."

That sounded right fine by me.

CHAPTER 6

Kabe pulled up in front of the courthouse. I swung outta his truck and then leaned back into the cab. "Give me an hour or so, I should be done by then."

I got a big smile. "No problem." He needed to pick up our haul from this local, kinda hippy-dippy food co-op thing. "I'm going an hour early to volunteer." It revolved around eating what grew in season and local. "Of course you just make me do all the hard work, while you're hanging out in an air-conditioned building." He'd dragged me along once to help portion and pack. The actual work went fine, a few of the folks I had to do it with, well that got a little testy.

You know, I like my meat and don't think pot should be legal... call me ol' fashioned that way.

"Okay." I grinned back at him. While I teased Kabe about the whole thing, I actually was kinda on board with the keeping it local and getting it cheap. I'd even ordered one of the crates for my folks. "Call me when you get done. I'll hang out and we can run whatever files I find to the station." I liked the program, I just didn't want to interact with some of the other participants all that much. Of course, the rules asked that you help out once in a while. I usually did my part by taking the leftovers 'round to folks who needed a bit of a hand.

He saluted. "Will do."

I shut the door and pounded on the side of his truck as Kabe pulled away. Then I jogged across Main Street. Since this equaled official business, but I weren't on duty, I wore the not quite duty uniform of a polo shirt with embroidered department logo on the chest and a pair of jeans. 'Cause everyone around these parts already knew me, I just carried my badge in my pocket. Wasn't armed or nothing neither; Kabe didn't like me carrying my piece in his truck. Once I got in the building, I headed to find the maintenance chief. Had to explore all through the building to find him—the new courthouse and county offices were attached to the historic part of the building. Made it a bit of a maze.

Found him up on the second floor of the old courthouse coming out of one of the rooms. Knew that large frame, bald head, and swaggering walk. "Hey, Duncan," I called out to catch his attention.

"Afternoon, Joe." Duncan turned and nodded, holding out his hand to shake mine. As I took his grip, he asked, "You sure you want to go digging through all the junk stored around here?"

"Don't have much choice." I fell into step with him. "New boss wants it done."

"Alrighty then. I was gonna have Bill help you out on this one. He's the one who recollected he saw the stuff, but he said something disagreed with him this morning so I sent him on home." From his tone, I kinda got that what disagreed with Bill weren't nothing he ate. Oh well, I'd been learning just to let that water roll right off my back.

"Where do we start?"

"Old cells in the basement." He shrugged. "Mostly record storage now days. That's where Bill thought he ran across it. Said he saw three or four boxes marked sheriff."

"Great," I grumbled. Not the nicest place to spend my morning.

Duncan held out an old jail key. "Last one on the end." As I took it he grinned. "Hope you don't mind if I don't join you, but I got other things to do."

"I understand." Tucked the key in my front pocket. "My cross to bear on this."

He nodded and took off. I headed on downstairs. Once I got down there I had to let myself into the cell block with the big, old fashioned key. The first cell they kept cleared out for short holding periods during court proceedings when they didn't want to go through the whole rigmarole of transport back to the new jail. From there, I threaded my way between old desks and office chairs stacked in the corridor. Luckily, it was pretty wide; meant to keep an officer walking the block outta arm's reach of the inmates. Most of the other cells contained file cabinets and outdated office equipment. In county government, you never wanted to throw nothing away. You never knew when you'd need it and whether you'd have the budget to replace it. Got to the last cell. Same kinda junk occupied its confines. However, stacked on the old bunk frame at the back were three cardboard boxes with Garfield Sheriff scrawled on their sides.

The first two I opened up didn't hold much more than some promotional material and old desk junk. We actually might be able to use some of the file trays and letter sorters in the new building. Paper likely'd end up trashed. I carried those out into the hall to take back to the station for sorting later. Went back in for the last carton...one of those old banker boxes. Cracked the lid enough to figure it contained files, although I wasn't sure of what. The light back there, well terrible didn't equal the half of it. I picked up the box of files to carry it out into the hall where I could see better. The dust off of it made my nose twitch, brought up this need to sneeze.

Started to snuffle it back when this big ol' brown spider, all scrabbling legs and the size of my badge, ran across my hand. "Holy—!" I jumped, bumped my butt against the bars and tossed the box away from me. Files and papers went everywhere. Didn't care. I'd been bitten by one of those nasty Hobo Spiders before. Stomped a couple of times trying to smash the darn thing. Fast little bugger, it scurried into a hole in the bricks, the kinda places they liked to hide: crevices, cracks, woodpiles...underneath boxes that hadn't been moved in ages.

Poisonous critters. Everyone worries about widows and recluses, but a Hobo once gave me a quarter-sized sore that took six months to heal up. Made it personal and all. More common than the other venomous types, more aggressive than most of its kin and more likely to be hiding where you weren't expecting them.

That bit of time wasted, I looked around at the mess I made.

"Darn it!" Knelt down and started to gather the papers off the floor. Lucky for me, most hadn't spilt out of their brittle folders. These looked to be old employment records. While I was down there though, I looked over and caught sight of an old metal box shoved back under one of the bunk frames. It had one of those big lock-plates on the front. What really made me think I found something: the strip of ancient evidence tape across the lock. Someone hadn't wanted anyone without the right need-to-know in that box.

Since I didn't much want to find the cousin of the spider I'd encountered a moment back, I got up and snagged an old broom-handle I'd seen propped off in a corner. Knelt down and gave the box a good couple of whacks, insuring that any critters would head for the proverbial hills. Then I reached under, bracing one hand on the lip of the old bunk frame, and dragged the heavy box out into the cleared area.

An old style fireproof and somewhat waterproof small document safe came out into the thin light. I blew the dust off the top to reveal an old badge sticker, the kind we still handed out to kids at parades and such, and a property tag taped down with evidence tape. Someone's pencil scratch spelled out *G.S.D. for temporary storage* and gave the department's address from before the new county courthouse had been built back in the eighties.

Temporary, my left nut.

I did not have the key. Likely no one at the station even knew whether the key even still existed. Since the box appeared to belong to my department and it seemed the type of box that you'd keep important files in, I figured I should get it open. The locksmith in town might have the correct bump-key to open it, so I got out my cell and made a call. He was out and nobody knew when they expected him. Well, the county had maintenance folks and they were on premises. Went upstairs, hauling the box, and tracked down Duncan.

"So what's in the box?" Duncan played with a set of picks he'd pulled out of his kit. "It's not going get me in trouble is it?"

"Naw." I shrugged. "I mean, I don't know what's there, but I got a good suspicion it's what I'm looking for." While he worked, I rocked the chair I'd commandeered onto its back legs. "And if it ain't something the department wanted opened, then we'll re-key it and lock it back up."

"Hum." He let out the non-committal sound and focused back on the lock. Another couple minutes later, I heard the lock pop and Duncan stood up. "All yours."

"Thank you, sir." I pulled open the lid. Files. Old files. My hunch was likely right.

"If that's all you need, I got to go fix the john in the jury room."

Looked up from the files I'd already started thumbing through. "I'm good." I, hopefully, was more than good 'cause if this was what I needed I didn't need to go back down with the dirt and spiders. "Can I use the room? Little more comfortable up here."

Duncan saluted me as he opened up the door to let himself out. "Knock yourself out."

Dragged the chair on over, pulled out the first file and opened it up. The details of an unsolved hit and run along the highway confronted me: serious injury, not a death case, from around seventy-five. Jackpot! I dropped that one back in and grabbed one from around the middle. Late sixties, commercial burglary with penciled in margin notes referencing the Ross boys, but again unsolved. Definitely the old case files I was supposed to retrieve. Fingered the edges of the files to find the place where I'd pulled the file. Went right past it and then my brain registered what I'd seen. I set the file I'd been holding on the table before pulling out the one that caught my eye.

Peterson, Rosalie - 1979.

Too much coincidence to be coincidence. I opened up the brittle manila folder. The first thing there, staring out at me, my sister Rose's face. The same school photo that hung in the hall of my parent's house, except at home a little card with Jesus and the children occupied one corner of the frame. Couldn't quite wrap my mind around it. Rose drown. Accident. Why was there a file for her? Accidental death, drowning, that's a closed case. Solved.

Except, sitting there, holding that file and thinking back on my memories, nobody'd ever said direct that it was an accident. They'd just always sorta avoided the subject.

I flipped up the photo. After the first few lines, I guess, I now knew why. Suspicious death all laid out in the details. I swallowed hard and started reading the cold, hard particulars of an unsolved homicide.

The basic facts: she'd been missing a day, hadn't made it home from school the afternoon before, when an old man out fishing saw something in the weeds on the edge of the lake. That was about seventeen miles away from where she should have been. When the department arrived, they found Rose face down in the water. Her panties were gone and a gash crossed her left temple. The summary didn't go into too much detail. That'd be contained in the investigator's notes. Went on to the next page, getting lost in the reading of it.

The office of the medical examiner had only been in existence for a few years when Rose died. Frankly, the report left a little something to be desired. Of course that could just be me with the twenty-twenty hindsight that thirty odd years of advances in forensic pathology afforded me. It'd gotten me used to OME reports five to ten pages long. This equaled a sheet and a half.

Official cause of death was asphyxiation, but the medical examiner had been hesitant to call whether it was due to manual suffocation or drowning. Well, actually, what he said was it appeared to be a combination of both given what he could see— just he couldn't rightly say which, if either, happened first. Either way, she'd died way before her time.

Evidence of asphyxiation included the telltale pin-point red dots of burst blood vessels the doctors called petechiae across her cheeks and in her eyes. Anyone who dies from lack of oxygen will likely have those and drowning is asphyxiation because you're breathing water. However, a longish bruise, possibly made by a thumb up along the left side of the nose and a series of small round bruises marked the skin of her right cheek. Which is why manual suffocation could be the cause. Rose also had a bit of foam in her mouth and nose and water in her lungs, both signs of drowning. Wasn't much, but it was all I had to go on.

I mean, all of what was there gave me three quick and dirty theories, each with pluses and minuses. Someone could have tried to suffocate her by putting their hand over her nose and mouth and when she passed out put her in the water to finish the job. They could have tried to drown her and if she wouldn't stay down under the water did it up close and personal. Or they could have held her like that and used the grip to push her under the water, holding her nose so she'd start panic breathing and suck down water faster.

None of it meant a pretty death.

It's never easy, reading through the report on some child's murder—'cause that's what this sounded of. Usually, it grabs you and shakes your sense of right and wrong, makes you feel connected to that poor soul.

I'd like to say that I felt something deeper, harder with this file. Truth be told though, I found it interesting, but kinda in a detached like manner. I didn't know Rose. A few comments I'd heard here and there about how Rose liked the old tree out back or how she read far above her age were about all I had that was more than the original investigators would have known. Heck, they might have known her better—from church or her playing with their own kids.

I knew mostly faded photographs and silence every time her name was mentioned.

Still, in just that little bit, the bug got into me. Any officer who's worked a case knows when it happens, when you land one you know you're going to dog until you solve it or it haunts your sleep because you cain't. I wanted to know who did this. Somebody'd gotten to my family and that bothered me something awful. Filled my childhood up with hard silences. Whoever it was hurt my mom and dad so deep they could barely stand to talk about their daughter. They deserved better. They deserved justice. That got me. Made me care.

That, that made me mad.

I had time and technology on my side. I thumbed through the pages checking for what the file contained and what it didn't. From what I could see, they hadn't taken a rape kit. The ME didn't see any physical trauma associated with that kinda abuse. Standard procedure now is to do one anyway. There's lots of ways for sickos to get off that don't...well, it hadn't been taken so no use my thoughts going down that path right then. Did see that she'd scratched up her own face a lot. Again confirming that she was probably alive when the hand was on her face.

The ME indicated that they'd clipped her fingernails and scraped underneath. Best they could do back then was type the blood found in the cells. It all came back as O which meant either she'd only scratched her own skin or she and her killer had the same blood type. If they'd saved the samples in evidence, we might get a DNA read, something that was still science fiction in the seventies. Of course, that'd be nine months to more than a year from now since this case was glacial cold.

Flipped the pages around until I found the evidence log. They'd dried and saved her clothes, stored the clippings the OME taken and some fibers they'd found twisted in her hair. Most evidence, if she'd been in the water almost a full day, would have washed away. Still, again, new science might pull things out of those slim pickings that the original officers would have thought impossible.

What science couldn't help me with: what they'd seen, recorded and thought. Lost myself reading through the thin investigative report, sifting the skimpy details through my brain. I wasn't even halfway finished when the rattle of the door knob jerked me back to the here and now.

"Dude." Kabe stepped in. "There you are. I've been waiting outside for like fifteen minutes."

I blinked. If Kabe was done, it had to be close to noon. "Why didn't you call?" I'd completely lost track of time.

He screwed up his face with a sour look. "Guess who forgot

to charge their phone?" Crossing his arms over his chest, Kabe leaned against the door jamb. "Straight to voice mail."

Realized I didn't remember putting my cell on the charger yesterday. Normally I wouldn't have forgotten, but the excitement of everything with my folks, plumb slipped my mind. "Sorry. Got caught up in things."

"Really." He sneered, not mean like, but sorta in the I'm-not-quite-buying-it way. "Like what?"

A picture's worth a thousand words. "This." I let the pages drop down, folded the file back on itself and held it up so that Rose's school photo stared out at Kabe.

"Who..." shock worked itself across his face, "that isn't? Is it?"

"My sister," I confirmed.

"You said she drowned."

Mulled over how to say it. Finally, I kinda snorted down a breath. "I don't think everyone's been all that honest with me." Or themselves from what I could see.

CHAPTER 7

Lacy wiped her hands on a dish towel and heaved up a deep breath. Kinda knew something was headed down the pike, since our mom did the exact same thing whenever she had something on her mind. "Joe." Lacy sat down next to me. "What are you thinking?" Almost like something frustrated her, she tossed the towel on the table between us.

I so didn't want to be talking about any of this. Managed to avoid it all through dinner with my folks. We all avoided it. This big ol' elephant in the room—Kabe and I sitting next to each other—and nobody wanting to talk about much other than the weather.

Licking the last little bit of gravy off the back of my fork, I mumbled. "What do you mean?"

After messing with the towel a bit, wiping invisible spots off the table, she finally hit me with, "He's so young."

"Oh," I'd been expecting a ton of other judgments, but not that particular one, "I thought you were going to get on me about Kabe being a he." She'd claimed to be all right with it, the other night. Figured that might just be acting polite 'cause a set of ears she didn't know listened in.

Lacy honestly looked surprised by my observation. "Why would I do that?"

"Well," I shrugged, "everyone else seems to want to take a shot. Figured sooner or later you would too."

"Joey," Lacy used my kid name again, like she always did when she felt in a place to yank my bit. "I cain't say that I wasn't shocked when I learned." This time she just wrung the towel through her hands for a bit before adding. "But I wasn't really surprised by the news neither."

That rocked me back a bit. "You weren't?"

"No, no I wasn't." Lacy reached out and squeezed my hand.

"I mean, between when you were a kid and all." A sad, sorry smile graced her face. "You never dated in high school," yeah, she hit that nail on the head, "not unless somebody else set it up for you." She worried the towel through her fists. "Not at all when you were living with me in St. George. And when you did live with me, well I found some things..."

Talk about a two-by-four between my eyes. "What things?" My heart darn near froze in my chest. "I never brought anything like that into your house, Lacy." I hadn't. Not at all. I'd never brought my habits into Lacy's home, not ever. I'd never, ever do that to her and her own. "I respected your family."

"I know, Joe." That calming, motherly voice I remember from my childhood. I'd heard Lacy's voice far more than my own mom's back in that day. "Nothing ever, well, not appropriate." She patted my hand. "But a few times I went to search for something on the Internet and things would come up as things someone had looked at." She shrugged. "I'm a mom. I didn't know who did the search so I'd look at them."

I palmed my face. "How'd you figure it was me?"

"I had a house full of girls who were all crazy for boy-bands and pop-stars." She laughed. "It didn't take a lot to figure it weren't Carl looking up gay sites. That left one option."

"Never used your computer for looking up anything nasty or nothing, I swear," I repeated, more for her benefit than mine.

"They weren't nasty," she reassured. A heavy pause settled between us for a bit. Finally, she asked, "Did any of those groups help you?"

"Yeah, some," I admitted. "Gave me folks to talk to that'd been down this same road. That helped me settle things. Taught me I didn't have to hate myself."

"I wish you'd felt comfortable coming to me." Lord, she sounded sad.

"Lacy, do you know how long it's been," kinda swallowed a laugh with that, "I ain't been comfortable talking to anyone about this. I know if Kabe hadn't come along and it all hadn't got pushed out into the open, we wouldn't be here talking about this now. I'd decided it was something I weren't gonna burden no-one else with." Tossed my fork on my plate. "'Sides what would you have done if I had told you, say, when I was twenty-two?"

"I don't know exact." Reaching out across the table, Lacy grabbed my plate and then stood. "I do know," she talked as she headed over to the sink, "I would not have turned my back on you." After rinsing the plate and putting it with the others in the dishwasher, she added, "And, like I said, I had some notions long before that."

'Cept for the dating thing, I didn't know what would have given her notions about me. "Like what?" I'd been pretty much like all the boys I'd grown up with.

Lacy turned, crossed her arms over her chest and rested her butt against the edge of the sink. "You used to steal my Barbies."

"Dude." Kabe's laugh caught me off guard. "You played with your sister's dolls." I hadn't heard him come up to the back door. He pulled open the screen and stepped inside.

I turned and glared at him as he set the box he'd brought in on top of a couple others. "I did no such thing."

Lacy snorted out, "Liar."

I didn't answer her. Instead, I growled at Kabe, "I thought you were going to stay out of this?" He'd kinda promised me that the other night, letting me deal with my kin how I saw fit. "Weren't you, like, gonna help June move some furniture or something?" We were trying to get my folk's place back to rights after two years of strangers messing with things.

Kabe grabbed a chair and pulled it out from the table. "Not with this kinda dishing." He swung it around and sat down on it backwards.

Felt the heat rising across the back of my neck as I denied, "I did not play with my sister's dolls." I hadn't really. Not like she implied.

First she hit me with, "Oh yes, you did." Then Lacy smiled

and explained to Kabe, "I kept them all arranged on a shelf in my bedroom. I was really too old play with them by then, but they were still sentimental, kinda a collection. I'd get home from high school and they'd all be in the wrong place."

"What?" He teased me, "Did you like change their outfits?" His voice went all high pitched. He even threw in a bit of a lisp for a deeper dig. "Take them shopping?" Sounded like that TV host that got all these pretty boys to dress up like gals with no fashion sense while trying to outdo each other in being over the top outrageous.

I glowered. "You asking me to put a hurt on you?"

His grin went wicked. "In front of your sister?" He didn't let up on the San Francisco accent none.

Lacy raised her hands almost pushing the thought away. "Not even going to say nothing on that one."

"Okay, look," I took a deep breath. Frankly, I'd have rather been discussing me and my excommunication with my folks than having this conversation. "I didn't, like, play with the dolls, not like girls do." Rubbed the bridge of my nose and kinda mumbled into my hand. "My GI-Joes needed someone to rescue."

Kabe looked at me all funny. "Are we talking about the little action figures?" He held his thumb and index finger in sorta a C indicating how tall he was thinking they must have been. At least he'd dropped the affected speaking pattern.

"No." I reached over and popped the side of his head with my fingers. "I had the big ones, my brothers' hand me downs." Showed him by holding my hand about a foot off the table. "And they'd go on missions to rescue the tourists down in South America or wherever."

The tone came roaring back. Added to it: his head tossed back, his wrist flipped out and a roll of his eyes towards the ceiling. "Oh, boring macho boy stuff?" By the way Kabe said it, the emphasis he threw on those words, he meant the exact opposite.

My sister stifled a laugh at his outrageous behavior while I just tried to ignore his digging. I knew that's why he did it: playing to a new audience. 'Cause it sure weren't like him normally. There were times when I knew, one-hundred-percent, by how he said something or did something that the boy was queer. But even then it weren't quite so balls-to-the-wall.

"And then, you know, the girl dolls would all go off somewhere and the couple boy ones would hang around," I kinda coughed into my hand, "and thank the Joes."

"Ha!" Kabe slapped the table with both hands. "The Hallmark moment is officially over!" He crowed.

"I am so glad I had no idea back then." A big ol' smile broke over Lacy's face. "Oh, Lord, Joe." She managed to sputter it out while snickering into her palm.

I snorted. "Like what were they all going to do?" Could hardly keep a straight face myself as I teased her. "Come on, they didn't even have bulges." All Mormons ain't prudes, especially when you're just among adults you know. Nobody likely be telling any off color jokes, but a little blue barb now and again...

"Joey." She rolled her eyes and huffed out like she scolded me, "What am I ever gonna do with you?"

That so did not put me in my place. "Cain't dance, too wet to plow, might as well laugh, right?" I grinned.

She barely gave my tease the time of day. "So, that early, huh?" Lacy shook her head and pushed away from the counter. "Wow." She shook her head again, like she really was having a bit of a time processing it all. After grabbing some plates outta the cupboard and forks from the drawer, she set them on the table. A quick turn around to grab the strawberry-rhubarb pie that'd been cooling at the back of the stove then she came and sat down with us. Without asking if we wanted any she just dished out slices. While handing over one to Kabe, she asked, "When did you know, Kabe? You know, about how you were?"

He shrugged and said, "When didn't I?" like it was nothing.

Lacy cut herself a far thinner piece than either that she'd served up to us. "How did your family handle it?" She asked as she picked at the lean slice.

"Grams?" He shrugged again. "She was cool about it. It was never an issue with her." He took a bite of pie and chewed on it a bit, like he was thinking. "My dad...he came home from this overseas business trip and I had this guy over for dinner. My Grams just introduced him as my boyfriend. Dad rolled his eyes, sat down with this stack of reports and pretty much ignored us all."

"That's so sad." Lacy set the fork down not having actually eaten anything.

"That's how my dad handled everything." Kabe sorta rocked his chair back and blew out a breath. "I can remember my seventh birthday. We're at the zoo. They pulled me up to do this wildlife show." He kinda mimicked tracing this big thing laying across his shoulders and twisting around his arms. "I've got a snake as big as I am hanging on me...and my dad's got his cell phone to his ear on some conference call. If it wasn't business, it didn't really matter." I'd heard snippets of similar things before: a little here, a little there. He'd never given me the whole story though. Of course, I'd never prodded him like Lacy did.

I figured he'd tell me when he was good and ready for me to know.

Lacy'd gone back to smashing her pie up, making it look like maybe she'd could fool us into thinking she'd taken a bite. "Where was your mom in all this?" Whenever things got a mite stressful, her appetite would go on hiatus. With four girls in her house, that meant she stayed rail thin.

"Rehab." Kabe said it like it didn't matter much. "At least when I was younger." Knew him well enough by now, however, to catch that the memory cut him some. "I stayed with her a little when I was like twelve and she'd cleaned up at that point, but it just didn't work out." Again, I sorta sussed out that it probably equaled more than just not working out. "I'd been with Grams since I was three, so it was like visiting some distant relative."

"Since you were three?" Lacy looked completely floored by

that revelation.

"Yeah." He kinda offered up a not quite smile. "My parents were real young." When Lacy seemed to look a little skeptical—I mean Lacy was married and all of nineteen when her first girl came along—he rushed out, "Seriously, my mom had me like when she was barely eighteen. Her birthday is, like, a week before mine." He managed to get it out while chewing. "My dad was maybe seventeen, maybe still sixteen, although he didn't know at first. I mean, about me."

Lacy reached across the table and touched his arm. "Oh, sweetheart."

"It's what it is, you know." Kabe gave up one of his lopsided, but still stunning grins. "She didn't tell my dad he had a kid until I was already a year old."

About that time I jumped in and pointed my fork at Lacy's plate. "You gonna eat that or just beat it to death with your fork?" Her husband, Carl, and I had worked out the system that if you pointed out that Lacy wasn't eating, she'd start putting food in her mouth just to prove you wrong. She glared and took a nibble, so I turned my attention to Kabe. "So how did you end up with your Grams?"

He looked at me like I gone and grown two heads. "I told you."

"No," I denied it, "you ain't never told me."

"Seriously?" It came out like he thought I yanked his chain.

Mumbled, "Yep," as I shoveled a forkful of pie into my maw. Strawberry-rhubarb wasn't one of my favorites, but I'd missed my momma's cooking.

"Wow." He kinda snorted and scratched the back of his head. "Okay, look, my mom...ah...did my dad as this total sympathy thing at this party. Not that he wasn't good looking, but he was a total dork."

Lacy's mouth darn near fell open. "That's awful."

"What, that he was a dork?" Kabe laughed. "How else do

you rebel against a hippy mom? My Grams was all free love," he flicked his fingers out like he shot off sparks to punctuate the words, "and ashrams and community sings when my dad was a kid." Then he kinda flipped his hand out almost brushing the thought off. "So he went total conservative over-achiever. But, he's a teenage guy and a totally hot chick is offering." He leaned in, sharing the joke. "What straight guy wouldn't go for it?"

"No." She scowled at her plate before looking up at him. "I mean it's so sad that they were so young and lost."

"Oh." He nodded, kinda getting what she meant. He'd been around me long enough to know that she'd be coming from the church's point of view. "I feel bad for Mom." Now it was Kabe's turn to stab at his pie. "I mean she wasn't innocent, let me tell you." That little bit of antsiness gave off a hint, at least to me, that bugged him some. "But, you know, not a bad kid at that point. Then, when her parents found out my dad wasn't," he sucked in the last word, "white." And now I knew why. "Oh man. They kicked her to the curb." He huffed, cut off a big hunk of pie and shoved it in his mouth. Somehow, he managed to talk while he chewed. "What do you do when you're that age with a kid and no job and no support? She hooked up with some folks. It wasn't good, from what I've been told."

A pause settled down around us while Kabe and I ate and Lacy nibbled. Finally, I found the question I wanted to ask. "So what happened when you were three?"

"Mom was pretty racked up on shit by then." Kabe pushed his plate away, pie only about half eaten. "A bunch of people living together and I was one of five kids there. Someone called social services on one of the older kids. She was in middle-school and showed up, bruised up from being, ah, sold off for a high." The strangled sound that came outta of his throat hit like a stick digging into my gut. "They pulled us all out." Crossing his arms over his chest, he leaned back in his chair. "My Grams says I was in foster care for a few months before they tracked down my dad—and he's in MIT at that point—so he called Grams and she came and got me." As he said that, he relaxed outwardly, some.

Lacy reached over and grabbed his plate as she stood up from the table. "They didn't call your mom's folks?" I went ahead and passed over mine as well.

"From what I've been told, they did, and those jerks said that I 'wasn't their problem.'" The last three words came out all nasty.

It was nasty enough a tone to stop Lacy in the middle of taking the dishes to the sink. She turned and hissed out, "That's horrible."

"No it's not." He smiled big and bright. "I got to live with my Grams and *Dadaji*." That Kabe actually sounded, I don't know, pleased with.

"*Dadaji?*" Lacy asked that question over her shoulder as she rinsed off the plates.

"Hindi for grandfather." Kabe jumped up and yanked open the dishwasher. "If I'd grown up with those jack-holes, my mom's parents, I'd be some closeted, self-hating ass." He racked the plates that she handed to him. "She let me be who I was." He leaned close, like he shared some special secret with my sister. "I never, ever felt unloved." Lord, the conviction in his voice, it was enough to make me actually believe him. "In fact, I felt like I was the most special kid in the world because they always managed to spin it like some fairy tale." He pushed the rack in, letting the dishwasher slam closed. "Now that I'm grown up, yeah, looking back, the situation sucked." Bracing his hands on the counter behind him, he rested his butt against the edge. "As a kid, though, she made it seem like the whole world converged to deliver me to her doorstep so she could show me a wonderful life."

"Never unloved, at all?" I didn't buy it, at least not one-hundred percent. "Even with your dad? I mean, he made your Grams go get you instead of him."

"Okay, my dad yanked my chain," he conceded, "a lot. I probably did a shitload of stuff my Grams wanted, that he didn't, because it was my immature flip off to him." He pointed to his chest. "But, although I've screwed some shit up, I like me. Lots of people out there can't say that."

"That's true." Had to agree with him on that issue. I got up from my seat and started pushing all the chairs back under the table. Kabe said something about getting more boxes from the shed and headed out the back door. I fumbled around in the still bare cabinets looking for a storage container to put the leftovers in while Lacy wiped down the table. Once I found something passable, I stuffed the remnants of meatloaf and potatoes in and snapped on the lid. As I shoved it in the fridge, I decided to tackle what I'd found that morning. "Hey, ah, can I ask you something, Lacy?"

"Of course." She'd grabbed the pans off the stove and was rinsing them out.

I picked up one of the boxes off the floor and set it on the table. "Did our folks ever talk to you about what happened to Rose?"

"Rose?" Lacy turned off the water and came up beside me. "Whatever brought that up in your head?"

"Some old stuff I found." Managed to shrug and pull out newspaper wrapped dishes at the same time. "Got me thinking on things." We'd bought a cheap set of china for use while the house was rented out. But my momma would want her stuff, what had belonged to her momma, back.

"You know the same as I do, Joe." Lacy picked up the first set of plates I'd unpackaged. "She drown, over in Panguitch Lake."

I stopped what I was doing and looked over at her, kinda hard. "Do you remember that day?"

Suspicious, she drew out the word, "Some," as she set the plates she'd just picked up back down.

"What do you remember?" I sorta slid into Deputy Joe mode. Not quite as harsh as I'd be with someone who weren't my own kin, but pretty much down to brass tacks. "Anything at all. I'm just trying to straighten some things in my head."

"We get talking about your friend's childhood and you gotta pull that outta yours?"

"Something like that."

"Lord," she looked a little confused, "make me think all that time back." Somehow, she must have caught how serious this was off my tone and how I held myself right then. "Let's see. I remember it was warm, it may have been summer vacation...no, I remember, we had school that day, so just right before school let out that summer." As she pulled one of the chairs back out and sat down, Lacy chewed on her thumbnail. Worrying the memories back through her mind. "I don't quite remember why, but I didn't walk home with her that day. I think maybe Jim did, but I'm not real sure about that. Tina was living with her husband at the Air Force base in California, I think. Know what? I was at Jessica's house, my friend Jessica, 'cause I remember Mom called over there, I don't know what time, because Rose hadn't gotten home yet. I think she called back a bit later and Jessica's mom got kinda upset and took me home." With a deep sigh, she rushed out the last bit. "I remember Mrs. Frank stayed with me and everyone was out looking for her. And then the next day they found her in the lake."

"Lacy," I kinda crouched down next to her, bringing us somewhat eye-to-eye. "Did you ever stop to think about how a seven year old girl got seventeen miles down the highway?"

"Ah, sorta. I mean, she was gone all night." Her voice went a might defensive. "I just kinda figured she maybe started out just playing." Lacy shook it off with a hard, almost defiant, toss of her head. "She was always going off into where she wasn't supposed to be, down by the creek and all." Still, I could hear her choking up with the memories. "Thought maybe she got turned around and when it got dark, got spooked and lost." Thirty-some-odd years of repeating that to herself, I guessed, and it probably started to become the truth in her mind. I mean, the other way of thinking, that would be pretty awful for a little girl to remember.

"I don't think she got lost." I had to give her something on why I'd gone down this road of questions. "I think someone took her there."

Lacy's eyes went wide. "Why would you think that, Joe?"

My bum knee started protesting so I stood up. "'Cause I was going through the departments ol' open cases, it's what they got me doing since I cain't be on full duty, and I found Rose's file." Started pacing to work it and my thoughts out. "By what I read, somebody did something to her."

That brought Lacy up out of her chair. "What?"

Thought through what I should tell her. Not much. She was a witness, kinda, and Rose's death was still an open homicide. "I'm gonna spare you the details," I shoved my hands in my pockets. "But it weren't no accident. And I aim to find out who did it."

"Why now?" She pulled her arms against her chest, like she pulled her memories tight around her in defense. "It's been all these years. If it wasn't an accident then how's picking at it now going change things? What's it gonna do for anyone? For you?"

"Why now?" The question flustered me for a moment. "I don't know exact." I really didn't. But something about it, the injustice of all these years, got under my skin. "Maybe 'cause I didn't know the truth before. Everybody talked it off like it'd been some tragic accident. Tragic yes. Accident no." Paced a bit, trying to drum down my thoughts into something that might be an answer. "I don't know what it's gonna do for me, 'cept maybe answer why most times I had you as my momma instead of Mom, 'cause she'd get so down she couldn't even get out of bed. Don't you want to know?"

"It ain't gonna change nothing." Lacy pressed her knuckles into the side of her mouth. "It ain't gonna bring Rose back."

How could she just be willing to let it go? "Don't you wanna see justice done?"

"Heavenly Father will see justice done."

"Sometimes God needs help." He helps those who help themselves. "That's why we have law enforcement."

"Stirring up everything after all these years, Joe." She almost looked like she wanted to cry. "Especially now."

"What do you mean, 'especially now?'"

"With all you've got going on?" I got a glare on top of her hissed out sorta question. "You've been excommunicated. You just told Mom and Dad about...about you and Kabe. They haven't even started to get their heads around that. All the problems you've been having with your job lately."

I hadn't told her much of anything about my job. "What problems?" A little bit about my accident, yeah, but not all the other troubles that went before and after. I mean, we were close, but it weren't nothing she could fix, so I saw no sense burdening her.

This glare was even more righteous than the last. "Don't be stupid, Joe. I grew up here. I walked into the market to get the milk I forgot to buy the other day and I ran into three people I went to high school with." She stepped in close, letting me feel how angry she was by being caught flat footed and embarrassed. "And every one of them wanted to know what I thought of all the trouble my baby brother's gotten himself into."

Couldn't really even answer her on that. Just stared out the back window into a yard full of moon cast shadows. I should've figured that would happen. Maybe I just tried to fool myself into believing everything was alright. If I didn't say anything then it wasn't really happening.

She almost sagged against the edge of the table. "Why would Mom and Dad lie?"

The question weren't directed at me, but I answered it anyway. "They never really lied; they just didn't say the whole truth. Maybe to spare you?" I guessed at some reasons, making it easier on her. I had my own questions about that though. "You were only nine. Spare themselves? Don't know. I figured you might have known different, but by the time I was old enough to understand, y'all decided to spare my little ears."

It rubbed me wrong that they'd, my folks, kept it from Lacy. She and Rose, from what bits I'd heard, were as thick as thieves back then. Stewing on that issue wouldn't get me nowhere right then. "But, okay, I want you to really think back on that time for me, okay, over the next couple of days, and see if anything else comes up in your mind about it. If you think of anything, just call me, it don't matter what time." Said that with as much conviction as I could muster. "Okay?"

Lacy hesitated, but finally nodded. "All right."

"And don't just yet say anything to our folks." I walked up to her, took hold of her sharp shoulders, and looked her straight in the eye. The more I tried not to think about what happened to Rose, the more I realized I couldn't let it be. I felt wronged, somehow cheated out of a normal life, one that wasn't filled up with ghosts. And it angered me, something awful, that someone had taken not only her best friend, but Lacy's childhood along with it. "I want to come at them fresh."

"What?"

"It's nothing big," I reassured her. "I just don't want their recollections clouded by yours, okay?" Ripped me up a little to realize I was going to have to question my parents. "Police stuff, Lacy, just trust me on this." What was worse, I had to keep open the possibility that someone, one of blood, might have been involved. Didn't think it likely at all, since, from what I'd read in the file their whereabouts had been sufficiently verified. But you cain't get tunnel vision on any investigation. You miss things that way.

"Why now, Joey?" She looked like she might be ready to cry.

Finally I told her what I'd known the moment I realized there was a file. "I just have to do it. I have to know." It wasn't much of an answer, but it was the truth.

She went back to biting on her nail. "I don't like it."

"I promise, I won't hold you silent for more than a couple of days. I swear." I even crossed my heart with my fingers. Same way I'd done when I was little and she took care of me.

It took her awhile, but finally she gave me a short jerk of her head and whispered, "Okay, Joe. I'll trust you on this."

CHAPTER 8

Gave myself, and Lacy, an out by grabbing up one of the bins Kabe'd brought in and heading upstairs. Didn't much want to think on the mess I'd made of my folks' life right then. The whole whitewash of my sister's death needed to have the scabs ripped off and aired out. Lot easier dealing with that, than the fresh wounds I'd laid into them the past couple of days.

I figured I'd come at my dad first. Head on 'round back here about lunch tomorrow. Like I told Lacy, I didn't want to have to hold her silent any longer than absolutely necessary. I don't think I'd full on convinced Lacy to go along with what I planned. I could tell she weren't happy, not at all.

Still, she let me have my way. I mean, not like Lacy knew nothing about police work, she had to trust me on this. And I didn't think for a moment that my family was involved in the killing, but years of memory were gonna fog up the recollections something awful already. I didn't want them talking between themselves, convincing each other what really happened or didn't that day.

As I came up the narrow stairs to the landing, I caught sight of June, off to the left of me, sitting Indian style on the floor. Jeans and an over-sized college sweatshirt made her look almost as fragile as her momma. June, though, cougar blood ran through her veins. I'd actually gone and seen her play once. And while I didn't much understand rugby, I could understand that thrill: baring your teeth, screaming your soul and taking some poor buck who didn't have the sense to get out of your way right down into the mud.

'Course, right then, June occupied herself with far less aggressive tasks. She pulled out the towels, sheets and things that we'd got for use as a rental, folded them up and stuffed them in the empty bins for the trip to the thrift store. My parents' things were stacked next to her, still in the air-tight bags and waiting to be arranged on the shelves.

"Hey, Uncle Joe." She pushed a bit of hair behind her ear and waggled her fingers at me in greeting.

I set the bin I carried down at the head of the stairs. "June, how's the team doing?" Her college rugby team made it to the championships and then had to forfeit when it ended up that someone scheduled their game on Sunday. They took a stand on principle—I mean the coach let them vote on it and the whole team agreed. It cost them. Felt bad and proud all wrapped up together. If the sport had been NCAA sanctioned *the BYU rule* would have kicked in and the game would have been moved to a non-Sabbath day...no matter what day that Sabbath fell on for a particular school.

She smiled up at me. "We're going to make it next year." Oh, Lord, she looked like Lacy at that age, 'least my memory of my sister then. I couldn't help but echo her grin. "Nice to see you smile."

That caught me up. "What?"

"You're happy." She shrugged and went back to folding. "You're smiling."

I took a step over and thumped the top of her head with my knuckle. Didn't sound hollow. "You ain't around me a lot," I corrected. "I smile quite a bit."

"No, Uncle Joe." This time she didn't look up. "Not like you're smiling now." I could hear the conviction in her voice, though.

I crossed my arms over my chest and leaned against the wall. "What are you on about?"

I got another shrug. "I can tell, you're happy." She started on opening up the bags. "Not like, just content, but really, really happy. We'd all talk about it. All the cousins when we came to visit. How you always seemed a little down." After a bit of a pause, June shook her head and gave a snort. "Well, not the boys, they were clueless. But, now, it's like this light has touched you. And I'm happy for you, that you found someone."

"You're okay with it...me and him?"

"God sent you someone to complement you, be your partner." I got one of those looks like June thought I'd gone a bit off my rocker. "Why wouldn't I be okay with that?"

I didn't want to bring her down to what I'd been dealing with this past year, so I hedged, "I'm not used to people being okay with it, right off."

"Twenty-first century." June twisted her mouth all funny and rolled her eyes. "Get over it already." She must'a caught my sour expression and kinda read through what it meant. "Oh, you mean the whole church thing." I got a nervous little laugh in apology. "Sorry. I didn't...I shouldn't have brought that up."

I shrugged. She hadn't intended anything by what she said. "It is what it is."

Another eye roll told me what she thought on that. "Well, what it is, is run by a bunch of fussy old white dudes." Lord, my sister would have a heart attack if she heard her youngest going off on the President and the Apostles of the church like that. "I mean, come on, they didn't admit African Americans to full membership until almost the eighties." She snorted. "Can you say, 'way behind the times'?" Then, like she wanted to reassure me, June added, "It may take a while, but the revelation will come." I don't know as I'd ever been that young and earnest.

"You might live to see it." Shrugged again. "Not sure I will."

"Well," her huff spoke to some deep things she must be mulling over, "several states have civil marriage...you know for... ah, well." June chewed on her lower lip some. "Not all states recognize it, but, there's ways around some of them, if someone was of a mind too."

There were times I talked in circles. June had me beat by a mile. "What are you dancing around?"

After scratching the back of her neck, shifting around on the floor some, I guess June found the stones to just say what she wanted, "You shouldn't be living together." Like she thought I might get mad, she wrapped her arms over her chest and kinda hunkered into herself. "At least, you know, now that there are states where you could make it honest."

Whoa, so we were headed down that road. "Okay, and Utah ain't one of them." I reminded her. "You got a wad of cash in your back pocket to get us to Washington or New York? 'Cause I sure don't."

That rated me a glare. "If I did, would you go?"

Was not a bridge I wanted to cross right then. "Ah, well." I sorta swallowed down the panic the mention of the possibility drove into my gut. "I'm not sure I've thought that through all the way." Actually, I was darn certain I hadn't thought that through at all. Wasn't about to admit that to my niece.

"And that's why." With a grunt, she unfolded her legs. "You know," she whispered like she didn't want anyone to overhear her chiding me, "you really shouldn't be living together, Uncle Joe." I stepped in to help her up, but she'd already clambered off the floor before I could move much. "I'm going to get some water. Want anything?"

I'm glad she saw fit to change the subject before I had to invent some cockamamie excuse to get away from the conversation. "Naw, I'm good." Probably said that a might too eager to be polite. To cover myself, I kicked the bin with the side of my boot. "Got to take this stuff into Mom." I got out of June's way, listened to her thunder down the stairs, as I grabbed up the stuff.

She and Kabe, both rushed through life pell-mell. 'Course that made me remember that, really, he weren't all that much older than my niece. That thought, it weirded me out a might. I mean, I was all of eight when my sis met this lanky cowboy who would set me up on his horse and let me ride it around the pasture—excuse to talk with Lacy. A year later, she'd married Carl and the one after that had her first daughter Kelly. Kelly was all growed up now, with kids of her own. But still...

I crossed the small landing, boards creaking under my weight, and caught sight of my mom sitting on her bed. Looked like she'd been sorting through the personal stuff I'd kept over at my place these past couple of years. Valuables we didn't want kept out in the shed. Not that my folks were smothered in diamonds or nothing, but some personal jewelry and my daddy's guns were safer with me. I knocked on the jamb since I didn't want to startle Momma none.

When she looked over at me, I dropped the bin and rushed into the room. "Mom, what's wrong?" She looked like she'd seen a ghost, her face kinda pale and her eyes looking all lost.

She put her hand over her mouth for a second and then let it drop to her chest. "I just." She drew in a ragged breath, "I just, I was putting things away."

I slowed down as nothing seemed to be all that wrong. "Did you hurt yourself?" Maybe she'd found a spider like I had earlier—spring after all, brought 'em out with all the other bugs. Sat down on the edge of the old metal bed covered in patchwork quilts. "You all right?" Right there next to her, I could feel how she shook just a bit. "Something startle you?"

"No." Her hand drifted back up to flutter against her lips. Resting on the bed and covered by her other hand was a little box. I recollected seeing it before, but I couldn't remember when or why. "I came 'cross something."

"Oh." I don't know what she might have run across that'd make her look so stricken. "What?"

Instead of answering, she just lifted up the box and handed it over. Her hand shook a little, I could feel it as I took the box. And, honestly, she seemed, I don't know, miserable wasn't it, but anxious didn't quite equal her mood neither. I guessed it was maybe a bit o' both. Sucked down a deep breath and, 'cause it seemed to be what Momma wanted, I opened the box.

A set of rings. I knew 'em. I'd seen 'em before. I shook 'em out into my palm and turned them over a few times in the light. The man's ring: simple, solid rosy-tinted gold with the etching of my gran'daddy's name—Joseph Price—still just visible inside the band. The sorta matching engagement ring, same gold with a round bit of robin's egg turquoise and four bluish tiny pearls. My gran'ma was buried with her band, but she'd worn my gran'daddy's on a chain after he'd died so she could remember him as he was before he went down into not remembering who he was.

Hooked my pinky in my gran'ma's engagement ring and held it up. "What made you upset about these?" I don't know, might have been just a memory or a flash of something. Still, Momma seemed more worked up than just that oughta do.

It took a while before she could speak. She started a couple of times and then couldn't spit it out. Finally, after some gulps of air she managed to get the words through her teeth, "I was saving them for you." After another kinda ragged breath, she pushed my hand back towards my chest. "For when you got married." Her hand dropped to my knee. "I don't know what use they'll get now, but just take them."

Wasn't sure where this all had come from. Well, I knew, but why the rings had done it, that I weren't certain about. "Do you want me to give them to Lacy, maybe for June?" Maybe it really drove it home for her, that little bit of a life I'd come to realize long ago that I'd never have. She'd be tackling this all with the wound still fresh.

"I don't care what you do with them." She couldn't really even look at me, just kept patting my leg and seeming like she held back tears. "Sell 'em. Melt 'em down and make something else outta it. I saved them for you." Her other hand fluttered up to her mouth. "They're meant to be yours. Just take 'em away."

My face got hot and I couldn't even hardly swallow. No man ever wants to see his momma cry. And you ain't supposed to be the cause of it. I'd done this to her. My fault. Not that I would, or could, change what I was than I could change my blue eyes to brown. But it was all on my head that she'd had to find out. My mistake, getting caught, set this fire running and it burned up everyone I knew in its path. I managed to kinda breathe out, "Mom—"

"Take 'em." That's when she gathered up the other bits she'd been sorting and dumped it all into her jewelry box. "They were special 'cause they belonged to my daddy, named you after him, and my momma." She stood then walked over to her dresser, back to me. "And it was gonna mean so much when they went to his namesake and your bride." I could see her knuckles almost white around the edges of the wood as she set it down. "And it's gone. All gone."

I tried again, "Momma..." My voice sounded like a scared little kid's.

"Joe." I caught her strained expression and trembling upper lip in the mirror's reflection of her face. "I need to have some time. Just take it and go right now." She rubbed her eyes with her fingers. "I need time alone. Please."

Almost couldn't get it out. "Okay, Mom." Somehow, I managed to find my feet. "Want me to get Dad?" Instead of answering with words, Momma just shook her head. "All right." Swallowed the word, along with my pride, some. Wanted to say more. Wanted to yell *look at me, talk to me* and I just couldn't. My balls crawled up inside me like a dog's tail curling between my legs. Almost in a stupor, I shoved the box in my pocket and stumbled outta the room. Amazed I didn't pitch myself head first down the stairs with how my legs shook. Felt as if my bones turned all to jelly. Thought the other night was bad...this equaled a hundred times worse. I'd never, ever imagined those kinda words coming off my own momma.

As I staggered into the living room, Kabe stood up from where he'd been straightening some things on a bottom shelf. He turned and must'a caught sight of me. "Joe, what's wrong?"

"Nothing." Stuttered it out so low that I hardly heard myself. "I..." Couldn't even bring to mind what I really wanted to say. "Not right now."

"Dude," Kabe huffed, "don't pull that stoic crap." About two steps closer to me, he blinked. "Holy shit, you're shaking." He reached out and grabbed my upper arm.

I swallowed hard. "Kabe, I. Oh, Lord." Leaned into his touch enough I though I might fall over.

Somehow, he managed to keep me from toppling to the floor.

"Shhh." He put his cheek up against mine and whispered, "I know. Don't worry, I know." And I knew he did. Not what just took place. Not any of the words my momma said. But he had a sense of what happened. "You can't even process what went down, I bet." He tugged on my sleeve. "Look, let's go home." He kinda pulled me towards the front door. "I know your sister needs help, but what everyone needs more right now is space." I only half heard him ask, "Okay?" 'Cause at that point I was staring over Kabe's shoulder at my daddy, his face all set hard. Only got a moment of his eyes on mine before he turned on his heel and walked back into the kitchen.

I swallowed and fished in my pocket for my keys. "Yeah, we should get." Once I pulled out my keys, I realized how bad I shook. Kabe weren't lying. The bits of metal jingled like sleigh bells in my hand. "I think you're gonna have to drive."

CHAPTER 9

I lay on the bed, my left hand pillowed under my head, and stared at the open box with the two rings resting there in the bottom. My nerves were so shot, I hadn't even bothered with getting undressed…tactical boots up on the covers and everything. Had 'em on 'cause I'd been moving furniture and such at my folks place. Kept thinking back on what went down just a short time ago. Nothing prepared me for hearing those words outta my momma's mouth.

I guessed I ought to just give the rings onto Lacy, keep 'em in the family so they could be put to their intended use. Set the box on the bed beside me, plucked out my gran'daddy's band and held it between my ring finger and thumb. The old gold caught the light bleeding in from the great-room and went all rust colored. I couldn't see the inscription, but I could feel the worn letters with my fingertip.

All my life I'd been told who I was in terms of who came before me. Felt the connection to Joseph Price and all back through our generations in that little bit of metal: the family eternal. Together always on earth and in heaven. Treasured connections of spirit.

I didn't want to let it go.

I shouldn't have to let it go.

It was owned by my gran'daddy, it'd been left for me, his namesake, and was mine by rights.

I took a deep breath and let it settle onto my right ring finger, pushed it down into place with my thumb. I might not be able to ever use it for the reason my momma saved the band, but I could honor his memory by wearing it; carry on with the values of Heavenly Father and family above all that he'd taught me when he'd still possessed enough of a mind to do so. Before his thoughts got eaten away with Alzheimer's.

Nobody'd take it for a wedding ring on my right hand and

it was simple enough that it'd pass muster with the department. I know it was sentimental and some folks might say stupid, but I don't know, I just felt like I needed that connection right then. Maybe 'cause how raw I'd been cut. I might rethink it all tomorrow. My gran'ma's ring, I'd give that on to Lacy, she'd been her favorite, so that was fitting. It'd mean a lot to my sister.

Reached down and snapped the box shut on the remaining ring, before I rolled over some and slid it onto the nightstand.

Heard Kabe's bare feet on the steps. "You don't have to be quiet," I called out to him. "I ain't sleeping."

He jogged up the last few treads. "Figured you might have crashed while I checked my email." He'd jumped on the computer for a bit when we hit the house. Told him I'd needed a moment or two by myself.

The day before, with my folks at dinner had been hard. "Gonna be awhile before I get to sleep." Today, with my momma, I felt like somebody'd shoved a grenade down my throat and pulled the pin. My insides were all ripped to shreds. "Even as tired as I am."

Kabe sat down on the edge of the bed. "No." He reached over and ran his hand along my thigh. His touch was warm even through my jeans. "You're not tired," Kabe insisted, "you're upset."

"I'm fine," I insisted, although I didn't even try to make it sound convincing.

"Bullshit, Captain Rock." He teased me with the name he used when he thought I was holding back. "You just had it out with your mom. In case you've somehow spaced the last hour, I had to drive your ass home you were so rattled."

"I was just a little frazzled." I denied the fact that he'd hit the nail on the head. "I'm fine now."

"Frazzled?" He scoffed. "Dude, you were shattered. I just knew the other night went down too easy. Took a day for the situation to be real for her, but the shit hit the fan. Somehow, I knew your mom would pull the you-ripped-my-heart-out routine."

Again I minimized. "It weren't all that bad." Weren't sure if that was for him or for me.

"It's bad enough that you're lying to me." Kabe pulled off his shirt and dropped it on my head. "You kinda suck at that, you know." As I chucked the shirt onto the floor, Kabe bent down over me, one arm on either side of my body supporting him. "Know what, you need to lie to me to save face, okay, but, dude, stop lying to yourself. 'Cause you got to deal with what happened and face the distinct possibility, no probability, that your dad is going to let you have it with both barrels sometime in the near future."

Lord, he was right. "I don't even want to think on that." I pushed him away, sat up, swung my feet over the edge of the bed and stared out at the night stars through the back window.

Kabe clambered up onto the bed, sat behind me, sandwiching my thighs between his. "Come here." He wrapped his strong hands over my shoulders and worked his thumbs into the base of my neck up under my shirt. "Let me relax you some."

I rolled my neck into the touch. "Feels good." Painful and good all at the same time; maybe that's how he felt when I played around with him. All my muscles just started un-fraying.

"I'm sorry it went down like that, dude." He leaned in and kissed the back of my head. With how he was up against me, I could feel his dick getting solid along the line of my butt. "But, seriously, Joe, just toss it."

"What?" I didn't quite get what he was aiming at.

"Let it go." He tugged my shirt out of my jeans, got his hands up under it and kneaded along my spine with the butts of his palms. "It doesn't matter."

Laced my fingers together and cracked my knuckles out in front of my chest. "It matters more than you know." Even the muscles in my hands were wound tighter than a top. Went ahead and unbuttoned my shirt and slid it off.

"No. It hurts." He kept the hard touch going along my tensed up back as I shucked the shirt. "But it doesn't matter." His fingers worked a deep magic into my bones. Not just the physical contact, mind you, but the fact that he was there for me when I needed him. "You can't change what she thinks. She has to get through it on her own and you can't let yourself get all wound up in that. You have to let it go or it'll drive you nuts."

Ran my right hand over my skull. "I don't know."

About half-way back, Kabe caught it in his grip. He brought my hand forward, in front of my eyes...and his, I guess. Ever so lightly, he brushed his finger over the band on my hand. "Dude?"

I sucked in my breath and closed my fist. "Just an old ring that belonged to my gran'daddy." I weren't up to talking to him about it right then.

Must've caught my vibe, 'cause he didn't say nothing else for a while, just kept that deep, hard massage going up and down my back. After maybe, ten minutes, or so Kabe leaned in and rested his chin on my shoulder. "I know what'll take your mind off of things."

Knew what he was suggesting, but I didn't think I was quite up for sex right then. "I don't know as I could even get my head in that space." 'Specially not our kinda sex. 'Cause, heck, even with how he'd been working on me you could have plucked my tendons like guitar strings.

"Sure you can." Kabe turned in closer and ran his tongue up my neck. "Trust me, dude," he whispered, "you need to."

I got my hand on his forehead and shoved him back. "You're pushing." Of course, my dick kinda protested since the touch started pumping the blood between my legs.

Kabe unwound himself from around me and scooted off the bed. "You need to be pushed." He knelt down in front of me and ran his hands up my thighs.

Didn't stop him. "What are you doing?" Like I didn't know.

He leaned in. "Pushing." That got mouthed over my prick

trapped in my jeans.

I shoved him away again, kinda half-heartedly. "You're getting me hard." That was pretty obvious at that point.

He unbuttoned my fly and pulled my jeans down enough to get at the tip of my dick. "That's the point." When his lips touched the skin, my soldier came to full attention, ready and willing for action.

He and my body were both against me. "I thought you're 'sposed to be the, like, submissive, half of this party?"

"Between you and me," he laughed, "doesn't mean I can't start something."

"You ain't gonna stop prodding, huh?" My grumble was half hearted at best.

I got a big ol' grin. "Nope."

"You're a brat." I swatted the side of his head with my open hand. "You know that, right?"

"I know." Kabe's smile went all sly, 'cause he knew he had me on his line.

Well, he might have hooked me, but I weren't going to let him think he could run the whole show. Brought my knee up fast enough that I cracked him on the chin. Then I set my boot against his sternum and shoved. Kabe went sprawling backwards onto the floor. I got to my feet as he rolled over onto his hands and knees. Before he could even make to getting off the floor, I got my boot on his butt and shoved again. He pitched forward, stopping the fall just short of his face kissing wood.

"Oh, big, bad deputy! Push me around." Kabe raised his face up and sneered at me. "Like you can even handle me."

I swiped his knuckles with the toe of my boot. "You got it, bring it on."

"I got it." Kabe lifted his hand and licked where I'd scraped the skin. "And then some." I got a flash of teeth. "You're the one short in the sack, asshole!"

My blood started to bubble, not quite boiling, but sure as shooting not calm neither. "I got more than you can handle."

"I can handle a fucking lot." He hadn't gotten up off the floor. "You're the one who holds us back."

I booted his knee. "I ain't holding back now." I barked it out. "You wanted this. Let's go!"

"All right, Joe." Kabe didn't sound either contrite or scared. Yeah, it was what he wanted too. "Let me get up."

Once again, he made like he was getting off the floor. This time I caught him on his hip, pushed him sideways. He rolled onto his back, right at the foot of the bed. "What's your problem, boy?" I laughed at him. "Cain't get it up?" Took two steps over to him, put my left boot right on his crotch and pressed down hard. Didn't put my full weight on his dick, but I didn't ease back much either.

Kabe's face went tight and his head jerked back pushing his shoulders up off the floor some. "Fuck," got hissed out through clenched teeth. "Asshole."

"I thought that's what you wanted?" Rolled my foot around some, grinding his dick between the sole of my boot and his own bones. "You can dish it out, but you cain't take it none." Yanked my foot back and popped his knee with the steel toe, just hard enough that he'd feel it good. "Get those jeans off."

Kabe yelped out, "Shit," and started struggling with the fly on his jeans.

The boy hustled, but not near fast enough. "I meant now!" I hauled back and kicked his leg, turning my foot just a bit before the blow landed. I wanted to rev him up…and me. I didn't want to make it so's he couldn't walk tomorrow. It still landed hard enough that he grunted. "Come on." Now I put my boot back on his crotch, this time with his hands pinned under the waffle treads. "You light a fire, you better be prepared to put it out."

Kabe squirmed beneath me, managing to get his fly open despite the predicament I had him in. "Yes, Joe."

I don't know why I so liked the sound of that. His simple, '*yes, Joe,*' sent heat rushing all through me. Meant he was mine and he knew it. "You need to hustle, boy." He wanted it. I wanted it too. "If I got to wait too much longer, I'm just going to jack myself off and make you sleep on the floor." Barked it out hard and nasty enough to file the edges off my nerves. I pushed off, making him grunt in pain again, and grabbed my junk through my jeans. "Move."

He writhed around a bit, but managed to shuck his jeans and hiking shoes pretty darn quick. All the while, he's looking up at me like I'm the king of the mountain. I knew that getting rough with him like this was what got him off, big time. And knowing I could give him that and enjoy it myself, well, it made it all a hundred times better. When he was buck nekkid, his long, fine dick all hard and wanting between his legs, this desperate look of want on his face, I growled, "I don't see no lube in that hand." Added a nasty laugh, just 'cause. "You got about five seconds to find it or I'm just going to do what I want to do without it."

"Fuck, Joe." Kabe scrambled to roll over and damn near fell over himself getting on to the nightstand, crawling along on all fours. "I'm getting it."

That nasty mouth of his made me want to teach him a lesson… one I'm sure he wanted me to learn him, 'else he wouldn't have egged me on like he had. I followed behind Kabe counting off backwards and every couple of steps shoving his ass with my boot again. "Three, boy." Another shove almost pushed him into the little table. "You're at two and I'm about to just pin you down and shove it in."

Kabe grabbed the bottle off the back of the nightstand, knocking the box with the ring off onto the floor. He almost fumbled the lube as well. All pleased with himself, Kabe turned and sat, holding the bottle up for my inspection. His knees were bent, butt and feet on the floor, with his back resting against the bottom rail of the bed.

Instead, I looked down at the box he'd knocked over and frowned. Guess I didn't have to say nothing, 'cause he grabbed it up and quickly slid it back on the top. Kabe twisted back around and smirked. Lord, I was going to have to smack that look right offa him.

"What?" I set my boot against his shin. Then I leaned on in, putting my weight all on his leg. "You think that makes you something special?" I folded my arms across my own bent knee and moved down closer. His eyes went all wide and bright as I growled out, "You better get your head on straight."

"My head on straight?" Kabe opened his hand up just enough so the lube slipped down into his palm. Then he closed his fingers around it. "Bite me," he snapped.

I reached out and grabbed a fistful of that wild black mass on top of his head. "I did last night," I reminded him as I raked the toe of my boot down the length of his shin and brought his face up close to mine.

"Ha!" Kabe licked his lips. "Whatever, dude." Not even intimidated, he moved in even closer. "Then do it again."

His breath flowed hot over my lips. I could almost feel them moving against mine. Lord, the boy knew just how to turn my crank, get me, and him, all worked up. I twisted my fist, pulling him back by his hair. His hiss of pain got all mixed up with a groan of pleasure. It ran like lightning all through me.

My eyes narrowed down into a snake dead glare. "Give it." I held out my free hand. I could taste him, Kabe was so close.

There it was, that shudder, his eyes drifted almost closed. Kabe stilled. My Kabe, who drummed out a random beat on the sheets when he was dead asleep. My Kabe, who couldn't sit for two minutes without his leg going a mile a minute. That's how I knew I'd done it.

Sometimes it was all the pain that got him there.

Tonight, I guess it was a mix of both. And I'd done it. I'd created that stillness. That quiet in him. I drank it in. Let it settle into my soul. I honestly could've almost stopped there. I should have stopped right there. It was just that satisfying.

Unfortunately, I had this critter between my legs demanding it get a piece of him too. My dick weren't about to be happy just 'cause my brain was. Sometimes the small head gets me into trouble the bigger brain knew to leave well enough be.

I reared up, shoving him down as I stood, twisted and straddled him. Then I yanked him back up onto his knees…I hadn't let go of his hair…and growled. "Give it on here."

A harder shudder hit his frame and almost rattled my hand. Almost shaking he held up the bottle for me to take, which I did. 'Course he leaned his head back right into my crotch as he moved. When Kabe did, I could feel it, I swear I could, that deep sense of self he'd fallen into. I stared down into a face so calm angels must have kissed it for what felt like forever. Green-brown eyes stared at my own face like heaven looked down on him. Then he took a deep old breath and blew it out, long and hard. Every sliver of air passing his lips slid that serenity into a wicked, come-get-me grin.

"Fuck," he drew out the words, "you."

I laughed, "That's kinda back-asswards, ain't it?" That place I'd sent him too, well, wanting to see him get farther on made me stupid, I guess. Knew that Kabe's sinful smile meant he wanted to double down and dig in. See what he could pull outta me. All I had left was a barely stitched together set of nerves. Time to pat his face, suck each other off and promise him that this was just foreplay for another session later on.

I weren't up for it. He'd been right earlier. I was wrecked as good as if I'd been run over by an eighteen wheeler. My whole sense of self lay shattered in the bottom of a ring box.

And I just, kinda, ignored that.

I let go his hair and shoved him down. Popped the last couple of buttons on my fly. He started to slink off, looking over his shoulder as he did so, making sure I was watching. I had to put my boot in the middle of his back.

"Don't you dare think of going nowhere," I ordered as I pulled out my dick. "I got plans."

"God speaks." He taunted me back. In a snot-ass voice, he repeated my order, "Don't you dare…" then he tried to get up. "Go. To. Hell."

I didn't like the blasphemy one bit. I could deal with the nasty language most times, sometimes I even liked it. "Shut up."

Got my foot off, but replaced it with my hand and the weight of my body as I got to my knees. Darn near stuck that bottle up his butt and squeezed a stream of slickness all over and into his ass. Didn't go far, but once I rubbed my cock all in that shine, I was slicker than oil on ice. Dropped the bottle to the floor and grabbed his hips with both hands. Hard, but slow like molasses in winter, I pushed my dick on into his hole. That heat. That softness over a load of muscle. All of it swept through me like a fire through bone dry forest. The sense charred my overheated senses to cinder.

Kabe dropped his head on his arm, his ass up in the air meeting thrust and taking it all. He shuddered out a, "Fuck."

When my pelvis met his cheeks, I stopped. Lord, I knew I was done for right then. My head already spun. The room around us closed in to a fist size box while seeming so huge it could swallow the earth. My mind already closed up shop two minutes ago. I didn't even think, I couldn't think, as I started pounding him hard.

He took me. Did he ever. Shoving back with as good as I gave. Snarling all sorts of curses at me. I'd done gone beyond even knowing what I said back to him. I smacked his butt I don't remember how many times. Not like gentle, playful swipes, but good, solid belts that stung all the way up to my elbow with how hard they landed. I dug my fingers into his skin so hard, keeping him where I wanted, that I think I drew blood. Got to the point where I was fighting to stay in him like a cowboy breaking a wild mustang.

"Stay still, boy." I yanked up a fistful of his hair. There were times when I liked how he fought me and other times, like tonight when I just weren't up for it all the way through. Didn't realize I weren't, but this little part of me really kinda knew it.

"Ha!" Kabe almost bucked against me. "Fucking make me, jerk."

I don't know how it really happened.

All I know is I was beyond aggravated at Kabe, but not mad. I'd wanted a fight, but couldn't stomach a battle. The little bit of glue my thinking mind managed to patch on my shredded soul melted. It all just unraveled right then.

Normally there's that point with Kabe when the battle of wills between he and I, well, it ends. I *break* him, at least temporarily. He settles down and rides the wave. And tonight he wouldn't go there — at least not this night, not like this. With all what happened earlier, what he'd meant to relax me from, the whole jumble of myself in dealing with it all. I'd been of a mind just to pack it in and go to sleep, but Kabe pushed and pushed. And then even while I'm pounding his ass like a freight train, he's got to go take a dig on me, see if he could push me, and him, a little farther, a little harder, than I was quite comfortable with.

That's just kinda when things went wrong.

We're on the floor, both on our knees and him down on his elbow with his other arm back between his legs by then and jacking himself off. I got one arm braced beside him. And I just lost control of my thinking self. This big ol' growl slipped outta my mouth...like nothing I ever heard from me before. I slid my left arm round his throat like I'd been trained to do, you know, keeping his windpipe in the crook of my elbow so I cain't crush it, and latched my left hand on my right bicep, kept him under control so I could ride him like I ought. I cain't say that I thought none about it, I didn't plan nothing. But then it hit, not the biggest or the hardest I'd ever cum, but enough that I tensed up good and shuddered.

Somewhere under the blood rushing in my ears, I heard it. A wet sorta half-snort half-choke. I knew it meant something, but my mind was all wrapped up in melting down. I heard it again as Kabe shook hard. Then he was nothing but dead weight against my arm.

That brought me right out of it.

My left arm was all tensed against the sides of his neck. Immediately I let go, so fast I almost dropped him. Managed somehow to get him down and on his back without cracking his head on the floor.

I'd choked him out.

Good Lord, I'd choked him out.

He lay on the floor with a little streak of white eyeball showing through his eyelids and this stupid, creepy grin on his face. "Kabe!" I yelled and slapped his face. Don't know why, he'd wake up when blood got back to his brain no matter what I did. If'n I hadn't really hurt him. Still, I was freaked beyond any panic I'd ever been through. I rocked back on my knees and shook like a dog about to get beat. My chest locked up so tight I couldn't hardly breathe and I thought everything I'd eaten for the last five days might come back up.

That's about when Kabe started to come to. Felt like forever, but it weren't more than fifteen seconds, maybe. A rush of relief washed from my head down to my feet. I leaned back down, still shaking to beat the band, and whispered his name, "Kabe," I tapped his cheek with the back of my hand a few times, "come on, boy, come out of it."

Kabe's eyes fluttered full open. He blinked a couple of times. Then he started to choke some. Quick as I could, I rolled him onto his side and held him while he puked up a little bile.

"Shit." Kabe propped himself up on one elbow and used the back of his hand to wipe the taste off his tongue. "That sucked." After another couple seconds, he kinda laughed. "Holy fuck, I've never cum so hard." He sounded loopy as all get out. As he looked up at me, Kabe's expression went all weird. "Joe?" Kabe tried to sit up and I helped as much as I could. "What's wrong?"

"You passed out." I sounded far more calm and in control that I was. My insides still jangled. "Scared me witless." He could talk and that was a good sign. "Let's get you up on the bed."

"Hey, I'm good." Kabe protested as I helped get him and

myself off the floor. "I'm okay." He sat down on the bed and glared at me like I was an idiot. "It was no big deal."

"Let me just take a look at you and make sure." I brushed Kabe's hair off his face with the back of my hand. "Okay?"

"I guess." Kabe shrugged like it didn't really matter to him. "Gonna pull up your pants or are we playing doctor now?" It didn't register until he said it that I was standing there with my boxers and jeans shoved down some and my pecker hung out. Of course, Kabe was buck-ass nekkid.

I hustled a few steps over and grabbed my t-shirt off the floor. Cleaned off my dick as I walked back, righted my clothes then tossed the shirt back on the floor. It took me hardly any longer than Kabe'd been out. Still, long enough for it to hit me hard what I'd done. Kabe didn't understand, I could tell. Being that I'd been trained to do what I'd done, I knew.

I could have killed Kabe.

One thing goes wrong in a sleeper hold like that and you can cause a blood clot, crush the windpipe or snap a guy's spine. Both my department and the Utah Department of Prisons where I once worked banned the maneuver because of the risk.

I reached out and Kabe swatted my hand away. "What are you doing?"

"Just let me look, okay?" I used my thumb to pull the skin down under Kabe's eye. "Want to make sure you're all right." Studied Kabe for a moment, looking for broken blood vessels and whether his pupils had dilated. Neither of those signs showed. I pressed around his throat, listing for the tell-tale crackling or popping that would indicate broken cartilage. None of that seemed present. "You look okay." I stood and crossed my arms over my chest. "Do you have a headache?"

"Not really." Kabe seemed completely annoyed with me. "It's just like a fuzzy head rush, like hitting poppers or something."

I'd never thought of Kabe as one to use drugs, he'd always said he didn't like 'em because of how they wrecked you up. Still, I also knew that a lot of folks didn't think of inhalants, like the nitrates in poppers, as drugs. "We should take you over to the emergency room." Even with me being an EMT, well, it just weren't good enough to know for sure whether he was okay or not. "Have them run some tests or something."

"I don't need a fucking emergency room. I just passed out." Kabe pushed me away. "Why are you acting like it's such a big fucking deal?" He didn't yell, but he sounded pretty irritated with me and my concern.

"Anytime you pass out there's a possibility of problems." Kinda fidgeted from foot to foot. I swallowed hard. I did not want to be remembering how stupid I'd been. Ran it through my mind again. He'd puked, but that's actually a pretty common reaction after passing out. He didn't seem to have any cognitive problems…he was with it enough to be irritated at me. Still, I wanted a second opinion from a professional.

"Dude," Kabe reached over and flicked my chest with his thumb and finger, "why are you so freaked out?"

Rocking back on my heels, I just stared at him for a moment. "I choked you out, Kabe."

"I just passed out." He snorted. In that sound, I could tell he didn't get it. "Nothing major."

I rubbed my forehead with the back of my hand and tried to figure out how to explain it so'd he'd understand. "Passing out is always major." That didn't half cover it, but it was the best I could manage right then.

"It was major *wicked*, Joe." Kabe's laugh sounded like he thought I'd given him the best ride of his life. "All of a sudden you got your arm around my throat and it's like my body wasn't really a part of me. Then whammo," he slapped his hands together, "I'm spewing spunk and my head just exploded." Flopping all boneless on the bed, he kept talking in that fast, excited patter. "I don't remember anything after that, except then I had this weird fucking dream that I'm hogtied like a freaking animal and you're all dressed like a cowboy and branding your name on my ass." After a huff and another laugh, he rolled his head and looked at me. "Only downside is the rush did give me a little headache."

"I'll bring you something up." I managed to pretend at calm as I headed downstairs into the bath. Oh Dear Lord, the boy thought it was a game or something. It was *my fault* it'd gone wrong…not that he should have been pushing at me and all, but it was on me, I should have stopped, gone and slept on the couch or something. My head was not a place to be doing what we'd been doing.

All I could manage right then was to lace my fingers over my skull and try and keep my head from exploding—not in a good way. Like a little pack of coyotes, the fact that I could have really hurt him, hurt Kabe bad, kept circling me, nipping at my mind.

No matter how riled up he got me, there weren't no excuse for it.

Nothing to do but go face what I'd done. I dug into the medicine cabinet and found some pain killers. Cradling those in one hand and little paper cup of water outta a dispenser on the counter I headed back to Kabe.

"Here you go." I handed them over into his waiting hands then rubbed my palms on my butt before sitting down heavy on the edge of the bed. Kinda let my hands dangle between my knees for a bit. I was never very good at this kind of thing. After a little more hemming and hawing I managed to mumble out, "I promise, it ain't going to happen again."

"What?" Kabe almost spit the water he was trying to drink out. He'd already swallowed the pills while I sat there working up courage to speak. "Why not…you mean the fucking choke hold?"

"'Cause it's too dangerous, Kabe." I couldn't even look at him. "People die from that kinda horseplay."

I felt his touch drift down the middle of my back. "You wouldn't ever hurt me, Joe."

I shrugged. "Well I'm glad one of the two of us believes that."

Chapter 10

Kabe stood up from the table and stretched a bit. We'd headed over to this little breakfast place on Main Street we both liked. As I fished in my wallet for enough cash to cover the check, he stated, "You shaved this morning."

"I shave every morning." Pulled out a twenty and figured that would do with tip and all.

The huff told me he was not amused. "You shaved it *all* off." He ran his finger along the line of his own jaw.

"Just felt like it." Stood up myself and kinda held out my hands. "Not like it's permanent one way or t'other." If'n I wanted to stay clean shaven, I'd have to scrape the whiskers off my face tomorrow.

He rolled his eyes. "No you didn't." I got another derisive huff. "You did it because your mom said she didn't like it the other day and then you got in a fight with her last night."

I turned on my heel and started towards the door. "Believe what you want to." Didn't want to admit it, 'cause it stung some that he might be right.

"Whether you have a beard or not will not be the deciding factor in her acceptance." Kabe followed me out. When it must've gotten through to him that I weren't gonna talk about that, he hit me with something else. "You know, we could have had breakfast at home." I guess he just wanted to point out everything I was doing out of the ordinary that morning. "You usually don't like to eat out when we're together." Our trucks were just down the road a bit and we headed over to where we'd parked side-by-side. Would have driven in together, but both of us needed to head in different directions after we ate.

I shrugged. "Just felt like something different." The food walked the line between traditional fare that kept me happy and funky offerings satisfying Kabe's need to be different. As long as

I got pancakes, I could deal with them made out of oatmeal and pecan flour. "Well, you know," I hedged a bit before just kinda jumping in to what I'd been thinking about most all morning... and all last night, "hey doc's just down the road." I shoved my hands in my pocket, spun and smiled at him. "I called, he's up, we could go see him."

Kabe stopped short. As his face went all hard and sour, he crossed his arms over his chest, cocked his hip out and shot me a glare. "Would you get the fuck off it?"

"Watch your language," I stepped in and hissed, "we're in the middle of town." What I'd put up with in our house wouldn't be tolerated on the street of our small little town.

He pushed past me, kinda holding his hand up like he was shoving me away. "Okay, get off my back." We'd gone round and round most all morning. Breakfast had been my peace offering. "I'm fine." Kabe shot that over his shoulder. "You checked me out."

"I ain't a doctor." I might be able to keep injured folks stable on their way to a hospital, but I sure as shooting weren't no doctor.

Fishing out his keys, Kabe shook his head and offered me a glare. "You worry too much," he chided. "I'm fine."

I came up next to him and rested my butt against the side panel of his truck. Kept my voice kinda low even if we were about the only souls on the street right then. "I ain't going to sleep right if I don't know you're okay." Studied my fingernails as I admitted that.

"Look," he huffed, "after shift tomorrow, I'll go to the doc-in-the-box in Cedar City, where nobody's going to ask too many questions." He smiled, but his body language told me he weren't gonna do no such thing. "You really want Doc Snow to know what we do in the bedroom?"

"I guess." Actually, I knew I *didn't* want Doc Snow to know nothing about it. Didn't want anyone to know. "Let me know, okay." I figured we'd just both live with that little lie. If we pretended it was truth, maybe it'd come to be true...unless he dropped dead because a blood clot loosed out of his neck and shorted out his brain. Shuddered even thinking on that possibility.

"Yeah," He fussed with the tongue of his web belt. "Okay." I think he caught on that I knew he lied and we just played this game to keep us from fighting. "Look, I got to run and get to the station. Shift starts at eight, supposed to get there around seven to start the change."

Twenty-four on, forty-eight off: the life of a Forestry Service fire-fighter round these parts. I checked my watch, about six-thirty, he'd have to hustle and he'd still be late. "All right. I'll see you tomorrow when I get off work." I might have leaned in to kiss him, but not in the middle of Main Street—I like keeping bullet holes outta my skull. That meant we'd have to leave it at this uneasy place.

He unlocked his door and pulled it open. "I'm going to run by the super-store before I head back home tomorrow." He kinda stood there, hesitating some. "Coffee, rice and crap. Anything you can think of we need?"

"Ah, let me think..." Wanted to answer *yeah, we need to get you seen by a doc*, but didn't. Stuck my hands in my back pockets, shuffled my feet, and stared off along the street. Right down the center came three boys swerving and cutting wheelies. Snapped me right out of the conversation with Kabe. "Hey!" Not even thinking on it, I quick timed it right into their path. "Hey!" The first boy had to swerve not to run me over. "Neil!" I pointed over to the dirt shoulder, telling them with tone and attitude where they needed to high tail their butts to. "Tom! Jake!" Knew them all...I'd taught them all Primary through the Ward for the couple years I'd been called for it by the Church. They all skidded to a stop as I swaggered over—cop move, pull yourself up, puff out your chest and act like you're about to whip some butt. "What are you doing?" I didn't have to ask where they were going. Knew that. Six-thirty a.m. in a Mormon town, the boys all in high school, they were headed on their way to Seminary at the church.

Neil threw off attitude. "Riding bikes." Kid liked to pretend he was tough. He had no idea what tough really was.

While they might sass a little to gain some ground among their friends, not a one of these boys would give me any real trouble. They'd all been raised not to. "No, idgits." I glared and just that was enough to shut Neil down. "What are you doing out in the middle of the road?"

Jake bounced his front tire in the dirt a few times before giving me a non-answer. "There ain't any traffic."

Tom chimed in. "It's not even seven yet." In the LDS church you're taught not to lie to authority figures...don't mean that Mormon kids don't try and hedge their way out of trouble like any other teen would.

I let my gaze wander up the road a piece, hover there, like I saw something way more interesting than these boys. Let the minutes tick off until I could feel those boys fidgeting. Fidgeting 'cause they was teens and just couldn't keep still too long. Fidgeting 'cause they'd been called to the curb by a cop. Fidgeting because if I didn't cut them loose soon, they'd be late to Seminary and then, then they'd have to stand up before the class and explain what delayed them. And that would be worse than any hell I could put these boys through. "Right now." I didn't bother to look at them, just pointed down the road and expected they'd pay attention to me. "But someone comes barreling up," swung that finger to almost brush Neil's nose and bored my gaze right through him, "'round that curve at ninety what you think is going to happen?"

He rocked back a little and shrugged. "It ain't that big a deal."

"It is if I got to be the one tell you boys' parents that I had to scrape you off the pavement." Let that thought sink in a bit. "It'd be a heck of a big deal." I hit each one of them dead in the eyes with my stare. Held that contact just a might longer than most folks found comfortable, made them drop their gaze to study their shoelaces. Finally, I drew myself up and kinda shook the stern attitude off. Not all of it, just enough that the boys' brains might catch on that this was as bad as this time would get. "Just don't do it again. 'Cause next time," the bear in my smile came out, "I'll call your folks and we'll just see what happens." Most of their folks would tan their hides if any one of them got a call from me. I jerked my chin in the direction of the Ward Hall. "Now get."

After I watched the three boys ride a ways down the road, I turned to walk back to my truck. Kabe waited, standing on the running board of his little pickup, arms draped over the top of the door frame. Surprised he'd waited. I know I'd just taken off pretty abrupt like, almost in the middle of a conversation, but not one that meant much of anything. Figured he'd jump in his truck and head to the ranger station down in Cedar City so he wouldn't be too late.

As I got closer, he called out, "Dude, that's it!"

"What?" All right, my brain did not make the leap from here to there.

Like it was real important, he insisted, "It had to be someone local."

"Huh?" I still didn't follow what he was on about. "Local?" Okay, before I'd gone over to chew those boys' butts, we'd been talking about groceries. One of those momentary, two-by-four upside the head moments hit as I realized how normal and natural it'd gotten to be yakking about such mundane things with Kabe. Managed to shake that feeling off before, I hoped, he could tell. "I don't understand what you're getting at."

"Your sister." He rolled his eyes and huffed, slumping a bit against the door frame. "Whoever did that to her had to be local."

After I found the file yesterday, Kabe and I hauled it and the metal box of ones like it to the station. Then I'd gone and made a copy of the reports, pictures and such it contained so I could really hunker down and mull over the facts on my own time. Last night, the two of us had gone over it a bit before heading to dinner at my folk's place. Right now, he knew about as much as I did about my sister's death.

"No." Shook my head. "No one local would have done what happened to her." I couldn't imagine it. I mean, yeah, I was a might younger than her, but still, there'd be people, families I'd known all my life who'd been here, alive, then. And while I well knew what harm my fellow men could do to each other, even those counted among the Latter Day Saints, I couldn't quite wrap my head around that. I'd hauled in guys I'd played football with in high school for beating their wives or driving drunk. Seen the ravages of drug addiction wrought into the face of a former prom-queen selling herself to truckers to feed her fix. Not all the Saints were saints. Still those, while not petty, weren't nothing near as monstrous as what I'd read in that file.

I did not want to believe I knew a monster.

"Except..." Kabe ran his hand through his thick black hair like I frustrated him, "Look, you got on those three kids for riding their bikes in the middle of the highway." He waved his hand off in the general direction they'd taken off to, then swung it around towards the rest of Main Street. "Ten people kinda glanced up or walked right by and didn't say anything."

Of course they wouldn't have, I was a deputy. "Yeah, and?" Nobody would stick their nose in my business like that.

His hazel eyes went wide. "And," he drew out that one word, "if I had been the one jumping on them, at least half of those people would have stopped and said something."

People corrected other folks' kids all the time in these parts. "You're smoking something." Small town America, everybody looked out for everyone else. You don't pry, least not overtly, but you wouldn't just stand by and let some child poke a rattlesnake neither.

"No look." I got another exasperated roll of his eyes as Kabe stepped down from his perch on the mini-pickup. "I'm not local. I mean, I've been here nearly a year. I'm not a local, even after ten years I wouldn't be considered *local*." That he hit dead on. It took about two generations before a family might be considered settled in to town. "People don't bother me much, cut me slack, because I'm with you. But if I was seen talking to a bunch of kids from town, everyone would notice." He kinda bobbed his head a little and a not quite grimace twisted up the corners of his lips.

"Somebody would come out and say something."

Hated to admit it, but Kabe was onto something there. "Okay, I'm listening." I knew who all in this town should be where and with whom and when they were up to something they weren't rightly supposed to be. Kabe'd been a topic of conversation as the *new arrival* for a good month after he hit these parts. Probably would have been so longer except, well, then he and I'd gone and gotten caught messing with each other and that whole nest of snakes was a heck of a lot juicier than just him being new to these parts.

Kabe straightened his shoulders a little. I got the sense offa him that he liked besting me one, especially if I acknowledged it. "Your sister was seven." That she was. "No way a seven year old got from town to the lake on her own." Both of us turned, looking off towards where the lake nestled in the mountains beyond our views. "Someone who could drive had to take her there."

Seventeen miles was a long distance to travel on foot. "I see that."

"Yeah." He swallowed, almost unsure of himself by his tone, but he plowed on ahead. Police work weren't his line of work. Still he had a good head on his shoulders. "So she got in someone's car. She knew the person. She trusted the person at least as much as those kids trust you. If you offered them a ride in the back of the truck...they'd get in." That thought churned my gut a bit, but he'd hit the nail square on the head. "And no one around here would think anything of it."

Still, I had to rub him a little...didn't want him to get to full of himself. "No one?" I teased.

My tone made him laugh. "Okay." I knew he got my implication by his next sentence. "Well a few who equate gay with sicko would be on the phone to all the neighbors or out on the street trying to blow your tires out." He socked my arm kinda playful like. "But that proves my point. If someone saw her with someone who didn't belong, who wasn't local, they would have noticed, remembered, said something or come out to see what was going on. Nobody did."

Okay, that part fit. Another thing didn't though. "But nothing like that ever happened again." I'd been reviewing all the cold case files for months. Even the new batch, I did a quick scan of them before I left the station yesterday. "Nothing similar cropped up." I didn't have to be some highfalutin FBI agent or hot-shot big city detective to know that what had been done to my sister equaled more of a *need* than a *want*. "A guy who could do something like that to a little girl...they don't stop unless they're put away or they die." Addiction, like meth for a tweaker...a guy like that might be able to wait, control his need some, but it'd surfaced again if he'd stayed in these parts.

"Okay, well, there's something to check. Kinda easy, right?"

Computers and the net made my job a lot easier, but it certainly did not solve my cases for me. "Not exactly easy, death wise there's the obits." There might be youngsters' deaths in neighboring areas that might fit, but didn't ring alarm bells at the time. "I don't know exactly how far back they're searchable." Kept stumbling over the big issue. "But I really don't think he did it again." People 'round here might not mention one awful death...but a string of them, all similar, that would have been town talk for decades.

"That you know," Kabe insisted.

"I've been inputting all that information into the Fed's databases on our cold cases." Had to remind him how I'd been spending my time recently. "Similar cases would be in there."

"Dude, you haven't even put her information in." His turn to remind me. "She died in '79. How many other departments have cases just as old, sitting in some storage area waiting for someone to have enough time to enter them into the system? Or, they entered information wrong, I've heard it happens."

"You've been watching too much TV." Teased him, but in the back of my head, I knew Kabe had a point.

His smile broke big and wide. "I'm right...right?"

Just 'cause it's me, I couldn't let him have that. "You're

pushing."

"Hah!" I think he knew I just wasn't giving in because I didn't want him to get too big for his britches. "I'm right...okay, I'm not being a total doofus." He leaned in to my space all pleased with himself. "It's worth looking into."

"Yeah. Yeah." Finally let him take his piece of well earned pride. "Definitely worth looking into."

CHAPTER 11

Nadia stood, her thin, dark hands braced on the lip of the narrow table between us, and scanned the topographical map of Panguitch Lake spread out on the surface. Off to one side rested a sketch of a bit of lake shore with an alleged set of directions and a big X where Rose's body had been found.

Almost absently, she mumbled, "I can't believe someone at your department didn't mention it to you."

I looked up from the stack of crime scene shots that I'd been studying, "Mention what?" I wondered what she'd seen on the map that I might have missed. Hoped it was better than the photos I'd been shuffling through. Some of the edges of the Polaroids already faded off into ragged white lace. The surfaces of others I studied glistened with that off-color washed out sheen of decay: greens moving off into yellow, blues turning rust and odd stripes of haze cutting across the surfaces. Most of the black and white pictures were still clear, but they didn't have the kinda detail color shots brought out—things like why did that patch of grass seem darker than the rest? Just wet or did something coat it? Not all of 'em were that bad off. Still, sitting around in a box, in a paper envelope at the back of a storage room hadn't done 'em many favors.

I hadn't gotten around to unpacking the whole thing, just cut the tape, lifted the lid and pulled out the photos and some papers. Didn't do a whole heck of a lot to expand on what little the file I'd already reviewed contained.

The lack of detail in the photos, and everything else, frustrated me something awful. Almost like they'd purposely tried to avoid it, I couldn't hardly find any shots of the full body. What there were had been taken from off angles where her face remained obscured or that shot along down towards her feet so you could tell her dress was rucked up, there in the water, but not whether that might be because it caught on the reeds or got pressed into the mud or something. The only reason I knew the little wad of white fabric in the grass that someone saw fit to take a picture of was her panties, was the note scribbled on the back. And that was it. Not a one showing that bit in relation to the body, the lake or the road. There were shots of the men pulling her outta the lake. Those didn't mean much to me other than to help try and pinpoint where my sister'd actually been found.

And that was a problem.

The patchwork jurisdiction covering most all of Southern Utah extended up into Panguitch Lake. Dixie National Forrest counted about half the shoreline within its borders. The other half belonged to various resorts and private residences meaning my department kept the peace. Get out on the water and who really had control equaled anyone's guess. I did know that if I got called out to a private residence and then saw some kids setting off bottle rockets on the park's side, I wouldn't just call it in to the rangers, I'd go handle it. Likewise, if a park ranger caught sight of some idget trying to get behind the wheel of a truck while three sheets to the wind, I expect they'd haul 'em off. Maybe they'd swing by to drop them off at our drunk-tank, but we had each other's backs. Cooperation, a little bit of fudging now and then, well it meant the bases got covered.

Frankly, neither the hand drawn map nor the faded photos I found in the file helped me much as to exactly where the body'd been found—our jurisdiction or theirs. First off, most of the roads hadn't been there in the seventies. Marking latitude and longitude back then wasn't as simple as pulling out a hand-held GPS and taking a reading. Water levels in the lake came and went depending on how dry things got over the years and more silt flowed in from upstream each season, meaning what the lake looked like now wasn't really how it looked back then. So's I didn't get in trouble by inadvertently stepping on toes, I'd asked Ranger Slokum to stop on by the station and confer with me on the case. Figured Nadia wouldn't yank the file outta my hands and she'd work with me on anything involving the feds.

"That your sister was murdered, Sugar." She spoke like I

might be slow or something. Maybe I just read that into her sweet southern drawl. With anyone else, I'd have got my back up. Nadia and I went back enough, not time wise, but having worked a few cases together...including her helping me just after she got transferred to Dixie National.

"I doubt any of them really knew." I stuffed the photos into their sleeve and shrugged. "I mean, possible they'd heard some rumors about a little girl who'd been attacked back in the seventies." Since nobody'd ever mentioned it, I figured the case slipped through the cracks, hazards of a small, regional department. Every four years equaled a potential change of the guard, new Sheriff in with his folks. At least that's the way it used to work. Now, while our department might still be small, we functioned like any modern law enforcement agency. "But, honestly, how would they know?"

Nadia laughed. "Cops and elephants have long memories."

"I give you that," I conceded the point, some, "but you got to understand where you are."

"What do you mean?" She picked up a stack of papers and shuffled through them.

Took a moment to think about it before I tried to put it in words. "Right now we got seven sworn deputies on patrol; all courtesy of the war on drugs and the big marijuana farms we get up here now. When I started working corrections, not quite ten years ago, there were only four deputies in Garfield." I'd always thought I'd like to get on with the department back then, but hadn't held much hope since there weren't many openings. "I came in the second round of expansion." Counted myself lucky on that. "See, all this is real new." I sorta spread my hands out to indicate the little interview room we'd commandeered for our confab and on out through the rest of the station/jail complex. "Back in the seventies, it was all *Mayberry* around here: an elected sheriff and *a* deputy. They might have had a part-time guy to serve process, but I don't know for sure about that far back."

She crossed her arms and stared down at me with that momma bear glare of hers. "So?"

I rocked back as much as the little metal chair would allow. "Probably, by maybe the nineties, nobody in this department had been around back when she died." Old guys went out, taking what was in their heads with them. New officers came in and shuffled the old, cold cases to the bottom of the pile. The colder a case got...well, there wouldn't have been enough manpower to chase even a hand-full of 'em down. "It was just one of a bunch of boxes down in the basement of the courthouse sharing shelf space with county assay books and Christmas decorations. We wouldn't have even known about it except for me being on light duty and the new watch commander coming on board and making sure all our old records made it to the new building with us. Going back through the old cases gave him something productive to do with me."

"Okay," She didn't sound all that convinced, "but wasn't it like the town gossip or the family gossip?"

"This was an insular Mormon town back then. And I mean *Mor-mon.*" Felt I needed to really put that fine a point to it. "If the town decided that it wasn't something to talk about because everyone just needed to heal and move on, nobody would have said nothing. They'd all have hung together." At least not outside of small whispers between maybe married folks... and the neighbors, and the gal who worked the checkout at the grocery— all right, but nothing they'd have shared with me. "My Uncle John was the Bishop back then. If my parents weren't up to talking about it, he'd of shot everyone else down." Knowing Uncle John, how protective he was of my momma, he'd have shut them up with his fists if necessary. "And generally, we don't talk about the bad things." Pointed at my chest and then at her. "Not in the family."

Nadia snorted. "Seriously."

"Heck yeah." My own little chuckle turned her derision back on her. "Least wise in my family." Especially in my family. "We ain't much for talking like that."

Earned me a shake of her head as she sat down in the other chair. "My family could never keep something like that a secret."

"Some of it, I think, had to do with how my folks took her death." Put a few things in my life, well, not in perspective, but threw a bit of light in some dark corners. "I don't know as anyone would have recognized it. Heck, it's only starting to make sense now, over the last few years, how my momma was when I was little. This opens up the *why* of the *what* I pieced together in my head."

"Sugar." Nadia, looked up at me, her eyebrows pulled together and her lips kinda thin, like she couldn't quite suss out what I meant. "I've interrogated tweakers who've made more sense than you just did."

"Look, Nadia, we've both been through training; how to recognize when another officer is in trouble, going down a bad road." Mandatory continuing education, most law enforcement agencies subscribed to it. A lot of the classes were about substance abuse and suicide prevention—and how to tell when a fellow officer might not be handling life well. "I look back at how my momma acted when I was little. The next door neighbor always over helping her clean and stuff." Guess I had to explain that. "The nineteen-eighties, Molly-Mormon, it should have been too embarrassing for Mom to accept that help. House-proud don't even begin to explain it, that was her calling from God, take care of her family and the house. Cain't say I think that I ever really bought into that mindset, but LDS of my parent's generation wouldn't have known no other way." Mormons, back then, were seen as a cult so they stuck together like glue. Tradition meant everything. But in our house, my sister, Lacy, was the one who always got me up, fed and off to school. Sometimes my momma would still be in bed when I got home from Kindergarten. "She was depressed, there ain't no two ways about it, maybe my dad too. My house, it was always dim, like the lights never worked right or something." I breathed into my fist a few times. "Sometimes, well, it's like the sun didn't quite hit all the corners of my life."

Crossing her arms over her chest, leaning against the wall, Nadia stared at me. Heavy minutes ticked by. This silence, like silted well water flowing through a pump, passed over my shoulders. "Well that explains some things." Her face, Lord, sadness added a cut to the fine lines of her face, drawing out the age I always knew was there, but never really saw. Like all outdoor folks, fresh air kept the wolf of time at bay, but sun stripped years off her skin.

My turn to look at her cross-wise. "Like what?"

"Sugar." She shook her head. "You were old before your time."

That didn't solve nothing for me. "I don't get you."

"You're not far past thirty." Nadia tapped the table with the report and leaned toward me. "You act like guys my age. Too cautious. Too stern." Then she tossed the paper on the table. "You don't laugh enough."

"I laugh plenty." Caught myself scowling at her.

"Not like you should." She snorted, knowing she'd caught me proving her own point. "Not free and easy. Nothing in your life is free and easy."

"Well," I corrected, "Kabe's pretty *free and easy.*"

That earned me a finger pointed at my chest. "And that's why I've always said he was good for you. You need that in your life. That breath of fresh air. I think, before you met him, you darn near suffocated under your life."

I hated it when she was right. Made me down right grumpy. "My life was what it was."

"I guess." Nadia didn't sound all that convinced. "I think you're far better off now."

"Yeah, yeah, I am." As much as I didn't want her to win, if I didn't concede the point, she'd never let up. "Even with all the things that have gone down." And truth was, he did make life so much better. "You're right, I get a deep lungful of air that tastes like the earth after the rain when I'm with him." Corny as it all seemed, the world shined a little brighter with Kabe around. I'd catch myself just staring at him, grinning like a fool. Our morning runs felt like the sun rose just to throw gold all over his skin. Sitting on the couch, watching some junk TV show... heck, as long as he leaned up against me, I could watch snow float across the screen and I'd sit for a lifetime drowning in his heat, his weight, smelling his skin. "I don't know what he sees in me." I really didn't. All I knew was that whenever he smiled at me this warmth bloomed in my chest and made me forget, for a moment, how hard the world treated me sometimes. "But I thank Heavenly Father every time I see him smile at me."

"I know." She sat down in the plastic chair and shifted a bit. "Teddy Bear picnic." She teased me with her standard barb. "Okay, and that brings up the whole 'why did no one talk about this.' You all were news not more than a minute after Ramon heard you over the walkie-talkies." Yeah, months back, early part of the morning out in the middle of nowhere, over a set of walkie-talkies, Kabe and I started teasing about us getting hot and heavy the night before in the back of my truck. Ramon Piestewa caught wind of what we said. By the time we'd made it back to town most everybody had some version of just what we'd done and what that meant I was. "Why had you never heard of this? No one thought it might be your business to know?"

There's gossiping about other folks and then there's getting up in someone's face. "You didn't poke your nose into other folks' lives like that." I shrugged. "Not unless you wanted to risk getting it shot off." People might have whispered among themselves, but it'd taken a set of brass balls to come out and ask me. Plus, the guys and gals I grew up with, they'd have been years removed from it all, just like me. Their parents wouldn't have said nothing to them or me.

"That's insane." Flicking the corners of the pages on the table, Nadia vented her frustration at the situation.

"It just is. I'll mind my business and you mind yours." I picked up Rose's photo from the top of the file. A bright smile shining out the future she'd never have. "I'm figuring Lacy probably had a hint, although she says nobody told her direct." Kinda brought Nadia back to where we'd started on this road. "By the time I hit school, it was a ghost story, the little girl who died over in the lake.

And not like there haven't been a fair share of drownings over the years: Panguitch Creek, the Sevier River, Panguitch Lake and all the little ponds and feeder streams. I cain't remember hearing a story about my sister, but I know if I had, I'd have asked my folks and they would have just said Rose drown."

"And you're okay with your folks lying to you all these years?" I guess she weren't gonna let me be and change the subject.

That thought hadn't really crossed my mind. "Am I okay with it?" Guess it was a lie. One by omission. "I don't know as *okay* is the right word." Slid the photo onto the table between us and tapped the edge. "Honestly, I only knew this girl in the pictures around my house. She was a name, and that was about it." For someone who wasn't even alive, she took up a lot of space in our lives. "But, I mean, my brothers, Lord, Lacy, to be told don't talk about how your sister died." I couldn't really imagine that. I mean, I'd lived it, but I still couldn't imagine it. How could my parents do that to my brothers and sisters? I guess I kinda understood it, they dealt with their spooks as well right then, I guess. "What a burden went down on them."

Nadia shook her head. "They ever get counseling or anything like that?"

Figured she spoke of my brothers and sisters. "You mean like a shrink?" I knew a couple of sworn officers who had to go through counseling, but even that was few and far between. Professional help, well it weren't seen as particularly helpful 'round these parts. "Probably not." 'Specially not back then.

Nadia split her attention between the report and the map, but kept talking to me. "Your church?"

I figured what she meant by the question. "I'm certain if they reached out someone would have talked to them." One of the perks of living in a small town, folks were there to lean on if you needed them. Looked up from map to catch sight of Nadia scowling. "Oh, you mean, like professional through the church?" Snorted back my laugh. "LDS is all lay clergy." Listed off some of the folks I knew who'd done the term of running the wards. "Uncle John served as our bishop on and off until I was almost five." It was a calling most adult men in the Church experienced at some point. Usually a couple-three years of the duty so as not to burden any one family too much. "My daddy did it for a while. Doug Rane, ran the grocery, had the job for close on six years, before his heart gave out." They'd all done well with the congregation. The newest guy, best that could be said about him was he got the job done; by hook, crook or just plain bullying. "Most recent it's been Pete Sampris." Felt my face go all sour. Pete'd kicked me out of the church, presided over my excommunication. Not that I'd gone to the hearing, but as the bishop of my Ward it would have fallen to him. "Also was the principal at the high school until he retired from that. Not a one of them has any formal training...well maybe Pete has a little, because, you know he was a teacher."

"Just," she huffed and rolled her eyes, "it's just weird."

"It is what it is." I shrugged. "Can we go back to the reason I invited you to my party?"

"Uh-huh." Nadia flipped through the report. "This is thin, thin, thin. No fingerprints." Back then, prints wouldn't have meant much until they had a suspect. The FBI's fingerprint database, AFIS, didn't come about until the late nineties. You studied them with magnifying glasses and only had time to compare lifted prints to actual suspects. "Limited blood typing. How did we ever manage to solve crimes back in the stone ages?" DNA, heck, back then was science fiction. Best you got was blood type, you know, A B O with a positive or negative and again it only mattered if you had a suspect.

"No sense wasting our wishes with what we cain't have." I took a deep breath. "What do we have?" I'd done an inventory, but I wanted to bounce it off someone else's brain, see what we could shake loose outta each other's heads.

"Okay." Nadia picked up the photo, looked at it for a moment, then set it down on one end of the table. "A dead child." Tracing the outline of Rose's face, Nadia's eyes narrowed and her jaw went a little tight. "That's normally a low risk victim." Victimology. You could have said Voodoo back when Rose died and the cops back then would have looked at you the same way. "Not somebody who's going to fight back much." I'm sure they processed some of it the back of their heads, but in those days nobody really thought all the way about the ins and outs of why a perpetrator chose this one victim over another.

I nodded. "And someone who could get her off the street and over to the lake." Nowadays, with TV and school, kids are a lot more cautious...as a group mind you. There were still ruses, lines and people that might overcome that stranger-danger training, but for the most part the little ones didn't trust like they used to. Even in these parts.

That meant we had to look at the time period.

Things were different back then. And Panguitch, well bucolic didn't even begin to describe the Pollyanna bubble they lived in. Insular little town. Mormon little town—and that rang odd. Nobody in none of the reports said nothing about strangers or drifters or nothing. Like Kabe'd said, someone who didn't belong would have stuck out like a sore thumb.

And even if folks hadn't talked to me, they would have talked with each other about what had been off that day. Somebody had to have seen something, noticed something. The town would have closed ranks and passed it back and forth in whispers. The decade though, that also played havoc with time lines. Nobody would have thought nothing if Rose wasn't home right off. Lots of friends to stop and play with. With the whole town, supposedly, keeping an eye out on everybody's kids, people wouldn't worry like they might these days. Not until close on towards evening would Momma have started to worry. Not until the third or fourth phone call would panic have started eating on her.

Nadia's voice broke through my thoughts. "Someone with a vehicle." Her finger traced the big map we had spread out, drifting along the line of the main highway between town and lake.

"Truck or car." I tapped the area where Rose'd been last seen. In a land of Molly-Mormon, cookie-baking, stay-at-home-moms who knew everyone under age twenty by name, age and who their friends were, someone had slipped her away under the curtains of normalcy. "Couldn't control her on a bike and it'd take a long time." At least an hour to go that far with one person pedaling and even a small one riding. "Motorcycle'd have the same problem, control-wise. ATVs weren't around much back then." I remembered the first Honda three-wheeler that hit our neighborhood: pricey thing with junky balloon tires that kept blowing out. "Either way, someone would have noticed a seven year old girl on the back of one of those."

"Okay. Someone with a vehicle." Nadia tapped her teeth with her thumbnail. "A closed vehicle. Car. Truck."

I heaved in a deep breath. "And someone who'd done it before or after." A shudder ran down my spine. "This might have been the first...but, this kinda crime, it ain't no one-off. He might have stumbled into this victim's death. But, likely, it weren't his first, or his last, along this line."

"Yeah. Don't like to think it, but, yeah, there'd likely be more."

CHAPTER 12

As I walked Nadia out of the station, across the lot and towards the white National Park's vehicle, with its green stripe along the side, she nudged me in the side. "Why are you so on edge?"

I'd been acting skittish all morning. More than once, she'd commented on me obsessively checking my phone. "It ain't nothing." I shrugged it off, hoping she'd buy the white lie.

"Okay," she huffed, "well the last time it *weren't nothing*, I ended up playing host to your boyfriend in my spare room...over Christmas."

Yeah, Kabe and I'd had a blow out. He'd caught me coming out of a hotel with another buck. Mind you, Dev was a friend from way back and nothing happened, but Kabe hadn't known none of that. Kabe, actually, got far more hot over the fact that I'd been discussing *us* with Dev than the thought of Dev and I having gotten it on. Said it meant I was holding out on him, not confiding with him. Took me a while to realize he was right and I was a moron.

"It really ain't nothing." This weren't quite the same thing as then. "Kabe's annoyed because I'm pushing on him go to the doctor." We'd got to her vehicle by then. I stopped next to the back fender, ready to shake her hand and see her off.

While Nadia stopped too, she didn't make to open her car door. Instead, she leaned against the side panel, crossed her arms over her chest and glared. "And..." she prompted.

It was bad enough having to deal with Kabe about last night. Wasn't sure I wanted Nadia knowing it all as well. "It ain't nothing," I repeated, hardening the tone in my voice to tell her to drop it.

The slight roll of her eyes told me I didn't intimidate her at all. "Tell me now or you can spend the next twenty minutes having me pull it out of you." This time she shrugged. "Your choice."

"You know, I really hate that about you." Mother bear, I couldn't get away if I ran all the way to the Siever River.

"Ha!" She reached out and goosed my arm. "I'm the one who usually gets caught in the middle of this, so I think I have a right to know."

"Look, he and I were horsing around last night and things just got a little out of hand." Maybe if I gave her a little of it, she'd let me be. "He had a bit of an accident." Soon as I said it, I realized that'd just feed into her more.

"Jesus Christ on a Crutch, Joe." She pushed away from the vehicle and set her fists into her hips. "Okay, so that we don't play this round and round shit," her voice, though not loud, cracked like a whip, "let me translate that out of Joe speak: you were having rough sex and you hurt him, somehow." She must've seen the red shoot up my neck and into my face. "Don't look at me like that, Sugar, you're the one dating a guy with no filter...at least when he's talking to me."

I really, really didn't want to discuss this all with her. "It ain't nothing." About as close to a plea to let me be, as I could manage.

"We just went over this, your 'ain't nothings,'" she snapped, "equals my routine disrupted by your boyfriend."

"Nadia."

She held up her hand to stop my hedging. "Seriously, no filter on that boy. I know pretty much everything you do in bed. And, really, I wish I didn't. Dick is not my thing after all." This time, like I was some bit of trouble, she smacked my bicep with the back of her hand. "So stop beating around the goddamn bush. What the hell happened, Joe?"

My face just kept getting hotter and hotter. "Talking on it with you..." I might tease a bit blue with my sister, but actually talking on what he and I did, well, I didn't want to take that path. And even if she said she *knew*, well, it just weren't how I was raised to talk on such things.

Nadia laughed, "I lived in the land of Folsom Street Fair and leather bars. Ain't nothing I ain't seen or heard. My girlfriend had a thing for gay porn, okay?" Nadia'd lived in San Francisco while working Alcatraz, up until her long-time partner died of cancer. "You gay guys think you got the whole tougher-than-you thing going." I got another laugh. "Honestly, you ain't seen nothing until you've seen a set of leather dykes after they play. Their bruises are massive and they're proud to show them off." I guess she'd told me that so I'd feel more comfortable. Didn't quite help. "So you can keep trying to pretend I'm all innocent, don't know nothing Kabe's told me, and it'll just drag this out or you can suck it up and tell me now. Few things are going to shock me. Especially between you two."

"I choked him out." I almost swallowed those four words. The rest came out as a rush. "I don't know as I hurt him. But I need to know that I didn't hurt him."

Nadia tipped up her chin, narrowed her eyes and looked at me down the bridge of her nose. "What do you mean you 'choked him out'?"

"I put my arm around his neck," felt myself kinda shrinking into my own body, "and he passed out."

"So you wanted him to go to the doctor."

I couldn't hardly manage a whisper. "Yeah."

Instead of yelling, telling me I was a low coyote or maybe plain stupid, Nadia asked, "How? What exactly did you do?"

Took me a few moments of staring at the purple-blue swipes of the Panorama Mountains off in the distance, before I could manage. When I finally worked up some nerve, the words flowed out in a rush. "We was just, you know, going at it." I kept my voice down, though, didn't want anyone I worked with overhearing if they came outside. "And he started getting mouthy and pushy like he does. Normally, I like it, but my day hadn't been going too well aforehand so maybe I weren't thinking all that straight." None of this was meant to justify what I did, 'cause there weren't no excuse for it. "And it all went wrong."

"Oh, Lord, Joe."

My face went all tight. "So he starts in at me, teasing, and I put my arm around his neck, kinda like this." I showed her on my own body, resting my chin up in the crook of my left elbow and my hand kinda wrapped around the back of my neck. "Sleeper hold, you know." Weren't exactly right, but good enough for Nadia to get the idea. "I didn't think on doing what happened. I'd just wanted to restrain him some, get him back under control." I swallowed hard. I did not want to be remembering how stupid I'd been. "Then I, ah, when I," all right she said she knew things, but I just couldn't quite spit that word out to a woman so I hedged, "ah, you know tightened up in that moment, I, Lord, choked him out."

Nadia rubbed her eyes with her fingertips like she was thinking on something hard. "You've been trained in that hold?" I mean, she knew. She was LEO same as me. Part of most departments' standard defense training included all the various head locks, leverage maneuvers and quick take down techniques. Some were recommended, some not so much.

"Yep." Without waiting, I answered the question I figured would come next. "And then been told the ten thousand reasons why it ain't a good idea to use it."

"Why do it then?" The crossed arms over her chest and that cold whisper told me I was talking to another officer, someone who thought I should know better. "Why do it on Kabe?" She hissed it out. I could see the tension racking up her whole body.

"I don't know. I just did." I felt like some little kid who's about to get whooped for being bad. "Lord help me, it was an accident. I didn't mean to hurt him none. He likes it, you know, kinda on the edge while were messing around."

It was Nadia's turn to stare at the horizon. "Ah shit, Sugar." She didn't even look at me as she hissed it out.

"And then, this morning," I scuffed the toe of my boot against the asphalt, "I'm trying to get Kabe to go on and get seen by a doctor. I mean, he came out of it quick, didn't seem disoriented and, I got EMT training, so I didn't see anything obvious, but..." Reined myself back in from rambling off on a tangent. "Now he's all convinced I'm worrying too much and just being a thorn in his side."

"'Cause he doesn't know any better." The long drawn out sigh told me she kinda wished she hadn't poked at me quite so much. "Shit. Sugar, do you want me to call him?"

A little bit of tension seeped out of my shoulders. I didn't do cartwheels or nothing at her offer, but it meant I weren't in this alone. Still, Kabe might not be so keen in me involving Nadia. "That's going to piss him off too."

"Yeah, it will," she agreed. We both knew how stubborn my boy could get. "But I think it'll get through to him that if you were talking to me about *sex* then you're damn worried and maybe he should be too." I hoped so. "He may be a pig-headed as you, but Kabe ain't stupid."

The knots that twisted up my stomach all morning started to unwind. "It'd be a load off my mind, Nadia."

"What are friends for?" She smiled as she finally yanked open her driver's side door. "I've got to get." Sliding into the seat, she reassured me, "We'll talk later, okay?"

Bracing my hand on the roof of the cab and the top of the door frame, I leaned in and said, "Thanks again." Then I stepped back. As she shut the door, I added, "For all your help today."

The little salute she gave me told me not to worry. I stepped away as she backed up. Didn't watch her pull out of the lot, I had things to get back to in the station. I hustled through the front door, slid my pass key to unlock the interior security door, and headed on towards my desk.

Lieutenant Lowell darn near yanked me by the collar as I walked past him. "Why did we just have a visit from the park rangers?" He didn't actually look up or even touch me. That voice alone was enough to make me stop mid stride and back up just a hair. Lowell spun his chair so he faced me and massaged the arms with his hands, making me feel like even though he'd accosted me, that I was interrupting him.

"Who, Nadia?" Thought maybe I shouldn't sound so familiar with her, so I corrected myself, "Ranger Slokum?" I don't know why he felt a need to pry. The rangers stopped off here every so often—get a drink, use the can, there were long patches of road 'round here with nothing but trees and mule deer to fill 'em. Like I'd said before, though, I tried to play nice with the man who took my job. "Ah, well, I asked her to come in and look at one of my cases. There may be some overlap on jurisdiction."

"Your cases?" The question didn't sound snide, but it got my back up a little all the same. "You're on light duty. Been moonlighting on me, deputy?" And that tease didn't do none to help my attitude.

Drew in a deep breath and pushed the resentment down. "No, sir." I think I even managed a smile. "It's one of the cold cases you handed off to me." Crossed my arms and settled into a wide legged stance. The 'I'm an officer and you ain't going to intimidate me' stance.

I heard a snicker from over near the counter; that'd be Deputy Jess Garts. He and I went a long ways back. Caught him out of the corner of my eye making a face like he'd swallowed a bushel of lemons. He was about the only one in the department that I'd told how low this whole arrangement made me feel. Glares off both me and the lieutenant made Jess mumble something about getting back out on patrol.

Once he'd ducked out, I finished my thought. "This one kinda got in my head." Hopefully, if I ignored Jess, Lowell wouldn't put no stock in his behavior. "I mean, I'm almost done with the data entry part of this and since it's an old case that needs cleaning up..."

Lowell licked his lips and narrowed his eyes like he might want to start grilling me on what was all on with Jess. After a moment, he shook his head and asked, "What's the case about?"

Blew out the breath I didn't know I'd been holding. "A little girl's murder back in the late seventies." I don't know why I hedged that some. Maybe because I didn't want him to think I was letting my personal business slide into my job.

"You think you can solve it, after all this time?" It didn't come off, too much, as a barb. More of just an honest question given how old the case was.

"I don't know as I can, sir," I admitted. "But, I'm about to run out of desk work and I figure dogging it for a while ain't going to mess with my light duty requirements." Plus, it'd give me a chance to stop looking at these four walls. I'd had my fill of being cooped up at the station. I needed to get out and about before I went crazy.

"You never know." He relaxed some, kicking one foot out and stretching a bit. "What got you on this one? New piece of evidence? Similar case turn up in the database?" Again, I couldn't tell if he prodded because of interest or to dig at me. "What?"

"Ah, I know the family of the girl." Again hedging. I decided it was mostly 'cause I didn't want the lieutenant that much in my head. "I seen what it done to them." I'd lived with what it'd done to them. "Kinda makes me wanna set it right, if'n I can."

"You might not be able to. Know that, right?"

"I know." I really did. "I got about as much chance as snow in July." I'd need a pile of blind luck, some dogged work and a smile, or two, from Heavenly Father to put my sister's killer behind bars. "But, new technology could shake something loose from what we got in evidence. Plus, I'm thinking that, maybe, people who might not have wanted to talk back then...things like that weigh heavy on a mind after all this time." Those were the thin strands most cold cases were stitched together with. "Or, with a little digging, there could be someone out there who the killer talked to long after the fact. Time changes things."

"All right." He nodded and straightened himself up. "Go ahead and keep on with it, but don't let it take too much time from the other assignments I've given you." He started to turn back around.

"I won't, sir." I was glad to be out of his sights again.

As I walked away he added, "Keep me posted."

I didn't bother to say nothing in return since he weren't even looking at me by then.

CHAPTER 13

Pulled up to my parents' house a little after eight in morning. Knew my folks would be up already. Early to bed, early to rise and all that hooey. Didn't want to be here, especially not after what happened two nights ago. Beyond the throw-down with Mom, painful as that had been, I still jangled over what I'd done with Kabe. Lord, I hoped he was on over to see the doctor when he got off shift today like he'd told me he would. Couldn't hardly sleep last night with the worrying on it. There's a difference between wanting to hurt my boy and actually damaging him. I'd walked right up to that line and almost across it. My belly cramped up every time I thought on it.

On top of all that, I had to go deal with Pa. I'd have put it off longer if'n I could, but I'd promised Lacy I'd get to it sooner rather than later. I knew this was akin poking a stick into a hornets' nest and I weren't going to come out of it without getting stung. At least the worst was over—me actually telling him I was gay. The rest just meant trying to keep my head above water as the flood pushed me along. Didn't mean I wanted to throw myself on the rocks along the way, but sometimes there ain't no helping it.

Talking about Rose's murder would likely be me throwing myself on rocks.

Pulled off into the drive and got out of the county vehicle I'd been using. Weren't mine. I'd wrecked mine, darn near totaled me out along with the Explorer I rolled. They'd replaced it with a new-to-us Charger bought offa the Layton PD. We hadn't even had time to change it over yet: they did white, our vehicles were all black. Made me feel kinda odd, rolling in a vehicle that didn't match none of the others. 'Course, not like I was supposed to be chasing folks down or nothing.

Didn't see my dad around as I settled my class B Stetson on top of my head. I heard him though. Rather I heard him working;

the rhythmic whoosh of air and the crack as the maul hit wood. Yeah, I'd made sure they had some logs and I'd split a bunch down for the fire, but Pa probably didn't think it was near half enough. I headed around back and caught sight of him. Lord, I hoped I was half as spry when I hit his age.

As he set the maul head on the ground, near his feet and leaned over to toss a split log onto the pile of others, I called out, "Morning!"

Alls I got in return was a grunt. Pa picked up another log and set it on top of the chopping block. Then he twisted it around looking for knots and natural splits. When it seemed like it was where he wanted, he stepped back.

Before he could take a swing I jumped in, "I need to talk to you, Dad."

"Why?" He swung the maul in a nice overhand move, letting gravity take half the work out of the project. The log split pretty much dead center. "You gonna get all in my face about you and that boy of yours?" He picked up one of the split sides and put it back on the block. "Obviously that's done." I got a glare as he walked the couple paces back to take another swing. "You've gone and decided where your life and your soul stands. Let everybody know it." The last sentence came out as the maul connected with the wood. "So there ain't much to discuss about that."

This was not the time to get my back up. "Actually, no, Dad, not about that." Still, my tone got pretty hard.

He dropped the head of the maul between his feet and leaned on the handle. "You ain't here to rub my nose in your sin?"

I think my growl startled him. "Dad." I'd never wanted to be treated or talked to like a child. The day after I had my high school diploma in my hand, I'd bought myself a broken down Chevy Cavalier for a thousand bucks, thrown all my gear in army duffle bag and taken off into Las Vegas to work with my cousin building fake chimneys on new houses. For the year before my mission, I'd paid rent to Payton so's I could sleep on his floor and sent a hundred a month to my gran'ma to pay on the auto loan she'd made me. "Don't you talk to me like I's five and in the dog house." I'd made my own way since then and the only reason I'd taken my parents' laying into me these past few days was 'cause I'd gone and blindsided them. "I got business with you that don't got nothing to do with that."

He turned his back on me and headed towards the shed. "About what?"

All right, I wasn't about to let him get away that easy. I followed. "About Rose."

"Your sister?" He stepped in and set the maul by his feet, then he turned, leaned on the door frame and crossed his arms over his chest. "What the heck you want to know about her for?" He looked at me like I'd done lost my mind. "That's what's got a burr under your saddle today? Hauled yourself over here in uniform and everything?"

I could work that stance too. Set my legs wide and crossed my arms over my own chest. "I need to talk to you about how she died." An interrogation stance. Not like this were really one, but Pa needed to realize that when I put on this uniform, it meant I wasn't going to treat him like my daddy.

"No." He hefted the maul and pointed the flat side at my face. "She's dead." I could have cut a hair on his voice, it went so sharp. "Ain't nothing going to bring her back so no use talking about it."

That burst rocked me back some. "Dad, she was murdered." Tried to gain back my ground by letting him know that I'd found out. "Someone killed your daughter."

He flipped the maul in his fist, let the shaft slide through his hand so that the head hit the shed floor with a bang. "Rosalie drown."

"Sorta." I choked up a derisive laugh. "If you look at it sideways." Sarcasm, about the only way to deal with that load of horse apples. "Someone held her down." I hit him with the cold hard facts. "Whether they pushed her under the water or knocked her out so's when they put her in the lake…either way…"

I snorted. "Yeah, right, she drown," couldn't keep the whip crack outta my voice if I tried, "with help."

Saw it. The red bleeding into his cheeks and forehead. Pa's shoulders went all tight. He drew himself up to where he stood tall and straight. "Why would you even say something like that?" A rattlesnake's hiss couldn't have been colder.

"'Cause I read the darn department file." Again, facts. He had grit, I had truth and we were buttin' heads like mountain goats in rut. "The one about her *murder*!" Drew that one word out and threw in all the poison I could muster. "The one that landed on my," pointed at the badge pinned on the uniform I wore, "desk."

He shook. "And she's just as dead." He let the handle of the maul drop as he stepped out of the shed. He came up all into my face. "You going to get all on me about why we didn't tell you?" Felt him shake, the air just vibrating between us. "Why we thought it best to spare you the details?"

"Yes." I think I registered it before my brain actually processed it: I had a good two inches on him. "No." It hit me, like shot in the gut with buckshot hit me, my daddy was an old man trying to hang onto his pride. Made me soften up my tone a slight bit, "Dad, it's still an open case." Forced myself relax just a hair. "I've got orders to investigate her death." This slice of time held still for a moment and then everything I knew...flipped.

Suddenly, I was the top dog, kinda. This swarm of white water bowled me over and kept flipping me in the mashed up current, bouncing me off the bank and raking me across the boulder covered bottom. I didn't know what was up or down.

"From who?" He spat it back. "Not from me."

"My department, the ones who matter."

"I'm your father! Her father!" Spitting mad, I felt the flecks of it hit my skin while I stared him down and he yelled. "I matter! I say drop it."

"No." My neck went all tight. Could feel the veins in my forehead bouncing under my skin. "I owe it to Rose to see if I cain't find her killer."

"You owe it to Rose?" His laugh was all full of bitter. "*You* owe it to Rose? She was dead and gone long before you could walk, boy." The air just seemed to bust out of him, and Pa sagged. He took a couple of steps away and shot over his shoulder, "What perverse sense of pleasure you getting out of this?" When he got to the chopping block, he turned and sat down heavy.

Took a moment to let the fight drain out of my system before I answered. "Justice ain't pleasure." Weren't all gone, but I didn't feel like I was gonna snap.

Pa let his hands drop between his knees. "There ain't but one person in this universe who has a right t'demand justice."

Been raised too long in the Church not to understand that he thought I was stepping on God's toes. "All right." Sucked down another slow breath, still trying to back myself down. "I owe it to Lacy and the rest of them, to you, to Mom." Been years since he and I'd had a throw down like this. "Let your minds rest."

He didn't say nothing for the longest time. Just stared off at the back of the house. When he did turn his attention back to me, his face had gone hard again. "Don't you dare bring this up to your momma." There were levels of threat in that tone that had nothing to do with a man and his son. "Let the dead be." All quiet and tensed up again, and scarier for it. "Rose is with Heavenly Father and we'll be a family in the next life...at least some of us." Cut me deep to know what he meant there; just bit my lip as he kept talking. "Whether some buck ends up behind bars on this world don't matter a hill of beans in the next."

That last arrow aimed at me was a lot harder to get past. I'd rather he'd have punched me than say what he had. My sore feelings weren't about to derail me from what I'd come for, though. "Why?" End run around his attack, I tried to root up what made him dig in his heels...more so than Pa normally would. "What are you hiding, dad? Why is this so raw?"

He pointed at me, his hand shaking just that little bit. "You," he almost had to take a breath between each of the next words, "will not talk to her about this."

Took my mind flipping that last order over a few moments to get he spoke about mom. "Why?"

As his jaw went hard, he stood on up. "I will not have you ruining the last few good years your momma has left with us by dredging this all back up."

There's times you think you've been arguing about one thing and then realize that weren't what it were about at all. All his anger kinda fell into place and then dropped right through the bottom of my gut. "What do you mean, 'last few good years'?" I'd thought maybe I'd hit a slow point in the stream, but this swept me back into white-water where I couldn't even tell which end was up. "Is Mom sick?" A good twenty years of my life vanished and, suddenly, I was a scared little kid. "What she got?" Asked questions like I was grabbing at the bank for my life. "How sick? Cancer? What?"

"She ain't sick." I could hear in his voice that he hadn't intended to tell me, least not then. "Not like that."

I weren't about to let him go. "Then what?"

"Not your problem, boy." All the fight from earlier came rushing back into him.

Came rushing back into me too. "Dad!"

"Drop it!"

"No." Wasn't going to back down earlier, and I sure as shooting wasn't gonna back down from this. "Dear Lord, Dad, what's going on?"

"It ain't nothing to concern yourself over." He couldn't even look me in the eye as he said it.

I pressed. "Whatever it is, it got you to coming at me...that means it's something."

Another long look at the house, then at the mountains and finally at me before he almost whispered, "Her mind is going."

I stepped back. That was it? "She's fine, Dad." Thought back over the last few days, the cheery letters and couple emails I'd gotten while they'd been away. Same Momma I'd always had;

just older and slower. "Nothing's wrong with her." He had to be imagining things, worrying too much. "You're both getting old, but..." Maybe all the stress of traveling and such got him spinning yarns in his head.

"Don't tell me what I know and what I don't!" The whip cracked through his voice again. "The doctors told me. It's coming on and it's going to start coming on faster and faster."

Doctors, nobody said nothing about them going to any doctors. "What?"

I hadn't meant it that way, but I guess my dad thought I wanted a diagnosis. "Alzheimer's." The scariest word in our family history. "Same thing that took her daddy." He kicked a log next to the chopping block with his boot and sat down again. "They say Heavenly Father has a reason for everything. I'd have never figured it out if we hadn't been called into Russia. I mean, we got the mission calling and I thought there's something wrong here." A lost, lonesome chuckle found its way out of his chest. "Old folks like us get called to do local Temple work or into Salt Lake for genealogy research." Except for your first mission as a young man, most other Church callings, even missions, took place close to home. "We don't get sent half way across the world to help set up a new ward on the edge of Siberia." Still, missions were a random thing. A single man might find himself on a two year duty at the Missionary Training Center, a unmarried young lady might end up helping feed children in some poor corner of the world. Not the usual, but not unheard of neither.

Still, wound up as I was in the blow I'd got, I didn't see how two and two equaled four right then. "I don't understand."

"If we hadn't have been in that little two room apartment away from everything we knew, everyone we knew, she coulda hid it from me."

"Hid what?"

"The little things." He cracked his knuckles by pressing his fingers against his palm. "Waking up and not remembering where we were, not just once or twice, but over and over again.

Getting lost, in maybe a block, trying just to get things for dinner in that little neighborhood. Those were the little things." Then he palmed his face with both hands, pulling his skin tight across his cheeks. "She'd forget and leave the stove on, things cooking. I thought she was gonna burn the place down at least twice." He heaved up a big breath. "That's what really scared me."

"That's just being forgetful." Over thinking it: my dad would do that from time to time. "I mean, you said doctors. You took her to some doctor in Russia?" I heard horror stories of medical care over there. Even if I only believed half of it, I'm not sure I'd put a lot of faith in a doctor over there. "They probably just guessed or you misunderstood." They'd have had training in Russian language before they went over, but big medical terms were not usually included in the general instruction of how to say, *please, thank you,* and *have you found God.*

"No, it was worse than that. She'd be talking and forget what we were discussing. Couldn't remember people's names, folks she'd met two or three times." In most folks, that'd be normal even if you weren't old, but not Mom. "She's always been the one good with faces and names." She'd meet a person once and remember them if she saw them three years later. "I found these stashes of reminder cards where she kept stuff written down." He huffed again. Lord, it seemed like all the strength in him just oozed out around his boots. "It was like snow falling." Fluttered his fingers in the air so's I'd get the picture. "All these little flurries drifting past you until you realize that you're knee deep in trouble. Not a one by itself seems like a problem."

This couldn't be happening, not to my momma. "Oh, Lord, Dad." I dropped my butt down on a sideways log, put my elbows on my knees and my face in my hands. It pushed my hat back high on my head.

"We got back to the States a while back, asked to come home early. She was so mad at me." He kept going, like he'd kept this all bottled up and now that the cork had been popped pressure kept it spewing out. "Told me I was being an idgit and a worry wart. I didn't tell nobody, not even y'all, because I, well, I hoped she was

right and I was wrong. We've been staying with your Uncle Eloy
for the last couple months, in Scottsdale. Took her to the Mayo
Clinic. PET scans, CAT scans, MRIs, I lost track of all the tests.
The doctors figure it's Alzheimer's because they've pretty much
ruled out all the rest."

Mayo Clinic sure as heck weren't no foreign doctor on the
edge of Siberia. "Ah," tried to lasso the thoughts spinning 'round
like dust devils through my head. Looked up and asked, "I mean,
what do they say?"

"Say?" The glare he shot me told me he wondered if I'd been
listening at all, "She's got Alzheimer's, boy, that's what they say."

I shook my head, "How long?"

He shrugged. "They don't know." Every word he said seemed
to add another year to his shoulders. "Could be years before
she's gonna need more care than I can give her. We could have a
few years beyond that before she's gone. Her mental symptoms,
they say it ain't as bad as the progression of the other things
happening to her body. She always read a lot, three, four books
a week if she could get 'em. Liked to do word games and mental
puzzles, really involved in Church work, even above and beyond
her callings, always keeping busy and helping folks...doctors say
that's helped." He wrapped his hands around in the air like he
tried to tie up his thoughts. "You know, keeping active and all."

"Lord. Oh, Lord." That might have stalled it some, but there
weren't no way to stop it.

"And I think she's known for a bit that it was happening to
her. I mean, she lived through it with her daddy. You remember
when he was with us, when it got so bad we couldn't handle
him." I remembered and wished I didn't. Pa-pa getting ugly and
violent. Everybody in the house ducking for cover. "She's always
had this book, different ones over the years, but where she keeps
everything, every scrap that's important. Birthdays, Ward events,
appointments and such. I think she's been training herself since
she was younger to go there, look there everyday." Like trying
to drain the Great Salt Lake with a tin cup. "That way, if it
happened to her, she'd be used to using that book to remind her.

She wouldn't forget it."

"Dad, I'm sorry." Don't right know what I was apologizing for, maybe just that it had to come out this way. "Tell me what you need me to do. You name it. I got it covered." I'd do whatever it took. My family didn't see eye to eye, most all too stubborn to give into the others, but didn't mean we didn't love each other in our own ways.

"Joseph." He reached out, grabbed my shoulder and pulled me close. "Don't take her last memories down into Rose's death. She don't need to be dropped down into that heartache again. For your momma's sake, leave it be."

Didn't want to remind him that her mind might likely get stuck back there anyway. "I've already caught the case." Lord, I wished I hadn't found that file. I wish I'd just done what I'd been asked and put the stats into the databases. And I wished I'd never gotten Nadia involved or the Lieutenant. "My boss wants me to work it." Even as I wished those things, I knew I would do the same thing all over again. "I cain't just drop it." Worst part of my own mule streak, I couldn't let something like this drift off in the wind.

"Well, do it without her." He squeezed where he still had ahold of my shoulder. "Promise me, you won't talk to her about it."

"But what if she has that piece of this puzzle and just don't know it?" And I might have protested, but already, I was trying to figure through ways not to have to talk to Mom about any of it.

"Going on thirty-odd years, Joe." He reminded me as he let go of me and stood. "That's how long Rosalie has been gone. Another ten, twenty ain't gonna change much of nothing."

Got to my feet as well. Took my hat off and ran the brim through my fingers a few times. "Don't you want to know?" I felt like a nest of snakes had moved into my chest and belly, everything all twisted up inside.

He rubbed his eyes with one hand. "I've spent more than half my life without the police solving it." There was a weariness, a resignation there like I'd never caught offa my daddy before. "It ain't gonna change nothing." He repeated, a little harder this time. Then he sorta sneezed like he wanted to blow out bad memories with the air. "Won't ever change my nightmares: coming up on the lake and looking down seeing all my kids' faces, your'n, your brothers', the three girls, all of you all there, blue and lifeless. And it ain't never stopped hurting," he tapped over his breastbone, "it's just gone from that feeling of a coyote ripping through my chest to this dull ache like my arthritic knees—always there, always reminding me that I buried one of my children." Then he shoved his hands in his pockets and frowned, just a bit. "You figuring out who killed her ain't gonna ever ease that."

CHAPTER 14

Drove on back to the station. Luckily, it weren't far, 'cause I didn't even remember how I got there. One moment I pulled away, the next, I sat in the parking lot of the station with the engine running. Didn't even know how long I'd been sitting there. Turned off the Charger, took a deep breath and got out. After I took two steps, I realized I'd left my hat in the vehicle. Turned around to get it and saw I'd left the door open too. Where the heck was my head? Squared everything away, pulled my Stetson on down and humped it towards the station all while studying the toes of my boots.

"Howdy, Joe." I heard Jess Garts call me from the station door.

I hardly looked up as I passed him. "Howdy, yourself." Mumbled it out. Didn't even think on him much as I wandered over to my desk and sat myself down. Took me a moment or two before I even had the will to power up the computer. Opened a file, stared at it a bit and then shut it. I thought maybe I'd done that one already. Cracked another and thought it sounded like the first. Then I wrapped my head around the fact that it was the same file... and I hadn't entered it. Tried to get into entering data from the files to keep my brain occupied. Mindless task in some ways, but I'd keep losing the information outta my head from the time I read it to when I put my fingers over the keyboard to type it in.

Don't know how much time I wasted before Lt. Lowell wandered over, pulled up a chair and sat down next to me, "You okay there, Joe?"

I looked up. "Excuse me, sir?"

Something about his face didn't read right to me. "Jess told me he saw you just a bit ago and you looked like somebody'd shot your shadow." He leaned in. "Sitting here right now, you don't look so good."

Tried to deny the obvious, "I'm fine." I didn't even believe myself with how it came out.

He snorted. "You sure don't look fine."

I shrugged and entered in some more data. "Doing all right."

Lt. Lowell tapped the desk to get my attention. "Wanna try punching in that same number a few more times?"

As I lifted my hands off the keyboard, I blew out a breath and rocked back in my chair. "Sorry, sir."

Crossed arms and a cop stare down were tempered some by the lieutenant's tone. "What's eating you?"

I knew I couldn't shine him on, not with where my head was. If I tried, I'd just muck it up. "Got some news about my momma." Rubbed my eyes with the fingers on one hand. "It ain't good."

He thought for a moment. "You need to take some time?"

Almost thought about calling off work for the rest of the day, not that I had a lot of time banked after my accident this winter. I didn't know how I was going to function at my duties with my world just falling apart right at my feet. "No, sir." I realized though, that if I sat at home, staring at the walls, I'd go crazy with worry. Probably be out splitting wood just like my dad. "I'd rather be at work, if it's all the same."

Any trace of sympathy vanished. "Not if you're going to screw it up."

Alright, I deserved that. "Yeah, I probably need something a little less..." searched for the word a bit and couldn't find what fit right, "something a little more interesting."

"What about that case?" He jerked his thumb towards the evidence storage area. "The one the ranger came by to talk about."

"I still haven't cataloged that box of evidence." I mean, there was a list of what was supposed to be in there, but didn't mean it was. Given what short shrift the reports in the file got, I wasn't real optimistic on what the box might hold. Not only what might have gone missing, but whether it'd been stored in any way that kept the integrity of the evidence. "I got to see what state of preservation it's in."

"See what's in there from your sister's murder?" I hadn't told him that. Guess he caught the flash of shock of my face. "You think I don't take a thumb through the files on your desk?" He stood and rapped the desk again. "Look, I'm fine with it, but I don't like you not being straight with me." Some departments had strict rules about who could investigate the deaths of people they knew. Honestly, we were small enough, most anything that happened 'round these parts happened to someone at least one deputy was friends or kin with. "Jess kinda brought me up to date on all you been through." He actually reached out and gave my shoulder a friendly squeeze. "But, deputy, I gotta know you're being above board with me." Like a coach in the fourth quarter rousing his players to his side and their best effort. "Understand?"

"I, well." Stopped myself. Excuses wouldn't work. I went for a more direct route and apologized. "I'm sorry, sir."

"I get it." He stepped back. "I'm trying to understand y'all. Y'all are trying to figure out me. I'll give you a pass on this one." I got a warning finger pointed at my chest. "Don't do it again."

He could have chewed me a new butt for holding things back. "Yessir." I might not like the man all that much, but I had a little more respect for him right then. "Understood."

I got a nod in response before he walked off. Maybe he was just one of those folks that said his piece and then once he'd said it, he was done. In the back country, well there were a lot of men just like that. One of 'em was my daddy. I shut down the computer and straightened my desk. Then I went back to the evidence locker.

The other day I'd cracked the seal on the box to pull out the photos. The rest of the things in the carton, I hadn't even looked at. Most of the stuff in the box had been collected back when folks weren't too careful about handling evidence. The items had gone to the OME and come back to us to store, who knows how many hands had touched the contents. Still, I wanted to keep any new cross-contamination to a minimum. We had a table back there for sorting things, so I set it on that. Then I pulled a sheet of butcher paper from the roll attached to the end and spread it across the surface. Got a pair of those purple gloves outta the little box on a shelf before I opened up the box for the second time.

After I wrangled the gloves onto my big ol' hands, I removed each manila envelope, slit the seals, pulled out the contents and set those out on the paper. Wasn't much. One packet held a little yellow dress with red patch pockets and a run of the same red fabric offset on the side hiding the buttons there. There was a picture of Lacy wearing that same dress when she was about the same age...likely the clothes had been handed down to Rose, same as I'd gotten the hand-me-downs from cousins. White knee socks, white panties and red shorts were all packaged on their own. A paper bag held a small pair of light brown leather, lace up shoes.

I frowned 'cause something weren't right. I picked up the file and read the description of how they'd found her. There weren't nothing on those pages about shorts. And a little bit of clothing might not matter, but it might matter big. She weren't wearing her panties, but was she wearing her shorts?

If she wasn't, then where they were found would be important since it might indicate exactly where she'd been attacked. If the shorts were quite a ways away, then the killer might have tossed them and that would tell us a direction he fled. If she was wearing them that raised other possibilities. Did she have them on backwards? That would suggest redressing by her attacker. If they were on correct, she might have put them back on herself and tried to flee or he'd used the distraction of letting her dress and thinking he'd free her for compliance and then killed her.

Then there weren't any samples of the water she'd come out of and they should have taken that. A little packet I didn't open was labeled *fingernail scrapings*. No reason for me too. I'd just send it off to the Office of the Medical Examiner. I also found a rape kit. There weren't no mention in the file about having taken one.

There were tapes with fibers on them. Basically, the box held a lot more than the file mentioned. I didn't know why those things weren't on the list, but I set it all to the side to go to the OME as well.

Made me wonder, though, what else got left out of the file.

CHAPTER 15

Almost couldn't handle the whole news yesterday. I'd been a robot at the station today. I headed back to my desk. Left my phone charging there while I was working on other things. When I got there, I flipped the display on hoping Kabe'd called. He always teased me about my dinosaur, but I never felt I needed nothing fancy. One message left about an hour ago. The missed call was a number I didn't recognize. Pulled the phone off the charger and headed to clock out. After that, I went round by the post office to collect the mail. Got a P.O. box this past winter. Problems with us getting our mail, finding a few surprises left in with what we did get, and my mail box winding up bashed in and quarter mile down the road prompted that move. Might have been a bit more of a hassle, but at least my electric bill didn't end up with dog crap all over it. About that time, I remembered the message on my phone. Listened through the intro as I unlocked my box and dug out the mail: June's voice came across asking me to call her.

As I flipped through the stack of bills, credit-card offers and junk, I went to the call log and hit the button to return the missed call. As soon as I heard the hello, I jumped in, 'cause I recognized the voice. "Hey, what's up? I got your call." Dumped the junk in the trash can next to the door while we talked.

"Hi, Uncle Joe." June always sounded so upbeat. "I needed to go to the pharmacy for mom's medicine. She forgot it. Mom's upstairs with one of her migraines." I didn't know if she could even take breath with how fast she talked. "Gran'pa told me not to leave Gran'ma too long on her own. And I wasn't sure how long it'd be."

"Where's Dad?" Corrected myself for her. "Your Gran'pa?"

"He had to go over to the church for something." A pause, and then she started talking with someone near her. June must've moved the phone away from her face 'cause I couldn't quite make out the conversation. Then she was back, "Sorry. Dealing with the whole getting the prescription transferred thing."

"I guess you got it sorted out then?" I kinda mumbled that 'cause I'd come across a letter addressed to Kabe with the return address of Weiss, Bulger and Noble, PLC, in Salt Lake.

I heard her tell someone thanks, then, "Yeah, Kabe came over."

"Kabe?" His name jerked me out of my daze.

"Yeah." She laughed. "I called your house phone too. Kabe answered and volunteered."

"He's there?" Realized I hadn't specified where I thought he might be.

She confirmed. "Should be." I guess she knew what I was talking about. "I'll be done in a bit, so I can send him back to you."

"All right." Thought for a second and then added, "You know, I'll run by the house and see what's up."

"Okay, whatever, I got to shoo."

"Right." I tucked the lawyer's letter into my shirt pocket. "See ya." I signed off. Folk's place weren't too far off, could probably walk it, but I decided to drive anyway. That way, if Kabe wanted to head on out, I'd just stick around. Or if June was back, I'd pass on by and go home myself. Took me longer to walk to my truck and start it up then it did to drive on over. Kabe's truck was parked on the edge of the road. I pulled in behind him and parked.

Put my game face on along with a positive attitude as I headed round back. Best I could manage right then. Headed up the back steps and pulled open the back screen. Most all the time, I came and went through the kitchen door... habit built up over thirty odd years.

My stomach twisted up a bit the moment I put my hand on the latch. Used to look forward to heading here, but with all that had gone on recently, well it tainted my feelings a bit. Put a little dread in my heart. Weren't nothing to be done but to work through it though. Swallowed it down along with hope that things would just be perfect when I walked through their door.

Nothing would be perfect ever again.

Might not get to perfect, but I could try and help keep it okay, at least on my end. When I stepped inside, the kitchen was empty, so I called out, "Mom?"

"Living room," Kabe answered. "We're looking at photos."

Why were they looking at photos? "Photos?" Maybe from their mission. They might have had time to get those developed. I walked into the living room. Like everywhere in the house, it always seemed filled with a bit of shadow. Kabe and my mom sat on the old green couch, a bunch of albums spread out on the spindly coffee table in front of them.

"Have a seat, Joseph." My mom smiled up at me. "I was just showing," she paused and I could swear this ghost of panic crossed her face. Then it was gone. "Your friend the albums from when you were little." That certainly settled that she still weren't easy about none of this between he and I.

"Yeah, see, you as a little baby." Kabe waggled his eyebrows and pointed down to a page. "First day of school." Lord, I'd cried the whole way to kindergarten; there it was captured forever, me with my flushed up face looking like I was about to be shot. "Running around in your sister's dress." Kabe's grin tore up his face.

That one was even worse. Lacy'd dressed me up like I was her doll or something. "Mom!" I didn't yell it, but I did belt it out in my embarrassment. Felt the heat creeping up the back of my neck.

Barely able to contain his amusement at my being flustered, Kabe snickered out, "Oh come on, you *were* cute." I think he saw that I was about to up and have a coronary, right then and there. He let himself have one more snicker at my expense, then asked my mom, "What's this album, Mrs. Peterson?"

She just shook her head as she reached for the book. "That's more family photos, older photos." Guess she weren't going to get in the middle of Kabe and I. "A little older than the last book we looked at." She opened it up to the first page, a lot of faded photos, grins frozen in time. Knew that it hailed from before Rose's death because there was one of my mom and dad out in front of the house and both were smiling.

"Who's this?" Kabe pointed to a picture of three boys sitting on the steps out back: oldest of them had to be, maybe, six, the tiny child, around a year old.

"That's Sam holding his baby brother James." My momma's finger traced the outline of the boys' faces. "Last one is Tucker. He was all of four then." Spent another fifteen minutes looking through my family's past. Some of the photos even made me laugh. Kabe managed to pull a muted smile outta my momma a couple times too. After a while though, Mom began fussing that she needed to start on dinner. She got up and hustled into the kitchen.

Kabe started putting away the albums they'd been looking at on the bookshelves by the fireplace. "Looks like the gig with BLM is going to happen."

"What gig?" I gathered the others off the coffee table and handed them over.

"Dude." His tone said he thought I might be getting senile 'cause I didn't remember every word he ever said to me. "I told you, I'm going to get to train with the BLM Smoke Jumpers."

Vaguely recollected him mentioning something about that. "Oh, right." Once he stood up, I fished the letter outta my pocket. "Here, this came for you."

"I'll read it later." Kabe didn't even look at it before going to tuck it in his back pocket.

"It's from your attorney." I don't think he'd noticed that. "We got that hearing coming up." Figured he needed to remember that. "I think it's important."

Earned myself a roll of those hazel eyes of his. "Here." He stopped and tore open the envelope with his index finger slid through the flap. After a quick scan of the contents, he balled the paper up and tossed it into the wastebasket by the arm of the couch. "Okay, it's just a reminder." He kinda nudged my hip with his as he walked by. "You got the time off?"

"Well, yeah," made sure I'd have the time to go support him in this, "I'm off shift anyway that day."

"Okay." He turned and walked backwards a few steps, smiling at me the whole way. "Well I'll get off shift at eight." That smile pulled a world of sunlight into the room. "Probably easiest if I take my good clothes with me to the firehouse." He leaned against the folded-leaf table with its crocheted round cloth and rested his palms on the top. "I can leave my truck there for a day. It'll be a little bit out of the way to swing back and pick it up, but easier."

"Makes sense." Sometimes the boy's head was set right on his shoulders. "I'll pick you up and we'll drive up to Salt Lake."

"What are you two boys conspiring about?" I hadn't heard Mom come in from the kitchen. "Where you got to be?" She patted his arm as she wandered past toward her flower print chair.

"Nothing, Mom." Kinda rocked back and crossed my arms over my chest. I knew it came off all defensive, but I couldn't help it. "Kabe's just got an appointment in Salt Lake day after tomorrow. We were going to drive up together."

After straightening the doilies on the arms, crocheted by my daddy's mom, she settled down into the worn seat. "Is it important?"

"Ah, naw," I minimized. You know, I hadn't really talked with them about Kabe's legal problems since the other half of our being together and me getting tossed from the church seemed to matter more. "Not that big a deal."

Kabe seemed to catch my vibe, "With our jobs, we don't have a lot of time to spend together, Mrs. Peterson." He lit up that smile of his again to help ease the half-truths on through. "We thought we'd drive up, do lunch. I'll take care of my sh..." he caught himself before he cussed in front of my momma, "stuff, and have dinner together on the way back." We actually did plan that. Neither of us deluded ourselves in thinking we'd have something to celebrate or mourn, but we thought we'd need to work through the stress of the day.

I tried to edge her into comfortable denial. "Don't worry about it, Mom."

The look I caught off her told me that if'n I wasn't almost thirty-three and twice as big as her, she'd have bent me over her knee. "Last time someone told me it 'wasn't nothing' and 'not to worry about it,' they ended up with cancer." She hit me right between the eyes with a hard look. "That was your aunt Pearl."

Well, at least she went so far off course I could actually be a little indignant in my denial. "Nobody's got cancer."

Kabe followed my lead. "It's nothing like that, Mrs. Peterson." 'Course it was easy considering how far off base she was.

Momma frowned. "Is it a specialist or something?" I think she thought we lied to her.

"No, Mom," I insisted. "He ain't sick."

"I have a court hearing." Just shoot me now, how could he tell her that? "In federal court."

"Are you in trouble?" She came off far more concerned than the judgmental I'd expected.

"No, Mom," Lord, I hated the little kid in my voice, "it ain't like that."

Kabe walked over and sat on the arm of the couch nearest her. He took a deep breath, "I screwed up a few years back." I didn't know as I could handle this as well as he did. He added a little tease to cut the pain some, "I can't believe you haven't heard about this already, with the way people talk about things around here."

Mom sat up straight in her chair. She licked her lips and wrung her hands in her lap a few times, "A couple folks mentioned you'd had problems with the law. I didn't pay them much mind." Yeah, that fit with her. She always tried to think the best outta everyone until she knew better. "Thought it might be just spite."

"It ain't." I stepped over and knelt down next to her chair. "I should have told you a little sooner, Mom, but with all the other rocks I'm dropping on y'all, well thought I'd space 'em out a bit." I really had planned to do that. I'd lied to them enough up until now. But there's times to bring the puss to the surface and times to let it sit for a bit.

She took a hold of my hand. "Is it something important?"

"No, not really." That was a lie. I didn't want her to fret none about that.

Again, Kabe backed up my story. "They're just going to review my case and see if my relationship with the justice department can be done." It was the truth, but watered down and made palatable.

Threw on some more reassurance to make it go down a little easier. "Pretty routine, you know."

"Don't worry about it, Mrs. Peterson." Kabe smiled again. "It's just something I have to take care of."

Right then the back door banged. Either my daddy or niece had come home. It gave us a way to cut our losses and run. "Hey." I jumped in. "We should bolt and let you all get to dinner."

"You're not going to stay?" She used her arms to help push herself up outta the chair. "You sure?"

"Yeah," I stood too. "Kabe's got to be at work early." I helped her the rest of the way up. "We'll show ourselves out."

She walked us to the front door. As I opened it up, she said, "I always figured on Sam being my Prodigal Son." Then she gave me a quick hug. "Night boys." Kabe got a pat to his back. "Be safe."

We said the rest of our good-byes at the door. We headed down the walkway, Kabe slightly ahead of me. He stopped and hit me with, "What's she mean by that?"

Figured that he meant the *black sheep* comment. Still, I didn't want to deal with the whole issue. I just shrugged and kept walking. Someday, I'd broach that whole thing about my older brother with Kabe. Didn't feel like getting into it right then though. Instead, I teased, "Race you home!" and started jogging towards my truck.

CHAPTER 16

"Good morning, Joe." I looked up from my paperwork to see a woman with washed out bob of short blonde hair and a practiced smile walking towards me. An understated layer of makeup hid all but the most obvious signs of pushing past fifty. "Long time no see." She held her arms wide causing the ruffles on her flowered blouse to flutter as she walked. I'd heard the buzz up front but hadn't paid it no mind. Guess somebody'd let my sister Tina on back.

I pushed away from the desk. "Tina!" I hadn't seen my oldest sister in what felt like forever. Recognized her mostly because of the photo of her and her husband tucked into the Christmas card she sent, 'cause I hadn't actually seen her in, maybe, six years. "What are you doing here?"

"You mean in Panguich?" She teased. "Or bugging you at your job?"

I got a quick hug when I stood up. "Okay. I know why you're in town." Family reunion and all. "But I'm on duty right now. I don't really have time to talk." Especially, if this were the kinda talk I figured she might want to have. Did not want to be discussing my relationships, with her, at the station.

She pointed at my chair. "Sit down, Joe." I sat. She was my oldest sister after all. "I got in last night." Tina gathered her ankle length skirt up in her fist before she sat down in the chair next to my desk. Then she proceeded to smooth out the blue fabric as she talked. "Lacy and I got to gossiping after dinner." Yeah, Tina would cop to gossiping since she stayed in the church to be *in the church*, and not because she really wanted to live by the strictures. "You want to know about Rose."

"Yeah." I huffed it out. In one way I was mighty relieved, she'd come for business. On the other hand, I was a bit annoyed. I know I'd told Lacy not to talk about it with my folks, but I thought she'd have enough sense to extend that out to our sibs as they arrived. "But, I, well..."

"I thought I'd come by and get it over with." She settled her hands into her lap. "I have a lot a things to take care of in the next few days, so let's get this done."

Yeah, she and Lacy were in charge of making sure we had everything for the reunion coming down the pike. "All right." Marshaled myself into something resembling relaxed, but attentive. "I guess." I'd never been all that comfortable around my eldest sister. I mean, she'd been married and off with her Air Force husband a year before I'd been born.

"Ask away." She smiled.

"All right." It was hard to catch me flat footed, but Tina blindsided me. "Well, ah, what do you remember about that day?"

"Not much, I'd already met Frank and moved away." My sister had gone into Ogden for a summer with a group of girls from the church for a service project. A young Air Force engineer caught her eye in church. My mom hadn't been thrilled to see her going into a nomadic life, but Frank was a nice enough guy. "But, I remember talking with the family."

"Okay."

"I came back right away and was helping Mom with things, arrangements and such." She thought for a bit. "So, I mean, what things I remember were all from after the fact."

"What kinda things?"

"Well." She pursed her lips together, like she was rummaging back through her brain. "There were some things, things that the gals I grew up with were talking about. I mean, besides Rosalie."

"Like what?"

"There was this boy." Now her look went sour. "I don't even remember his name." Might have been from the memory he brought up or that she was annoyed she couldn't remember his name. I didn't know Tina well enough to really be able to gauge. "But they all," she paused, and then rushed out the rest, "well he didn't seem right. Following girls. Got caught peeking in windows."

Peeping tom behavior, well that could lead to other things... usually though way down the line. Still it gave me someone to look into. "You don't remember his name?"

"No. I don't." Seemingly sorry she couldn't dredge that up, her voice got a little nervous edge to it. "I think he might have hung around with Tucker. It feels like, in my head, that he was about that age."

Given how much time had flowed down the river since then and now, I was surprised folk recollected as much as they did. "Think Tucker would remember?"

"He might." She didn't seem all that confident. "Enough that it'd be worth a call to the Middle East."

Tucker worked for a military contractor over in Iraq, did security for them. "I could probably swing it." He weren't coming home for the reunion, although his wife and younger kids were headed down. "Have to make sure I don't try and call him at two a.m. or something."

Tina steepled her fingers together and tapped the bridge of her nose. "There was also this guy who kinda blew through town. A bunch of the gals talked about him as well, kinda not right. Think he was a cowboy name of Walker or Walters or such—the name reminded me of that Texas Ranger TV show." She nodded to herself. "I think he might have worked over on the Martins' ranch; they always had a lot of hands back then. Vanished right after."

"Sure about that?" Knew it was stupid the moment I said it.

"Not really, it was thirty years ago and I had a lot of other things on my mind." She reached over and flicked my ear with a manicured hand, reminding me that I might be in uniform, but I was still her baby brother. Then she got serious again. "There was talk that maybe the Martins told him to hit the high road. That maybe they suspected something and didn't want nobody like that around their family." She rolled her hand in the air and added a bit of a shrug. "But, that might be me mixing things up in my head."

"I understand." I jotted down the names she'd given on a slip of paper. "Anything else you can think of?"

"There was the campaign to run off some of the hippies camping out in the park." She looked even less sure about that. "That, though I'm not certain if it was before or after, you know, what happened." Thirty-three years down the line and nobody wanted to even really whisper the word *murder.*

"I'm impressed you remember all that from so long back." I was. Of course she'd probably been thinking about it most all night since she and Lacy had talked

"The hippies yeah. I think it was just before the funeral." Tina chewed on her bottom lip a moment and then gave me a tight lipped smile. "I mean, they were probably just a little counterculture." A little laugh followed. "You know, 'cause I felt it too. Felt weird, showing up in my pantsuit and Farrah Fawcett hair." She held her hands up around her face like she was pushing up a big old mess of curls. "It was what everyone who wanted to be anyone was wearing on base, back then. Big bracelets, big earrings...half the old timers thought *I* was a hippie."

We both got a chuckle off the memory. "I can't even imagine you like that." Actually, I kinda could. Frank rose pretty quick through the ranks. I'd known Tina years down the line, the few times I'd visited with her, as the wife of a junior officer, she'd come across formal and conservative. But more because she was the kinda gal who took on the manners and such of who she wanted to be. "Okay, I can see how that part stuck, but the rest of it?" I tapped the pen on the desktop.

"It was hard, Joe." What little bit of tension we'd relieved by the fun memory came roaring back. "That time. I was raw and felt like I, well I should have been there, you know, maybe if I hadn't moved away." She crossed her arms over her chest and rubbed her biceps with her hands. "I know it would have happened with or without me here. But, I think because of that, I guess, guilt, I was really paying attention to all the other stuff going on." Then she must have realized the nervous tick she'd settled into. Deliberately, she unwound her arms and set her hands back in her lap. "Distracting myself. My way of not really dealing with how awful it all was."

I offered her the best sympathy I had, my understanding. "That happens." I hadn't lived it, but as a cop I'd dealt with that same reaction in a lot of other folks I'd come in contact with. Gave her a moment to compose herself a little more by looking down at the spare bit of notes I'd jotted. Under the couple names, I added a line about creepy teenage boy and squatters. Felt weird in this day and age to be using the word hippie for folks in '79. "Anything else?"

"No, not really." She stood up and I followed her lead. I know I must have said something about walking her out and getting together with the family as we headed towards the front. Just as we reached the security door, Tina hesitated. "Ah, Joe." She kneaded her knuckles with the palm of her other hand. "There's been something else that always bothered me."

I turned towards her, rested my hip against the lip of the front desk. "What?" The front of the squad room looked more like a bank teller's counter than a police station.

"I, ah," nervous tension came out through a thousand little tells. "Forget it, Joe. Really, maybe it's nothing."

Obviously something important got triggered by our little chat. "If it's bugged you, it's something." That was God's honest truth.

She stared at her hands, didn't even look up as she mumbled, "Dad and Uncle John."

A little trickle of ice wound its way down my spine. "What?" I don't know why, but their names and how bothered Tina seemed by whatever our talk dredged up, well I got a little nervous myself.

When she did look at me, Tina's face was pained. "I got home about two days after it happened." She stepped in close. "Frank was stationed at Edwards, over in California. Drove in. Through the funeral and all of it felt normal." She snorted. "Well, not normal, but like grieving folks should." Again, she crossed her arms over her chest, like she wanted to retreat from the memory. "Maybe three days after the funeral they both got real quiet, withdrew."

"Well, they probably just did what men do." Stoic, keeping up a brave face for the rest of the family.

"No. This was real odd." All right, I could only look at their behavior now, years after the fact. Tina's sense of them, at the time, probably was better than mine years after. "I don't know how to tell you just why." She shrugged. "But I think they knew something. I don't know what."

"Okay." I reassured her with a hand on her arm. Then I opened up the door. "I'll look into all of it." Figured I'd walk her to the exterior door.

Only got a few steps through the lobby when I felt Tina's hand on my shoulder. "How are you holding up?"

"Excuse me?" I paused at the exterior door.

She took hold of my arm and guided me outside. Before she spoke, Tina glanced back into the station and then around the lot. "Lacy and Mom told me about what's been going on with you."

Lord, there it was. Knew I shouldn't have gotten my hopes up about skating on the *me* issue. "Oh, good." Sarcasm flooded my words. I know I should expect it. They'd all, my brothers and sisters, if they had half a brain would have figured the basics. Still, I'd hoped against hope that they'd keep out of the rest of my life.

She blew out a deep breath and fished in her shoulder bag for her keys. "Are you sure about this?"

"About what?" I knew what she meant, but I was sick of being the one who had to explain it all.

The hard look she gave me knocked the chip off my shoulder some. "That this is what you want out of your life?"

Couldn't do much more than repeat the question back to her. "What I want out of my life?" I knew this was going to happen with whole family coming in for the reunion. Still, I wasn't prepared for the constant questioning. The raw way it stripped my emotions. How defensive I felt and then how angry it made me that I got backed into the corner.

"You want to buck the system that much?"

I knew Tina tried to be sincere, but I couldn't hold back the bitter. "The system bucked me, not the other way around."

"I don't understand why." She drew herself up into the ramrod stance of a career officer's wife. "I'm just going to be honest with you, I don't get it." She shook her head. "Just 'cause I don't get it doesn't mean I judge it. I've lived all over this planet of ours and there's a lot of things I don't get." Frank'd been stationed all over Europe and Asia. "And there's a lot of guys who've gone through Frank's command, that everybody, well, it was an open secret. But you don't dump a good soldier 'cause of who he goes to bed with."

"Yeah, it always comes back to that part, huh?" Sex. Not who I had feelings for, but that we both had the same set of plumbing.

"Joe." She didn't yell, but her tone jerked me up like bit chain pulled short. "You and I don't really know each other that well. I'm not all that comfortable with all this. But, let's be honest, the only thing we really got to tie us together is our family. So, I don't care about you in that way, fine by me." Another shake of her head. "But, it has floored Mom and Dad. I know Lacy keeps saying she's all okay, but she's not." Her face tightened up again. "She's trying. You were her baby, before she had babies. She won't abandon you, no matter what."

"And you would?"

"Joe, I," sounded like I caught her flatfooted, "no, but honestly, it's 'cause I don't know you that well. I held you when you were a baby. I held a lot of my friends' kids when they were babies. I want you to do well because that makes Mom and Dad happy. I want their lives to be easy, especially now." A huff worked its way out of her chest. "You've made them...not easy."

Managed not to raise my voice. "My fault then?"

"Fault?" She laughed. It sounded bitter. "It ain't nobody's

fault." A bounce of the keys in her palm and then she added. "I wish it hadn't gone down this way."

I might have said something else right then, but I decided to bite my tongue. Just nodded my good-bye and watched her walk off. Honestly, the thing I hated most about that last little talk; I'd lived my life knowing exactly what she meant. I hadn't wanted to burden my folks with this. I was willing to live my life as a lie to protect my family from what I was, the pain of it, the shame of it. I'd darn had my fill of shame. Tired of living with that weight. While I didn't want to pull them all through the mud with me, well, weren't nothing for it and they all could figure out how to handle me and Kabe or choose not to. That was on them though.

CHAPTER 17

The hardest thing about the day, besides Tina coming by the station, was not having Kabe at home. Actually, it was hard because she'd come 'round the station and then he wasn't here to help me sort through it. I know I'd been a little standoffish with him since I screwed up. Still, when he weren't around, the house felt hollow, empty. Came in, threw my keys in the bowl on the breakfast island and stowed my arms in the gun safe under the stairs. After that I changed, I did a little workout, took a shower and warmed something up in the microwave.

Hard to remember that, until Kabe came along, this was how I lived my life. And I'd thought I had a pretty good life like that. How wrong I was.

I sat down in front of the computer with a plate of leftovers. Fired it up and started in on paying bills online. 'Nother way I dealt with people messing with my mail. They'd have to try a heck of a lot harder to waylay an electronic bill. Got through a load of payments when a chat box popped up on my screen.

Dev's screen name appeared next to: *Poke!*

Toyed for a moment with just ignoring him, but we hadn't spoken in forever. *Don't poke at me.* I typed back. *I don't know where that finger of yours has been.*

Up my ass. Oh yeah, that was Dev all over.

Nice. 'Bout that time my phone range. I fished it off the desk and hit answer. "Hey, Dev."

That warm, always seemingly happy baritone came over the line. "Typing sucks."

"I guess." Figured he used the same hunt and peck method as I did. "And I guess you got something on your mind other than just annoying me." Sussed that out from how fast he picked up the phone and dialed my number. Most times, even when we did talk, it was a few quick lines, short text or a quick conversation.

"Holy shit, I ain't actually talked to you in, like, two months and you're all 'get off the phone,'" he teased.

"Sorry." Went ahead and shut down the computer since everything I'd wanted to do, I'd finished. "I'm on edge some."

I earned a laugh for that. "Since I've known you, when have you not been on edge?"

Grabbed the plate with my free hand and got on up. "Bite me, Dev."

"Shit." The derision came through loud and clear. "Excuse me." Then Dev switched gears. "So how's the hottie?"

"Kabe's doing all right." I knew he was just messing with me. We joked around like that. Easy friendship, neither of us expecting too much outta the other. "Just got back from working a fire in Great Basin." Dropped my plate and fork into the sink. "Was gone for more than a week, been home a few days now."

"I knew that." Dev laughed. "Crap. I mean, he actually updates shit on the net." The few times Dev had tagged me online it was always about me not keeping in touch. "I get to find out what my little bro Joe is up to by following his boyfriend." Let him talk as I grabbed a glass and filled it up at the sink. "Doesn't tell me how things are going though."

Walked out onto the front porch. "So you called me just to shoot the breeze?" I took a swig of water.

"Am I keeping you from something?" The tone said he doubted it. "With this attitude it better involve lube."

"Kabe's on shift." Wish he wasn't, 'cause, you know, something involving lube sounded pretty good.

"Well, then," Dev sounded smug, "you obviously don't have anything better to do than surf the net for porn and talk to me." Porn weren't one of my things. Dev knew it and figured it made the perfect topic to rib me about. "It won't even bug me if you jack off while we're talking. Multitasking is good."

"You are a dog, Dev." I might not have agreed with his life choices, but I didn't judge him. Still, didn't mean I couldn't tease him right back. "You know that, right?"

"Woof." Then he fell into one of those kinda sing-song tones that told me he had more in store for me. "So, Dev, what have you been up to lately?" He talked for me and then switched over to himself, "Not much, Joe, I was in the City this weekend."

Cut him short with a question. "The City?" Really didn't know what city he meant.

"San Francisco, dude. The only city that matters." Dev sounded disgusted with my lack of culture. "Hanging out with some old friends—"

Threw his joke back at him. "And making new friends with lube?"

"Actually, yeah, blond guy with tattoos and a lip ring." I should have known better, after all, I talked to Dev. The man had more hook-ups in a weekend than I would in a year. "But anyhow," he jumped back into the previous thought, "I'm catching up with these friends of mine and my trip to Brian Head at Christmastime came up." Stepped onto the front step and leaned my butt against the handrail as he worked around to his point. "So then I talked about you and you not letting me meet your new hot piece of ass because you were worried that I'd steal him because I'm so much better looking than you."

Had to dig into him. "You wish." Always said, Dev was the ugliest good looking buck I knew.

"Well, look. I ah," All of a sudden he got kinda skittish, "I was teasing around so much that I had to put my money where my mouth was." A heavy pause flowed over the connection. "I showed them his profile."

Between the pause and how weighted his words were, I knew something tugged at the back of his mind. "I'm sensing an *and* in there."

"Yeah." He huffed. "Ah." Another heavy breath stalled the conversation. Finally, Dev started talking again, "They knew him, kinda. I mean, your boy grew up around here and there might be other guys who look similar, but his name kinda stands out."

"What, you going to tell me he had problems with the law?" Maybe they were worse than Kabe let on. Then I tossed that thought, because, I'd accessed his record when he first hit my jurisdiction. "We both know that. I told you that."

"No, Joe." He backed me off that thought. "And, look, I don't really want to stick my big nose in your business," with that, of course I knew he'd gone and done so, "but, I mean, I really think of you like my gay little brother. If I had a brother, I'd want him to be you." I often thought of him as more of as an older brother than any of my own blood ever managed. "And, you know, if you were my brother, I'd want you to tell me about certain things."

It couldn't have equaled good, not with Dev going the long way 'round the mountain to get to what he wanted to say. "Spit it out, Dev." Set my glass on the rail.

"Right, Joe." He drew in a real deep breath. "Let me tell you a little story about a boy who cried rape."

Felt like I'd been gut shot. "What?" My legs went all to rubber and I slid down until my butt rested on the tread of the step. "Oh, Lord." I mean, I knew it happened. And, I knew, reasonably, it could happen to guys and gals all the same. But, my boy? Kabe?

He let me get a few breaths down before he added, "It gets better."

I knew by better, he didn't mean in a good way. "Better?" Acid bubbled in my gut.

"Yeah, see, there was this kid named Kabe wanting to get in with the kinky crowd." I didn't want to hear this story and yet I knew I needed too. "And he hooked up with this older guy who was supposed to be real good at showing newbies the ropes."

"Okay." Well, it was far from okay, but when you've been kicked in the head, few words really convey what chaos your mind churns through.

"Then, from what I understand, things went to hell." Dev's voice sounded as worn and weary as I felt. "Kabe accused the guy of going way too far." Unfortunately, this story or variations on it were much too common in our line of work. "He blamed

Kabe for not being clear on his limits."

Huffed like I'd been punched in my sternum. "Date rape."

"With handcuffs and floggers." Dev's laugh rated far more bitter than amused. "The icing on this cake." Oh Lord, there was more. "This all went down maybe six, seven years ago."

"What?" That didn't make a lick of sense. "Wait, Kabe's only twenty-three."

"I know." That came with a load of *he wished he didn't*. "Figure Kabe was maybe seventeen at the time, if you squint real hard and kinda tilt your head sideways when you look at it." Dev paused then, for a bit, let me get my head kinda wrapped all he'd dumped on me, before he continued. "Apparently, the whole thing caused a lot of bad blood between a bunch of folks. And then when Kabe was actually old enough to be screwing around like that, he tried to go back in the scene and found himself kinda black-balled."

Went back to things I knew, things that made sense in my world, "Any charges ever filed?"

"No, not that I could find." Of course, Dev would have checked up on the story. In a cop's blood to verify any allegation, new or old.

Swimming under the complete and utter confusion, this little snake whispering that someone'd hurt mine coiled in my chest. "What was the guy's name?" I tried to get it out as neutral as possible.

"I'm not going to fucking tell you." Dev knew me all too well. "You'd drive out here and shoot him. If you could find him."

"Maybe," I conceded.

"Yeah. Not maybe." He snorted. "You also should know that when Kabe went back in the scene, the guys I know says it was as a real power player. Pretty much claimed he had no limits."

"Lord."

"I hate to drop that bomb on you," Dev really sounded sorry, "but I thought it's something you should know. Especially, 'cause if he's a power bottom...well, dude," this time his laugh was directed more at me and actually carried a little amusement threaded through it, "you don't know jack-shit about what you're really doing. He's teaching you everything, right?" Dev didn't even wait for me to answer. "You really need to get him to understand that he knows a lot more about this shit than you, 'cause you don't want to step on that land mine. Expectations being different and all."

Way to go with the late warning. "I might already have." Wished I could take those words back the moment they slipped between my lips. Knew Dev would latch on.

"You want to talk about it?" he asked.

Clambered up off the step, grabbed my glass and headed back into the house. "Nope." I needed to think on things some and I didn't want the world to see it.

"Has he walked out on you?" Dev wasn't the kind to let things just drop, especially if it had to do with me. "Like he did at Christmas?" Kabe and my first blow up, Dev had gotten an earful of that fallout.

"No." It wasn't that bad, not yet at least. "He's just pissed right now. I keep backing things off and he keeps pushing. It's messed up." I walked over to the breakfast bar and hooked a stool with my heel. Sat down kinda heavy, propped an elbow on the counter and kneaded the bridge of my nose with my free hand.

"Okay, Joe, I ain't a shrink." No, he was a deputy in California, but sometimes our jobs and those of counselors crossed wires. "I'm just your friend. All I can say is it looks like, whatever happened, Kabe's managed to work through it some..." I could almost hear the shrug over the line, "Maybe he got therapy or something." Maybe. Kabe had his ticks, but seemed reasonably together. At least as much as any buck his age. "You guys enjoy doing what you do, and I know you don't want to stop it. I also know, you'd rather swallow broken glass than talk about your feelings, but if you don't: big mess. You're going to have to talk to him. You decide whether to tell him you know about this thing that happened, but at least it'll give you some bead on where his head is at."

That it would. "I got to process this." I don't know as it would tell me where I was, but, well, it gave me some things to chew on. "I'll talk at you later. Okay?"

"All right, Joe." Dev knew that I needed time to think on things. "You know how to find me if you need me." Then the line went dead.

Dropped the phone on the counter and then slid down until my forehead rested against the cold, hard surface. There were times, early on in our relationship, that I realized what it meant that Kabe'd done time. Some days, I'd head out to my shift and when I'd get home...well, things were put together. Institutional put together. He'd make our bed up with hospital corners and a six inch sheet turndown—I'd measured it by the palm of my hand. I could eat off the counters in the bathroom and kitchen. All of his shoes got lined up against the wall and, well, Kabe started to fret if I kept the lights on past ten at night.

I always teased that Kabe seemed to somehow muddle through his time—learning how to walk the walk of being locked up without being broken. And now, well all that fell into place a little bit more. It gave him control. A control he'd lost over his life, in a hard and unforgiving way long before he'd wound up behind bars.

When I added up all those little things, they sliced my heart apart in tiny slivers. 'Cause, see, the thumbprint of time behind bars had gone and marked itself on a brain already flailing about for an anchor. I don't think he probably even saw it.

CHAPTER 18

I sat at the breakfast bar for I don't know how long, tumbling things around in my head. Lots of folks would think, well, that a boy who been abused like Kabe'd been, that he'd never give up control ever again. But that's a funny thing about people's heads. If you give up something, then no one can take it away from you. In a way, you gain power back. And you get a hundred folks who experience something like he had then you're going to get a hundred different reactions. Some things: fear, sleeplessness and reliving the event—those are pretty common right after. Seven years down the line, especially when it looked like he must have gotten some help, had people who supported him, yeah, everyone develops a different way to cope.

With him, I could see it. You go that deep in yourself, that you accept the lack of control. Pull strength from down inside. The world becomes a bit more manageable if you don't expect to manage it. Couple that with the outward little ticks. His need for organization on things that ain't living. The thrill seeking behaviors Kabe engaged in, like free climbing and base jumping where skill counts for your life...literally, you screw up, you die.

And the rough sex he liked, we both liked, that fell into the thrill seeking, the living on the edge. Both of us, two sides of the same coin. Climbing, best example, I guess, Kabe talked on about it as losing yourself in the mountain, drowning in it. For me, that thrill rose from overcoming myself and pushing beyond the limits of gear, terrain and weather.

But we both sought out that rush.

And I, I'd always kept control, over myself. Always been the good son. The trusted officer. And yet, I craved that kinda wicked, the power to control. Thought about it as long as I could remember, as long as I'd could remember consciously knowing I liked bucks. Not the specifics, mind you, but that depraved little whisper in my ear that told me how sinful I really was.

And somehow we'd found each other. While I'd figured out that I didn't necessarily drive the wagon, I chose the route. I knew what I wanted to happen. I also knew, no matter what, if he looked cross-wise, I wanted to be able to handle it, back off and be there for him. Now, that said, I screwed up. But it weren't like I went in intending to hurt him or that I disrespected his choices or his boundaries.

I just blew it.

With anyone else, you go in and say *I screwed up*. But with Kabe, I would have to walk along a greased log over a rushing river and somehow make it across.

I couldn't come at it like I thought he couldn't handle things. That'd just piss Kabe off to no end. And I couldn't go off in the direction, well, that made me seem inconsiderate, 'cause that might tie into what happened to him before. Lord, I didn't know how I would handle this whole mess.

As my brain tried to process all those thoughts, someone banged on my door. Jarred me so hard I almost fell off the stool. I glanced up at the clock. Nine in the evening, that couldn't be right. Who the heck would be banging on my door? I got up and turned to walk over; then it hit. What if something happened to Kabe? I'd done my share of notifications. Whoever it was only got in one more pound on my door before I had it yanked open.

I breathed. The man at the door wasn't in uniform. Silly of me to think that anyway.

Even more so, I knew the guy. A heavy, squared face sported a reddish, horseshoe-style mustache. That pretty much represented the only hair on his head. Plaid shirt, a ball cap with a trucking logo, jeans and work boots rounded out the whole picture. My oldest brother Sam weren't the most stylish man on the planet.

He boomed out, "Hey, Joey!" Then Sam pulled the ball-cap off his head, opened his arms and gave me a broad smile.

"Sam." For a one syllable name, it took me a while to spit it out. "What are you doing here?"

"Ah, family reunion." He reached out and thumped my

forehead with his thick fingers like he tried to jumpstart my brain. "You told me I could bunk here tonight, remember?"

Lord, I had, months ago. "Oh, yeah, I did, didn't I?" Sam had to drive down from Ketchikan. Even from the southeastern most tip of Alaska, that meant a three day drive.

"There a problem with that?" Sam had asked if he could crash on my couch until his oldest boy Payton made it in with his twins and their RV. Planned to go fishing and camping for the week prior to the reunion. "Drove almost twelve hours a day to get here." He pointed at his feet. "I'm beat and I don't feel like trying to scare up a room right now."

"Ah, no, it's okay." My reassurance sounded downright thin.

Sam rolled his eyes, blue like the rest of our tribe, and pointed into the house. "You gonna let me in?"

Shrugged, but I didn't move aside. "I guess."

"What?" He stared at me like I gone nuts. Then he rocked back and his face went a little slack. "Wait?" A sly smile twisted his lips. "You got a girlfriend or something with you?"

The tease was about as far off base as he could manage. "You don't know?" Everyone had heard. Or maybe it was just Sam's twisted sense of humor.

The smile faded to a frown. "Don't know what?" Sam sounded irritated too.

All right, maybe he really hadn't gotten the memo. Moved back and kinda waved him in, "Don't you talk to none of the family? Follow us online or nothing."

"Internet, no." Sam shouldered past me as he talked, "I called Tina last month to make sure everything was still on." He dropped his sleeping bag and knapsack at his feet. "That way I didn't have to deal with Lacy and the load of judgment that comes down with that conversation." Sam had been out of the church for a good twenty years. Not like me, he just stopped caring and going. "I hate the 'net." He scanned the downstairs, looking more puzzled with each passing second. "You got married or something?"

Even more off base than the last. I almost laughed out, "No." Of course, I could see how he might get that. I weren't no slob, but Kabe kept the place pin neat and, I don't know, put together in a way I never even thought about. It felt like a home more now than just a place to store my stuff.

"You shacked up?" Even Sam couldn't keep a straight face while he said it.

"I got someone living with me." Tried to keep my voice even. Thought of maybe a hundred things to say, and couldn't come up with a damn thing. Flustered, I huffed out, "But, ah, you really don't know?" I couldn't believe Sam didn't have a clue. "You ain't like seen the family blowing up all over their pages and stuff?"

"Told you," Sam flopped down in my couch and threw his feet up on the coffee table made from deer antlers and burled wood for a top. "I don't read that crap." Then he folded his hands behind his head. "I don't need to know who's gran'baby just puked all over the dog. My kids want me to know something, they call me." He snorted. "Like real people." After a bit of a pause, Sam squinted his eyes, rolled his head and kinda looked at me side wise. "What the hell is going on with you? You're living with a gal?"

Almost thought about lying, but he'd find out soon enough. I sat down on the arm of the couch. My whole body slumped and I dropped my hands between my knees. "I'm living with a guy."

The loaded stare told me he thought I was making mountains outta molehills. "A bunch of fuss over a room—" I think about that time all of what I'd been saying and my body language, hesitation and such kinda percolated through the layers of his brain. Sam sat bolt upright and his feet hit the floor with a thud. "Holy shit!" He leaned forward, this look of utter consternation flooding his features. "You? And a guy?" He pointed at my chest. "You're?"

"Yeah." Swallowed that one word down. "So you know, if it's going to be awkward for you, I can make some calls and find a place for you to stay." Wasn't sure what was going through my brother's head.

That narrowed eyed stare came back. "You going to be, like doing it in front of me?" I think the pure horror that washed over my face answered him. Sam nodded. "Then I'm okay with sleeping here." Then he shook his head. "Cain't say I ain't floored. Little creeped out by the whole thought of..." He cupped his hands in the air and moved them around each other like he tried to figure out where pieces all fit. Finally, he just gave up and sat back in the chair. Sam chewed on the inside of his cheek before belting out a laugh. "Holy shit, does Jim know?"

"What?" Where did that come from...either the humor or the question? Shrugged again. "I guess." I was doing a lot of that lately.

"Ha!" Sam thumped the arm of the chair. "That would have been worth the price of admission."

"Huh?" I was as lost as if I'd been wandering Dixie National in the middle of a moonless night with no flashlight or compass.

"Oh, my God." Sam leaned in and slapped my leg. "I bet when he heard, his asshole puckered up so tight shit came out his eyeballs." That thought humored him so much he kept busting through the words with laugher.

I just shook my head and let it work through his system. When the guffaws died down a bit, I commented. "You're taking it well."

He thumped his own chest. "Hey, I can't cast stones." Many of our family conversations, before my little coming out, revolved around Sam's shortcomings. "The only reason I still talk to Tina much is she's such a Jack Mormon she don't give me no grief over having three ex-wives."

Yeah, Tina kept up appearances of being in the Church more than she actually participated. Then one of the things Sam said hit me. "Three?"

I got another laugh. This one equaled far more bitter than amused. "The latest ball and chain served me with divorce papers last month."

"Oh." Cain't say that I was surprised. "I'm sorry to hear that."

Offered the thin veil of sympathy to him.

"I ain't." He almost physically brushed it off with his hand in the air. "What can I say, I'm the marrying kind." Another snort. "I'm just not the staying married kind." Oh, Lord, weren't that the truth. "Guys, wow. Never would have thunk it about you. My baby brother is gay. Holy shit, I changed your diaper. Maybe it was all those times I dropped you on your head."

"That don't do..." I realized Sam might be half serious. "Wait, you dropped me on my head?"

"No." Sam stood and stretched. "Lacy did."

"What?" I couldn't have heard that right. "Really?" He had to be having one on me.

"Yeah." He rapped on the top of his skull with his fist. "Right there. You were probably about one. Your head bled like crazy and freaked Mom out." Brushing the air, dismissing any concerns...at least on my end. "Obviously didn't do you no real harm."

"So you ain't talked to nobody but Tina and me in the last few months?" I didn't know if I should tell him about our momma.

"No, haven't." Sam rubbed his skull with one hand. "Something up? I mean, besides, this thing you got going on?"

"Naw." Lord, I didn't want to lie, but I didn't think I should broach it. "Well, yeah, you need to talk to Dad."

His whole body stilled. "Something bad happen?" His voice went low and suspicious with the question.

"It ain't an emergency." Put as much reassurance as I could into that. "But, you need to talk to Dad."

Sam licked his lips. "Don't hold out on me, Joe."

Wished I hadn't said nothing. "It's Dad's piece to say."

"I could," he glared, "just beat it out of you."

"Oh, Lord," I huffed. I'd started and Sam wouldn't let it be until I told him. "Mom's started down the Alzheimer's road."

Sam covered his eyes with his hands, almost digging his palms into his cheeks. "Shit." That came out all muttered. The second,

"Shit," was darn near a yell. Sam'd been around enough, on and off, to remember Pa-pa and the misery the last few years of his life had been on the family. I'd never managed to reconcile the memories of my namesake teaching me to ride a bike and throw a ball with those of my teenage years dominated by an angry-scared man who called me by my uncle's name and drown our home in chaos. It filled me with fear for my momma and where she was headed.

We just sat in silence for a while; the only sound the crickets and cicadas serenading the moon outside. I let Sam have his peace to process it. Lord, knows I still hadn't processed it.

Maybe three, four minutes later, Sam sucked in a big ol' lungful of air. He got off the couch, glanced up the stairs and then headed into the kitchen. "So where's this guy of yours?"

It sounded forced, and likely was. I figured Sam weren't in no mood to talk about Mom and needed the distraction. Honestly, I didn't much want to dwell on it neither, much less discuss it. Talking about it would make it that much more immediate and inevitable. If he wanted to change the subject, I'd oblige him.

Wasn't like there were a whole heck of places to hide in my place. If Kabe had been home, Sam would have tripped over him. "He's working." I got up and followed him on into the kitchen. "He's on an NPS fire crew."

"Oh." Sam started rummaging in the fridge. "Local?" He came up with a can of root beer in each fist. "Or you meet him on like studfinder or something?" He held out one of the cans for me.

Grimaced as I took the pop. "A studfinder is a little box you use to find where the posts in your walls are." I pointed towards the side of the house. "And no, he ain't local, not really."

"Not really?" Sam leaned against the counter and popped the can.

"You know the Hardings, with the ranch up the way?" They'd lived in these parts as long as my family had. "And you know Sandy, T's wife, had a sister Gail that ran off in the sixties and married a guy from India?" When he nodded, I added. "It's her gran'son. So not local himself."

After he took a drink, he added. "Local family though."

I walked past and shoved the can back in the fridge. "Yeah." Wasn't all that thirsty for pop.

Silence kinda wound through the room for a while. Sam went and fussed with his stuff, setting out his sleeping bag on the couch. I tidied a bit; doing dishes and putting a few things away. My brother flipped on the news. A lot of sorrow in the world got served up with way too many smiles. Then Sam excused himself for a bit to go outside. He didn't say nothing, and I didn't see fit to comment, but I knew he headed out beyond where I could see from the house so's he could smoke. A little fiction. Sam pretended he hid it. Most all of us pretended we didn't know he had a nicotine habit. My brother Jim would have said something snide about Sam flaunting The Word of Wisdom. Not to Sam's face, mind you, but he'd have commented.

I sat down at the breakfast bar with the deposition transcript and started reading through a few more pages. Heard Sam come back in. I shoved the pen in the page and turned around.

Sam stood at the door, his hands in his pockets and stared at me for a long, long time. Stared back since I didn't know what he wanted. After a while, he shook his head, chuckled and kinda muttered out, "Thank you."

"For what?" I cast around in my head. "A spot on the couch? It ain't that big a deal."

"No." That got me an actual laugh. "Taking the heat off me, moron." Sam walked over to the couch, sat down hard and started to unlace his boots. Kept talking to me over his shoulder. "Now I can actually enjoy myself," a pause before he added, "some. Nobody's going to give a rat's ass about my drinking and why I haven't been to church in, well forever."

"You're welcome." Didn't know what else to say.

"You ain't in the church anymore." That had to be obvious since I was out.

I confirmed it. "Got excommunicated." Got up, wandered over to my chair and took a seat.

"For you, that's gotta suck." It had sucked. The church meant more to me than just a set of worn scriptures. "I mean, I always knew you wouldn't give me shit about my life. I thought it was just, you know, you respecting my age over yours. But it was because you had this dirty little secret." Sam grabbed his pillow by one corner and flipped it at my head. "And there you were pretending to be one of the Saints."

I pulled it from the wedge between the back and arm of my chair where it lodged. "Bite me, Sam." I tossed it back at him and hit Sam in the stomach. I had better aim then he did.

He flopped back, shoving the pillow behind his head. "No thanks."

All right, weren't a perfect acceptance, but I'd take Sam's attitude over hatred or scorn. Even, actually, over Tina's lukewarm I don't care 'cept you're screwing up our parents' lives attitude. 'Course thinking on Tina made me remember that I wanted to ask Sam about Rosy, just like the rest of them...before he'd had a chance to talk with my sisters. I scooted forward in my chair until my butt just rested on the edge of the seat. Dropped my hands between my knees and tried to come off as casual as possible. "Hey, Sam."

"Yeah, Joe?" He answered through a big ol' yawn.

"Look." Had to stop myself from following his lead. "I know you're worn thin, but can I talk to you about something?"

Hard to shrug when you're laying flat on your back, but somehow Sam managed. "What?"

Eased out her name as an answer. "Rosalie." Tina hadn't been around when it went down, Lacy'd been all of nine. Sam though, he was almost eighteen at the time. Hoped his memory might be a little clearer than my sisters' recollections of the events.

He sat up and looked at me funny. "Rosy?" As he eased his feet onto the floor he added, "What about Rosy?"

"The department's re-opened her case." Fudged the facts a bit. Seemed to be a sore spot for my kin that I wanted to dredge it all up. "Can I talk to you about it?"

Palming his face and leaning back into the seat he grumbled, "Right now?"

"Good a time as any." Actually, it equaled a pretty good time. Folks who were tired were less guarded about what came out of their mouths. Any witness, not just suspects. A sleepy mind didn't try and put structure on thoughts.

"I don't know much of anything," he insisted, rather hard. "Really, I don't."

I started getting the same vibe off him as I'd gotten off my dad when we'd talked. "You may not know what you know." Not as intense, mind you, but there just the same.

Sam stood. "Sheriff Wright talked to all of us, back then." He walked behind the couch. Then he leaned on the spine kneading the worn fabric with his fingers. "I was at school most of the day and then cleaning brush after school at the Smith's place." The words came through all rushed. "I didn't get home until late."

I don't know where that flood of nervous energy welled up from. "I'm looking at the big picture, Sam," reassured him a bit, "not just that day." Maybe he just got flustered 'cause his baby brother asserted his presence as a cop, an attitude he was used to throwing around. "What was going on a few days before, a few days after."

He snorted. "After?" Came off like a forced bit of disbelief.

"Yeah." I tried to not read too much into the way Sam acted. "Putting the puzzle together." I noted it, but I needed to steer my brain from inserting my own ideas into it, just yet.

"I don't know why what went down after would matter."

"Doers often attend the funerals." Pop science actually, but I figured Sam would buy that explanation.

That earned me a genuine, not forced, derisive roll of his eyes. "Joe, the whole town came to the funeral."

In a town of fourteen-hundred, not everyone would have shown. "Did you notice anyone acting strange?" Still, a good chunk of the residents would have come by. "That kinda thing."

"Look, Joe." He leaned in over the couch. "I'm beat." Knew he wasn't lying about that. "Can't we do this another time?" Plus I'd hit him with two big emotional zingers in less than an hour... Mom probably being the bigger gut punch. Physically tired and emotionally wrung out.

I wanted to get his thoughts. Wanted to get them before they got polluted by the rest of the family talking about things. And I didn't like that jumpiness that came on all of a sudden in him. Still, the case weren't going to get any colder by waiting a day. Pressing now weren't going to buy me anything that decades hadn't buried. "All right," I conceded as I stood up. "We'll talk later."

"Maybe tomorrow."

I'd have to track him down since he weren't staying here more than one night. "We'll have to touch base after Payton comes and gets you." Shoved my hands under my pits. "I got someplace to be tomorrow."

"Yeah." He yawned again and nodded. "We'll touch base."

CHAPTER 19

I shoulda gone with Kabe's more casual attire. Although, I'm not sure I could ever pulled off what he tended to wear and wear right well too. In keeping with the import of his hearing, he'd donned a suit, sort of...at least pieces of three different suits. Khaki slacks, a black vest and a camel colored, narrow fit suit jacket over a white t-shirt and loafers seemed all pulled together on him. I'd have looked like I was dressed by a blind-man pulling clothes outta the Deseret Industries charity bin if I put that on.

Me, I stuck with my Sunday-go-to-meeting clothes, navy suit with necktie Kabe'd bought for me: white fingerprint whorls on sky blue. That meant, though, when we went through security, I felt like I were gonna be strip searched. Beyond clearing my pockets, I had to remove my jacket, watch, belt and boots. Kabe just kicked off his loafers and tossed his jacket into the bin. I might have cut to the front of the line and seen if they'd give me courtesy, let me avoid the hassle of the search as a sworn officer, but I was off-duty and here to support Kabe. Plus, I didn't really feel like drawing that much attention to myself.

This whole thing had me so nervous that I'd sweated through my shirt and under-shirt the first fifteen minutes I'd had it on. We were here to see if we could get him off of probation early. Kabe's life would ease up like a spring thaw if he could be done.

For me, if it came up again before the Peace Officer Standards Committee, the fact that I, as a law enforcement officer, was now living, in the biblical sense, with a guy on probation, I might not come out of it so clean as I did the first time. Although I'd got off by the skin of my teeth when I got called in for an administrative hearing about Kabe's and my relationship, I could get pulled in again. We were still together. If some official, like my new Watch Commander, got a burr up their butt they could report me for repeating my offense—well, never actually quitting it.

I needed this as much as Kabe did.

Once we got past screening, the Fed courthouse felt different from the county and justice courts I normally was in. There chatter and chaos ruled the halls—bubbling out from the courtrooms themselves. This building almost held its breath. Even my boots landing on the marble floors as I walked seemed to hush themselves. Didn't help my nerves at all. We got to the courtroom a might earlier than we really needed too. I paced a short bit of the hall in front of the courtroom while waiting for Kabe's attorney, Aaron Bulger, to show up. Kabe just sat on a hard wood bench with his knee going a mile a minute and worrying his fingernails with his teeth. Every second the clock ticked by set my nerves bouncing against each other all the harder. Finally had to sit myself down next to Kabe and grab his knee to stop the shakes, since his nervousness wracked me up too.

Normally, they'd have held the hearing in the same court as Kabe'd been convicted in. Mr. Bulger pulled some lawyer magic and got the case transferred to the Federal District of Utah. He told us getting it done had a lot to do with Kabe's original judge retiring, the original prosecutor being promoted to the bench and the convenience of witnesses, specifically, Kabe's probation officer, 'cause none of the rest of us counted for much.

At four-hundred bucks an hour, that was some expensive magic, let me tell you.

Had to pull a small loan outta my credit union to make this happen. You get what you pay for though, and all the folks I'd talked to said Mr. Bulger was one of the best. Anyone who has to throw himself on the mercy of the public defender...well that can be a total craps shoot on talent. People on the wrong side of the criminal justice system were always better off hiring their own lawyer.

Kabe paid me back like clockwork over the last couple of months. Although I told him that he only had to pay me back about half of what actually got spent and we'd call it even. Getting him done early meant I could let out my breath about having to undergo any more reviews like I'd had that winter. I never wanted to go through that again.

Mr. Bulger walked on up not too long after we got there and seemed to recognize us right off. As I stood up, he shook my hand and said, "Afternoon, Joe." We'd met with him a couple times before to make sure he had everything he needed to make this happen, but most of our conversations took place over the phone. Then he shook Kabe's hand and patted his shoulder. "So, Kabe, how are you feeling about today?"

Kabe's answer of, "Nervous," came with a tense little laugh.

"Well, it's a big step, young man." Mr. Bulger had one of those TV lawyer faces with a serious smile and enough lines to let you know he'd been around a while. "I'd be nervous too in your shoes." His smile inched a bit brighter as he added another pat to Kabe's arm. "All right, boys, let's go over, again, what's likely gonna happen here today." I felt like we should be hunkering down into a quarterback huddle. "The judge may just rule based on the paperwork we've submitted without taking any testimony or," a heavy pause broke the thought, "she may want to hear from you." He shrugged like it didn't matter much. "You just never know for certain."

"Isn't it just routine?" Kabe bounced from one foot to the other. "I mean, these kind of hearings?" His nerves had me all jumpy too. We both fidgeted the whole way into Salt Lake.

"Yes and no." Another noncommittal shrug followed the first. "The forms are always the same, but behind those doors," he pointed to our left and the person awaiting us behind those doors, "a Federal Court Judge is the law of the land." Bulger laughed. "If she tells you she wants those forms on pink toilet paper and printed in glitter ink, you get it to her that way." Then his tone got a little more sober. "Remember, son, we went over this on the phone. Just be honest. The truth can't hurt you."

"Oh, God." Kabe groaned. "I don't know if I can handle this."

"Don't worry, Judge Mills is pretty easy going." He settled his briefcase down by his feet and then crossed his arms over his chest. "There are a few judges in this courthouse who, if we'd have drawn them, I'd have told you to give up and go home. No sense throwing money down a well."

I clung to that little bit of hope. "So you think Kabe's got a good shot?"

He gave me another bit of a shrug. "Nothing in law is ever certain, but I'd say, yeah, we gotta decent shot at prevailing. Kabe's probation officer is on board. The prosecution has filed an opposition, but it's pro-forma." When he saw the blank looks on our faces, he explained. "He filed one because he's supposed to, but it's boilerplate law and half-hearted arguments."

"Oh, okay." Kabe didn't sound all that convinced.

Like he caught Kabe's tone, Mr. Bulger reassured, "Don't worry, son. You meet the requirements." He ticked them off on his fingers. "Family support, stable residence and regular employment. Non-violent offence with no dirty drug tests or run-ins with the law since going on supervised release." He shook his head. "The only reason you're even at a two outta ten on the Risk Prediction Index is you haven't *finished* your degree, you ain't married and you're young. You're, in my opinion, as about as low of a risk for recidivism as my Great-Aunt Martha."

Mr. Bulger'd emailed us the tables for the Risk Prediction Index. How someone thought that nine *yes* or *no* questions, weighted with point values for how many times you'd been previously convicted and a person's age could tell you whether they'd commit another crime was anybody's guess. Other than the section on previous convictions, all of them seemed arbitrary and stacked against most folks. "Too bad it ain't your opinion that counts." I didn't mean it to come out as snippy as it sounded, but I didn't like that Kabe's, and my, future rested heavy on a bureaucrat's form.

Mr. Bulger didn't seem to pay my tone no mind. "Like I said, nothing's certain, but I got a good feeling about this." He took a deep breath and brushed a bit of lint off his coat. "Ready?"

"As much as I ever could be." Kabe leaned against me and I kinda rubbed my face against the back of his head.

As he picked up his briefcase, Bulger instructed, "Make sure your phones are off and let's go on in."

I powered down my cell as I pulled the door open with my other hand. Then I stuck the phone back on my hip and walked on in. This was one of the beautiful old courtrooms; the whole building was historic. Dark wood, soft lighting except for what was focused up on the raised area where the judge sat. In a few years, from what I'd read in the paper, they'd finish up a new courthouse for the civil and criminal hearings and this one would only handle bankruptcies. Kabe and I slid into one of the old wooden pews while Mr. Bulger went up to check in with the clerk. As we settled onto the seat, Kabe grabbed my hand. I squeezed his fist to reassure the both of us.

It only took a few minutes after Kabe's attorney sat down with us before the judge took the bench. The clerk announced the Honorable Jessica Mills' entrance. The whole courtroom rose when told to and said the Pledge of Allegiance. Then, as we settled back in our seats, the clerk started calling matters. We got to watch a couple plea deals, a guy brought in on a probation violation and a detention hearing while we waited for Kabe's matter to come up. If this judge was considered easy going, I wondered what hard-nosed would be. She did not seem the friendly sort.

Every ruling she handed down seemed a little harsher than the last. I thought she was going to come off the bench and pop one defendant upside his head. And I was used to a bit of friendly banter between the judges, staff and attorneys. Here they all deferred to her like she was the First President and they were members of the Twelve Living Prophets of the Church. All and all, it made my skin crawl with what we were up against.

When the judge finally called out, "U.S. versus Varghese," and read off the case number, my chest tightened up. Both Kabe and I needed this to go well. We'd both been living under this hanging rock, wondering when it was going to roll off and crush us. Yeah, it was a little selfish, but nothing in the scripture says I cain't be hopeful for myself along with wishing good for someone else. Mr. Bulger stood and motioned for Kabe to follow him up to the table farthest from the empty juror's box. Prosecution always got the table nearest to the jury, whichever side it happened to be on. Been in enough courtrooms in my time to know that.

"Good afternoon, your honor, Aaron Bulger for Defendant Varghese." Kabe's attorney announced himself.

"Good afternoon Mr. Bulger." The judge didn't even look up from her notes. "What are we on calendar here for today?"

"Petition for early termination of probation."

She raised her eyes to stare, disapprovingly, at Kabe. "And you are the defendant probationer?"

"Yes ma'am," Kabe swallowed over his mistake, "I mean, your honor."

"Ma'am is fine." Her voice came off like dust coated her vocal chords. "Counselor, your client is petitioning for early termination of his supervised probationary period not having served a full year of the two years imposed." She tapped the tip of a pen against her tightly drawn lips. "Is that correct?"

I could see the tips of Mr. Bulger's fingers, pressed against the wood of the podium where he stood, go just a little white from pressure. "Yes, your honor." Nothing but that little tell showed his reaction to the judge's attitude.

The judge huffed. She actually sounded right bored. "You understand that the average amount of time served before early termination will even be considered is two thirds of the sentence of probation." Her eyes flicked up as someone came into the courtroom. I heard the door open behind us, but I didn't dare look away. Must've not been anyone important 'cause almost immediately she refocused her stare on counsel's table.

"When you talk in averages, your honor," the pressure came off his hands and his voice settled into even, confident and measured, "that means that there are those who are required to serve far more than that and those who serve less."

"Although I went into law, I did manage to pass math." From bored to kinda irritated...I didn't see the change in her tone to be a good sign. I knew he hadn't meant to piss her off, but he seemed to have done just that. "I understand what an average means." I started feeling all antsy in my seat with the way her attitude rolled over the courtroom. She said the next bit real slow, "Why is your client an exception to the rule?"

"As I explained in the moving papers—"

"I can read as well." The judge's eyes narrowed ever so slightly. So far the prosecutor hadn't hardly moved and barely breathed. I guess he figured he should stay out of the line of direct fire. Not a bad plan since her Honor picked up the file, leaned forward and dropped it with a bang into the well between the bench and counsel tables. The sound jerked me by my gut strings and I saw Kabe's head go back just a skosh. "Tell me what's not in the papers." She kept speaking as her courtroom assistant scrambled over to pick up the file and slide it back, discreetly, on the side of the bench. "Why does your client need to have his probation terminated early? Why does he deserve it?"

Bulger straightened his shoulders and kept his voice even. "Well, your honor, Mr. Varghese is a contributing member of the community in a stable residence and with family around." He'd warned us this would be a hard go, this early in Kabe's probation, I'd just discounted his caution as being overly careful in not getting our hopes up. Any hope I had pretty much said *see ya back at the truck* and hit the high road.

"Okay, let's dissect this." She rolled her eyes. "The family he has around is a great aunt, that's not generally what we consider close family." Dear Lord, she really, really read the moving papers. Most judges of my acquaintance left it to their law clerks to summarize arguments in briefs. I swallowed so hard I'm sure her Honor heard me up on the bench. See, Bulger gave us a chance to look them over, and I'd thought he'd polished all those not so great facts until tin shone like silver.

She kept going. "Since getting out of prison he's had seven jobs, one of them volunteer, and three different residences." She took a moment to pull the file back to front and center. She huffed and chewed her lip for a moment. When it seemed she might speak, she huffed again. Finally, she must have figured out how she wanted to ask what she wanted to ask. "Please explain to me how, in the space of eleven months, that equals stable?"

"Perhaps Mr. Varghese can explain it better than I seem to have."

A snapped out, "Fine," grudgingly accepted his suggestion. She looked down at her clerk and pointed towards Kabe. "Swear him in." It only took a moment for the clerk to recite the affirmation to tell the truth and Kabe to answer positive. The moment they finished, her Honor jumped in. "Explain this to me, how you're turning your life around bouncing around like this?"

Kabe inched closer to the podium where the microphone was. He shoved his hands in his pockets. Then, like he remembered where he was, took them out and crossed his hands over his chest. I winced. That move just screamed defensive. Luckily, Kabe probably realized that didn't look too good, because he uncrossed his arms, took a deep breath and grabbed the edge of the podium.

"Well," he almost swallowed that word, "ma'am, ah the job thing." I had no idea how he'd manage to untangle it all and make it palatable to the lady sitting in judgment of him. "The volunteer thing, with the fire department, I was doing it most of the same time as some of the other jobs here in Utah." He shook his head, I guess figuring he'd kinda jumped into the middle. "Look," he backtracked, "the first job on the list was one I got right away after getting out, you know slinging coffee in the Castro." Putting it in order seemed to quiet his nerves some. "But I had to get out of San Francisco." I wished it managed to quiet mine.

"Why did you have to?" She tapped the pen against his file. "Get out of San Francisco?"

"Because all the same people I knew from before were there and it just wasn't good for me. Not if I was actually going to do this." Kabe's body went all calm; I knew that as his *thinking* attitude. The boy fidgeted in his sleep and jittery didn't begin to wrap around his all-over-the-place natural waking state. But when he really got serious about something—climbing, snowboarding, studying—it was like this blanket of stillness settled over him. "My friends weren't bad, but they wanted me to go out and party. Nothing illegal, but telling me to 'call in sick so we can go to this club,' or staying out all night when I had work the next day. Sooner or later, I'd have majorly screwed up." He blew out his breath. "I so did not want to screw up."

"Okay." The judge smiled. Seriously, the upturn of the corners of her mouth cracked the stern mask of her face for the first time that morning. Although, honestly, the grin came off far more feral than friendly. "So you have more sense than most young men your age." She swung the pen in a circle in the air. "Keep going."

"So my Aunt Sandy and her husband offered to let me work on their ranch as a green hand and let me stay with them. So I moved to Utah where I can't screw up like I could living with my Grams...my grandmother." He scratched his head and kinda screwed up his face like he might be embarrassed. "But honestly, I totally blow at the cowboy thing. I couldn't cut it." Kabe kinda glanced back at me, almost for reassurance, and I gave him the barest nod of my head for support. "So a park ranger friend helped me get a job with this canyoneering outfit...something I could do, you know?"

"A what?" I swear, at that moment, the judge looked just like my high school English teacher trying to figure out whether what I'd just said equaled insightful or down right dumb.

Kabe explained. "Teaching tourists how to rappel off cliffs and climb to go down on tours into the slot canyons in the National Parks. When that season ended, I got a job at the ski resort, as a trail host. Basically, directing people to the right runs, making sure guests who fell didn't need medical assistance, running lifts and such." He spread his hands. "But, it was part-time gig and I was working on my EMT license through this program, so I started volunteering with the local fire department for my hours requirement." He kinda boxed the thought up with his hands on one side of the podium and then moved that imaginary box to the center of the space. "Then, in January, I also took a temporary job at the hospital while I was still doing those other two things. Three jobs at once." Now he moved his box to the opposite side of the podium. "And, then, when ski season ended, I was still with hospital for a bit and then I got the job with the forestry service on a fire-crew." He spread his hands wide and added a shrug. "So it wasn't like I was going from job to job, I just had a lot of balls in the air."

"Why wasn't San Francisco good for you?" The judge went back to what Kabe'd said earlier and I kinda winced inside. "Your immediate family is there and I know you said you had friends *pulling* on you. But, still, moving out to where you knew no one doesn't seem like the best choice."

"Yeah, but I don't think you understand the lifestyle I led then." Kabe almost sounded apologetic or maybe slightly embarrassed. I couldn't tell exactly which. "They wanted me to party like I did before I got into trouble—and I mean, there were no nights off. A different club every night until two or three in the morning. If I did that, I'd get in trouble again, especially on probation. None of them are bad people, but something would have screwed me up. A fight or not watching how much I drank and getting stopped walking back to the BART station." He chewed on his lip for a moment, I could see it from my angle. "I never want to go back to Lompoc...ever."

"So that explains the first move." The judge nodded, like she kinda expected that explanation. "Tell me why you moved from the ranch?"

"See, at the end of December, my boyfriend," Kabe glanced back at me again, pulling everyone's attention to where I sat. "Joe was in an accident."

"Your boyfriend?" I did not like the emphasis she placed on those words. Plus, my situation, if she knew anything at all about Utah law enforcement, wouldn't do him any favors.

"Yes ma'am." Nodding, he turned his attention back to the judge. "And it was pretty bad, not as bad as it could have been, but Joe was off work for several months. He needed someone to help him just get around for a while and pay bills and all. So I stepped up."

She paused for a while and tapped her pin against her lips. "Are you still living there?"

"Yeah," he caught himself, "I mean yes."

"What does your boyfriend do?" She pointed the butt of the pen out towards me. "Does he have steady employment or does he bounce around on jobs like you?"

"Ah," Kabe hesitated, "he's a deputy with the county sheriff."

"Really?" Her eyebrows went up and her mouth hardened back into a little line. "Given your situation, that may not count as a good thing." My chest tightened all up around my heart, I could feel it pounding, with how she said that.

Kabe blew out a hard breath. "Well, you know, that's one of the reasons Joe really needed my help. He didn't have any income for about three months, 'cause on top of the accident he got suspended for a while."

"Why was he suspended?" I fidgeted in my seat 'cause with the tone I caught off her voice, it sounded like the judge already had a inkling of why.

"For being with me." Kabe scratched the back of his hand with the knuckles of the other. "'Cause I'm on probation."

"I take it that is the main reason you need to get off probation?"

"Yes ma'am." He nodded. "Honestly, I could probably handle another year of this, even with the money I have to pay for my supervision, but I don't want Joe to have to worry."

For the first time her face eased up. She didn't smile, but the look came off far more open and friendly than any she'd worn on morning. "Thank you for your honesty, Mr. Varghese." If I had to guess, she'd gotten used to defendants being far less than honest with her. I was proud my boy chose that route, not even hedging over the not so nice things. I guess Bulger really did have a good sense of what would work. Why he was one of the best.

Kabe shrugged. "Lying just get's you in deeper, your Honor."

"Mr. Prosecutor," her honor swung her attention to a thin young man in a funeral suit, "do you have anything to say?" She kinda motioned between the lawyers using her all purpose ball-point pointer. "With what you've heard."

"No, your honor, other than, as you've said." The prosecutor sounded bored. "It's early." He paused to flip through a few pages of the yellow-pad on the table in front of him. "The Defendant has barely served a year of probation much less gotten near the two-thirds mark."

She seemed to digest the disinterest in his tone. "What about the low RPI score?" That stupid set of ten questions again. It was insane that they'd try and mathematically average a person's life to predict what they'd do next.

The prosecutor thought for a moment then offered, "He could have been at a zero."

Her honor snorted. "I don't think there's anyone under age thirty that would score out at a zero." Tapping on the file in front of her, she asked, "What do you think of the PO's report?"

"I think defendant's probation officer has a soft heart." That he didn't appear to need to think on.

"So, you don't think it's justified, an early termination?"

At this point, Kabe and I were trading the barest of glances and shrugs. There ain't supposed to be any communication between those up front and people sitting in the audience. But the prosecutor was mouthing back all the reasons Mr. Bulger explained meant we might fail.

"No, your honor." He flipped through his papers again. "Under these facts, I don't."

Pulling the file towards her, the judge seemed to be thinking on what she'd heard. Finally, she looked up. "All right gentlemen, I have some things to think about." She made some notes and handed the file down to her clerk. "You'll get my ruling through email notification off the PACER system."

CHAPTER 20

We made it about halfway down the aisle, towards the doors of the courtroom, when the sight of a pink coat caught me up short. Had to blink a couple of times before my mind really registered who I saw. I hustled over as she stood up. "Mom," I hissed it out, "what are you doing here?" I looked over my shoulder and caught the glare off the bailiff.

"I came to support..." she whispered as she made her way out of the pew at the back of the room, "support your friend." I shushed her some, politely as I could. Then, with my hand on her shoulder, I guided her out of the courtroom. She kept talking, at least real low, as I hustled her out. "He doesn't have family nearby. I talked to the Hardings and they weren't planning on being here, so I thought it would be, well, the right thing to do."

"You drove all the way here?" My momma didn't drive much in town much less down the highway and into the city. "Into Salt Lake?"

"Oh no." She looked horrified at the prospect. "Mary, you know Jane's daughter, she grew up next door, used to play with Tina when they were young." Mom nattered on like we were coming out of Church on Sunday not in the middle of the Federal Courthouse. "She and her husband, well their daughter just had a baby so they all were driving in. Jane was going along to see her first great-grand-baby. So I asked for a ride." The way she said it, well, made the plan sound about as reasonable as the sun rising the next morning. "I figured you boys would have too much to discuss that you would appreciate me hearing, so I didn't want to bother you."

"How did you even know where we'd be?" Instead of answering me, my momma dug in her pocketbook, pulled out a neatly folded bit of paper and handed it to me. When I unfolded it, I realized she'd salvaged that reminder letter from the attorney out of the trash. The one Kabe'd balled up and tossed while we were at my folk's the other day. She must have heard us going on about more than I'd figured then. "What if the hearing got canceled or you missed us? You'd be stuck in Salt Lake."

"They're all going home tonight. Late." It came out like I must be a little dull to not magically know that. "But Mary's husband came to the courthouse with me. Looked in and made sure you were here. I have my phone if there was an emergency." Bare bones basic with big numbers and pre-paid minutes. I'd gotten it for her several years back in case, well, she needed to get a hold of someone when she weren't near a land line.

That reminded me, though, to turn mine back on. Soon as it powered up, the darn thing went off like a five alarm fire. Ten missed calls in the last hour and a half, pretty much the entire time we'd been in the courtroom, about half and half between Lacy and Pa. "Mom," I tried to keep my tone respectful, "did you happen to tell anyone where you were going today?"

"I left a note for your father." She chided me, like I shouldn't have even worried about it. "Said I had some things to do."

It might not have worried her, but I bet my dad was more than a little bothered. "Did you turn on your phone?" I pretty much already knew the answer.

She huffed. "I didn't want to waste the battery."

"Mom!" I was about to say something more when my phone went off in my hand. My daddy. Punched accept and put it to my ear. "Hey, Dad—"

"Why haven't you been answering your phone?!" My daddy roared it loud enough that I might have been able to hear him all the way from Panguitch even if I wasn't on the line with him. "I cain't find your momma! She didn't come home for lunch! Nobody knows where she's at." Every time he took a breath I tried to jump in with *Dad*. Never even got half a syllable outta my mouth. Guess it weren't my day to sneak a word in edgewise. "I called everyone I can think of. Nobody knows nothing!" Honest, I thought maybe he might just have a coronary right there on the phone with me.

At least he'd paused. "Dad!" I rushed it out and hoped he'd heard. "She's here."

"What?" I actually moved it away from my ear so I didn't go deaf.

"Mom's with me." Tried to calm him down some with my tone. "In Salt Lake."

I heard him take a couple of deep breaths before he started in again. "Why in the world is she in Salt Lake with you? What are you doing there? Why didn't you answer your phone?"

"We were in court." Sorta answered all three questions at once.

Mom tapped my shoulder. "Is that your father?"

"Hold on a moment." Bought him off for a bit of time. Then I smiled over at my momma although, with the tension, my normal sarcasm rose to the surface. "No Mom, it's some guy you don't know screaming at me about where you're at."

She scowled and held out her hand. "Give me the phone."

"Just a moment, Mom." My daddy went off again, although I didn't catch what he'd said. "Dad, hold on."

"Joseph Price Peterson give me your phone." That's what we all grew up calling the *someone's gonna get a whoopin'* phrase. Whenever my momma used our full names somebody was about to get their hide tanned.

Rather Dad than me. "Here, Dad," I interrupted his sputtering, "Mom wants to talk with you," and handed the phone over.

"Hello, Walt." She started off nice enough, but snapped out of it real quick. "Do not use that voice with me." Okay, that tone weren't pleasant at all. "I am not a child, Walt. I left you a note. Because you cain't fix yourself lunch?" I have no idea what my daddy's side of the conversation was like, but I was darn happy I wasn't part of none of it. "I am perfectly capable of taking care of myself." And really, I'd never heard my momma take that tone with my daddy. Good Mormon housewife with *yes, dear, no, dear* and *do as your father says*. "Jane's son-in-law drove us all down. I've lived next to her all my life, of course I trust her. I don't know why she isn't answering her cell phone. I'm going home with Joe, we'll likely miss dinner." She scowled at whatever he gave her in response to that. "Well, have your daughter fix it for you," she snapped. "I am not going to have you yell at me over the phone. We will talk when I get home." She pulled the phone away from her ear and gave it a sour glare. I think it was meant to go over the airwaves and nail my father between the eyes. Took it a moment of fussing with it before she figured out how to hang up on him.

Kabe'd been over talking to Mr. Bulger. They shook hands and he headed back over to me as momma handed me my phone. "Hey. Everything okay?"

Like that whole exchange hadn't even happened, Momma answered, "Right as rain." She smiled over at him as she passed me my phone. "You boys hungry?"

"No." I stuck my phone back on my hip. "I'm not." Set my hand behind my mom's back and steered us towards the elevators. "Shall we head out?"

She waited until we were heading down before asking, "Are you sure?" I don't know why, but she seemed agitated to me. "We can find someplace nice."

"Yeah, Mom," my female kin and food seemed their cure all for stressful situations, "we'll eat along the way home."

She fumbled in her pocketbook for something. Once we got to the first floor, Momma pulled out a bit of paper. "Here." She shoved the folded note into my hand.

I didn't have no idea what was up with her and the scraps of paper. I stared at her and glared. When she just returned it with that righteousness that only a mom can muster, I unfolded it and looked it over. A set of handwritten directions ending at an address in Lehi. Along the route home, off the 15 at the edge of Utah Lake. "What is this?"

Her smile went all tight as she insisted. "We need to go there."

The tension made me suspicious. "Why?"

"Marshall's daughter lives there." It came out like I should know who that was and why I needed to take her there.

I didn't have a clue. "Who?"

"Marshall Wright." The name rang a little bit of a bell, but not much. She must have seen the confusion on my face. "He was the sheriff." The next sentence hit me like a two-by-four between my eyes. "He was the one who looked into your sister's death."

How the heck did she know about that? "Mom." I'd done as my dad said and not mentioned nothing to her about what I looked into. "I mean, Dad didn't want me to bother you with this." The only folks in my family who knew about the investigation were Dad, Sam, Tina and Lacy. I couldn't see Dad not shutting them down, same as he done with me. "How did you find out?"

"Do you think I wouldn't know what y'all were about?" She rolled her eyes up like she was asking God why he'd burdened her with an idget for a son. "I figured it out. Lacy's gone all skittish every time she looks at Rose's picture. She and Tina stopping in the middle of talking every time I walk past." A poke at my chest, told me off more than her words. Mom always did figure out anything we tried to hide from her. "You and your dad at each other the other day. Screen doors don't stop much sound." Of course she'd have been in the kitchen, probably making his lunch. "Then Kabe and I were talking about Rose, looking through those photos. He seemed very interested in that...and not you. I know what you're up to."

Kabe broke in, "But why his daughter? Why not him?"

She laughed with one of those almost embarrassed little sounds. "Lots of folks of my generation have already passed on. Marshall was older than Joe's daddy by a few years." Kinda taking him by the elbow, she started walking. "His daughter has his things."

Fell into step right beside them. "I have the file, Mom." What there was of it. I couldn't imagine what else there would be.

"Marline said he kept things." Her tone said she thought whatever would be important, but wasn't quite sure why. "She has 'em."

I still didn't know what the former sheriff would have kept. "Has what?"

"What her daddy didn't see fit to keep in the files." She patted my cheek, like it made it all better. "Let's get going. I told her we'd come around before five."

Kabe snorted. "Dude, Mom arranged a road trip."

"She's my momma." It wasn't that I felt territorial; more that it was a privilege she hadn't granted.

I felt it, just the slightest bit, as she leaned into my side. "I'm all right with your...your friend...calling me mom."

We stepped out into the gold of an early spring afternoon. I didn't want to think back to the other night, but I couldn't stop my mind from going there. Took me a few steps down Main Street, heading towards Post Office Place and my truck in the public lot, to work up the stones to say, "You told me to trash Nana and Pa-pa's rings." Realized, as I said it, I fussed with the ring still on my right hand, spinning it around my finger with my thumb.

A few steps and my mom stopped. She ran the strap of her bag through her hand a few times. "I'm sorry, Joey." A big sigh found its way between her lips. "You caught me flat footed. That, well, it cut me raw and I bled all over you. You," her hand wrapped around mine and squeezed, "you're my baby boy. I buried your sister. I ain't going to walk away from you when you're still breathing."

"Mom." I almost couldn't find my own lungs, my chest tightened up so much. Wanted to believe her, but it was so hard. "I don't know."

"All I can say is, I'm sorry." I got a sad smile. "I probably hurt you bad, but I..." she grabbed her mouth with her hand for a moment, took a few steps before she turned back to me. "I guess we'll have to work on that, huh?"

If she'd make the effort, I would too. After all, I never

expected them finding out about me and who I was, to go down easy. I figured there'd be a bunch of stumbling and a whole heap of hurt feelings in the months to come. We'd just have to pull through it the best we could. Hopefully, we'd all come out the other side, maybe banged, bruised up, but still a family. I'd just have to keep putting one foot in front of the other to get there.

Didn't say much as we walked the rest of the way to the car. Kabe kept pace with me, occasionally running his hand along my back. I didn't catch anything off Mom, although I'm pretty sure she saw. Once we got in my truck, I made Kabe sit next to me instead of squishing my momma between the two of us. She gave Kabe the directions, let him navigate.

At least we were all dressed up for a visit.

Once we got off the interstate, Mom made us swing by a grocer. Fried chicken, pasta salad and peanut butter squares: enough food for a whole herd of folks. 'Course I didn't know how big Marline's family might be. From there, Kabe read me the directions until we pulled up in front of a two story brick house with a manicured lawn and two car garage. A boat and RV were parked off in a field of weeds on the other side of a white split-rail fence. There weren't no cars in the drive, but if you had a garage round these parts, you parked inside. Cycles of snow and sun does a number on paint jobs.

As I pulled onto the gravel shoulder, a teenage girl stood from where she'd been sitting on a screened porch. Hadn't seen her back behind the big tree in front of the house. I got out, jogged around to open the passenger door for my mom, and heard the girl yell, "Mom! Company's here!" over by the house. By the time I helped Mom out of the cab, Kabe had scooted out the driver's side and grabbed the food. We all walked up the path together.

A dark haired lady, who looked a little younger than my brother Tucker dressed as she was in jeans and a long sleeve t-shirt, held open the porch door. "Howdy." One of those angelic smiles graced a face not burdened by a lot of makeup or stress. "I'm Marline." She held her hand out to mom. "Liz?"

"Thank you for letting us impose." Mom took her hand and

patted it. "I hope you don't mind, we brought dinner."

"You didn't have to," she insisted. Then she looked over at me, "You must be Joe."

"Yep." I nodded. "This is my friend, Kabe." He smiled at her when I mentioned his name. "I wanna thank you for letting us disturb your evening."

Marline held the door open and ushered us inside. "If it was a bother, I wouldn't have offered."

As we walked in to a comfortable living room filled with department store furniture, she introduced us to Bethany, the teenage girl we'd seen a moment earlier. Also inside we met Jacob, a freshman at BYU, still living at home and her youngest son, Mark. Kabe passed over the bag of food to the oldest boy who took it off into the kitchen. We all got seated, accepted the offer of lemonade and got a little rundown on her and her kids since she'd moved away near on twenty-five years ago. Then Momma and I went through a round of Panguitch news—who was up to what and why. 'Course, none of us touched on the scandal that was Kabe and I. That was best left for other folks to gossip about.

Polite pleasantries meant we could all pretend this was a social call. Kinda how things worked in these parts, even the big city. I didn't have no problem just getting right down to brass tacks if I was on a case. This, however, weren't quite the same. So we all played that this was just a set of old neighbors stopping by to catch up. We all knew it weren't nothing of the sort, but you had go through the dance so's not to be rude.

When her husband, Rich, got home another round of introductions and niceties got passed about. Kabe and I danced around the whole reason behind the court hearing we'd been at. Of course, they kinda knew I was law enforcement, so I suspect they just figured it had something to do with my job. And once we asked Rich about his work, well, folks tend to like to talk about themselves, especially if you play like accounting is the most interesting field in the world. We got saved when Bethany came in a little later and asked if were hungry, since dinner was ready.

After we'd said blessing, eaten and spent enough time talking about the weather to be polite, Rich excused himself to go change and make a phone call. The kids started clearing plates and Marline stood up. "Come on." She beckoned us to follow her. "What you wanted is out in the garage." Like I said, we all knew that this weren't no random visit.

Kabe and I both stood, but Momma didn't. Instead, she smiled and sorta brushed us off with a wave of her hand. "You boys go on, I'm a little tired, just gonna sit here."

As we followed her out, the oldest boy started chatting with my mom about Russia. I caught up to Marline and asked, "So my mom called and got this all set up?" I'd been kinda curious about how this all happened. I mean, my mom weren't the most assertive person on the face of the earth. She got things that needed doing, done, but, I couldn't see nothing this elaborate. I don't know, maybe I sold her short on some things.

"No." Marline shook her head, "Jean Schlosler called. We probably talked for three or four hours about the whole tragedy and what my dad knew." Almost as an afterthought, she added, "I did talk with your mom a bit."

Seems my mom had a conspirator in this whole scheme. Stood to reason, I figured, with the way Dad acted, she'd have had a bit of trouble putting all the pieces together. Desire, drive, yep, but the actual making it all happen, that would have been like trying to weave snakes into a basket for her.

Marline walked us through the kitchen, a utility room, and out into the attached garage. "Sorry about the mess." The apology didn't mean much, I coulda eaten off the concrete it was so clean. She pointed to a set of shelves against the far wall. "It's up there. The blue trunk on the third shelf."

We scooted around the bumpers of the two compact cars. "This box?" Kabe asked as he reached up to grab the old footlocker.

I stepped in to help; weren't large, but it looked wedged in with a bunch of other junk. Figured if it wasn't the right one she'd have said so. Took us a moment to wrangle it off the shelf. Once we managed, he and I carried it into the laundry room. The light was a sight better in there. Crouched down beside the trunk after we set it on the floor. A padlock, beat up as the trunk it was attached to, was clamped tight in the hasp.

Marline fished a set of keys out of her pocket. "Don't know which one works on that, but one of them should."

"Thanks." I took them, discounted a few right off as not the right kinda key. Of the three left, the second one I tried sprung the lock. I opened it up. A whole mess of manila envelopes, file folders and notebooks confronted me.

Kabe leaned up against the dryer, one of those looks like a kid who just opened up a package of socks on Christmas morning twisting his face. "That's the junk that's so important?"

"My dad insisted I keep them, just like this." Marline shrugged. "He used to go through it every so often, but I haven't even opened it up since he died."

Pulled out one of the notebooks and kinda flipped through it. "Why'd he keep all this here?" Looked like his case notes. "I mean, not keeping this stuff with the files at the department."

That earned me an embarrassed and slightly bitter laugh. "He and the guy who came in after didn't quite see eye to eye on some things."

"Like what?" Kabe asked what I'd been thinking.

"Dad kept notes." The evidence of that was right in front of us. "On everything. What he thought, ideas that played through his mind. The new sheriff, he believed in organization."

Pulled out a folder and opened it up: 'nother set of notes on looseleaf paper. "Not a bad thing." Mumbled that kinda absently, 'cause the envelope underneath it caught my attention. A block printed *Rosy P.* in pencil had faded almost to illegible.

Not paying me much mind she kept on, "Well, according to Dad it was when it meant the files had to be winnowed to the 'pertinent facts.' Whatever that means." She tapped the side of the locker with her toe. "Instead of tossing it, Dad took it all with him when he left. He said someday, someone would come looking for his files. Someday, folks would want to know."

Hope that meant I got to take the whole thing on home. "Like me?" I grinned up at her. It'd take a while to sort through the whole mess to see what I needed.

"Like you," she confirmed. "You can take the trunk too. It's nothing sentimental."

"What's in here?" I knew physically that it held papers and such, but I wondered if these files were special or was I going to have to sort through logs of his camping and fishing trips as well.

"All the big solved and unsolved cases he worked on." I got another shrug. "That's what he told me."

Since I had permission to haul the files away with me, I shut the lid. "Did he ever say why the solved ones too?" Then I stood up and handed her the padlock.

She bounced it around in hands for a bit before answering. "Because you never know what's going to be important in the long haul. Maybe what he had might someday link back to something." She moved to the kitchen door so Kabe could step in and help me lift it up. "He always told me that cases were like jigsaw puzzles; sometimes a piece wouldn't make sense until you had just the right section of the puzzle done. Twist it. Turn it. But sometimes you have to just step back and see the whole picture. Sometimes that whole picture is another case."

"I can see that." I grunted as I hefted my side. Weren't big, but paper always seemed to weigh far more than it should.

Kabe cocked his hip and rested his side on it while he arranged the weight a little better. "One bin for all those cases?"

"Not all that many actually." We followed her voice through the kitchen. Her daughter, Bethany, was washing up the dishes. Jacob sat at the table talking with my mom while helping his little brother Mark with his math. After a quick check on the dishes, Marline went back to our conversation. "Sleepy little place back then. People used to call the house at night if there was a problem. They didn't run a night shift."

Mom looked up, "Panguitch?"

"Yep." I confirmed what we'd been discussing.

She stood up and kinda kneaded the knuckles of one hand with the other. "It was such a nice town back then."

CHAPTER 21

"Come on, dude." Kabe followed me up the stairs and shucked his jacket. "We haven't had sex in days." The house was cold and empty. Sam's SUV weren't in the drive and I figured he'd gone off to stay with his son at the RV park in town.

Thank goodness, 'cause Kabe'd started teasing on me while we drove home after dropping my mom off. I kept kinda pushing him away the whole ride. It hadn't stopped when we got out of the truck, neither. I reminded him, "We messed around a few days ago." I'd removed my tie and jacket before we'd even gotten in for the ride back to Panguitch. Figured we'd go back for his truck sometime tomorrow, when we both weren't so beat.

"That was almost a week ago." He grumbled behind me.

Got up to the top of the stairs, turned and glared back down at him. "You keeping score?"

"Bite me." He walked on past me, pulling the shirt up over his head as he did so. "Come on, dude, my balls are blue."

What if I screwed up again? What if it turned out worse? "Look." I tried to put him off. "We had a long drive today and it's late." Not that I didn't like having sex with him, but I knew what he fished for and I didn't want to go there.

"And neither of us has work tomorrow," he pointed out, "so we can sleep in or take naps." Kabe toed out of his shoes and wiggled out of his pants. He grabbed it all up, set the shoes along the wall and his clothes in the hamper. "Come on."

I knew I couldn't really brush him off. He'd had a big day and he had to be needing to be touched and connect to something that made everything right. Something I couldn't deny him. Took a few moments to think things through. I knew of something, we'd done it before and Kabe liked it. Weren't exactly *rough,* but it was as far from vanilla as we were from Mars.

This though, what I thought of, in the scheme of things,

was relatively idjit proof. Not enough electricity came out of the TENS box to kill someone as healthy as Kabe, no heart issues or nothing, especially when all the equipment was placed south of the border. The specialty lube would help conductivity while preventing burns to places I sure didn't want injured on Kabe. It'd give him the kinda pain he liked and I'd get to watch and know I gave or denied it.

I walked into the closet and opened up a box I kept there. "Get on the bed," I ordered as I pulled out a couple of carabiners and a few webbing loops: two blue, a yellow and a red.

"Now you're talking. "Kabe dropped his drawers and headed over to the bed.

Wished I felt as gung-ho as he sounded as I strode on over to him. "Give me your arm." As Kabe sat down, he held out his right arm to me. I took the red webbing loop, wrapped it around Kabe's wrist a couple of times going inside the loop each time. Slid the working end through the big loop and then pulled it snug, a prussic knot of sorts. Normally, prussics are used for sliding along another rope. Push the prussic up, yank it tight and it sticks...they can tighten up, they're meant to tighten up. That wouldn't work for keeping blood flowing through Kabe's fingers.

Took a deep breath and tried to get myself excited. "You ready?" Somehow managed to dredge up a leer to go with my question.

He smirked. "Like you got to ask."

I went back and slid the working section under itself and around to knot the line so it wouldn't tighten up. Took me longer to think on how I do it than it took me to do it. Looped the free end 'round one of the far headboard posts and clipped onto itself with a carabiner. Then I laid him down and got his other arm trussed up the same. Wrapped that web round the other side, unclipped the first from itself then clipped them together behind the headboard. Same routine for his legs down at the foot board.

There he was, trussed up all spread-eagle. The sight of him sent fire up my spine, made me remember just how hot Kabe really was. Of course, that got dampened down a notch from the chill of anxiety eating at the back of my thoughts. Still, I was starting to get some into it. Hard not to since Kabe equaled sex on a stick.

So he couldn't see what would happen next, I tied a red bandanna across Kabe's eyes. Then I reached out and just ran my palms down his chest. Kabe sucked in his breath and arched into the touch. His skin was warm over his hard chest and ripped belly. Just enough fur ran from his pecks down to his navel and beyond to rock my mind. I hated that whole shave-everything-off look.

Now that Kabe was trussed and blindfolded, I figured I'd get naughty with him: in kinda a safe way. You know, no chance of me getting so physical that I hurt him. As long as I used enough lube and kept everything below the waist, what I planned would stay pretty safe.

He called to me, turning his head towards the direction I'd last been in. "What are you doing?"

"None of your darn business." I reached out and smacked his middle. "Shut up."

Got the TENS unit from where I kept it in my nightstand. Doctor gave it to me after my surgery. Something about the electrical current helping my muscles and pain levels and I don't know. Didn't know why that supposedly helped while those ab-belts on TV didn't do diddly-squat. Still, when Kabe first saw the darn thing, you'd have thunk it was Christmas his eyes lit up so big.

See, apparently, he'd gone and injured his arm back when he was around fifteen or so and a doctor friend gave him one. Being that age and curious in the kinda way that he was, he'd put those little electrode pads on places the doctors never intended. I knew what that current felt like at the back of my knee and I was certain I wouldn't want it coursing through my nuts. He, on the other hand, liked it.

Said it made his dick feel like a thousand tiny mouths sucked him off...one's with little tiny teeth.

The unit I had took two sets of wires, four electrode pads total. We'd had to shop around to find a few things, on the cheap, to make it more interesting, 'cause I still paid down some of the credit card debt I ran up while I was off work. Kabe's paychecks didn't really stretch that far. We'd managed to survive and still have fun.

One of them, this little black and silver thing about as long and wide as my thumb called a torpedo-plug, we bought online and on sale with a few other bits. Pulled what I wanted to use right then out of the same case the TENS unit occupied. Then I lubed up the plug and put it where the sun don't shine. With as small and, well, torpedo shaped as it was, it just kinda slid right in.

Kabe grunted, "A little prep might be nice."

He just teased me 'cause he was a brat. My boy had taken that and more many times before. "Yeah," I teased back as I rolled the torpedo around in his ass for a bit, "I forgot the foreplay... telling you to bend over." I kept him blindfolded 'cause I didn't want him to know what was coming when, but I liked his mouth. All uppity and down right filthy at times. It turned over my crank something hard.

Had to feel around a bit to make sure I got it right at that place 'cause I wanted to create this little current loop between prostate and dick. Then I slicked up his already hard cock, stroked him low and slow until he felt nice and solid in my fist, and slid this rubber sheath over the shaft until his head popped out the top. A few tugs on the lacing snugged it up nice and put the contact points lining the inside right up against his meat. 'Course I pulled it a little harder than necessary just to hear him grunt.

Next, I choked his balls with an electrode studded nylon strap. Kept thinking how this would charge Kabe up and that thought ran chills down my spine. The final connection was one of the normal sticky-pads, like a doctor might use, stuck on the skin just below his belly button.

That set up would create all sorts of sensations as the current rippled through his lower half. Made sure all the control knobs were off before I plugged the two leads into the TENS. Joined the wire from Kabe's butt and the one leading to his prick with the right hand Y lead, the other bits I hooked up with the left.

Then I stepped back for a moment. There was something a little sick, but a hell of a lot sexy, about seeing Kabe like that. His arms and legs tied wide apart, just enough slack to let him struggle. Him all nekkid with his chest rising and falling in slow but excited breaths. And all these little trembles jittered across his brown skin as he anticipated what he knew was coming, but didn't know when or how it would go.

All the gear—different colored wires, black rubber encasing all but the head of his dick and the medical-blue strap on his balls—looked like some mad scientist prepped his junk for an evil experiment.

Reached down and rubbed my own dick through my slacks. I hardened up some as I'd been working on him. Even my reservations couldn't dampen the smell of sex dripping off his skin. The whole package of him trussed, shot the rest of my blood straight south. Made me kinda crazy, I guess, with how much I liked seeing him like that. Un-tucked myself so's I could give my cock a few good strokes, then I picked up the unit. I had the little box in one hand, my own dick in the other, just stroking, thinking on what I was gonna do. Gave time for Kabe to really sink into his own head, spin off the *what-ifs* in his imagination.

I was starting to realize that the anticipation, uncertainty and anxiety that weren't quite the level of real fear, played heavy into why Kabe liked this so much. And knowing that he gave me that power over him. Lord it shot sparks up my spine every time the thought fired across my brain. Just up to me, though, to understand I couldn't let it go too far…like I had the other night.

Kabe trusted me.

I didn't know as I could trust myself.

I could trust myself with this though. Released the grip on my dick and rolled the top knob on the left lead. Kabe, and I, tensed up at the buzz of current sliding down that wire. There's this moment of panic at that sound, your mind can't help it, 'cause it means a shock is coming and you don't know how fast or how bad it'll be until a second later when it hits. I could see it in his face. Kabe's fear of the unexpected drove this rush of heat tensing up every muscle in my body.

A trickle of current crept down the lead before sliding across the nerves in Kabe's cock and ass. His abs tightened up, every little feather in his six pack visible for a fleeting second as he hissed and shuddered long and hard. Knew that meant he liked it.

This TENS had four knobs; top of the line. Top two controlled the amount of power slipping down each lead, how strong the shock was. The bottom ones modulated frequency, whether that zap would come in slow pulses or rapid fire bursts. Started off low and slow. Practiced playing with the different combinations on my own knee, read up on things a lot, so that when I moved to doing what I did right then, I had a good sense of what sensations I created in Kabe's far more sensitive areas.

Waited for a while with just that low, light pulse making every third breath of his a little more intense than the others. Set the frequency a little faster on the second lead so that when I let the power rip, it hit Kabe's nuts off-time and with a bit more charge than the current twisting the nerves from his butt through the center of his dick. His hands, already wrapped around the ropes tethering his wrists to the bed, went white knuckled as that wave hit. He let out a hard grunt. His jaw clenched up.

Kabe rolled his head back and a lower, slower and far more satisfied groan carried him through the wave of that shock. Knew then he fell into that space in his head where the whitewater rush of his senses jumbled any sense of up, down or sideways. When we'd really go at it, I'd get there too. Different rivers charging down the mountain, both ending at the same lake.

"You okay there?" Wanted to make sure that Kabe was doing fine. This type of sex was all quiet like. No big yells. Just hisses and grunts and groaned out versions of *fuck* slipped through clenched teeth as things ramped up.

He gave me a thumbs up. "I'm good." He hissed. "Real good."

All right. After that, it was all just messing with him. Changing levels and duration. Keeping things in or out of sync. Loved watching him like that…every time I'd find a fun setting that made him react, I'd take my fingers off the knob and jack my own dick for a bit. At one point, his hips popped off the bed for a second and twisted back and forth.

Bent down then and kissed him on his cheeks, his forehead and mouth. I could feel his jaw vibrate, his teeth not quite chattering with the inability to stop himself. Kept it quick, just long enough to let him know I was there, so's I wouldn't end up completing a circuit up through his heart.

Not likely, but possible.

That risk, no matter how small, was part of what fed the edge, the need to do these kinds of things with him. The bigger part of it was electricity was an untamed beast. Something we're taught to be scared of as kids, fear more than rattlesnakes or strangers with candy.

That deep down fear, settling it in him, it was like a drug.

No matter how I gave that to Kabe, it kicked in the endorphins in my brain into high gear, changed the wiring in my head, so that I got to needing it, thinking about it, wanting it when I wasn't doing it. Like when you're hungry, all you can think about is what your next meal will be and your mouth starts to water and you can almost taste it. For me, I'd pick up something as simple as a ruler and a thought would whip across my mind about putting that and Kabe together, my pulse ramped up, my dick warmed up and I'd start to smell him on my clothes. Didn't matter when or where I was for that to happen.

Figured we'd done enough of this teasing, it was time to get down to brass tacks. Eased the power a bit higher on both leads until Kabe arched his back off the bed and groaned out, "Fuck," in that Lord-I-need-this tone.

I turned the frequency down so that he got drummed with these long, slow pulses. I ran the back of my hand along his abs, savoring the sensation of muscles twitching under his skin. Every so often, I'd up the power a hair more. Finally got it to a level where Kabe started breathing pretty hard, his back arched and pelvis thrusting up almost like he rocked in time to my dick in his ass. Writhing and rolling, like you might trying to get a partner hitting the right spot. But it didn't do a lick of good, 'cause it was all just current and straps.

And that's what made it fun all around.

The more I jacked up the current the more frantic his movements got. I had him on the line where his thinking self headed for parts unknown and all that got left was a raw bunch of nerves and need. Just exactly where he needed, wanted, to be. He started grunting out, "shit," or "fuck," more often. Moved the power up to the highest setting I was willing to use, one that seemed to keep Kabe right on the edge of pleasure and pain. Went back to stroking myself. The sight of him, the charge of knowing I did that to him, pushed me a heck of a lot farther along. My balls already started to tighten up and my dick felt so hot it might explode into flames at any minute.

I reached out and ran my hand down his leg. If I created any circuit there it'd just add to the feelings surging through his nerves. Then there it was, a little drop of fluid oozed from the tip of his prick. Sucked in my breath as I watched it pool there and then slowly slide down his head and collect on the thin rim of black rubber just at the neck of his dick. This rush of chills hit and I started to shake almost as much as Kabe did. Any moment now. The anticipation of the rush he'd feel and that would wash over me seeing him overcome, jangled my nerves.

His breath caught and my whole body went tense with expectation.

A jerky indrawn hiss sucked through clenched teeth. Another grunt. Kabe's dick jerked. His hips shot off the bed. Every muscle in his stomach froze hard into mountain cut relief. Cum welled up out of the hole. Not a big spray, but this bubbling fountain of white, coating the red head of his cock, streaks of white running over the black sheath like a slow motion volcano. All through it, his hips bucked out of control.

Lord, few things ever looked so incredible.

Let him go through it a little longer, made sure that he'd shot his wad, then I powered the whole thing down. Kabe almost collapsed on the bed, like his bones had turned to jelly or something. As I yanked the leads out of the box, I leaned over the bed and kissed him again. This time long and slow and with my tongue all in his mouth. He tasted like sex. The room pulsed with that thick, heavy, sensual scent. Came up for air and began getting him out of all the gear. Left him tied up though.

"Fuck," Kabe sounded sleepy, "that was awesome dude."

I yanked the torpedo out with one tug. He was so relaxed there weren't even a bit of resistance. "Better than me pounding you?"

He laughed, sorta, it almost merged into a yaw. "No. Getting fucked by you is way better. This was just," he sighed, "intense. So fucking weird to get off with nothing actually touching you. You know?"

"Like the feeling?" I reached up and pulled the bandanna off his eyes.

"Yeah." He grinned. "It's like your body's dancing all over this not quite pain, but nobody's touching you and my dick feels like it's going to split. It's just erotic as hell."

Clambered up on the bed next to him. I'd flagged a little, but I knew what would get me back up. "I know you feel like you've just run five miles in five seconds, boy." Straddled his chest, my knees right up under his pits. "But you got one more job."

"Yes, Joe." He licked his lips and stared up at me.

I'd never had no one look at me like he did. "Open up." Made me feel all warm and jumbly inside.

When he did, I leaned forward and slid my prick into Kabe's mouth. So hot and wet all at once, lit up my senses like a Roman candle. He sucked hard and, like I thought, didn't take me long to get my cock all ridged again. Once I got to that point, I grabbed hold of the headboard, shifted so all my balance rested forward and started to pound his mouth with my dick.

Kabe managed like a trooper. When I'd pull back he'd suck against the draw and on the push back he'd open up so I could get as deep as possible with the angle I was at. Built the heat in my belly to an inferno. Already completely jangly over watching him, didn't take me long at all. Everything tensed up as I was pulling back and there it was. My whole body shook as I filled his mouth with cum.

Held onto the headboard for a moment while my nerves got steady. Then I got up off him, swung off the bed. Took me a while to get him all undone, although once I'd freed his hands, Kabe helped some. Tossed him a t-shirt off the floor and he cleaned his dick and the sheath up while I put the rest of it away.

We didn't say much of anything to each other. I don't know. I didn't feel quite right. I mean, I'd gotten off, but it hadn't settled me down none. Found my shorts and a pair of jeans and hopped on into them.

"What are you doing?" I heard him ask behind me.

"I just cain't settle down." Looked over to where he sat on the edge of the bed, his hands between his knees and a not-quite put-out expression on his face. "Been kinda a roller coaster day. Think I'm going to watch the news until I get sleepy."

Kabe snorted. "Dude, news is the last thing that's gonna make you sleepy."

"Maybe an old movie." Had to get myself another shirt outta the drawer since I'd handed him mine to clean up with. "You go on to sleep." I reached out and rubbed his cheek with my knuckles. "I'll be back up in a bit."

He didn't say nothing, just kept looking at me funny. I didn't know what else to say back to him, so I just mumbled, "Night," and went on downstairs. Settled myself into my old recliner and started flipping channels. All I could really think on was how hot that could have been between us and how cold it left me…like I'd climbed to the top of the mountain only to find a bigger one still behind it.

Sore.

Unsatisfied.

And unhappy with myself.

CHAPTER 22

"Hippies, in Utah?" Kabe mumbled around a mouthful of this stuff he called muesli: a mix of yogurt, bran, oats, sunflower seeds and Lord knows what else. He caught a bit that spooged out of his mouth before it could fall on his tie-dyed t-shirt.

Speaking of hippies, one sat at my kitchen table. I stopped reading through the notes I'd culled out of the trunk. While we ate breakfast, Kabe and I had been sorting things, comparing notes of what we found and organizing bits into piles. Honestly, Kabe weren't law enforcement, but he had fresh perspective… that of an outsider, someone who hadn't been here then or didn't have family embedded in the area. Nadia, Sheriff Simple and, Lord help me, my new Lieutenant, they also had it. But he was here and he was now. Also Kabe wasn't LEO. A guy from the other side of the bars, without the years of training, culture, and mindset to level me and pull my head out of the structured way of thinking cops were prone to fall into.

Cold cases took a different way of thinking to puzzle them through.

I stacked some of the papers and then tapped them on the counter to straighten the mess. "That's what Tina said." I had three different piles going: photos, Marshall's notes, and reports.

He took a couple more bites then nodded like he settled something for himself. "You should talk to Leah," came out all sage-like.

I couldn't recollect anyone named Leah. "Who?" I mean, the name rang a few bells, but nothing specific.

"Leah." He rolled his eyes and huffed. "The woman who runs the food co-op we belong to."

I remembered why I didn't recollect anyone named Leah. I drawled out, "Oh." I'd worked hard to *forget* Leah. Leaned back against the counter and crossed my arms over my chest. "I don't think she'd want to talk to me about nothing." Maybe blow my head off, but I didn't think Leah'd say much to me before she did it.

"Why?" He shoveled another mouthful in. "I mean you guys got along *so* well." Even he couldn't keep a straight face saying that. "Seriously." Using the spoon pointed at my chest to drive home the point, he added, "You called her a 'whack-job, vegetarian, bleeding-heart liberal,' and she called you a 'neo-fascist pig.'" And then some. "You ended the *best of friends*."

Not one of my more stellar moments in dealing with folks. But, Leah just rubbed me the wrong way. "What would she know?" Nothing I hoped, 'cause I didn't really want to have to deal with that woman.

"Well, she's from that generation." He got up and headed over to the sink with his dishes. Kept talking to me as he walked. "She and I got to talking once and she told me about being in the area in the seventies." I scooted over so he could rinse his bowl. "I mean, she wasn't from here, if I remember right, but she hung out a while, then went off and got her GED and went to college. She came back in the mid-nineties. She might have been around or knows someone who'd been around then." Kabe flicked a bit of water off his fingers into my face.

I grabbed his hand and wrassled him for a bit. Wound up with my arms wrapped around his chest, my face pressed into the back of his neck. One of his hands was shoved into my front pocket, the other held onto my arm. He smelled good. Always did. Like wind and pine and lazy days spent swinging in a hammock.

The weight of his body pressed against mine, how the line of his hip melded into my own, equaled just this side of heaven. I could stand there all day wrapped up around him. His skin, where my lips brushed it, bloomed with the promises of spring and the coming summer. Light, easy life.

Kabe twisted in my arms and I moved up to meet his kiss. Deep and slow and even hotter than the rest of his skin. His kiss tasted of adventures we'd had while whispering promises of those not even in our dreams yet. I slid my hands down to cup his butt. Pulled him hard up against me. Felt so right. Felt so good.

Then as I'm kissing him and he's kissing me back my mind flashed to *that* night. All I could see behind my eyes was Kabe on the floor, unconscious with his eyes rolled back in his sockets. I jerked away.

Kabe cocked his head sideways and looked at me like I'd done lost my mind. "What?"

"Nothing." I stepped away, kinda shrugged.

"Something wrong?" The suspicion in his voice told me he already believed there was.

"No." I swallowed. "We just should get going on the day."

"Dude, it's our day off." Kabe leaned against me, pinning me between him and the counter. "We've got all the time in the world."

"Yeah," I hedged, "Well, you know." I hooked my fingers through belt loops on his jeans and gave a tug to tease him. "If we get all involved, then I'm not going to want to get back out of bed." That wasn't much of a lie. With my hands where they were, I just sorta pushed him back. Smiled while I did it. "And we'd have to shower before going out amongst folks." Not that I was a prude or nothing, but I didn't want to head out smelling like I'd just got laid. Enough problems followed us around to keep me from advertising that we messed with each other.

Kabe rolled his eyes, but backed off. "Buzz kill," he grumbled.

Caved in to first his suggestion to derail him from the second, "When we get back." I bought him off with a vague promise and a smack on his butt.

Took us a bit to get everything settled and out of the house, especially with him sniping at me about earlier. Easiest route over to Parowan was the twisty old highway. Went from the alpine forest where we lived down into sparser scrub pine in the first two-hundred feet of elevation. The lava flats along the 143 sucked the sun into its jagged pores. Ragged stands of aspen didn't do much to keep the sun at bay. We dropped close on another six-hundred feet in the space of an hour. When we finally broke through into the dry flats around Parowan the sun hung about mid way up in the sky.

Turned off onto one of the dirt side roads and headed along through a couple more turns. About another mile down the way, I could see an old farm house settled next to the orange frame of modern metal barn. Off, in one of the pastures, another livestock barn had chickens pecking about. Finally, we rattled over a cattle grate which split a fence far more intricate than those of scrub poles and barbed wire most ranchers used. A small heard of about ten alpacas fled from the truck, even though more of that heavy fencing lined the side of the track. Three large dogs, all white and that looked more like polar bears than dogs, bounded across the field to wiggle under pass through gates as we pulled into the main area near the house.

Just ahead of us, next to a battered Outback parked in front of the house, a steel haired woman with a hard figure moved about, fussing over boxes of produce. She'd pulled her long hair back in a ponytail secured with a stamped strop of leather pierced by a carved wood pin. A longish denim skirt, a man's plaid shirt over a red t-shirt and moccasins—ones that looked like she wore 'em every day of her life—pegged her as one of those folks who moved up into God's Staircase to commune with nature. As we pulled to a stop, Leah stood up and shaded her eyes with an outstretched hand. The three dogs, darn near as big as she was, swarmed around her. I think she recognized my truck because that look of curious expectancy faded to a good, solid frown.

Kabe flashed me a smile before jumping out of the cab. "Hey, Leah!" He called out the greeting as he slammed the passenger door shut. I followed him out a little more slowly.

The dogs padded on over to us ahead of her. "Kabe," Leah started on towards us, "how are you?"

"Fine." He bounded over and gave her a quick hug then leaned down to muss the ruff on one of the dogs who'd doubled back to follow him. "How's Winter and Jasper?" Leah and I might not get along with each other, but I didn't choose his friends for him.

Enough bits and pieces of his dealings with her had dribbled out that I kinda recollected those were, maybe, the names of her kids, or her dogs. I weren't all that sure.

Kabe got a smile. "They're doing okay." I got a glare. "You brought him." The dogs seemed to catch the vibe off their mistress as they kept a wary eye on me.

"Yeah, ah," Kabe rocked back and shoved his hands in his pockets, "we need to talk to you about something."

Came up on beside him and crossed my arms over my chest. Realized that made me come off harsher than I wanted. I uncrossed 'em and then didn't know what to do with my hands. "I need to pick your brain." Ended up with one in my back pocket and the other rubbing the back of my neck.

Slowly, Leah crossed her own arms over her chest. "And why am I going to let you pick my nose, much less my brain?" I'm guessing she meant her stance to come off harsh and defensive. One of the dogs added a bark to let me know he thought I was a bit suspicious.

Okay, so we didn't get along much. Still, she never came across as one who truly hated cops. "It's about an old murder." More of the *leave me alone* attitude that even the most law and order folks around these parts tended to nurture. "I need to see what you might remember." That, and she was a dyed in the wool, bleeding-heart liberal. Thought I should give up my guns and everything.

Kabe sensed, I guess, the rising tide of tension flowing between us. He jumped in with, "Joe's got a personal interest in this."

Leah snorted and ignored him. "I have yet to figure out how a gay man can have a stick as far up his ass as you do." She stared at me with an invitation to take her on. "Just don't make sense." 'Bout that time the dogs must've figured I weren't no threat to their human. One flopped down against the tire of my truck while the other two trotted off back to the fields.

I didn't need to take Leah on in a battle of will or words.

Licked my lips and thought for just a hair. "Well," I drawled it out, "I kinda thought that having things shoved up your butt was, I don't know, the essence of being gay." Said the whole thing as flat as if I'd been asking for change at the gas-n-shop in town.

She blinked. She uncrossed her arms and set her fists against her hips. Then Leah looked over at Kabe. "Did he just make a joke?" Leah turned back towards me and narrowed her eyes. "You just made a joke." The words came out like she accused me of running nekkid through her barn or something.

Kabe laughed and smiled big at me. "I told you that Joe wasn't a total prick."

I found myself grinning back at him like a fool. His smile, it vied with the sun for how much it dazzled me. In fact, so much so that actually took a fair bit for his words to percolate through my brain. "Wait," I glared at him. "What do you mean a 'total prick?'"

"Dude." He slapped my back. "You have your absolute tool moments."

"Which I have witnessed." Leah gave me a tight lipped smirk. "Here," she pointed to the crates she'd been inspecting. "Grab a couple of those and bring 'em back into the barn. It's a little cooler in there." She hefted a box herself. "Most of it's going right back out for site delivery in Escalante."

"Yes ma'am." I snapped out the answer. Kabe rolled his eyes as I grabbed up a couple of boxes of the first rounds of snap peas. Guess he thought I was sucking up or somethin'. I replied with a sour stare for him and a, "Lead away," for Leah.

As we walked, she talked to me over her shoulder. "Candice says you pick up the leftover produce and distribute it."

I'd been over to the barn plenty of times. "Yep." Just always timed it when only Candice was around to show me what to take before it spoiled. She and I got along well enough, mostly because we didn't say more than three words to each other.

"Where to?" Leah stopped and turned. "Not like we have a shelter around here."

"Around." Managed to shrug with my arms full of boxes. "There's a lot of folks about that don't have a safety net." This weren't the most well-off place in the states. "The church takes care of its own." If you were LDS, they wouldn't let you starve. You might not eat well, but the folks in your ward all chipped in to make sure no-one went without. "Not everyone, though, belongs to the church."

Almost suspicious, Leah asked, "And how do you know who they are?"

Didn't let her attitude rile me up. Easy, friendly, I answered, "It's part of my job as a neo-fascist pig to know my beat."

Leah belted out a laugh, "Cute," as Kabe stifled a snort.

Decided to keep things light. "I hear things." I heard a lot of things. Whispers through the area of folks hard on their luck as well as things gone more criminally wrong. "A ranch family over in Ticaboo lost their dad a few months ago." When your job is keeping the peace you learn all sorts of things about the people you're keeping it for. "There's a few older folks who I check in on that live out alone. I drop a few things off when I head round."

As we walked into the shade of the barn, she shot over her shoulder, "Okay, I guess." Leah shoved the box she carried onto a table. "Candice never had any problem, but you know, this is my show. I want to know what's going on."

"I get that." I stacked my boxes next to hers.

Kabe came up beside me and asked, "You get what?" as he set his boxes atop of mine.

I leaned over and in a whisper meant to be heard by everyone, I said, "She's checking up on me."

"Oh." Kabe nodded like he weren't surprised at all. "So did you ask her?"

"Ask me what?"

"Ah." Took a deep breath and thought about how best to approach the subject. The barn smelled of onions, radishes and fennel. All of it had been in our last box from the co-op. "Well,

I'm looking into a murder."

"A murder." Leah leaned back on one leg. "I haven't heard anyone say nothing about a murder."

Kabe braced his hands on the low workbench and hefted himself up to sit on the lip. "It happened years and years ago."

"Yeah." I leaned up against one of his legs. "Old case I'm looking into."

Leah ambled over to one of the boxes filled with radishes. She pulled out a few that must have fallen off the bunch. Talking with her back to us she said, "'Fraid you're out of luck with me." She turned and offered up a sorry-you're-out-of-luck smile. "I've only lived up here, maybe a decade."

Nodded, 'cause I kinda expected that response. "Kabe says you were here once before, long time ago."

Shock flashed across her sun-lined face. "That was, God, almost thirty years or so ago." I think she actually laughed a bit as she said it.

As I'd talked, Leah walked over to a small sink and rinsed off the radishes. "I know." Had to agree with her there. "It's a murder that happened in '79."

Radishes cupped in her hand, Leah kinda shook her fists at me. "Why do you think I'd know anything about some age old murder?" Droplets of water stained the concrete floor with little dark pin pricks.

"Look." I straightened up, shoved my hands in my pockets and offered her the basics of the case with a shrug. "Back, 'round about the year I was born someone killed a little girl."

That stopped her in her tracks. "What?" Literally, she was walking on over to us and darn near missed a step.

Kabe popped me in the thigh with his foot. "His *sister* was murdered over at Panguitch Lake."

Leah belted out, "How old were you?" Then a little quieter she continued. "I mean, you don't look much past thirty."

"I ain't." Thirty-three in less than two weeks. "I weren't even crawling yet when she died." The last of my siblings, all seven of us. "But I want to lay her ghost to rest, give my family some peace."

"Look, Joe and I have been going over the file." I could almost feel Kabe's scowl burning into the back of my head. "He talked to his older sister and she mentioned, well, a hippie encampment over around the lake." Kabe pushed me to the side and bounced off the table. "I told Joe that maybe you might have heard something. You told me you were around back then."

"Encampment? Hardly." She snorted. "Yeah, I passed through the area around then." Leah walked over to me and held out her hand, the one with the radishes. I pulled my own hand out of my pocket. "A group of us hitchhiking across the states." She dropped the vegetables into my palm. "Me and my two girlfriends hooked up with a couple of guys with a VW Van." She belted out a deep old belly laugh as she moved her free hand up and down the air in front of her torso. "Back when I was young and cute and free love abounded. We stopped here, camped for awhile. Local law ran us off after a few weeks." The deep smile the amusement brought on faded ever so slow. "That's right." She dropped her hands to her hips. "A little girl died around then. That's why they harassed us."

Pulled out my folding knife, flipped it open and cut the ends off the radishes. Then I popped a small one in my mouth. "Were you camped by the lake?" I asked as the first bite of sweet and heat exploded across my tongue. Cleaned the others off the same way and parceled them out between Kabe and Leah. Saved a few for myself, of course.

"Well, kinda." She took a bite outta half of one and chewed a bit. "I mean back then it was just a lake. Not many houses or anything out that way. No campgrounds that I can remember, so I think we were between the lake and road." Holding the half eaten piece in front of her eyes, she seemed to study it, like that bit helped her think. "The guys did some odd jobs. I cleaned houses for a few people. But, yeah, I remember this big stir out by the lake. All these cars coming and going. There usually wasn't a lot of traffic beyond a few fishermen."

"All right." I prodded, gently, trying to stir her memories but not add anything to 'em. "That's good. What do you remember about that day?"

"Not much," she admitted as she popped the other piece between her teeth.

"Think back." I didn't quite plead, but I did ask pretty hard.

She jerked her head up like I'd cracked a whip behind her and looked back at me. "This is important to you?"

"Yes." I guess I must have asked even harder than I thought.

Kabe added his plea. "Please, Leah, think." Came out a little more earnest and a lot more personal than mine.

She thought for a long, long time. Puttering around the barn. Messing with things in boxes and tossing some of it out. I let her have that time. This was about pushing at the right moments to release the things held in the back of her brain. She weren't a suspect so I didn't need to drill.

"Mostly what I remember was this big line of cars going on around the lake about midday." She scowled. "And then, a few hours later, a bunch of folks, one cop car, and some others, dragged us all down to the jail." That statement got a nasty roll off her eyes. It was a look I'd caught off a ton of folks who felt they'd been hassled for no good reason. "We got yelled at for hours and hours." She picked up a leek outta one of the boxes, pinched it in a few places, scowled and tossed it in a big trash bin marked *compost*. "I guess though, they finally figured we didn't know anything. We heard that a little girl died. They drove us to the county line and just dumped us there with our stuff." She shook her head as she came up in front of me. "Didn't leave a great taste in my mouth."

"But you came back," Kabe reminded her.

"I followed others." She laughed, easier this time. "Time changed some things." Leah reached out and tapped Kabe's nose with his index finger. "Hell, Cedar City has one of the biggest Shakespeare Festivals in the west. The counter culture revolution is slow but steady."

"All right." I brought us back to the topic at hand. "Think back to the day before all that happened."

Kabe added, "She disappeared the day before she was found."

I scowled a bit. Hadn't wanted to prompt her in that direction. It might mess up the flow of her recollection. I didn't say nothing, however. That would just interject our issues into this whole case. Tried to think a bit on how to steer us back from that feed of information.

Leah saved me by hitting me with a question outta left field. "What was her name?"

"'Scuse me?" I crossed my hands over my chest.

"What was your sister's name?"

Took in a deep breath. Hadn't wanted this to go to the all-about-me mode. Kinda grudging, I huffed it out. "Rosalie." Put my attitude in my pocket and tried to recover by spitting out, "Everyone called her Rosy." Tried to make that flow easier and less irritated.

"Rosy." She seemed to mull the name over in her head. "Pretty name." She offered up a sad smile. "You know what. There was something strange the day before."

"Really?" Kabe seemed shocked.

"Yeah." Leah nodded. "Like I said, usually only fishermen braved those roads out there. All dirt." Half the roads through the Dixie National were still dirt, but around the lake, they'd since gone and paved the major ones. "But, I remember I was walking in from the highway along one of the roads and I got passed by this little red sports car, kicking up dust and heading for the highway. Italian or English make; like an MG maybe." She sounded downright unsure on that last bit...about the type of car, not that it was a foreign job. "I remember I told the sheriff back then. He got real quiet after that. I think we'd been in questioning for what felt like days," she almost chucked with her own exaggeration, "and he just stopped and stared at me when I mentioned the car." Her face all serious, Leah crossed her arms over her chest and kinda rolled her shoulders like the memory spooked her. "He asked me, maybe, a few dozen follow up questions and then walked out. The next day they drove us to the county line. The guys' micro-bus was there. They cut us loose and told us to hit the road."

"A red sports car." I could feel my lips tighten and my eye's go a little narrow. "That's what made Marshall stop?" Mostly 'cause I hadn't seen nothing so far in anything I'd read about a red sports car. Weren't in any file or case note. Not another person had motioned it to me so far.

She gave me a come-again look, "Marshall?"

Explained myself, "The sheriff at the time. Marshall Wright." Licked my lips and asked again, "But you told him about a red sports car and he cut you loose?"

"Yeah, he really drilled me about the car." Confirming her conviction, Leah nodded. "Everything I could remember about it. Didn't care about anything else." She smacked her palms together like she was dusting them off and then held them out to indicate that was all she knew.

I pressed a little bit more around that subject. She couldn't answer me more, really, given how long it had been. She said she did tell Sheriff Wright some deeper details, like what state the license plate was from, but didn't recollect none of them now. Just this memory of a bright red sports car of a kind you didn't see round these parts back then.

Heck, even now days, a car like that would stand out. Pickups, SUVs, mommy-vans and maybe a hand full of cheap, compact imports made up what folks drove. Back then, again, pickups, station wagons and big all-American boats would have been the norm. And that meant, if the car had ever been registered in the county I actually had a shot at finding it.

CHAPTER 23

On the way home, we talked over what we knew. Frankly, weren't all that much. Rosy disappeared walking to the house from school, she'd been found by the lake and a red sports car might, or might not, be connected to her death. Of course, that was strange that it hadn't been in Sheriff Wright's report. Both of us puzzled through that. For as thin as the official file was, the unofficial version we'd picked up in Salt Lake held a lot more details. Still neither of them mentioned a red sports car.

Given how Leah talked about how it shook Sheriff Wright, pulled his focus, there should have been at least some mention. Even if he ran that lead down and it didn't pan out, a good officer kept those little facts 'cause you never knew until you had everything wrapped up what mattered and what didn't.

"All right." I huffed out my frustration. "Can you think of anything else about this death that we haven't run into the ground?"

Instead of answering my question, Kabe asked one of his own. "Why are you distancing yourself from this, from her?"

"What do you mean?" Kinda scowled across the cab at him. "Distancing?"

He rolled his eyes and shifted his butt on the seat so he could see me better. "Well," his voice went up about two pitches on just that word, "you picked this case, out of all those old cases, you picked this one."

I had no idea what he was fishing for. "So?"

"Every other case you've handled, you get to know the victims." He said it like it should be so obvious. "Like that kid last winter." That was the case that I was wrapping up when I got suspended for being with him. "You dug to find who he was, what his life was like and how he interacted with his friends." Kabe'd been around, not intentionally, for some of the suspect interviews. I guess he thought he knew my style from just that bit. "You've been acting like you're doing that with your sister's case, but you're holding yourself back."

My scowl dropped into a full on frown. "I don't get you."

A strangled sound preceded the next statement. "You're not pushing." His tone called me an idiot for not seeing what he did. "You're not prying. You're not questioning like you would."

"You get involved in two of my cases and you think you know how I do this?" I think I sounded as frustrated as he did. "I'm doing what I always do."

"No," Kabe insisted. "No, you're not."

"What, exactly, are you on about?" Took the turn up our road a little harder than I should.

Kabe grabbed the door frame so's as not to get thrown against the door itself. Didn't stop him from digging at me. "Your brother blew you off. I wasn't there, I didn't hear the conversation, but he blew you off, and you let him."

Sam had been dead tired. Driving for that long would wear anybody out. "I'm going to talk to him again." Hadn't had a chance to talk with him yesterday, being as we'd been in court, but I'd get back to him.

"The Joe I know would never have let him walk away from that conversation without digging into why he didn't want to talk right then," he pointed out. "I know it was late. I know the excuse, but you and I both know that's BS. You made him uncomfortable and that made you uncomfortable because he might know something you don't want to hear." He popped the dash with the palm of his hand a few times. "You don't want to think about it. You're drawn to this case. But you won't let yourself really think about it."

"You're smoking something." Yeah, Sam seemed a little antsy, but like I'd said, it was late and he was exhausted. "I am thinking about it," I insisted. "Trying to puzzle it all through."

"No." I could feel his frustration all the way over on my side of the truck. "You're not thinking about what happened."

"I am." Turned onto into our drive and the trees closed in around the truck. "I'm working the angles."

He rolled his eyes and turned his head to look out the window. "Maybe in the intellectual sense, but you've always gotten in to people's heads." Kabe talked to me without looking at me. "You tell me that. It helps to think like the victim or the jerk who did it. And you're not letting yourself go there."

I think I was just as frustrated as he seemed. "How the heck do you know?" I snapped a little harder that I normally would.

Kabe shook his head. "'Cause you're not talking to yourself."

Stopped the truck and threw it in park before I hit him with, "What?"

As he unbuckled, he explained, "When you get into a case, and you're processing it through, you walk around talking to yourself. Not out loud, but I can see it." I had no idea I did anything like what he was talking about. "Your lips move, the expressions go across your face. You don't even know you're doing it. And this time." Kabe popped the truck door open, but didn't get out. "You'll start and then you shut it down. Plus you're talking in your sleep. The only time you ever do that is when shit is bugging you." He got out then, but kept talking as I clambered out of the truck and we both started towards the porch. "After your accident you did it a lot." Shrugging, like it bewildered him a bit, Kabe added, "Each time you have to go through deposition or they have you go to another medical exam, you'll do it for a few days before. Makes it really fucking hard to sleep." He snorted. "This, you can't let it come out when you're awake so it's invading your dreams." Kabe stopped on the bottom step of the porch and turned back towards me. "Not good. Since you found the file, the only good night's sleep I've managed is the few times I've slept over at the fire-house."

"Look," I tried to brush him off, "I'm working this case at my pace." But I kinda suspected he might be onto something. My dreams lately, while I couldn't really remember them, left me all uneasy in the morning. Meant I weren't sleeping good.

"My ass." He spat. "Your sister was found drowned, her underwear some five hundred feet away." Kabe thumped his chest with two fingers. "I'm not a cop and I know what that means. She was seven. She was raped." That last word came out all hard. "You're not facing that, at all!"

"The OME didn't find any evidence of forcible contact." 'Course the medical examiner hadn't really tried from what it looked like.

He barked out a laugh before thudding up the few steps to the door. "With that craptasitc file, that doesn't mean it didn't happen. Tell me I'm wrong."

I fished the right key on the ring as I followed him. "Okay, yeah, the official file left something to be desired." Didn't used to lock my place, but since meeting Kabe, I'd become a lot more cautious about a lot of things. I didn't want the mischief happening with my mailbox to translate to the inside of my house.

"It's a shitty report," he insisted.

As I opened the door and walked in, I tried to rationalize, "But, they wouldn't have ignored that."

"Bullshit." He hit me with the curse. "You know they would have, back then." Pushing past me, Kabe headed for the kitchen. "Shit, you're the one who was telling me the formal medical examiner office hadn't been around very long then." Although his back was to me, he kept talking. "No protocols. Kinda winging it." Kabe made it to the fridge and pulled out a bottle of water. He slammed the fridge door to emphasize his next statement. "They fucked up the report, dude."

I propped elbows on the breakfast bar and leaned my weight to rest on them. All right, I'd said it myself, the file was thin. "So?"

"So." Snaking a chair out from the table with his boot before plopping his butt down in the seat, he spun his thoughts out for me. "You're avoiding that hell. The hell she went through." His eyes kinda drifted from looking at me to staring out the window. Quieter, he continued, "Can you imagine being seven and going through that? Think, dude. What was she thinking? Lay there. Let your mind go somewhere else and maybe, if you don't struggle, you'll get to go home." Those words kinda tightened up my own chest, 'cause I wasn't all that sure whether he was imagining what went on with Rose or remembering his own ordeal. "And in those last few minutes, fuck," the curse came out with a huff of breath, "what was going through her mind. Could you imagine? I can. I can hear her in my head. Pleading for your mom and your dad."

I'd heard enough. "Shut up, okay." Not about her, but about him. Made me remember what I'd gone and done. Struck me hard and made my gut bubble with shame.

Kabe ignored me. "And your family, your parents, your brothers and sisters. Every night they went to bed hearing that soundtrack in their heads."

"I said, shut up!" Didn't yell, but my tone was strong.

"For all these years, you've been spared that." Kabe wouldn't drop it. "And you won't let yourself go there."

Took a few breaths to keep myself even before I answered him. "I don't need to think on that to be able to solve this."

"Yeah," he took a swig of water in between the words, "you do."

"Look." I stepped back and palmed my face with both hands. "I don't got the perspective that you have on this. I can't just go there, like that."

"Perspective?" Now Kabe just sounded confused.

I don't know why I'd said that. Hadn't meant to. "Ah, well you know, identifying with her like that." Had a feeling that explaining my choice of words was just going to dig me in deeper.

Kabe slammed the bottle onto the table top. "Like what?"

Lord, I was gonna have to tell him what I knew. "Awe, heck, you know," I swallowed hard before continuing, "'cause of what happened with you."

"I'm sorry?" He stopped in mid motion, the bottle halfway back up to his mouth. Slowly, Kabe set it back on the table and leaned toward me. "What do you think happened to me?"

I came around on into the kitchen. "Okay, look." Grabbed hold of the back of a chair and kinda massaged it with my grip. "I heard about some things."

"What things?" All of a sudden, he was shouting. "Goddamn can't you just fucking spit it out?"

"I was talking with Dev and he was talking with some folks he knows…and," hesitated a moment trying to think of how to say it, "they know about you."

"What?" Kabe stood. "Fucking tell me, what?"

Let go of the back of the chair. "That you got into a situation when you were, maybe, sixteen." Tried to keep my tone even, make sure I didn't sound like I judged him. "Things got out of hand. The guy you were with took advantage of you…"

His face went slack. "Where the fuck did you hear about this?"

"I told you." Shoved my hands under my pits and shrugged. "Dev was talking with some folks and they said things."

His voice went all cold. "What right did he have to dig into my life?"

"I don't think he was digging." I really didn't. It had just come up, like things sometimes do.

"Holy shit!" Right then he blew: face all red and hopping mad. "Not his right!" He slammed his fist into the table. "Not your right! My life."

"What do you want me to do," I snapped back, "pretend I don't know?" Wasn't mad at him, had to be a shock, finding out I knew that about him. Still, him coming at me got my back up.

"Fuck, I don't know!" He bellowed back. A few moments passed where we both just thrummed like telephone wires in a windstorm. When he seemed to get a little control back, he asked, "What do you know?" May not have yelled, but he sounded like a rattlesnake telling me he might bury his fangs in my leg.

Rolled my shoulders a bit trying to shake off some of the tension. "A guy, an older guy, took advantage of you. Didn't stop when you told him to. And then, well, lots of folks didn't believe you, got messy." Again, I didn't want him to think I blamed him for any of it, although I probably weren't choosing the right words. "That shouldn't have happened to you. Shouldn't happen to nobody."

"Jesus Christ." Like all the air had been sucked right out of him, Kabe dropped back into his seat. "Can that asshole not mess in our lives? Why would he tell you anything about that? No don't even try to answer." He stood again and walked up to me. "Never mind, there's no answer." His face was all locked down. "Right now, nothing you can say means shit."

"Kabe—" There had to be something I could say to ease him.

He held up his hands like he was pushing me away. "Back off, Joe. I can't believe he told you. I can't believe you fucking didn't tell me immediately."

"I just found out the other day." Tried to be rational about it. "You were at the station, so I ain't going to pick up the phone and be all about what I heard." Didn't figure it was going to help much as Kabe had gone over the lip of the mountain and was full on committed to his view, still, I tried. "And yesterday, well we had a few other things on our minds. So, you know, it was the first time I had the opportunity to bring it up." I could understand him being a little upset, but, Lord, he was making a mountain outta a molehill.

"Godfuckingdamnit." He smacked his forehead with his palms. "Okay. I can't even. Gah!" The anger wound 'round his words and strangled them. "I can't even, like, talk to you right now." He pushed past me. "I'm going upstairs, watch *Touching the Void* then *Endless Summer* or maybe *Mango Soufflé* on my tablet." Stopping at the pass through by the breakfast island, Kabe turned and pointed at my chest. "I don't even want to see you until at least tomorrow morning." Then he stomped up the stairs, the booms on the wooden treads echoing through the cathedral space of the front room.

Okay, I ain't seen either of the other two, but *Touching the Void*, with all the intense mountain scenes and hard decisions on whether you try to save your climbing partner or cut them loose and let them fall…yeah, not my idea of a movie to watch if'n I was burned by someone. Unless maybe he wanted to imagine me as the guy hanging off the ledge and him being the one to drop my ass down the face.

CHAPTER 24

Spent the day at the station catching up on a lot of things I'd put off while tracking down this matter and trying not to think on the blow out with Kabe. Did mess with Rosy's case a little. Tried to run the car through DMV records. Not much luck with that: red, foreign sports car. Might have been a Porsche, MG or Fiat for all I knew. I knew it wasn't any newer model than a '79, but not how much earlier than that it'd been made. Heck, I didn't even know whether it'd even been registered in Utah. That search felt like firing blind into a forest and hoping there was a deer hiding in there somewhere.

About midday, Tina called and asked if it were okay that everyone came over to my place for dinner. James had hit town last night, so everyone wanted to get together and chew the fat. My folks though, they were already worn a bit thin. So it was my house or somebody's hotel room. Didn't want to deal with all of them at one time, given everything going on, but I couldn't avoid it all my life so, against my better judgment, I said yes.

Came home to a house that was all empty. Kabe'd left for work around six that morning, not even saying nothing to me on the way out. Hoped a day away from me might give him some time to process things, ease up on being mad. Seemed like, if I gave him some space, he could come back on things a bit later and not be as sore. Didn't know as it would really happen, but I could still hope.

First off, I turned on the oven to preheat; wanted to roast a loin of venison I'd pulled outta the spare fridge in the pantry. I'd pulled it out of the freezer a few days back figuring we'd use it sometime in the week. Then I changed outta my uniform into sweats and washed up last night's dishes. Not long after, Lacy and Tina arrived with a few grocery bags. Left them in the kitchen to do what they wanted to do while I went for a light run.

My doctor cleared me to run so long as I kept the pace easy

and chose even surfaces. I thought I was farther along than he believed, but I had better sense than to buck his orders. Wouldn't want to screw my knee up again and end up worse off than before. Probably was out a good forty minutes, 'cause when I got back a bunch of cars that weren't mine clogged my parking area. Said a quick round of hellos then I went upstairs and grabbed a clean pair of jeans and a shirt. After a shower made me a little more presentable, I headed back into the great-room to greet folks proper.

Sam looked up from where he and Tina's husband, Frank, knelt in front of my TV stand. "Joe," Frank's voice boomed with all the authority of a man who'd spent his whole life giving orders. "Come over and show us how this cockamamie set up you have here works." He looked like a guy who gave orders too. Stern, square jawed with a dark crew cut; even when he was out of uniform, you knew he wore one.

"Sure." I scooted around the couch, grabbed the remote off the coffee table and headed over. "What y'all trying to do?"

"Play this disk." Sam tapped the machine, I guess they'd already put it in. "Thomas had it made up from a bunch of home movies. You know, the ones Lacy had you dig out and some stuff we all had." I'd wondered what Lacy was up to with all that. She'd said something about saving them, but I hadn't really asked neither. "Tina wants to make sure it all plays right first so we can have it at the reunion."

"Oh, okay." I punched a few buttons on the remote and the TV came on. "Got a set up for it for the hall?" I sure didn't want to haul my flat screen and accompanying gadgets over to the social hall. Too much stuff to disconnect and reconnect.

"Yeah." Sam stood up. "Payton's got one in his RV." Good. I wouldn't have to mess with my system.

Frank got to his feet as well. "That set up alone," he pointed at my electronics, "lets you know that a single guy lives here."

Didn't quite consider myself single no more, but I was a long way away from ever being hitched. "I guess." Pressed another couple of buttons switching from satellite to the disk player and handing the remote over to Sam. "There you go." Up on the screen a grainy vision of my folks on their honeymoon at the Grand Canyon flickered to life. "Wanna watch the whole thing?"

"Naw, figure we'll just skip around some and make sure it plays." Sam jumped the video ahead a bit every so often. Watched my family get bigger and everybody age in bits and snips. There were a few sections with Rosy running about the yard or at birthdays. One of her laying next to me on a bed, giving my tiny fingers a kiss…I couldn't have been more than a month old. Wondered how my folks would react to that. Don't recall that they'd ever pulled those out when I was a kid.

We all looked over as the door banged open and Tina called from the kitchen, "Hey, Jim."

Lord, Jim, third brother in line who seemed to think it was his duty to make our family toe the line in faith. He's the one I most dreaded seeing. And it looked like he might feel the same way about me. His broad face was all drawn up like he smelled something bad. Button down shirt and khaki pants, Jim always dressed like he was on his way to some function that rated far more important than whatever you were up to. Jim barely acknowledged us with a jerk of his chin before heading into the kitchen where I could hear his wife Jenny talking with my sisters. When I turned back, Frank and Sam were staring at me. I'm certain they caught the vibe off Jim, same as me.

I was about to say something about it not mattering when the video jumped to some sporting event. A bunch of teenage boys stood in a group and tried to pretend they weren't being filmed. "Wait, go back." What caught my eye…a little reddish sports car parked off to the side and almost out of frame.

Sam hit fast forward instead. "What?"

"Give me the remote." I reached out and grabbed it outta his hand. After a bit of futzing I found the section I wanted. Stopped it on the clearest shot of the car. "There." I almost laughed with how dang lucky, I'd just got. I pointed to the left corner of the screen. "Yeah, there, that car!"

Frank looked at me like he thought I'd gone and lost my mind. "Car?"

"You done gone car crazy on us." Sam tone said he might just agree with Frank's assessment of my mental state.

"That red sports car." Actually, it was kinda pinkish-grayish. Time hadn't done any favors to the quality of the images. This section sported a sepia wash. "Well I think it's red, color is a bit off on this."

"Old film." Frank observed as he wandered over to sit on the couch.

"What about the car?" By his tone, Sam hadn't come to a firm decision about whether I'd gone round the bend or not.

I reached for my shirt pocket and felt for the pad I always kept in my uniform shirt. 'Course then I realized I wasn't in uniform. "Somebody get me pen and paper." I'm sure I was talking louder than I needed, but this was like finding a bag of money in the middle of the road: unexpected and unlikely to happen. "I need to write down the plate."

I guess the commotion had drawn Jim out of the kitchen, 'cause I heard him behind me asking, "Why are you writing down the plate for Clay's car?"

"Clay?" I turned around. "Clay who?"

"I don't remember." Jim frowned. "I didn't know him that well." He rocked back on his heels and shook his head. "I just know it was Clay's car because he was one of the few kids around town that had their own car."

"It wasn't like it was anything great as I remember." Dropping down into my recliner, Sam sounded dismissive. "All beat up."

"Yeah and we got to drive what?" Jim grimaced. "Mom's station wagon, sometimes. I didn't buy my first car until I was back from my mission." Jim didn't make any moves to come and sit down. "So I remember he was one of the few guys we knew that had their own wheels."

I headed over to the desk in the corner to get something to

write with. I could make out the state, Idaho, mostly because I could see the I and D. Couldn't get a handle on a full set of numbers either. But a make, model and partial plate, that would get me access to the registered owner and a chance to find this Clay fellow.

"Why are you so interested in that car?" Sam asked as I jotted what I could see down.

"'Cause I think it might have something to do with Rosy's death." No reason to lie right then.

"Clay?" He snorted. "Clay's car." I think Sam settled on me being crazy. "Your hat's on too tight. Clay was, I think, sixteen when Rosy died. He couldn't have had nothing to do with it."

"Okay, well, a witness I found remembers that kind of red sports car out by the lake the day Rosy died." Explained it out so they all didn't decide to pack me up to the funny farm. "It might not mean anything, but I got to look into it. Maybe he lent it to someone that day." That was possible, I also floated the other possibility. "Or maybe he saw something that he might remember now." I would think that, since most folks 'round here didn't have those kinda cars and Sheriff Wright would have recognized it as belonging to Clay, he'd have talked to the boy. Made it strange that I didn't find no notes about that. "You don't remember what his last name was?" DMV would give it to me, if he owned the car, but I rather have the information sooner than later.

"No," Jim answered. Still off across the room like he might get tainted by the air if he moved any closer to my general direction. "I didn't hang out with him, I was all of thirteen. I don't think he ever came to church, lived out on one of the ranches. The Richardson's place, I think." Like he tried to make certain I understood that the memory was cloudy he added, "We didn't see him much except at school."

"That was pretty much just passing in the halls." Sam jumped in with a confirmation. "Kept to himself. Didn't play sports." That was odd. With as small as the school was there was only one team, freshmen through seniors, and unless you were physically unable to play, you were on it.

At least now I had something to go on. While we waited for dinner, I tried a couple of times to get Sam off alone. Too many folks about especially when Payton and his brood arrived. The twins decided that the best thing in the word was sliding down the banister until their mom caught them at it and scolded them. Then she scolded all of us men for not putting a lid on the hijinx sooner. Don't know what she expected, we'd all have done the same thing at their age. A lot of nothing got talked about until Lacy called us all to eat. After Frank said blessing, Payton's family went to eat on the porch so the boys could burn off more energy outside. The rest of them settled in around the kitchen table while Sam, June and I occupied the breakfast bar.

About halfway through the first helping, Jim dropped his fork and knife on his plate and huffed out, "Ain't anybody gonna say anything?"

My gut went cold, 'cause I had a sinking sense of what he thought should be said. Weren't nice. Weren't pretty. And had everything to do with whose house they were in.

"Well." Sam chewed on a mouthful of venison before finishing his thought. "I was kinda thinking on the words of our Lord, 'let he who has no sin cast the first stone.'" The grin he gave Jim reeked of evil and smug. "Puts me right out of the running of saying something, even if I had a mind to."

Jim rolled his eyes and went after those he thought might back him more. "And, you're just okay with this Lacy?"

"I love him." She pushed the food around on her plate. She hadn't taken a lot in the first place and she'd eaten even less. "I love my brother," she repeated, this time looking Jim square in the eye. "I refuse to turn my back on him."

"But look what he's done to this family," Jim sputtered.

"What?" Sam grumbled, "Exist?"

Tina folded her napkin onto the table. She leaned towards Jim and spoke, quietly and more powerfully for it. "And whenever you stand praying, forgive, if you have anything against anyone, so that Heavenly Father may forgive you your trespasses. As His word says, of faith, hope and love…the greatest is love." Then she scowled at him. "Or have you forgotten that?"

"Don't y'all have something much more important to talk about?" Trust Frank to jump in and break up a potential fight.

"Really, Jim," Tina scolded him. "I mean we need to discuss what we're going to do about Mom and Dad. That's why we all decided to come over here."

"That's why?" I'd kinda wondered what got the wild hair in them to get together. "I thought you all just wanted hang out," I teased.

I earned a scowl this time. "I told you that's why we were all coming over."

"No, you didn't." When she started to open her mouth to argue with me, I cut her off, "But it don't matter."

"Well, okay." This time Lacy derailed a potential off topic argument. "So everyone knows Mom's got Alzheimer's." I had a feeling Lacy'd given them all the rundown throughout the day. "They're both up there. It's been great that they have been independent for so long, but somebody's got to take care of them now."

Okay, they weren't doddering old folks. "What?"

"They can't live on their own now, Joe." Tina talked at me like I was a slow witted child. "It's just not possible."

"Of course it's possible, Tina." Sam crammed a mouthful of potatoes into his maw and talked around his food. "You just don't think it's a good idea."

"Well you don't have to worry, Sam." Jennifer, Jim's wife, decided to jump in and say her piece. "They're not going to go live in some hovel in Alaska, so you can stay out of this." Jen's long suffering voice always had that nails across the chalkboard quality to it. "They're going to end up living with us, I'm guessing."

"Why would you guess that?" Tina wasn't any fonder of Jen than I was. "They could stay with us or Lacy."

"Right," Jen sneered, "because the feed store is so lucrative."

I guessed that Jen's barb landed right where she wanted it to and dug in deep 'cause Lacy hissed out, "We're not poor." If I had to guess, Lacy and Carl probably did better than Jim overall, but Jen would cut her own tongue out before she'd let anyone think that they didn't hit the top of the pile.

"Put a sock in it," Tina snapped. "This isn't about you, Jen, it's about our parents."

"As much as I hate to admit it." Frank leaned away from Tina just a hair, like he knew what was going to come out of his mouth next wouldn't sit well with her. "We're not really an option. Not yet. I don't intend to retire until they decide I'm too old to stay in. That means we could still get transferred again." When his wife didn't seem like she'd bite his head off, he relaxed a little. "Pulling up stakes as often as we do wouldn't be good for your mom."

Lacy nodded her agreement. "We have the room. The farmhouse is big." June was the only one in the room who kept her head down and didn't say nothing.

"Why do they have to move anywhere?" I couldn't understand what the urgency was.

"They need someone to take care of them." Jim drew himself up and tried to sound authoritative. "They'll need help and there's no one here that can do it."

Sam stopped eating long enough to yank my chain. "Hey, Joe, you're officially no one."

"I'm here." I rapped the counter next to my plate. "They don't have to pick up and move. This is their home."

Jen rolled her eyes. "I really don't think someone like you—"

Cut her off, and cut her off quick, "Pardon." I would have winced at the snot tone in my voice if'n I wasn't ready to spit nails at her. "You're right gay equals incompetent. Oh wait, no it don't. It ain't got nothing to do with whether I can handle it."

"Y'all have families." Sam pointed out the most obvious. "Joe's just got his guy." You'd have thought he poured lemon juice down Jim and Jen's throats by how sour their expressions went. "No kids. No other obligations than work. And he's a cop. How much more responsible can you be?"

"He's right." Frank sounded a little relieved. I think he liked my folks just fine. But there's a difference between liking your in-laws and wanting to live with them.

"It's a big job, Joe." Lacy looked pained. "You were there when Pa-pa lived with Mom and Dad." Both my grandparents had moved into our place when I was about seven. "It got pretty awful," she reminded me.

"Yeah, okay," I conceded. "But Mom ain't there yet. It may be years before she's that bad off." My gram'pa stuck around for several years before he passed. The last couple had been like living with a six foot, hundred and sixty pound two year old. One with a temper. "But that means I actually understand what I'm signing up for." I did, in spades. "Most of y'all had moved on by then. Your own places, own families." There had been quite a few days where, well, insanity didn't even begin to describe the chaos at the house. "I remember Dad and I having to bust down the bathroom door 'cause Pa-pa locked himself in and then panicked when he couldn't figure out how to get out. The time he went after the next door neighbor with Dad's gun 'cause he thought the guy shot his dog. One that had been dead, like a dozen years." There were worse things than those. I just tried to forget them as best I could.

"Joe," Tina chided. "You can't handle it. You don't understand what it takes."

"No." Frank and Sam shut her down at the same time, but Frank was the one who finished the thought off. "Joe's right. Being in their own home for as long as humanly possible is the best thing."

"But, with, well, the way he is," Jen sputtered while Jim just glared. "Immoral people shouldn't be around good folk."

That turned Lacy onto my side. "Joe's damn fine people." She snapped it out. "Mom and Dad should stay here, in Panguitch, until, like Joe said, it gets too bad."

"Right." I think Tina was as relieved as Frank at not having to shoulder the burden. "That's the plan then." She'd have stepped up, being the oldest and all. But, I guessed she was glad she didn't have to just yet. "We shouldn't tell them we talked about it."

Sam stretched, bumping my shoulder with the back of his hand as he did so. "We're all good at keeping secrets in this family." I wasn't sure what he meant by that, but I didn't have time to ask him as Jen decided to argue the point with Lacy and Tina. I just let them at it and went back to eating my now cold dinner. The girls had decided that this was how it would be and there weren't no way Jen, of all people, would convince them otherwise.

CHAPTER 25

The evening didn't get a whole lot better after that argument. The gals all sat arguing and not eating. I finally couldn't take it no more and headed out to the front porch. Sam joined me after he'd taken a walk down the drive to smoke. That meant I could talk to him like I'd been wanting.

Except then Jen barreled out of the house and made a bee line for their car with Jim not far behind. My guess she'd lost the argument and wasn't in a mood to stick around. That meant I had a choice between Jim or Sam right then…and given the way Jim felt, it'd be easier to run Sam to ground later. As soon as Jim stepped foot on the porch, I intercepted him.

Set myself right in front of him at the bottom of the stairs. Crossed my arms over my chest and spread my feet wide. "We need to talk." He couldn't get around me unless he decided to go right through me. James weren't one I feared that from. Out of the corner of my eye, I caught sight of Sam heading 'round the back of the house. I don't think he wanted to be part of what I had to say to Jim.

Jim looked down his nose at me. "I have nothing to say to you."

"You will hear me out." I had about twenty pounds muscle, that on my older brother was fat. "Look, don't give a rat's ass about what you think about me and how I live my life." And I'd bet my fitness level, even with not being able to work out full on, against his marked by desk work any ol' day. "I'm settled with it. You can be settled with how you feel. And we're just gonna leave it there for right now."

"I can't accept that." How he ever got so sanctimonious, I don't know.

"Too bad." I growled. "That's the way it is. And my business with you, ain't got nothing to do with this."

"Doesn't matter. I have nothing to say to you."

"Yeah you do. You're going to tell me everything you remember about the day Rose died. Everything you know about Clay."

"Why would I do that?"

"Because I ain't asking you as your brother. I'm asking you as a cop. And I'm asking you to pay me the little bit of respect that you'd pay anyone out there. What little bit that you need to show a man who just let you sit at his table and eat his food. Do I make myself clear?" Jim didn't answer, so I took his silence as a yes. "Tell me what you know about this Clay."

His mouth went tight and sour. "What I told you in the house." Came out grudgingly, like he really couldn't stand to be around me. Still, the church brought you up to respect the law. Jim may not have respected me, but he respected my uniform and I'd settle for that right then. "Mostly." He shrugged; shoulders all tight and hands jammed in his pockets. "And that the girls all thought he was kinda creepy. He showed up to a couple of Ward dances and it didn't go over well."

I made a conscious effort not to throw his attitude back at him. "Over well?" Came out as easy as I could manage. Don't get me wrong, it stung some knowing that hate rolled offa my brother.

"Rumor was he grabbed a girl. Middle School age, one of my classmates." Jim didn't elaborate on where or how, but any untoward physical contact wouldn't have gone over well. "Bunch of the older boys picked him up and tossed him out."

"Okay." I acknowledged what he told me, but prompted for more. "That's it?"

"Pretty much, he was a grade behind Sam in school. Between Sam and Tucker." Jim's attitude slipped a little, just a hair. "Didn't play football or baseball. Kept to himself." He didn't like me much, but I think this rested heavy on his mind, like it did for all the rest of us.

"That's it?" I prodded.

"About Clay, yep."

"All right." I let it go at that. I didn't think he knew much more on that subject anyway. "Let's talk about the day Rosalie went missing." Since I'd established that I was top dog, at least here, I moved aside so he could walk past.

Jim started to walk. "I was supposed to walk home with her that day." He heaved up a big sigh, like all the air in the world had been held in his lungs. "But I had practice. Told her she was a big girl and it was time to do it on her own." Jim stopped and moved the dust around with the toe of his loafers. "I should have walked home with her. Five minutes difference. Five minutes."

As irritated as I was with my brother, that was a heavy burden to bear all these years. Likely he was harder on himself than anyone else he knew. So I gave him what sympathy I could muster. "You couldn't have known."

"I should have walked with her." Jim sounded like he might just cry. "I'd have earned a couple of laps for being late. I run a thousand laps if I could roll back the clock, if it could bring her back."

"Did you meet her at the elementary school?" Older grades started and ended earlier than elementary 'round here.

"No." He walked a few more feet to his car. Jen already sat in the passenger seat, a tablet kinda thing on her lap that she read from. "Rose came over to the high school." Middle and high school were in the same building and everyone just called them both the high school. "I was on student government and we had some things we had to wrap up, end of the school year and all. Then I had practice."

We ended up by the back end of his car. "So you saw her at the high school?"

"Yeah." He leaned against the trunk. "I met her outside on the sidewalk. I spoke harsh to her." Jim rubbed the top of his balding head with his hand. "I replay that over and over in my head."

I didn't think Jim wanted my sympathy, but I guessed he'd

held in the guilt so long, he just needed to get it out. "I get that."

"Joe, I don't know." He huffed. "I still always think about what if."

"Yeah." The word meant nothing. "You were the last person to see her?"

"No." Jim shook his head. "A couple folks who lived across from the school saw her start down the street."

That jived with what I'd read. "That was the last you saw of her."

"Yep," Jim confirmed. "I'd give anything to redo that day."

"All right. Thanks for the information." I held out my hand to show him I didn't harbor any hate towards him.

Jim looked at my hand and then looked at me. He didn't take the shake. Instead, he walked around me and popped open the driver's side door. The only positive thing I got was his parting comment, "I hope you get whoever did it," before he slammed the door shut.

I moved back, let him pull out. Stuck all his attitude in my pocket. I mean, this little bit of conversation tempered how I thought of Jim's rigid and uncompromising nature. Didn't make me *like* him any more, but I did understand him a little better. Thirty-odd years of guilt about what he should have done equaled one heavy cross to bear.

As I walked back towards the house, I ran into Sam, Payton, Payton's wife Shelly and their boys heading out. "You all turning in for the night?"

Jonah lifted his head off my brother's shoulder. "Night, Guncle Joe." Almost all my grand nieces and nephews just called me that. It all started because my oldest grand-niece couldn't make the whole grand-uncle word come out right. It stuck.

I ruffled the hair of his twin brother Jacob as Payton passed. "You out of here, Sam?"

"Yeah." He kept his voice quiet. "Time to put the monsters to bed."

Hated to press at a time like this, but I did anyway. "I really need to talk to you."

"Tomorrow." Sam's promise sounded, I don't know, hollow. "We're taking the boys on a canyon trail ride in the morning, but sometime after that, we'll talk."

Kabe would get on me about not pressing, but you know, the little kids needed to get to bed. "I'll hold you to it."

CHAPTER 26

Got into the station early enough that morning. Did a little bit of paperwork until the clock rolled around enough for the high school to be open. I called over and asked if they had copies of the year book from '79. Took a bit to get the answer, but they did. When I offered to come get it, Lonni, who worked the front office and had graduated in my class, said she'd have someone run it over to me.

While I waited for the book, I ran the partial plate through Idaho DMV. Took a bit of messin' with data and a phone call or two to dig out that in 1979 the Fiat with that plate number belonged to a Darla Young of Boise, Idaho. Then, for a bit in the mid-eighties, it'd been subsequently owned by a Misty Young, also from Boise, before she sold it off. Possibly mom and then maybe a wife. Could be, if'n I was certain of Clay's name.

By then they called me up front, because the book arrived. Thanked the buck who brought it in, promised to return it when I was done, and headed back to my desk. I opened up the thin volume. Sam would have been a senior that year, Tucker a sophomore, so if this Clay was a year behind my oldest brother that would have made him a junior. But I checked all three classes none the less. I mean, it ain't like it was ever a large school. All of twenty kids made up my graduating class. Back in that year, only fifteen kids were in the junior class with one boy named Clay… Clayton Young. Had to go back to the middle school grades to find anyone else named Clay and they'd have been too young to drive. There you go: my guess was that momma bought him or lent him a car to drive while he was out here.

Picked up the phone again and called Lonni back. She pulled up Clay's records for me then faxed them over. He'd only been in Panguitch for two years. Back then, the school wouldn't have recorded his social. In fact, unless he had a job he wouldn't have needed to apply for one. Still name and date of birth were enough for me to run him through a records check…and strike out. I mean, I found a couple of Clay Youngs but none who'd ever lived in this area or had the same DOB. Likewise for both Utah and Idaho DMV. Odd.

Called over to my folk's house then. June answered so I asked her, "You seen Sam around yet today?"

"Yeah." She must have held her hand over the receiver to answer somebody's question 'cause I heard a muffled *Joe*, before she continued. "Uncle Sam's here right now, out back with Gram'pa." Then she kinda whispered to me, "They've been arguing most of the morning."

"Okay." I reached for my hat and keys. "Tell him to sit tight. I'm going to come right over."

"All right." I could hear someone talking at her in the background. "I'll see you in a bit."

I acknowledged, "In a bit," before I hung up the phone. Passed my Lieutenant on the way out. "Sir." I skidded to a halt since I'd been close onto a run in my rush to get over to my folks' place. "I'm headed over to talk with my older brother. I might have a person of interest in this case. The one about my sister's death."

He looked at me like my hat was on too tight. "Your brother's a person of interest?"

"No, sir." By the question, I realized how muddled my last words came out. "Someone my brother went to high school with. Going to go talk to him about it. Guy's name was Clay Young."

He nodded. "Good. Look, I want you to bring me up to date in the morning." The man sounded distracted. 'Course he always sounded distracted to my ears. I was starting to think maybe it was just who he was and not that he actually didn't listen to you.

"I could do it this afternoon." Not like my calendar was full.

Waving me off, he talked as he walked away. "No, I'm out this afternoon. Got to take my wife down into Cedar for this whole shopping, dinner and a movie thing 'cause I royally screwed up our anniversary this year." He paused and turned to look back at me. "So, unless the station burns down or one of y'all gets shot, do not call me."

"Yessir." I snapped to attention and saluted him like he was man headed out on a suicide mission. Watched him for a moment as he walked away shaking his head. I don't think he had any more read on me than I did on him. Sooner or later, we'd figure each other out. Jogged out the back of the station to the Charger. I'd started to kinda like driving it...big ol' muscle car grew on me. Didn't take me long at all to reach my folk's place. Sam's SUV weren't around as far as I could see. 'Course he could have lent it to his son Payton to drive since they were in the RV. Got out and headed 'round back.

First person I saw was my daddy...working hard mending a fence. Yeah, we'd made the right call, no way would he, much less my momma, take to that loss of independence. "Hey, Dad," I called out. "You seen Sam?"

Dad hooked the hammer on the rail of the fence and turned towards the sound of my voice. "He took off maybe ten minutes ago."

Just like Sam to run from talking; to me or anyone else. "Darn it." I yanked off my Stetson and slapped it against my thigh in frustration. "We're supposed to talk today."

"About what?" Wasn't his business, but since he was our dad, everything to do with us equaled his business.

Hooked my thumb in my duty belt as I set the hat back on my head. "Same thing I've been talking to everybody about."

"Joe, cain't you just let it go?" Dad ambled over. Noticed a hitch in his walk I ain't seen before. Almost like I frustrated him more than he could fathom, he asked, "Why are you doing this to your momma and to and everybody else in this family?"

"'Cause she was my sister, Dad." Gave him the same answer I done given him before. "And she deserves to have someone answer for what they did to her. The law gets its due."

He sat down on the picnic table bench, legs kicked out and

elbows resting back on the table top. I remembered eating dinner outside at that table when it got hot. Came over and sat next to him, 'cept my butt was on the table and my feet on the bench. Didn't say much for a while, just stared off at the blue-gray sentinels of the Panorama Mountains. Even here in town, it was pretty quiet. Nothing but the trees talking amongst themselves and a low tractor rumble off a few miles away.

Finally Dad spoke, "You didn't even know her."

"You're right," I conceded. "I didn't know her...not at all 'cause no one ever even talked about her." Didn't want to make this about me, but I wanted him to understand why it got so deep under my skin now. Why this was personal, went beyond my job. Why, like Kabe said, I had a hard time dealing with it myself. "I spent my whole childhood tip-toeing around this house, trying not to wake up the ghost of a girl who'd died the year my spirit touched this world." Took my hat off and spun the brim through my fingers. "God gets vengeance. Rose gets justice. And maybe I'll get a little peace from my memories of my mom hardly able to get out of bed some days or standing at the sink crying for no reason that I could understand."

"You figuring that out won't make those memories go away."

"You're right." Nodded and tried to work the thoughts around in my head so I could get the words out right. "It won't, but I think it'll help."

"I know and it don't help none with the loss." He sounded sadder than I could ever remember.

Still what he said didn't make a lick of sense. "You know what?"

"I know who killed my Rosy." He leaned forward and put the weight of his body on elbows cross over his thighs. "That got taken care of long ago."

Winter hit inside my chest and blew frost into my brain. I hoped he wasn't saying what I thought he might be. "What do you mean, Dad?"

Slow, like maybe I hadn't heard him right, he repeated, "We

took care of it."

That frozen feeling exploded out of my chest and swept through my veins. I swear the sweat on my head turn to ice, I'd gone so cold. "Of it?" Swallowed hard as I asked it.

Dad didn't look at me. "Of him." He dug dirt out from under one on his fingernails with another. "He weren't ever coming back here to do nothing again."

Oh, Lord. He couldn't be telling me what I was darn certain he was telling me. "Dad?"

Now he turned his head. Face all hard, determined, he asked, "You gonna arrest me, boy?"

"Don't know." My knee started bouncing at about a mile a minute. "For everything but murder, statute of limitations ran out long ago, even under the DNA revival statutes." Tried to give him, myself, a reason that I wouldn't have to. "So 'less you killed someone, no."

"Well, he weren't dead last time I saw him." Dad nodded. "Couldn't be sure he didn't end up that way after."

"When was that?" I should have called in another officer to take his statement. I couldn't. I just couldn't. I had to know. "What happened?"

"A while after. Marshall, John, me and a couple others took this boy, Clay, for a ride to the county line." He couldn't look at me as he told me. And Clay, Lord, my person of interest. As he talked I felt my muscles wind up around my bones until they thrummed so tight I thought they may snap me clean in half. "Taught him what it means to do something to one of our own." Something like that went against everything I knew about my daddy.

I couldn't believe the Sheriff had been on it. 'Course that would explain why a mention of the car and Clay's name hadn't made it to the file. Sheriff Wright buried it. And my Uncle John pretended like it never happened. "Who are the others, Dad?"

"Don't rightly recollect." His tone told me he knew darn well.

I had an inkling of why he might not want to tell me. "'Cause they're still alive?" Marshall and John passed long ago. If the others hadn't and if Clay died, they'd all be on the hook for murder. Be like my dad to admit to something like this, but not want to take no one else down with him.

He shrugged. "Could be."

"What happened?" I needed to know as much as I could. I'd set out to find who killed my sister. Now I needed to figure out if I could save my daddy. I sent up a silent prayer that this Misty person turned out to be Clay's wife, 'cause if she weren't, heck, I couldn't even let my thoughts go down that road.

Matter of fact, he laid it out. "We taught him a lesson." Stared off across the horizon all the time he talked. "A hard lesson, with a few ax handles and a lotta fists. Didn't kill him right then, although I wanted to." There was this cold, quiet, festering anger in his tone and it did nothing to stop the dread from chewing on my heart. "Like you couldn't imagine. Had my rifle out and pointed at his head." Dad pantomimed holding his thirty-aught-six and pointing it at someone lying on the ground at his feet. "All ready to do it." Now he looked up at me. "Marshall stopped me. Told me we'd got all the retribution God would grant us. A death was for Heavenly Father or the state to impose."

"What happened to Clay?" Maybe he'd made it back and then left town.

"Don't know," he admitted. "We left him there in a ditch by the road. Pushed his little foreign piece of junk off the road and down in there too. Look like an accident or something." That plucked a few more strands from the thin rope of hope I held onto.

My jaw was so tight, I didn't know how I managed to get the words on through my teeth. "If you knew who did it, why didn't you have him arrested?" I got that there was anger in my daddy. Who wouldn't be so angry they could kill someone who'd done that to their daughter? But why a lynch mob? Good law abiding folks who might have been foaming mad, but would have let the law handle it because that was the right thing to do. "Marshall was the sheriff; he could have just hauled him off."

"Back then we couldn't prove it. Not to a court. Not to a jury. It's what the prosecutor said, why he wouldn't file charges." All sad, he shook his head. "But we all knew."

If they couldn't prove it to a court, it meant they might have gotten it wrong. "How did you know it was him?" Bad enough that my daddy might go down for perpetrator's death, it'd be a hundred times worse on him if it turned out it was the wrong person. Even if they just beat him and he made it out, that guilt would wreck him.

"Odd boy, that Clay." That didn't make him a killer. "Parents sent him out here to live with his gran'parents, I guess 'cause he was getting into trouble back home. Always where he shouldn't have been." My daddy's jaw clenched up tight and he patted my knee with his hand. "Coach caught him in the girls' locker room, taking their things outta the lockers. Kicked him out of school for that. He'd follow the girls around. Couple fathers found him peeping into girl's windows."

All right, maybe. "How did he react when he was caught?" What used to be seen as harmless pranks we now looked at as gateway behavior to more serious crimes. Not every boy who raids a panty drawer becomes a rapist...but those who keep on with it, those you keep an eye on.

"Always blamed it on the girls, you know. They dressed too provocative, he was just walking by—*fifty feet from the house*—and there she was by the window." The more often it happened, especially after being caught, yeah behavior pointed to more serious problems. Still didn't mean he'd done this. "And that boy spun stories, all of them utter hooey about how important he was and things he claimed he'd done. While he was in school, before they kicked him out, he'd find reasons to rub up against the girls."

I moved down to sit on the bench. "So he was a creep." I heard things that made me suspicious in what Pa just told me, but it didn't settle nothing. "That doesn't mean he..." couldn't say that word to my daddy about my sister. "What made y'all believe he'd done it?"

He sat up straight. "We knew."

I prodded again. "How did you know?"

"Things that he did, said in the days after. Things that just weren't right." Didn't seem like dad wanted to elaborate more.

Honestly, right then, I was happy to let it go 'cause I had a much bigger question looming at the back of my brain. "How do you know you didn't kill him?" I wanted him to tell me it was okay, things were fine. Right then I weren't a cop, I was a little boy and he was my daddy—the one who was supposed to be strong and make things right.

"He was alive when we left him." Dad stood. "Never heard of no boy being found dead on the side of the highway 'round those parts…least not that year." I really hoped that was true. After a good long pause and a scowl, my daddy spoke again. "I need to go look in on your momma, so unless you're going to arrest me right now…" when I shook my head no, he continued, "I'll get to that. I ain't gonna run away. You know where to find me." Then he walked into the house.

Left me sitting there on that bench with my whole world dropped on its head and broken into pieces. Tried to sort it all out in my brain. Nothing made sense: about Pa, or Sheriff Wright or my Uncle John. It's like I'd focus on one bit and the rest reshuffled.

I'd been in a lot of hairy situations in my day: faced down drunks with guns, crawled in the hills to raid some big pot farm and take down the desperate guys who guarded it. I'd never backed down from none of it. This…this drilled that cold snake of fear so deep in my soul I didn't think I'd ever get the taint of it out. Like a robot, I got up from the bench and walked to my vehicle. Don't even remember getting in or turning the engine over. I do know I made it about a hundred yards down the highway before I had to pull over and puke my guts out all over the side of the road.

CHAPTER 27

I sat in the dirt near the fender of my vehicle, tasting my own vomit and wondering what the hell had just happened to my life. My phone went off a few times. I just ignored it. Didn't think I could talk to no one right then. I did go and find a warm, half-drunk bottle of water on the passenger floor. Used it to rinse my mouth and spit in the dust. Don't know how long I was there before my radio started paging me. Grabbed the mike off my shoulder, keyed it on, and gave my acknowledgment.

Noreen, our dispatcher, came back at me. "10-25 Ranger Sloakum on North Shore Road across from Rocky Point Boat Dock, possible 10-56." Every jurisdiction has its own version of the 10-code system. Since Utah had one overriding police authority that ran all the academies, ours were pretty standard across the state. Sill, why Nadia needed me to meet her for a drunk out by Panguitch Lake, I had no idea.

"10-10 I'm 10-7." Told Noreen I wouldn't respond 'cause I was clocking out. It was early. I'd get chewed for it, but I'd deal with that tomorrow.

A few minutes passed while I tried to collect myself then Noreen broke in again. "10-18 she says you need to be 10-17 now." I hauled myself up 'cause whatever it was equaled urgent and she needed my butt over there like yesterday. If it were anyone by Nadia, I'd have told Noreen that I wasn't responding no matter what. Instead, I hauled my butt off the ground and got in the Charger. Didn't take me all that long to get on over there. Drove round North Shore Road until I spotted the Ranger's truck and an SUV with Alaska plates. Kinda had an idea then why Nadia called me. Parked behind the white patrol car with the green stripe on side, got out and picked my way down towards where three figures were gathered near the shore.

Before I could say nothing, Nadia hit me with, "You lucked out that I landed this call."

"Thanks, Nadia. I owe you." Thanked her because I recognized the other two figures. One was Fred. The other, my brother Sam. Didn't think Fred was drunk.

"Well, you know." She slapped my back as we continued walking towards where he sat on a big boulder near the shore. "Easier to have you come pick him up than me spend the rest of my night doing the paperwork for drinking in public." She gave me one of her feral grins. "I'll let you haul him on home."

I just nodded and waved to Fred. Continued on down the bank to Sam's side. Half a six pack sat by his feet and he smelled like he might have primed the pump before starting on those. "Sam, what are you doing?"

Instead of answering my question direct, he pointed off down the shore. "Right over there."

Trying to interpret drunk wasn't easy. "What?" Given his state of intoxication, he'd poured it on fast and hard. Probably been drinking long before I even called my folks' place and talked to June.

"That's where they pulled her outta the weeds." He didn't slur too much. 'Course he'd been a hard drinker for years. "I'd offer you a beer, but they," he indicated the rangers walking back to their truck, "cut me off."

I reminded him, "You know I don't drink, Sam."

Sam gave me a bitter laugh. "So you'll put a dick in your mouth, but you tie yourself to the rest of it." Perplexed, he shook his head. "I don't get you, Joe. I don't."

Trying to explain things to a drunk was like trying to argue scripture with Satan. So, instead, I cajoled him, "Come on, let's get you home." Behind us, I heard an engine crank over and Nadia and Fred pull out.

He didn't move. "I watched it you know." Instead, his gaze tracked the shore of the lake until he came to a spot near where I'd placed the body recovery from the photos. "Them pulling her out. Eighteen all of a week and I'm standing next to my daddy watching them drag my little sister outta the water. Shouldn't have had to see none of it."

Nobody should have to witness nothing like that. Again though, I didn't try and engage his subject, I tried to talk him around to doing what I needed him to do. "And I don't need to see my big brother hauled off by my good friend 'cause he's three sheets to the wind sitting on a rock on the edge of Dixie National." I could be the sympathetic ear or I could be the cop right then. Cop was easier.

"You're gonna arrest me sooner or later anyway." Another bitter laugh choked its way outta his throat. "Why not now?"

"You're drunk, Sam." I knelt down and took hold of his elbow. "Come on home." Hoped that, as I stood up, the pressure on his arm would make him follow.

Worked okay. Sam managed to gain his feet none too gracefully. When he was upright, although not all that stable, he grabbed hold of both my shoulders. "You talked to him and you're just gonna let it slide? What we did?"

It all just lined up. Him leaving the church not long after his mission. What my daddy told me earlier and him not wanting to name names of those not six feet under. "You're talking about Dad?" The drinking. The fights. Running as far away from this little slice of Utah as he could get. "You were there." That weren't a question. At that point, I knew. And Lord, I wish I didn't.

"Beat the hell outta Clay." He gagged and I thought he might puke. Felt like I might even if he didn't. "They were all ready to kill him. And I was right there with 'em. We left him for dead. Surprised he didn't die right then and there while we were watching, we beat him so hard." Sam stepped back and presented his clenched fists to me. "So come on baby brother lock me up."

"I don't know that he's dead yet." I did not want to be here. I'd rather relive telling my folks I was gay a hundred times over than deal with this. "If he ain't dead, then I don't got to arrest you." I didn't want to arrest him or my daddy. I hoped like hell that somehow Clay made it off that road alive.

Sam mimicked putting a pistol between his eyes with his

fingers. "Daddy was all set to put a bullet through his brain." He clenched his thumb to the sound of, "*Pow.* The only reason we don't know whether Clay bought it, is the sheriff and good ol' Uncle John said to leave Clay's fate to Heavenly Father."

"How did you know it was Clay?" Don't know how much good information I'd get outta Sam right then, but a drunk would be less liable to mind his words.

"I don't know." Another braying laugh. "And, honest, I still don't know." Sam dropped back down on his butt. Guessing the only reason he didn't scream in pain was that he passed the ability to really feel it several rounds ago. "They all told me it was." He picked up a rock and tried to skip it across the lake. Didn't even make it to the water. "And stupid kid that I was, I believed 'em. So much so, that I was the one who lured him out onto that highway with a bottle of booze that Sheriff Wright gave me and a story about some girls up the way." His voice almost cracked as he spoke. "Got to a point in the road, told him I had to take a piss, then they hauled him out, kicking and screaming. I got into his little piece of shit car, drove behind them and pushed that son-of-a-bitch into the ditch. Make it look, kinda like an accident and all. In case, you know, somebody went a looking into it."

Now I knew who my daddy protected. "It's okay, Sam." I couldn't promise to make it all go away, so I gave him the best reassurance I could. "I'll try and sort it all out."

"It ain't okay." He jumped up and staggered towards me. "It ain't been okay for fucking near thirty years."

"Just calm down." Kept my voice neutral as I got my shoulder up under his pit. "Let's go home." Figured it would be my home, since I didn't want to pour my brother onto my daddy's couch. Especially not with him raving like this.

"Do you know what it was like?" He rambled as I walked him towards the road. "Riding home, smelling his blood all over me." Sam dug in his heels and almost dropped us both. "I'm sandwiched between Pa-pa and Uncle John, in the back of the sheriff's car." Okay, that was the other buck involved. My gram'pa was long dead, but Pa would never speak a word to tarnish his name in these parts.

Somehow, I managed to get us moving again. "No, I don't." I couldn't even begin to imagine what it would have been like for him. The fear settling down along with realization of what he'd just been part of. "Where was Tucker?" Jim would have been in middle school, but Tucker was only a couple years younger than Sam.

He tried to shrug. Hard to manage when my shoulder was under one arm. "They only needed one of us."

Weren't much I could say to that. "Oh."

"I left the day after graduation." Sam let me steer him and momentum kept us going. "Came back a few times, but I just couldn't stand to see this place no more." Again, he balked, but this time I managed to just use the halt to spin us round and then move forward a bit faster. "Thought, maybe, my mission might reconnect me to Heavenly Father, understand all this bullshit." By then we'd made it to my vehicle. I leaned him against the back end and fumbled with the rear door. "Didn't do a Goddamn thing other than make me hate the Church." Somehow, I got the door open and I tugged on Sam enough so that he almost fell into the back seat. "Know why I joined the Montana game wardens?" Sam served with the department of Fish, Wildlife and Parks for twenty years. I'd followed him into law enforcement 'cause he was my hero. When I didn't answer direct, he still gave me his reason, "'Cause it wasn't here and I could be out by myself most of the time."

"Okay." I didn't know what else to say.

Sam reached up and grabbed a fistful of my uniform. "I didn't want to be around nobody. I always thought they could see right into what I'd done."

"Don't worry, Sam." He had plenty to worry on, but telling a drunk that wouldn't get me cooperation. With one hand, I picked his feet up and shoved them into the back. "We'll deal with it." The other I used to try and disengage the death grip he had on my shirt.

When I finally got loose, Sam flopped across the back seat. "No matter how far I ran, my mind never left this goddamn town."

"I know." I shut the back door and dropped my forehead against the warm metal of the Charger. I lost track of how many minutes it took me to get to a point where I thought I could drive. Got into the driver's seat, took a few deep breaths and drove on to my own house. Don't know it I was relieved or irritated to see Kabe's truck parked out front. He was back off shift and home now. Probably should have returned the Charger to the lot, since it weren't my assigned vehicle, but I did not feel like going through all the red tape this boondoggle would entail. Easier just to suffer through a butt chewing for not sticking to protocol.

I went round to the passenger side and opened up the back. Sam had passed out somewhere along the drive. Given how much I knew he could put away…well, it might put a man with lesser tolerance into the hospital. Hooked my elbows under his pits and hauled him out. The thumps and scrapes as I drug his dead weight across the drive must have called Kabe outta the house.

I heard the front door open to a, "Holy fucking shit," at my back.

"You could help," I called over my shoulder.

Kabe ran past me, his cut brown body clothed in nothing but a set of low rise mesh trunks. Any other time, if I came home to him wearing that, I'd have been all over him like bees on honey. Right then, I noted his state of dress and continued with the effort to pull Sam into the house.

"What the fuck happened?" Kabe fell into EMT mode: catching Sam's legs at the knee with his elbows and using that grip in a two man carry to get him up the stairs.

"Okay." I anticipated and dealt with Sam's upper body weight falling full into my arms. "Apparently my daddy, uncle, gram'pa, Sheriff Wright and Sam here, drove this buck they thought was the doer across the county line and beat him like a bad hand of poker." Stumbled a bit getting through my front door and around to my couch. "He's drunk as a skunk." I stated the obvious. "And I couldn't let his gran'kids or my folks see him like this." We managed to heave him over the back of the couch. "So I brought him home, here."

"Really?" Kabe dumped Sam's legs over the spine. "He drinks?"

"Yeah, always has." I blew out a deep breath. "Long as I can remember. 'Course, now I know why."

"'Cause he got in a fight?" Kabe's look might have been more cutting if'n he weren't standing around with nothing but a little bit of net over his junk.

I shrugged and leaned over the couch for a quick frisk of Sam's pockets. "My daddy's not quite sure the guy survived." Found his keys in the left front. Helps to be a cop…sometimes. "And Sam, well, he wasn't more than a hair over eighteen. Having everyone you know and respect tell you that you got to man up and beat someone, maybe to death, Lord, I cain't believe he ain't more messed up." Somehow, I managed to get this all out calm and reasonable like. Nothing about my life right then equaled either calm or reasonable.

"You think they killed a guy?" Kabe's eyes had gone as wide as dinner plates and his voice jumped through about twenty tones as he asked it.

"Don't know." Dug Sam's keys out before I stood up. "I found Clay Young in one of the high school yearbooks. Tracked down his mom and maybe wife or sister through DMV records. If it's a wife, then he survived." That'd be obvious since a kid wouldn't have been married. "If'n it's his sister maybe he didn't. But somebody ended up with the car after the incident."

Kabe screwed up his face like he thought I was 'teched in the head. "Well then he survived."

"No." I corrected as I walked over to the gun safe under the stairs. "Don't mean he did." Realized most folks, like Kabe, didn't understand this stuff unless they'd had to deal with it. "What it means is some agency may have impounded the car, notified the registered owner and they came and got it."

"Well." He followed me. "But then you'd find a death report, right?"

Unlocked the safe and started storing my service weapon. "Maybe. If anyone's had time to enter an old death in the system. Let's face it, I'm just now getting to that era." Had to remind him what I spent most of my work days on recently. "Other departments maybe haven't. Or they ruled it a single driver accident." Slammed the safe shut, stood and unhooked my radio from my belt and shoulder. Piled that on top of the safe. "Dad and Sam both said they pushed Clay's car into a ditch alongside him, so if it took a few months to find the scene. I don't know where exact it happened, but I'm guessing on a back road, not the main highway." My grimace echoed my frustrations and fears. "Yeah, dead kid and sports car with no seat belt laws at the time, they'd have gone with the easy conclusion." I stood back up and bounced Sam's keys in my hand. "Most departments wouldn't enter what they believed to be a closed case into the systems." Wish I knew for sure. Don't think I'd sleep until I did…and if'n I got the wrong answer, I don't know if I'd ever sleep again knowing I dredged all this up and set the bar rocking.

"Holy shit." Kabe leaned on the breakfast bar.

Palmed my face and then ran my hands through my buzz cut. "I got to make a few calls." Fished my cell phone out of my pocket. "Can you get a blanket to throw over Sam?"

Kabe snorted. "Like he needs it." When I shot him a coyote-eyed glare, he conceded. "Okay."

Dialed up my sister and told her, kinda, what happened. Left out why Sam got drunk at the lake and any hint of the talk I'd had with Pa. She didn't need to have none of that until I knew for certain whether they were in hot water up past their eyeballs. She and June headed on over to grab the keys and then go retrieve Sam's car from Panguitch Lake. We could have left it there, but I'd rather not.

While I waited for her, I walked out to get the shotgun outta the front of the Charger and then brought it back into stow with the other weapons. I also called Payton and let him know I had his daddy at my place. He knew enough not to have to ask why his daddy was at my place and why I was calling. I figure he knew well enough why his momma left my brother. Never ever blamed Sam's first wife for that breakup. She did what she had to.

Heard Kabe thunder up and down the stairs a few times, as I dealt with things. When I got it all arranged and my sister swung by and grabbed Sam's keys, I looked around for Kabe. Couldn't find him anywhere. Considering that our house consisted of a great room with a kitchen that opened onto it, pantry, bath and mudroom all downstairs with one bedroom on the upper floor, there weren't a lot of places he could hide. Decided to look for him in the one place I always went to think.

CHAPTER 28

Found him up on the roof of the mudroom. Place I often went to clear my own head. I clambered up, setting my foot on one of the logs and my hand on the lintel over the back door and hefted my weight towards the sky. If you can climb a mountain, you can climb the side of a house. Kabe sat on the tin roof, his knees tucked up under his chin.

As I came on up I got hit with a poisoned stare.

I settled down with my legs dangling over the edge. As easy as I could I asked, "You okay?" Honestly, I don't know as I was ready to deal with him right then. But, you know, life never threw you the passes you expected. It was all about changing things up. My family life slid down into a slot canyon, but I had a chance to belay my romantic life off a free fall. I grabbed onto that line and held it for all I was worth. "Wanna talk?"

Kabe'd thrown on a pair of jeans and a t-shirt. "Not really." He huffed. "You got too much shit on your mind right now. I just needed to think some." A shrug added to the general air of indifference floating off him. "We can deal with this later."

Tried again, "I'm here. I'm listening." Hadn't even changed out of my uniform or nothing. "We can deal with it now."

He shrugged again. "I don't know."

I sucked in a big breath, held it for a moment, before I broached the subject myself, "I know you're a little sore." I wasn't used to talking like this...not with Kabe, not with anybody. Course, I'd never actually been in a relationship with anybody before him. Least handling this with him would keep me from running off screaming into the wilderness.

"A little sore?" Kabe snorted. "I'm still so fucking pissed right now that I could push you off this Goddamn roof."

Decided not to call him on taking the Lord's name in vain; he'd thrown it around way too much lately. Instead, I apologized,

"I shouldn't have brought it up; what happened to you." We both were close to the end of our ropes, frayed beyond belief.

"No." Kabe drew himself up, pushed his legs down, straightened them out along the line of the roof. "I'm glad you did." He folded his elbows behind him and leaned back. "Are you sure you're up to talking about this?"

"I ain't sure about anything," I admitted. "But it's going to be a bear dealing with that." Pointed back towards the house and Sam's general location in it. "If this rough patch keeps going on between us, I don't know as I can deal with everything else. I need something, if not right, then at least settled some."

"Okay." He sat for a while not talking, like maybe he collected his thoughts. When he finally did speak his voice was all quiet. "Look, I'm pissed at you, that you didn't tell Devon to shove it up his ass, but I'm massively pissed that he stuck his nose in my business." Another snort was followed by a shake of his head. "And I've never even met the asshole."

"I think he was just trying to help me out." I didn't know how else to explain it. I got that he thought Dev treaded on his boots. "Help us out." For me, yeah, Dev probably really believed I should know. He wouldn't have dug, but once he found something like that out, it wasn't like Dev to keep a friend in the dark. "For some crazy reason he seems to think you're good for me." Cop thing, I guess, you don't leave other officers hanging in the wind if you got the info they might need. No matter how you got it.

"I don't care why he thought that it was okay to tell you." His face was hard, his body language closed down. "It totally wasn't." Reminded me of the con I'd met before I discovered the wild and wonderful guy hiding under the surface. "It was my thing to tell you…you know, if I ever wanted you to know about it."

Chewed on the nail of my thumb for a bit and tried to put my thoughts in perspective. "You didn't think it was something I might need to know?"

He flopped back flat against the low pitch of the roof and stared at the sky. "I fucking don't know."

Above our heads, the fading sun ran golden fingers along the undersides of the clouds. I leaned up against the side of the house, my butt parked in the corner where the mudroom roof met the wall of the main house and stretched my legs out along the line of the eve so that our boots just touched. I'd screwed up the world enough that I just needed to listen to him. He was my only hope to hang onto sanity.

"Right now, no." He slammed his fist against the tin roof with a bang. "You didn't need to know it right fucking now." Then, like he was frustrated, Kabe ran his hands through his hair. "Down the road, yeah, maybe. But, you know, I needed to decide that."

"I'm sorry." If I'd thought it through, I probably would have realized me saying something, anything, wouldn't go down well. Kabe held his head high as was his right. My bringing it up, especially the way I had, wouldn't have sat well with him. "I shouldn't have mentioned it."

"No." Kabe sat back up. "Look. I'm pissed." He leaned toward me and bumped my ankle with the toe of his boot. "But I'd rather know that you heard about what happened instead of dancing around it for ages. I've gotten past it."

"You've gotten past it?" I bent forward too and grabbed his knee. "I mean, I don't want to question you, but that's a saddlebag full of hurt to carry around."

Not like I knew personal, but I'd had enough training in dealing with victims and survivors to understand that the pain never really goes away. It might fade. It might get buried for a time. Sooner or later, though, it breaks back up to the surface. Kinda fell back on that training, you know, talking through this here with him: how to be sensitive, not put your head or prejudices into it, that stuff. Of course, this mattered a heck of a lot more than calming a victim enough to get a statement.

"I've processed it, okay." Oh Lord, he sounded sincere. "I had a lot of people around me, who supported me." Okay, that would help. All the research said that gals who had a bunch of folks behind them came out better than those that didn't. Had to assume it'd be the same for a buck…since, you know, there were fewer studies on sexual assaults on men than there were sweet springs in the desert. "That helped a lot in being able to deal with what happened. I've come to own my part in it—"

That statement hit me like a two-by-four between the eyes. "Your part in it?" I think I was almost angry that he'd run that line between his ears. "Boy, that was none of your fault." I put every ounce of conviction I could muster into that statement.

"Shut up and listen to me, Joe." I could have sliced a hair on the sharp tone in his voice.

"Sorry." I think I messed up this attempt at working things out more than I messed up…well most of the rest of my life. I was trying, but the whole conversation felt like rowing upstream battling a whitewater current; a lot of effort without being sure you're making any actual progress.

"Look." Kabe rubbed his eyes with the base of his palms. "You have to own your mistakes. I was stupid and young. I shouldn't have gone out to that bar. That's all on me." When my jaw started to open a hair, he leaned over and shoved his hand over my mouth to keep me from saying what I was about to. "I deserved to have a really bad hangover and my Grams find out and yell at me. I did not deserve to run into a predator. I did not deserve to hook up with a guy who thought *no* meant *push harder.*" He pulled his hand back. "That's all on him, not on me."

The words sounded a little rehearsed, but I didn't doubt the sincerity behind the statements. That whole what he did and did not *deserve* line seemed like something drummed into his head through therapy. I grabbed his hand before he could take it all the way back. "All right." Heck, who was I to talk, whatever got him through it.

Kabe squeezed my hand in his grip. "I also did not deserve to have my name dragged through shit because he was an arrogant asshole with a rep he didn't deserve." He squeezed again. "'Cause I'll tell you, after all the shit blew up with me, I ran into other guys that told me things that happened to them." Yeah, guys like that, they never struck just once. Screw someone over and move on. "This douche-bag traded on his charming other people into thinking that it was a few whiny subs…when he was the fucking problem." He huffed, ran both hands through his hair. That mussed up, wild look. I didn't know he could look that sexy, especially talking about what we did and, mostly, what we didn't. "And, you know, there's a lot of guys who just didn't want to admit that they'd been taken advantage of. I hate to say it, but there's a resistance in the community too. No one wants to believe that someone they all put up on this throne of Dom-ness is really a creep."

"Not a lot of guys would have the stones to say anything." That was the truth if anything. Why sexual assaults of any nature went underreported with men, much less women.

"No." I could swear, Kabe sounded relieved. "And I wouldn't have said anything except, well, Grams was out of town on business so I was staying with some of her friends in the City." The explanation came out in a rush. "When they figured out that I'd snuck out they freaked out and were looking all over for me." He sucked in a massive breath and huffed it back out a few times before he could continue. "Finally, I drug my ass home and, well, I looked like hell, I guess." Kabe leaned in, stared me straight in the eyes. I couldn't have looked away…even if I wanted to. I sure didn't want to. "It took Bill a while to pull the whole story out of me, but he has a way of getting people to talk. Bill's the one who went after the asshole with both barrels."

I didn't know who this Bill was, but I didn't want to derail his thoughts by asking. Instead, I prodded in a different direction, "You didn't want nobody to know?"

"No." He rubbed his left arm with his right hand. "It took me a while to process that everyone were just doing what they thought was right. Bill never did tell Grams, either, 'cause I asked him not to. To get that, I had to agree to see this shrink that he knew." The grip on my hand never let go. "I didn't want to, but I went, because otherwise I'd have to deal with Grams freaking out."

Took me a bit, but I managed to spit out the most obvious question, "How did she not figure something was up if you're going to see a head doctor?"

"Ah, actually," Kabe bent forward, pulled the hand of mine he held up towards his mouth. Then he seemed to reconsider and stopped about halfway. "I had pretty bad test anxiety." Kabe bent forward and planted one solid on my lips. A hard, desperate kiss bubbling over with a need that didn't taste of passion or lust or even love. All I could feel was the want for me to accept who he was. Tried to convey that he owned that in spades back through my own touch.

When we needed to come up for air he pulled back and started talking again, "I think Bill told Grams he'd arranged it so I could learn how to manage that and get through my SATs." I'd rather he wasn't talking, although I knew we needed to air this out. "The therapist actually helped with that too. So, dude, I've dealt with it, okay." He brought his other hand up and gripped my chin. Then I felt his thumb run along the bone in my cheek. "I don't want it to be this black spot on what we've got."

"I understand, I think." I didn't know if I'd processed it all the way through, but I got the point. "I don't know what you mean dealt with it." You know, where he'd been and where he was now. "But I respect that you don't want to talk about it."

Kabe chided me, "Don't go there, Joe."

Okay, I got he didn't want to dredge up his past, but..."Go where?"

"That." He actually smacked my face. Not hard, but a little stinging tap to the side of my cheek with his fingers. "The stupid ass place you go where you're convinced you're doing the right thing and you're just fucking stuff up more." He kinda rolled until he sat up on his knees. Kabe got right up into my face. "Spit it out, 'cause that shithead screwed up enough of my life. I'm not going to let some ghost from my past wreck what we have 'cause you think you have to treat me with kid gloves."

"All right, look, you're right." Lord, I'd rather have faced down a rabid coyote than have this conversation. Still, I had to cross this bridge if'n I wanted him to be by my side from now until forever. "Know what, I don't know how to deal with this." Almost lost my nerve, but I somehow managed to spit it all out. "It makes me think back on all the things we've done together and wonder what I messed up. Kabe, I'm…I'm sorry for what I done."

"What you done?" He rocked back, rested his butt on his heels. "Can you please talk like a human being?"

I looked off at the horizon where the sun bled into the feathered clouds. "The other night, I should have been more in control." I reached for his hand again. "I let it get out of control. With someone like you…I mean someone who's gone through what you did." I needed to feel the warmth and strength of his fingers. The weight of his touch so solid in my hand, it grounded me like nothing else. "That, well there ain't no excuse for it."

"Joe, I pushed you." This time my fingers made it all the way to his lips. Kabe whispered the next words against my skin. "And sometimes I forget that I may be the sub in this relationship, but I fucking have loads of experience you don't. So, I was good with where we were going." He crawled over, just a hair, mind you, and swung one of his legs over both of mine. "You weren't." As he settled his weight onto my legs, Kabe reached out and set both his hands against the wall behind me. Pinned me. I could smell his heat, hear his heartbeat, he was so close. "I get that, I've got to remember that sometimes I'm training you."

I reached out, ran my hands down his chest until I hit the band of his jeans. "I still, I don't know, I feel like I let you down." Curled my fingers around the fabric.

"Don't go there." A sly smile spread across his mouth. "You are the one person I know won't screw me over." He moved closer still, until our noses almost touched. "You can be a jerk at times and I wish you'd pull your head out of your ass on this whole I'm in control crap…you know outside of when we agree that you're in control." A little closer and his forehead brushed against mine. "But, I knew, early on, you were different from anyone else I'd met."

I tugged on his jeans. "What do you mean, early on?"

Kabe laughed. "The first night we fucked."

"What?"

"Look." He kissed me quick. "I went into that first fuck thinking that, great, I found someone I can screw while I'm in exile so I don't have blue-balls on top of boredom." Another stealthy kiss. "And then after we fucked you said something, two words, and it changed everything on how I viewed you."

"Two words?" Wrapped my arms around his middle and pulled him until he sat in my lap. "What two words?"

"We got finished fucking." This time he just dragged his index finger down the bridge of my nose. "You'd tied my hands to a peg in your truck and it got so hot." The touch seemed far more intimate than the overt kisses had been. He moved closer, leaning in next to my ear and lowering his voice to darn near a whisper. "And then I'm basking in that I've-just-had-my-brains-balled-out-muscles-gone-to-jelly glow and you were working the blood back into my fingers. Then we snuggled down. You whispered in my ear."

"I don't remember that." I remembered tying him up in the back of my truck the first time we got it on. "I mean I recollect the sex." Pretty fondly actually. "And that I let your arms go numb like a stupid hick, but I don't recollect that I said something."

"You did." He rolled his head a bit until our foreheads touched. "Just two words that made all the difference in how I saw you."

"What?" I really couldn't bring anything like that to mind.

"You mashed up all next to me and whispered in my ear… you said," deep pause before he finished, real soft, "'thank you.'"

I couldn't have heard him right. I pulled back to look him in the eyes. "I'm sorry?"

He grinned and sat up. "You said, 'thank you.' And you *meant* it." Punctuated the last four words with jabs to my chest. "Lots of other guys would have just thought it was their right, or a fun toss in the sack. You, you got that it wasn't all you. Yeah, your dick pounded my ass…but not like it was this magic wonder rod." Both of us kinda laughed at that mental picture. "But, I mean you understood that it took two to tango there. I appreciated that you acknowledged it. I understood then, that you were different than most guys I knew."

I had to smile back. "You ain't like anyone I've ever known."

He kissed me again, pausing just long enough to whisper, "Damn straight."

"I ain't…" I stumbled on it all, "heck, I'm sorry. That's all I can say."

He bumped my head with his. "You think that means I don't get apology sex?"

Rocked back and looked him over. Even without the nekkid chest and mesh shorts he'd had on earlier, well heck, Kabe could wear workout gear five sizes too big and still rock my world. "No." I took a deep breath. "You want an apology, I will grovel at your feet. You want a roll in the hay, I'm down with that too." Kinda rolled my head back against the wall. "In fact might just be right what I need now. One of the reasons I didn't want to put this off between you and me. It'd have messed us up, you know."

"Okay." Kabe moved in close. "Then, I want sex on my terms. What I say goes." He jammed his nose right under my chin, his hot breath sending shivers down my spine. "I need you to understand why and how I want you."

Remembered that we had a houseguest. Kabe and I could get pretty loud at times. Still, Sam, it'd take a nuclear blast to wake his butt up. "All right," I promised him. "Let me get down of the roof and go change."

"But officer." The words blew hot across my skin. "I've been bad. And I need you to put me in my place."

CHAPTER 29

As Kabe vaulted off the roof, he hit me with, "Here's the plan."

I scooted to the edge and let my legs hang over. "The plan?" Once his feet met the ground, I swung off the roof. I managed much less gracefully. My knee still bugged me some.

"Shut up, Joe." He glared at me. Then his features softened. "I need you to just roll with me here." Kabe said it all earnest.

Normally, I took charge. "All right." But that ain't always fun. I mean, sometimes, letting him cook up the how and the why added a bit of spice to our dealings. Plus, right then, I sensed that he had some kinda idea in his head that went beyond my dick in his ass.

"Okay." As he headed inside, he gave me a bit of a run down. "We had sex, messing with breath play and I passed out and you're a lot more freaked out than I am about it." Once he hit the mudroom, he turned around and walked backwards a few steps. "I know the risks of what we do. I choose to do these things with you. I understand the chances I am taking." Kept his voice low, even though we could likely drop a bomb on Sam's head and not wake him right then.

"I don't know, Kabe." I didn't think he understood exactly what had happened that night.

"Yeah you do." He stopped at the kitchen table, set his hands on the top and propped his butt on the lip of it. "Dude." He flashed a grin. "What's my favorite thing to do in the world, besides sex?"

I didn't even have to think on that. "Free solo climbing." I settled myself against the door jamb between kitchen and mudroom.

"Yeah." He nodded. "And I do it knowing that with one wrong move, I'll end up as pizza at the bottom of the face of a cliff." In case I didn't get the point right off, he added, "I know the risk and I'm willing to take it."

Unfortunately, that weren't exactly how things were between the both of us. "But that's all on you. And this, what we do together, is like when we climb together. I know that when we go up a wall of rock," tried to explain it as best I knew how, "you and I know all the signals and if something goes wrong we got each other on belay. I know what the rules are, who expects what." Let out a breath I didn't know I was holding. "Sometimes, when we're together, I just don't know as I know that you want, what I want outta it." Sounded messed up even to my own ears.

"Okay." He stood up, came in close. "You know what I want?" Sliding his hands into my front pockets, Kabe leaned up against my chest. "I want you to be my Daddy." He breathed the words against my neck like it was the most sensual, most loving thing he'd ever uttered in his life. "I want to be your boy."

I had a kinda clue what those words meant, but still, "That just sounds kinda wrong to my ears." My heart beat in random time against my ribs. I couldn't hardly breathe with the weight of it.

"All right look, it's just a way of naming things." I could feel his mouth up against the curve of my jaw. "Now everyone has, like their own understanding of what this all means, but my take on it is a Sir or a Master expects a shit-load of more, I don't know, boot licking, from their submissive than a Daddy does." The weight of his body against my chest worked itself so deep into my soul that I couldn't tell where he ended and I began. "Daddies expect respect from their boys, but there's a lot more independence in the relationship." His head rested between my shoulder and ear, his arms gripped me stronger than a rock in a flood. "I can suggest sex." The whispers shot shivers down my spine. "I can push you into a scene. If I'm wrong, you might punish me, discipline me like a Daddy should."

"You're a brat." I wrapped my arms around Kabe's warm body. Moved my mouth until my lips pressed against his forehead. "You'd end up having your butt smacked a lot if I actually took you in hand."

"That's what I want." Our chests fell into sync, rising and falling like we shared the same set of lungs. "That's why I act the way I do sometimes. I'm looking for that reaction. Is that something you want?"

"I like taking a heavy hand with you." Couldn't do more than whisper that admission. "I just never knew…all right, but how do I know when you don't want to do something?" I slid my face down until we were nose to nose, forehead to forehead. "When I've done something wrong?" I didn't ever want to treat him wrong. "Or I'm hurting you in a way that's all messed up or something?" Rubbed my cheek against his. "Half the time I feel like I'm climbing without a belay."

"Okay." Kabe pulled back and stared deep into my soul. "I get that. You're right. I'm the kinda person who's good without safe-words and that kinda thing. You're more risk adverse." With a sly smile he whispered, "Pajamas."

I could not have heard him right. "What?"

"Pajamas." He said it louder this time. "It's a word I never say, at least during sex." Kabe stepped back just a hair, cocked his head to the left and tried to stifle a smile. "So if I say pajamas that means something's gone wrong." After a squeeze to my thigh, Kabe pulled his hand from my pocket and ran his knuckles down my chest. "Work for you?"

Sounded kinda silly, actually, and I could see a flaw or two. "But what if I got you gagged, how you going to say anything?"

"If you've got me bound and gagged, then you can put keys in my hand." He reached down to where my keys hung off my duty belt and flicked 'em with his finger, making them jangle just a bit. "If I drop 'em, that means stop. Or a shave-and-a-haircut knock." That he tapped out on my empty holster. "Those three things mean stop. Does that work?"

"I guess." Wasn't a hundred percent convinced. "Yeah, it would make me feel better." Probably wouldn't have stopped what happened the other night, but it'd help going forward. Even so, I'd screwed up bigger things, too. "Still, with your past, there's got to be things that make you uncomfortable, in a really bad way." I was glad I knew 'em, but it made me feel like I needed to step away from things, keep myself more in check than I liked. "I'll always worry that I'm going to cross that line." I hated having to second guess myself. It frustrated me and I figured it frustrated him or we wouldn't be talking like this.

"I don't think there's a thing you could come up with that I wouldn't be down for." Kabe ran his tongue over his teeth and grinned. Then he got serious again. "You keep reading things into my head about me being in prison and what happened with that douche-bag." He stopped talking for a moment and kissed me. Slow and easy, letting me know this was just a warm up to the rest of the night. Then he pulled back, from the kiss and my body.

Suddenly, he was all business. "If everything works out there won't be a line after tonight." Kabe crossed his arms over his chest and stared me down. "I want you to promise me that you'll roll with this." When I nodded, Kabe dropped the serious pose and walked over to the bathroom. I had no idea what he was after in there, well a little idea, but I couldn't ask 'cause he kept talking, "You won't stop unless you get the signal. And that you won't over think things. Remember I'm the one who cooked this up, so that everything that happens is what I set in motion." He came out shoving a small bottle into his pocket with one hand and carrying a wadded up bit of black fabric in the other. "Down with that?"

Took me a second to realize what it was in his hand. Why I needed the brace for my leg, I had no clue. "Okay." I hoped whatever he planned worked, got me over the hump of my own thoughts so we could be together like I wanted. Like he wanted.

"Here." He tossed me the brace.

I caught it with one hand. "I ain't worn my knee brace in weeks."

"Trust me." His grin was all wicked. "You'll need it." Like he lectured me, he pointed at my chest. "Put it on and meet me upstairs. Keep the uniform on."

Figured if I needed the stabilization on my leg, Kabe planned something involving serious calisthenics. "What if Sam hears something?" Our talking up to then had been kinda quiet. We could get loud if things started heating up.

Kabe laughed. "I could set bottle rockets off in his ears right now and he'd probably just roll over." Then he shook his head. "Don't worry, it's not going to be a problem," he reassured, gave me a wink and then headed up the stairs.

All right, I'd go along with him. I wanted to do this for him, and if he was setting it up, then I supposed he would be okay with whatever happened.

Sat myself down in a kitchen chair and straightened out my leg. The doc gave me the brace about a third of the way through physical therapy. Replaced the big, hinged, post-surgical one that I'd outgrown early. My doc said I pushed myself harder than most, had a better tolerance to pain, so I advanced in leaps and bounds rather than a slow crawl. This brace, the light one, was meant to keep support while letting me get more back to normal. Had on my BDUs so I unzipped the side of my tactical boot, loosened the ankle tie, pulled the leg up and wrapped the brace around my knee and secured it with the big ol' elastic cross straps. Then I worked the pants back over my brace before I tucked them back into my boot. 'Bout that time I heard a crash upstairs, like my jar of pocket change fell off the dresser.

I bolted out of my chair and took the stairs two at a time. Noticed out of the corner of my eye that Sam hadn't even moved at the sound. Good. I charged into the bedroom and skidded to a stop.

Kabe grinned at me from right beside the open bedroom window; the one that overlooked the mudroom roof. He raised up his right hand, flipped me off and then jumped out the window.

What in the heck was he up to? I ran over to the window and caught sight of him sliding right off the end of the pitch. He landed hard, stumbled to his feet and turned to look up at me. This time I got a, "Fuck you!" along with the bird before he spun on his heels and ran.

Why did he want me in uniform to play around if he was just going to—then it hit me. I needed to roll with this. He was egging me on, calling me out. This was what he planned and I needed to stop thinking and just move. I clambered through the window and swung my feet onto the low pitched metal roof. I didn't run, but I hustled to the edge and swung myself down easier than Kabe's full tilt crash landing. I was into this, but no way was I willing to screw up my knee again for a jump in the sack…no matter how hot.

My feet hit the dirt and I took on off after him. He headed into the woods surrounding our property. I'd actually bought the undeveloped lots in front and to one side of mine with the house. Dixie National butted up around the rest. Gave him plenty of room to run and not be seen. Especially as it was getting on towards dark. Threw most everything into blue shadow.

Kabe had a head start on me. I had a bit more practice on running men down and Kabe, well he weren't really trying to get away from me, running for his life or nothing. Still, dogging him through the trees got my adrenaline going. Started to feel like I really chased someone down. Him going out the window like that. I pounded after him. And I knew, in the back of my mind, it wasn't real, but every time my foot hit the ground, the edge of disbelief slipped just a hair farther behind me.

I wanted to get him.

I needed to get him.

Up ahead of me, Kabe grabbed hold of the top of a post and vaulted the barbed wire fence at the back of the property. Pounded up to it, dropped both hands on top of the post and jumped up, swinging my legs out and over to the side. I stumbled some when I hit the ground but I managed to keep running. Kabe shot around like a rabbit, twisting one way then switching back on his heel. Kept me on my toes. After a bit, though, I started anticipating which way he'd go.

Every perp has a rhythm. They may think they're being random, but they ain't. You got to learn to watch for it. Kabe favored his left, odd for someone who weren't a southpaw. For every one right twist he added two moves on the left. I started, I don't know, smelling how he'd move next. We'd circled back, hitting the road into the park just long enough to cross through the fence again. Shadows deepened. Let my eyes adjust, didn't try and force my sight.

There it was. He'd feigned right, but moved left. Poured on a bout of speed. Nailed him. Grabbed a fist-full of his shirt. Kabe stumbled. He went down. I went down. He grunted like I'd knocked the wind right out of him.

Landed on top of him and we rolled maybe three times. I struggled to my knees. "Can you talk?" I panted it out.

He spit out a mouthful of pine needles. "Bite me," came out as a growl.

I took that as a yes. Still we landed hard. "You all right there?"

I might not have been able to see it, but I felt that glare as he rolled his head to drip poison over his shoulder. "You can't make me say it."

I was about to ask what I couldn't make him say. Then it rolled through my mind that he told me he was fine 'cause he weren't going to use that word. Okay then. Kept my weight mostly off him, but used my knee in the small of his back to keep Kabe pinned while I got my center of gravity back. Then I stood, pulling him up along with me by the scruff of his neck. "Get up." I growled it out.

He spat back, "Fuck you."

When Kabe didn't move fast enough, I yanked him. He hissed. The sound shot shivers down my spine. I could smell the adrenaline fueled sweat rolling off his brown skin. "Move, now," I ordered. My voice sounded harsh to my own ears. And I liked it. He struggled to his feet. When he got both under him, I shoved Kabe forward keeping him at arms length. Planted his face right into the side of a tree.

With my right hand, I grabbed his and pulled until I had his palm right behind the base of his skull. Used my fingers to scrunch his together and the pressure of my grip, in and kinda downward, to keep him in place. Wrangled Kabe's left arm up to the same position. "Lace your fingers together." I barked it out. As he complied, I transferred my grip from right to left hand. Actually, the grip equaled a very effective way to keep a suspect in place. If they tried to fight, I'd shove down and forward. I could drive a guy to his knees that way.

He struggled some, but I could do this compliance hold in my sleep. Didn't stop him from mouthing off though. "Go fuck yourself."

I moved in close so my breath brushed the hairs at the back of his neck. "What'd you say, boy?" I knew what he said, but I wanted him to repeat it. I liked his nasty talk something awful.

He took a deep breath. "I said, 'fuck you.'" I could hear the sneer in his words.

"Wrong answer." I jammed my knee between his legs. He grunted as I bumped his balls. Didn't care. I'd lost the sense of where play ended and my job began. "Spread 'em." I hissed it out right near his ear. Had to kick his ankles to make him comply.

Of course, I did, in the back of my head, realize this was a game. So my next moves I played out slower than I might if'n he were a real suspect. Kept my left hand parked overtop both of his. The other I used to search him. Started with his hair... dragging my fingers all through it, hard. Regressed to my days as a correctional officer. Pat down searches in prison got a lot more intimate, invasive, than the quick toss for weapons and drugs I did as deputy.

Kept my grip hard, looking for things right up against the scalp. You'd be amazed what a con could hide in the space of your thumb nail. That done I worked over his jaw, feeling for things hidden against his teeth. All through it, Kabe sputtered cusses at me. Hard and slow, I drug my hands across his right arm and then down the right side of his body.

Then I slowed it down a notch further. I'd reached the interesting places. Everything below the waistband of his pants. Took my time. Felt around. I slid my hands under his jeans and shorts, something I'd never do in real life, but here and now, it worked just fine. He was all hard. 'Course I was too. A little adrenaline and a lot of want pumped through my veins.

And yeah, his hard, hot piece of meat, I ignored it. Instead, I moved under, around and passed it with my searching fingers. Tried not to bump it even. I wanted him just desperate for that touch. He tried to move right and left, but I had him full on in my control. So all it did was scrape up his cheek against the tree bark. That just sent a shiver down my back.

From where I was I could get pretty much all down his leg…I didn't bother. I mean, yeah, it felt real. Heat pounded all through me. But, well, Kabe weren't liable to be packing heat. Instead, I switched my grip over and repeated the search with my left hand. This time, when I got to his pants' pocket, I found something hard. Dug it on out. "What's this?" I teased, 'cause I knew full well. "What are you hiding, boy?"

"Bite me, asshole." Came out a little mumbled since half his cheek still kissed bark.

Held it up, off to the side, where he could kinda see it. "What you planning, carrying things like this around with you?"

"Fuck you."

"Yeah, well with this, somebody was planning on having that happen to them." I grinned, all feral. "I think, more like it's gonna happen to you though."

He started struggling, almost in earnest really. I just kept the pressure in and down and all he did was drive himself farther down onto his knees. "Get off me, asshole." Kabe twisted under me. Kept my right hand on him as I stowed the lube in my own pocket and then had to reach around to get my cuffs outta their holster at the back of my Sam-Brown belt.

Didn't have to fight too much to get the right bracelet of my handcuffs on his wrist. "Shut up, and quit struggling," I ordered.

"It's only going to be worse for you if you don't cooperate." Locked his wrist up tight, pulled that arm down towards the small of his back and went for the other. He struggled. My blood pumped. I grabbed his left hand and wrassled it around to his lower back. He fought me every inch…spitting and cursing and telling me I was an asshole. Ricked down the cuff on his other hand and settled my weight back on the balls of my feet.

I ordered, "Move." Used the cuffs like a leash to steer him around. I didn't want to be messing around where I couldn't see the coyotes or raccoons or far more poisonous critters that shared the woods. Night had dropped down enough that Kabe stumbled a couple of times on the way back towards the house. As we came out into the cleared space around the house, I got hit with an idea…an important one since I did remember that Sam, passed out or not, occupied my living room.

See, Kabe'd parked his truck off to the right of the house, out of the view from the front window. I pushed him towards his truck. "This your vehicle, boy?" Might have been a little more hot if I tossed him in the back of the Charger, but I weren't quite willing to break either the taboo or the regulations against misconduct in official vehicles. Lord knows I'd had enough close calls on losing my badge. No sense handing folks any more ammo.

When we got right up next to the truck, I slammed him against the hood. "What have you got to say for yourself? In trouble like you are?" Weren't in any trouble 'cept what we'd created, but I liked the sound of it.

"Fuck." All of a sudden, a backwards kick caught me square on my bum left knee. Barely heard him add, "You," to the previous word.

My eyes crossed, but I didn't drop. Instead I grunted out, "No thanks." I popped his head so it banged on the metal. "I got to teach you some manners, boy." Right then my adrenaline pumped enough that I didn't really feel more than a shade of pain. Still, I took him in hand. Grabbed his shoulder and flipped him over.

He spit in my face.

I hauled off and belted him across his mouth.

The breath froze in my lungs. I stood there a moment with my hand just shaking. I couldn't move none at all.

Like he sensed it, my deer in the headlights terror, Kabe hissed out, "No matter what you do, I will never, ever say it." Then, maybe just to goad me on a bit, he added, "You fucking stupid pig."

I stepped in, moving right between his legs. "What did you say?" With my thigh pressed against his junk, I could feel how hard he was. Of course so was I.

"Fuck you."

"You liking this, you little pervert?" Reached down with one hand and grabbed his dick through the denim. "Am I turning you on?" One by one, I managed to pop the buttons on his fly. I spread his fly open and looked down. Might have been a little dark, but I could make out that he still wore those mesh briefs he'd had on. "You're just a horny little perp, aren't you?" Twisted my fingers into the mesh and pulled. It gave easy enough, with that low ripping sound charging right into my own balls and making itself comfortable.

"Don't." He breathed it out and I hesitated.

It weren't that word though, so I guessed I could keep going. "I got you all good, boy." Stroked his dick a few times, the scraps of mesh dragging against his skin under my hand. "I'm going to do what I want to you and you cain't stop me."

"No." It almost sounded like he was pleading. "Stop." The fact that he humped into my touch though, yeah, he was into this.

"Let's have some fun." I let go of his dick and grabbed the front of his shirt, picked him up and walked him around to the side of his truck. Fished my keys offa my belt. I had one for his truck on my ring. Then I backed him against the side bed. Took me a moment to get the door open. Although there weren't no dome lamp in his truck, enough glow leaked around us from off on the porch that I could kinda see what I was doing. Took hold of his shirt again, hauled him around and dropped him face first onto the bench seat of his little mini-pickup. As he fell, I caught the back of his jeans. Pulled 'em on down so that perfect butt of his was all on display.

I knew just what I wanted to do to it, too. Hauled my baton out of the holder on my hip, rotated my wrist so that the line of the baton and my arm would end up mimicking the line of my leg. Hit the button as I moved and it snapped open. That hard, sharp, metallic clatter as the baton went from six inches to almost two feet long…heck I felt the sound shoot up through the bones in my arm. Rotated my hand back up without even thinking. Brought the baton up in front of my upper chest and head, kinda twisting my body to chamber it for defense or offense.

Growled out, "This is for kicking me, spitting in my face."

I twisted off my leg, rotating my hip and dropping my shoulder to snap the baton down across his butt. I do admit I held back just a bit—working more of a crowd control beat down than pummeling a suspect into the ground. Still that whack as the blow landed across his butt, covered in nothing but a scrap of mesh, it vibrated through my frame like a house on fire. I had to shift my prick, 'cause I felt like I'd split my skin.

His belted out, "Fuck," just added to the heat ripping across my belly. His, "No," whispered all sorts of naughty thoughts to my dick. Kabe jerked up and kinda forward as best he could. The rasp of his boots scraping like mad for purchase on the running board of his truck crawled up my spine and locked into the base of my skull. When he moved, I caught the shadow of his dick between his legs…still hard and pushed through the tatters of his briefs.

I whacked him again and again, the sublime merging of sound of the baton as it cut the air, the feeling of connection as the steel alloy hit its mark. It was like my soul fed off his each time the baton made contact. Each solid swat made him jump a little more than the last. Kabe protested, boy did he ever, but he didn't say the one thing that would make me stop.

Couldn't quite see what I did to him. But I knew that it'd be crimson marks over dark skin. I had to stop and reach out to touch. Kabe hissed as my fingers slid across his flesh. His ass burned with blows I'd laid on. I could feel each and every mark through the palm of my hand, one hot strip radiating on top of another with the little ridges from the sections of the baton. That ass would be a mass of black and blue come morning. The faded sense of the blows wound like snakes up through my arm, chest and then down into my belly to work fire through my dick.

I wanted him.

Bad.

I snapped the baton closed and slipped it back in the holster. Then I unzipped my fly and pulled my dick out. "I'm going to make you pay." I growled the threat as I reached over, hooked my fingers into where the torn mesh tangled up Kabe's balls and ripped it up the rest of the way. "Just like you know you want it."

Kabe shuddered. "Oh, God." I could hear the jangle of the chain between the cuffs. "Not that." The protest sounded half hearted at best.

I knew he wanted this as much as I did. It jazzed me up knowing I could give him his pleasure like this. "Yeah, that." I fished the lube out of my pocket and spread it on nice and thick. I grabbed both his hips and, with a grunt, pushed on in. Lord, he was so hot.

"Fuck, yeah." Came out all long and drawn out with his need to be used like this.

I didn't say nothing back. Couldn't really. All worked up like I was, I lost myself in pounding his ass. Short, sharp, desperate strokes. My fingers dug into his skin as he pushed back against me. Reached down between his legs and grabbed onto his prick. I don't know as I'd ever felt him that hard. I also didn't realize how worked up I'd gotten myself during all of this. I used to think sex was just about bumping uglies. With Kabe I'd come to understand it ran from when we both started thinking until we'd wrapped ourselves up for the night.

I'd been holding myself back from him for too long. Felt it in both of us, as that hot piece of meat slid through my fist, as he gave me back as hard as I gave him. Heck, he must've been pent up as all get out, 'cause when Kabe blew it was with a yelled out, "Fuck!" and a hard shudder.

Weren't all that long before my senses burned through like a forest fire. Had to grab the frame of the door to keep steady as I came. I barely heard myself whisper out, "Lord, Kabe." Somehow I managed to just breathe through it, my brain tumbling all over itself. I moved back, slipping out of him, and shook my head. "Wow." Didn't let go of the frame.

Kabe tried to roll over and slipped off the bench seat on to the floor of the truck. "You can't make me say it." His breath was heavy. "I can take you on all night and you won't make me crack."

I thought we was done. Guess I was wrong. "All night?" Both of us were panting as I finally stood, tucked my dick back into my pants and zipped up. Once I straightened up, my bum knee started to throb. Now that the excitement rolled into a lull, my knee decided to tell me that it weren't a happy camper.

"Bring it on." He kinda sat up and sneered. "I can handle it."

"Pajamas." Figured since it was his word, he'd get what I meant.

Kabe tipped up his chin to stare at me. "Pajamas?"

"Okay, yeah," I could hear the strain in my own voice, "I cain't keep going." Answered his puzzled look with, "When you did that mule kick back there, you caught me dead on my bad knee."

Like a switch, Kabe's attitude flipped. "Oh, shit!" His eyes got big. "Are you okay?" If his hands hadn't been cuffed behind his back, I swear he'd be trying to do first aid. "You're wearing your brace, right?"

"Yeah, I got the brace on." I eased down to sit on the running board and stretched my leg out. It pulled a little, and I could tell I'd be a bit sore, but it didn't feel like he done permanent damage. "If we stop now and I put one of those cold packs on it, it should be fine."

Kabe leaned forward and rubbed his chin and cheek over the top of my head. "Shit, Joe, I'm sorry. I got caught up in all."

"You and me both, boy." I motioned him out of the truck, scooting over a little to give him a bit of room. As he slid out, I fished my handcuff keys out of their pocket. "Let me get those cuffs off you and we can go inside and clean up." Got the bracelets off his wrists. Then, as he tugged his pants up, I got to my feet. We headed inside through the back door and I washed up a bit, got the cold pack out of the freezer, while Kabe jumped in the shower. I was a little slower than I'd been recently going up the stairs. More me being cautious than because I was in pain…'cause I weren't that much. Got out of my uniform and the brace, then into something to sleep in.

Wasn't too long after that Kabe came up the stairs toweling off his hair. He had on his jeans, but they weren't buttoned up or nothing. "How was it?"

I sat on the edge of the bed in my briefs and t-shirt, holding the cold pack on my knee. "Interesting." I was still trying to wrap my head around it all.

"Interesting?" He tossed the towel in the hamper before settling down next to me. A little hiss tightened his voice, "How so?" Kabe picked up the cold pack and rearranged it on my knee. Guess he though he knew better than me on how to treat it.

"Well, you know." I shrugged. "I couldn't quite get it out of my head that it was just a game. I get the points you were trying to make. My head ain't that thick."

He grinned and rapped the side of my skull with his knuckles. "It's pretty damn thick."

"Shut up." I swatted his hand away. "I cain't even get a word in edgewise without your mouth going off." Then I set my hand on his leg and rubbed it a little. "But, I get it. You ain't got any baggage from prison, at least none that's going to mess with what we got and mostly if you don't tell me to stop, then I'm doing stuff that you're okay with." I shuffled a bit where I sat, then I asked, "You sure you ain't got issues with the whole cop thing? I mean, some of the way you talked."

Kabe busted out a laugh and then stifled it quick. "Dude, lived in prison for two years…I may have kept my head down, but I learned how they talked about cops." The explanation was earnest, but he couldn't keep serious. "I'm not interested in living a bad porn script, but I got the reaction I wanted out of you, didn't I?"

"Yep, you did." Still needed to ask him, "You will tell me when it's not okay?"

"Yep." He put his hand on top of mine and laced his fingers through. Seemed like he might be thinking on something, 'cause he paused for a moment. When he started to talk again he pulled both our hands up so he could kiss my fingers. "Can you do me a favor though?"

"As long as it's not asking me to rob a bank for you, yeah." I'd do darn near anything he asked, 'cause he did everything I needed.

"Stop asking, you know, when we're in the middle of things, if I'm okay." His face was all earnest. "I will let you know if I'm not and it pulls my head right out of the moment when you do."

Took me a second to figure out what he meant by that. "Okay." There were a few times I'd stepped out of what we were doing to ask him that. "Cain't promise always, 'cause you may think you can take the pain, but I might be seeing something happening that you ain't." Broke me outta the head-space of it too, but I'd kinda felt like I should ask those things, maybe just not so much as I had tonight. "So did you get into what we were doing?"

"Some." He let go of my hand and flopped back on the bed. "I'm not big on role-play. It can be kinda fun sometimes, but not my big thing. Like service isn't my big thing. I like the pain." That he did. "If I need to do one of those two things to get to the pain I will, but that's why I really like what we have." He tugged on my shirt so I eased on down next to him. Got a smile and a light touch running up my arm for my effort. Kabe ran his teeth over his lower lip and smiled. "The bondage and submission you want is a vehicle to getting me locked down enough to send me into orbit in my head when you get going."

"Is that normal?" We were so far beyond my points of reference on sex, which, before I met him, usually hadn't even got serious enough where I found out the guy's last name. I wasn't stupid, I knew what they called what he and I did, but it didn't seem exactly the same as what I found when I tried to look things up. "I mean, what I read online it's all about the tying up and fancy clothes, Sir and Master, you know?"

All quiet and easy, he laughed. "Define normal." I'd kill to keep him laughing like that: content and full of the world. "It works for us, dude." Like it weren't nothing too weighty, Kabe explained. "We are in the S & M car on the BDSM train." He tapped the letters out on my shoulder. "You're a Sadist and a Top, I'm a masochist and a bottom and together we rock."

"Sadist?" Most times I'd heard that word was in continuing education classes when they talked about types of abusers and killers. "I ain't sure I'm liking that name for myself."

"Joe, you like causing pain." He turned the tap into a caress up and down my arm. "That's a sadistic trait. There's other ways you express dominance: you *own* a room when you walk into it, you like ordering people around." My mom always called me bossy, saying it was a great trait for a cop and a lousy one for whoever had to live with me. "But with you, it's inflicting the hurt that gets you off." I got a soft smile that lit up those hazel eyes of his. "That's okay since you don't do it to people who don't want it. And it's okay, 'cause I want it." He rolled over onto my chest and grinned down at me. "Good?"

"Yeah." Reached up and ran my fingers along the edge of his ear. "You okay?"

"Hey." He got stern for all of a second, but couldn't maintain that expression. Breaking back into a smile, he grumbled, "I told you I'll tell you when I'm not."

I thumped his head with my fingers. "Brat." We didn't talk much after that, 'cause he leaned in and kissed me. Fell asleep, like I hadn't slept in ages, just wrapped around him like that.

CHAPTER 30

Rolled out of bed that morning and hissed as my bum leg touched the floor. Not that I'd hurt it, but I sure was stiff. The house felt quiet, still sleeping in the darkness. The only light seeped in from the low moon outside. Bathed everything in a faint blue wash.

As I stretched, I heard Kabe blow out a breath and felt his knuckles run down my spine. "So," he kinda yawned through his words, "What was eating you last night?"

"What?" Thought back and couldn't remember much past the sex.

"Okay, you dragged your brother, totally fucked up, back to the house." He sat up. "You're calling everyone except your folks. And," he popped my shoulder with his fist, "you actually apologized to me." The word apologize came out with every syllable given emphasis. "Dude, you were stressed."

I fell back across his lap. "Oh, Lord." I ran my hands over my face. "You don't want to know."

"Yeah, I do." He leaned over me and flashed one of his thousand watt smiles. Even the darkness couldn't dim it back. "Tell me the whole story. You said something about a beat down and maybe more than that."

Reached up and wrapped my hand around the back of his neck. "I don't know." My chest tightened up again. "The problem is, they don't know if the buck they messed up ever walked away from the scene."

"What do you mean?" He pressed his thumbs against my temples and started to rub.

"I told you," I sucked in a big ol' lung full air, "they may have killed a guy." Even with all that breath, the words came out a whisper.

Kabe's hands stilled. "You really think they may have killed him?" He hissed the question. "I wasn't sure if I heard you right last night."

"Yeah, it's a distinct possibility." I used the grip I still had on him to pull him down 'till his hair brushed my face and his forehead touched mine. "I don't know what I'm gonna do." Just having him there, with me, made me able to face what might have to happen next. "I'm gonna have to tell the sheriff." Ran my other hand up his arm. "I don't know what's gonna happen after that."

Scooching around until his knees were next to my thigh, Kabe folded himself over my chest, wrapped his arms around me and just held me. All I could do was shake and hold on to him. Pressed my face hard against his and tried not to think. I knew was this was gonna be, likely, the hardest thing I'd ever done. I knew I couldn't put it off no longer.

Real gentle like I pushed him off my chest. "I got to get."

He kissed me. Just a short, soft thing on the side of my head. "You don't have to tell him."

"Yeah, I do." Matched his kiss with one a little harder. "I cain't keep it hid." Wrapped my fist in his hair. "If I just drop the case, the only other thing I can do, then they'll be asking all sorts of questions." Then I slid my hand down to cup his chin and tried to manage a smile. Knew I missed it by a mile. "That'll be all that much worse." 'Course not like he could really see me well anyway.

Kabe sat up. "Then you've got to find out if that dude died." His voice was all earnest. "If the fucker isn't dead, then it's okay."

"Maybe." Sat up myself. "I'm gonna get taken off the case though." Palmed my face. "They bent the rules enough letting me work my sister's death. There ain't no way they're going to let me keep working this."

"So." He put his hand on my leg, gave it a squeeze. "You can still try and find out if the guy lived. If he's alive then there's no problem."

"I don't know."

"Yeah, you do." He squeezed again. "Track this creep down. Make sure there's no problem before you create one."

Got up off the bed, made my way to the closet and flipped on the light. I got my uniform out. "I gotta tell." Came out all muffled as I pulled my t-shirt over my head. "But, you're right. As long as Clay lived, then my daddy, Sam, they're okay."

The light from the closet bled across the bed. Kabe smiled up at me. White sheets twisted around his brown legs. Sleep mussed hair fell 'cross his eyes. I don't think anyone could ever look so fine. Walked back over to the bed, reached over and brushed that thick, black mane outta his forest colored eyes. "I'll figure something out." Then I patted his cheek and headed off.

His, "I have faith in you," followed me down the stairs.

I grabbed a quick shower and got presentable. Somehow, I managed to get myself sorted out: shirt buttoned the right way, boots on the right feet and everything. Then I checked on Sam, still sacked out cold on the couch. He'd pulled the blanket on over his head at some point. Kabe'd probably fix him some coffee later. Figured Kabe knew a thing or two about nursing a hangover that I was clueless on. I'd have to trust Kabe to get Sam on home. Got my weapons outta the safe and the radio off the top although I had to use my flashlight to see what was what. Kabe banged around a bit upstairs, came down to use the can and gave me a big ol' hug as he passed.

Once I got outside the moon gave me enough light to find my way to the Charger. The whole way into the station, my mind kept twisting around the problem. Least with Kabe distracting me like he had, I'd managed to sleep. Probably wouldn't sleep much for the rest of my life if this situation went any farther south than it already had.

I got in even earlier than normal for me these days, good hour before the sun even thought about poking its head above the mountains. Since the deputy on the night shift hadn't come back from patrol, and the early morning shift wouldn't start for a while, I settled behind my desk and flipped on the computer.

I ran Clay Young's name through every database I could think of to see if I could find a record of his death. Wasn't any more successful than I had been the last time I searched. Again, a few Clay and Clayton Youngs peppered here and there, but nothing that felt like he'd be the Clay I sought. A social would have gotten me a direct hit. Heck, I even woke Noreen at home and conned her into calling up Mrs. Massey, the librarian, for me. Mrs. Massey could access the church records on births and deaths within the Latter Day Saints from her home computer…it was her calling for the Ward. Took a good hour of me chewing on my nails to find out he didn't turn up there neither. That just meant he weren't a member. I didn't recollect if his Gran'parents were Mormon, but it had been worth a shot given where they lived.

After about my fifteenth trip from my desk to the break room, I realized I needed to get out for a bit. Maybe the folks who lived near the Richardsons would know what happened to Clay. Since none of my superiors were in yet, I decided to head round to their farm. Or what used to be their farm. Didn't take me long to get over to the area 'round their old neighborhood; in the broadest sense of the word, since ranches and farms could be separated by miles.

I pulled over to the side of the road and got out. A tractor rumbled towards me. I flagged the driver down. He stopped the tractor, didn't turn it off, and waited for me as I crossed the road. Sorta recognized him as one of the Small family. I knew lots of folks round these parts. Didn't mean I was on first name basis with them all.

"Morning." He pushed his ball cap back on his head. "What can I do for you, Deputy?"

"Morning." I returned the greeting, pretty loud because the engine still rumbled next to my ear. "You're, ahhh…" I fished for his name.

He grinned and reached down from the tractor to extend me a hand covered in a beat up, brown leather work glove. "Robert Small."

"Morning Mr. Small." I took his shake. "Wondering if you

know the Richardsons at all?" It was too early to beat around the bush. "They owned the ranch down the way." Pointed towards a house set back, maybe, a mile off the road.

"Yep." He nodded. "They moved off maybe twenty years ago." Pulled his ball cap off his head and settled it back down. "My son lives there now. My daddy bought the place and combined our farms."

Great, that meant that his family been around for quite a bit. "You lived next to them?"

He shifted the tractor into neutral and set the parking brake. "Yep." Meant he planned to stay a bit.

The man looked close to my older brothers' age so I took a guess. "You remember their gran'son, Clay Young?"

He sat back on the tractor seat and shrugged. "Their gran'son, yeah, I met him a few times." His face took on a sour look, like something didn't taste right to him. "He was a few years older than me. Didn't like him much."

That confirmed my thought on his attitude. "Why not?"

"I don't know." I got another shrug. "He just always seemed odd." Mr. Small wrapped his hands tight around the steering wheel of his tractor. "His little sister was okay."

"Sister?" I prompted.

"Yeah." Took him a moment of thinking before he added. "Missy or something."

"Misty?" I prompted.

"Could be." He sounded very non-committal. "Don't remember exact."

I couldn't help but ask. "But he had a sister?"

"Yeah," he confirmed. "She visited a few times with her mom and brother, you know, before he came to stay. Nice enough." His face went sad. "Played with my little sister Jasmine." Then his expression faded into confused and concerned. "She always came over to our place, never wanted my sister to go there, adamant about it. It's why I even remember that." He let out a deep breath before he added, "They stopped coming after Clay moved up here."

Thought for a moment before I asked, "Do you remember his mom's name?"

"Naw." He shook his head. "Only remember his, 'cause he was in school ahead of me. Like your brothers."

That caught me a bit blind, not sure why. "You knew Tucker and Sam?"

"Tucker better than Sam," he confirmed. "Played football with Tuck."

"Surprised you recognize me." I didn't look quite like my brothers, but we looked related.

"If you'll forgive my saying it," he stifled a laugh, "but you are a bit notorious around these parts."

I didn't even know how to respond to that, so I just ignored it. "Well thanks for the info."

Seemed he was willing to gloss over his gaff as well. "No problem." Then he popped the tractor outta park, shifted it into gear and headed off.

Asked around to a few more folks I found. None of them had any more to offer than Mr. Small. Figured it was time to head back to the station and get the worst over with. Made it back around nine. Didn't see the Sheriff's car nowhere. However, I recognized Lowell's car in the lot. Would rather have talked to Myron Simple, but I needed to get this done. Parked and walked inside. Felt like I was headed to my own execution. Found the lieutenant up by the front counter, filling in forms. For as much as folks think that police work is all about running folks down, any more it's about forms and paperwork. Every ticket I wrote meant a report to be filled out after.

"Sir." Always felt like I was interrupting him. "I need to talk to you."

He didn't look up. "So talk."

Didn't know how to actually ask what I wanted. Scuffed my boots around on the tiles for a moment before I got up the nerve to add, "Prefer if we could do it in private."

Something in my tone jerked his head up. He studied me for a bit. "All right." Lowell stepped back and put his pen in his pocket. "Let's go in the sheriff's office." Followed him through the station over to the office. An old battered desk and cranky office chair occupied the space. Lt. Lowell shut the door, with its scarred up window, behind us. "What's on your mind?" He crossed his arms and leaned against the edge of the desk.

I guess neither of us felt comfortable in the space. I kinda set my hands on the back of the loan guest chair and rested my weight on my arms. "I think I have a major break in the case."

"And." He sounded annoyed.

"And, it…oh, heck," I couldn't quite force it out of my mouth. "My prime suspect is a buck named Clay Young."

He screwed up his face so that his mustache formed an upside down U. "Think he's a good suspect?"

"Pretty good." I knew I was hedging, but I couldn't dredge up the stones for more.

Lowell sounded frustrated. "You needed to tell me that in private?" With me. With this small town. With this case.

Sucked down some air and then rushed out, "It appears that I ain't the only one who thought about it." Fought the bile bubbling up in my throat. "I was talking with my daddy and my brother." Just the thought of what I had to say pulled the words outta my mouth. "Lord." Was all I could manage.

Everything about him softened. Lowell stood up and took a step towards me. "What?"

Managed to control my urge to puke. Somehow, I sputtered out, "They formed a lynch mob." Felt like my chest might collapse into itself. "They took him out to the county line. Beat him down pretty bad and left him for dead."

A lot of silence flowed through the room for awhile. Finally, real quiet he asked, "Did he survive?"

Couldn't lie. "Nobody seems to know, sir."

Again, a long pause wound between us. "Think he died?"

"I can't seem to find out one way or t'other." With everything else, there weren't no reason to hide it.

"Lord have mercy." He huffed it out in one breath.

Let the silence flow again for a while before I spoke again, "I guess you're going take me off this case."

"I don't know," he admitted.

I didn't understand. My bosses always had the answers. "You don't know?"

All frustrated, he blurted out, "Who else I got to put on this?" Lowell threw up his hands in frustration. "It ain't a good position." It came out as a near shout. "We're between a rock and a hard place."

Like I didn't know that. "I know, sir." His tone got my back up.

Could smell the tension in the small room. We sucked on it for awhile. Then he snorted and clapped his hands. "All right." He sounded confident. "Short term plan. We find out if this Clay fellow is dead. If he ain't, then there ain't no problem. If he died, we give it to the State Troopers." Lowell slapped the desk. "And frankly, I can probably only justify maybe two days, maybe not that much, before I should call them in to take over." He paced the small room, talking his thoughts out. "You got it. And this ain't no favor to you," he shot the words like a weapon. "I got to get my head around this and talk to Sheriff Simple."

Couldn't do much more than belt out, "Yessir."

Lowell headed to the door and put his hand on the knob. "Get on it." He shot over his shoulder before he opened the door and stormed out.

CHAPTER 31

My conversation with my Lieutenant lit a spark under my butt. Headed back to my desk and pulled out my notes. I only had a day, maybe a little more, to figure out if Clay died from the beating. If he did, being gay was the least of my problems with my family.

Dialed the numbers I'd gotten through various databases for the two gals who'd owned the car Clay drove: starting at DMV and working out from there. Went through a few and struck out. The next number rang three times before a woman picked up with a, "Hello?"

Wasn't certain who I was talking with. This was my third try on the list of numbers. "Ms. Young?" The voice sounded a little young to be Clay's momma, but I couldn't be certain.

"Who's this?" She sounded suspicious.

"I'm Deputy Peterson with the Garfield County Sheriff," I explained.

Now she just sounded confused. "The what?"

Repeated myself, "Sheriff's Office in Garfield County Utah." Then I asked a more focused question, 'cause the number I'd come across belonged to Misty Young. "Your first name's Misty? Misty Young."

"Still Misty." She came across irritated. "Young before I got married." A pause, and then she added, "And, yeah, went back to it for a long time after my first divorce."

That explained it some. "I was wondering if you had some time to talk?"

"Right now." A few muffled bangs and some odd sounds came across the line. "Not really, I'm on my way into work." I heard a set of keys maybe jangling in a lock.

"I really need to talk with you." Tried to keep my tone

reasonable, reassuring to get her to cooperate with a voice over the phone. "I'm working on a case and you might have some information I need."

An aggravated groan was followed by, "I don't know anything about any crimes or anything, especially not in Utah."

"Well," I took a deep breath and kept it friendly, "I just need to pick your brain for a bit 'cause I think you may know somebody who I'm looking for." Didn't want to spook her so I added, "Case file says they gave a statement, and I need to verify it, if I can."

"Okay, look, I'm really running late." Something fell. "I got to go." I heard a click and then a dial tone.

Darn it all. I toyed with calling right back, but then figured she probably wouldn't even pick up. I'd have to put it off and try again later.

Got up from my desk and headed to find Lt. Lowell. Took me a bit, but I located him and Sheriff Simple back at the garage standing over the Charger I'd been using these last few days. Coughed into my hand so's to let them know I was there.

"Yep?" Sheriff Simple looked over his shoulder. "Hey, Joe."

I counted Myron Simple as one of my friends, didn't make him any less of my boss. "Hello, sir." Always made certain I treated him respectful at work. "Can I have a moment with the lieutenant?"

"We're done." Lowell turned and stared at me kinda blank faced. "Just deciding whether we're going to keep this vehicle in the condition it is instead of converting it over."

The condition it was equaled painted white with no markings or light bar up top. "Not make it fit in with the fleet?" A set of blue and red flashers sat behind the grill and in the back window, but nothing else on the exterior indicated it was anything more than a modern souped-up four-door.

"Might be high time to have an unmarked vehicle in the fleet." Sheriff Simple shrugged. "What you need, Joe?"

"Ah, well, this case I'm working," I didn't know how much the lieutenant filled him in on the goings on recently, "I talked to the potential informant a moment ago."

Lt. Lowell gave me a cold grin. "The sheriff is up to date on your case."

"Your sister's murder," Sheriff Simple nodded, "I understand the conflict."

"Okay." Kinda antsy all of a sudden, I shuffled a bit where I stood. "Well, I talked to Clay's sister. At least who I believe was Clay's sister."

The lieutenant scowled, his mustache dropping down almost horseshoe like over his mouth. "Anything useful?"

I shrugged. "She hung up on me. Gonna try again later."

"Well, it might be better done in person." The sheriff pointed out the obvious.

"I'd prefer to interview someone face to face." I really did. "Since she's up in Boise, well, that's the better part of a day." Good eight hour drive up there…seven and a half if you drove like I tended to.

Sheriff Simple furrowed his brows and added a glare. "Then take the day and do it."

"You're all right with me working this case?" I reminded both of them that we were so far off book at this point that the rules could have been written in hieroglyphics. "I'm mean, it ain't procedure."

"No, it ain't," the sheriff answered. "But I don't got a lot of people to spare. And we don't even know, yet, if a crime has been committed at least as to Clay," he reminded us all. "We get to that point, I'll re-evaluate."

I had to remind him there was at least one crime that they'd both admitted to. "We know they were involved in at least an assault."

"Decades ago." Sheriff Simple shrugged. "Nobody's going to be prosecuted for that." He walked up to me and patted my shoulder. "You go up on into Idaho, Joe, and talk to that informant. I got the sheriff's offices in Paiute and Wayne counties looking through their old records." Yeah, that would take his level of pull. Not that a request from any one of us line deputies would be ignored…it'd just get pushed to the back burner. "Seeing if they have any reports from then of an unsolved murder fitting the facts, or even what they may have written off as a car accident with that vehicle. State Troopers too, although they're pretty up to date with their database entries, so if they'd been involved it'd probably have popped on a search. It's going to take a while."

I sucked in a big ol' breath and muttered, "All right."

"Keep track of your expenses," Lowell instructed. "You got a per diem for this kind of thing. Get a not-in-service sign from the garage and don't break any speed limits in a county vehicle. You'll probably want to head up tonight." He pointed to the clean, white lines of the Chevy. "Having that Charger unmarked right now kinda works out right for this."

We all started walking back into the main station. "I'll call Boise PD and let 'em know I'll be in their neck of the woods."

Sheriff simple nodded, "Good," before he peeled off to his office.

Once he was outta earshot, I asked Lowell, "You don't think I'm compromised by it being my family?"

"I do, actually," he admitted. "But I also know that you want desperately to find this guy and hopefully not six feet under. So I figure I can trust you with that interview. Like I said, though," he poked my chest with one meaty finger, "I find out that boy died, you're off the case."

"Yessir," I acknowledged before heading to my own desk. Realized if I didn't get on outta here soon, I wouldn't hit Boise until long past midnight. Made a quick call to Boise PD to let them know I'd be interviewing a witness up their way, in case someone had issues: good manners and all. Straightened my desk, shut down the computer and then figured I ought to touch base with Kabe and let him know what was up.

He picked up on the third ring. "Hey." I didn't need to say much of a greeting since the number I called from would show on his cell phone. "You're working tomorrow, right?"

"Yeah," he answered, "it's a shift day."

"Okay, well I'm going to have to leave the station in a bit and drive into Boise." Hoped I'd get to see him at home for at least a few minutes.

He laughed. "Dude, you're kidding me, right?" It sounded like he thought I pulled his leg something awful.

I had no idea what amused him so. "About what?"

"Dude." The tone of that one word chided me for being stupid. "I told you, I'm leaving this afternoon to go to Boise."

He had told me no such thing. "No, you told me you'd be training with the BLM smoke jumpers." That I remembered.

"Yeah." He drew out the word. "Their base is in Boise at the airport."

"Oh. I didn't realize that's where they're at." I hadn't really thought about it, I just figured they'd be more local than that if they had offered Kabe a chance to hang out with them for a day.

Kabe cut into my thoughts. "Why do you have to go?"

"Tracked down Clay's sister," I explained. "She lives outside of Boise. I'm going to go interview her tomorrow. It's an eight hour drive, so I figured I'd head over today instead of leaving at three in the morning."

"Great." I could *hear* his smile. "We'll take one truck."

I didn't want to rain on his parade, but this weren't no social visit. "Well, I'm supposed to take a sheriff's vehicle."

"Who are you talking to?" The lieutenant's voice snapped my spine straight and spun me around in my chair.

"Hold on." I muttered to Kabe before I put the receiver against my chest. "My ah, you know…" I fished for the word.

"Your boyfriend, deputy?" Came out all matter a fact.

"Yessir." I nodded. "I forgot he's supposed to go for training in Boise tomorrow." I'd already got chewed on for hedging the truth once. Didn't want to have it happen again. "He was talking about going up together. I was going to tell him not a good idea."

Lowell pulled on the ends of his mustache. "He works for the forestry service, right?"

"Yessir. Firefighter with them," I confirmed.

"I think you can give a lift to a US government employee." I might have almost gotten a smile offa that man. Couldn't be certain though. "Tell him to wear his uniform. Probably a few less questions that way."

"Okay." I hadn't expected that t'all. "Thanks, sir."

He pointed at the phone still clutched against my shirt. "You going to tell him, or you just going to let him spin in the wind?" Then he spun on his heel and walked off. Abrupt hardly began to describe that man.

I fumbled the phone back to my ear. "Hey, I'm back. Lieutenant says it's okay as long as you're in uniform."

"In uniform?" Kabe sounded confused.

Tried to explain it as best I could. "Yeah, I think 'cause then it don't look like I'm taking advantage of the situation or nothing. It's obvious that we're both on duty, sort of."

"Okay, whatever." That was his classic *I ain't going to argue the point with you line.* "I'll get our shit together. When do you want to leave?"

"I got a couple more things to clean up, but if we get out of here by one, we should hit Boise by eight." Kinda thought it through in my head. "Find a cheap motel so we're not completely wracked up in the morning."

"I'm supposed to check in tonight with BLM guys." The disappointment of not being with me for the evening rang loud and clear. He tried to cut the bitter tone with an explanation. "They're giving me a bunk, 'cause we'll be out early doing basic training drills."

"All right." At least we'd get to ride up together and have dinner somewhere. "Well I'll drop you off and then I'll go find a cheap motel." Wouldn't be quite a date, but it might get kinda close to one.

CHAPTER 32

It was about eleven in the morning when I showed to pick Kabe up at the HQ of the Bureau of Land Management in the region. Dropped him off there last night. Seemed kinda odd to me that he was supposed to be here for a day of training but would be done before lunch. Pulled up into a parking lot surrounded by landscaping that looked like a wilderness meadow. A pathway lined with concrete markers, often stamped with a name, a unit and a date they died fighting a fire lead me towards the entrance. Folks left little stones, flags and toys next to some. A memory walk, so you knew every day who'd given their life. Every step I took jangled with all the gear I wore, me being in full uniform and all. There was a big old rack of bicycles just to the right of the building entrance. Walked inside to the lobby where they kept a mannequin in full smoke jumper gear.

A man in a blue t-shirt with the word *FIRE* printed in white across the back, gray shorts and flip-flops on his feet knelt next to a case with pamphlets and straightened 'em. Something about his attitude, the way he held himself reminded me of Kabe. He turned and stood when he heard me come in.

Don Stoddart gave me a big smile, "Howdy." Black shaggy hair and a soul patch didn't make him seem quite the fire-fighter, but his bright blue eyes, they had that confidence of a man who'd stared down his death in flames and come out the other side. "You're here for Kabe. His *friend* the deputy from last night." He offered out his hand in a shake. "Nice to see you again." I'd met him the previous evening when I'd dropped Kabe off. They'd all insisted I stay for a fire-house dinner and let me know if they'd known I was a'coming too, they'd have found me a bunk somewhere.

"Yep." Took the proffered hand. "Beautiful day, Don. Especially since the world ain't burning down." Let go my grip and crossed my arms over my chest. "So, what'd you have 'em doing today?" Couldn't quite think of anything else to ask.

"Today!" He barked out a laugh. "After you took off, we sent them out." He motioned me to follow him as he walked back into the building. "Basic training, put the rookies through paces. They humped in." He looked over his shoulder and gave me a feral grin. "They dug fire lines until three in the morning. Gave 'em a couple hours sleep on the ground and then they packed out eighty pounds of gear this morning. Kabe actually came in under ninety minutes." Don sounded impressed. "Lot of the actual recruits didn't. Gave 'em some food and let them crash. We'll kick the recruits out of the sack in a bit and start 'em running drills." He paused by a desk among a sea of desks where every person manning them seemed busier than all get out. Another nasty grin flashed. "They don't call it hell week for nothing." He buzzed an intercom and asked someone on the other end to go fetch Kabe.

"So why'd you ask Kabe to come along?" I'd been curious about it and hadn't really had time to ask Kabe. And dinner conversation, well it'd never gotten to a place I could ask it.

Sitting down at the desk, Don shrugged. "Think of it as a pre-interview, interview." He pointed to a vacant chair for me. "See if he's got the stamina for this kinda work."

I settled down to wait. "You want him as a smoke jumper?"

Another shrug. "He needs at least a couple-three seasons of wilderness fire work under his belt before he has enough experience to apply." Smoke jumpers were the elite of the elite in wilderness fire fighting. "But you know, I keep my eye out for guys with that certain combination of anal retentive and *the bug*."

"The bug?" I thought I might have an inkling what he meant, but I weren't certain.

He pushed his chair up against the wall and folded his hands behind his head. "Yeah, takes a certain kinda adrenaline junky to understand that jumping out of planes into the middle of bum-fuck nowhere behind a fire line, humping a ton of gear and living by your wits is the best job in the world." This grin told me

Don lived that feeling. "We got to talking with him over in Great Basin. Lots of good wilderness skills, he already knows sport parachuting and base jumping. That's nutso shit, we'd have to break him of some bad habits, but it means he has ideas of the risk and no fear of jumping out of a plane." Like he knew he'd made the right choice, Don nodded. "Kabe's got the bug."

Kabe enjoyed things that might make a lesser man pale. "He free solos too." Liked to climb mountains with nothing but a chalk bag, his body and his wits. "But when he does traditional climbs, does rescue work, he's meticulous." He and I climbed together when we could. I insisted on ropes though. I did not believe in the fall-you-die style of climbing. Enough necessary risks were inherent in the sport without adding unnecessary ones. Of course, we'd added a few unnecessary risks of our own a few times, but those generally happened when we were clipped in or at the top of a mountain.

"Kinda saw that streak in him," he acknowledged. "So, you know, a little encouragement, let him know we're paying attention to him so that he remembers us when he's ready."

"You think he'd be good at this type of work?" Personally, I thought so. I thought he could do anything he put his mind to really.

"If he keeps with the firefighting I think he'd be a good addition to our team."

About that time, Kabe stumbled through the door. We both stood and waited as he walked over. I might have hugged him, but not in front of a bunch of folks I didn't know. "How you doing?"

"Beat." He yawned. "Fucking beat."

I did reach out and bump his shoulder with my fist. "Shall we hit the road?"

He said his good-byes and we headed out. His hair was a bit damp and his uniform clean, so he must have caught a shower just before I arrived. Might have told him how good he looked in his green pants and long sleeved yellow shirt—the uniform of the National Parks Service fire-fighters—but I didn't want to stoke his ego too much. I figured him being invited here and knowing he'd skunked some of the rookies that applied would make him darn near insufferable, anyway.

Didn't take us too long to drive over to the suburb where Misty Young lived. We pulled up in front of one of those older stucco type houses they'd slapped together just after World War Two. Little run down with a chain link fence and a concrete driveway. Didn't see a car so I parked along the road and waited. Kabe dozed while the minutes ticked by. Finally, about five before twelve a blue compact car pulled into the drive. A woman, maybe forty-something got out juggling a set of grocery bags and her purse.

I popped the door on the Charger and hustled on across the street. "Misty Young?"

She looked up. "Yeah."

"Morning, ma'am." I tipped my hat and slowed down. "I'm Deputy Joe Peterson." Behind me, I heard the passenger door on my vehicle open and shut. "We spoke on the phone yesterday." Figured Kabe must've gotten out.

"The deputy from Utah?" Her face echoed the confusion in her voice. "Why are you here?"

"Well," I smiled. "I told you I needed to talk with you."

She looked over my shoulder towards the Charger. "Why is the ranger here with you?"

Figured she couldn't distinguish the uniforms when I looked back at Kabe. He'd come around the side of the vehicle and leaned up against it. I guessed he just didn't want to sit, but weren't about to get in the middle of this. "Oh, yeah, him." I turned back to her. "Well we both had business up here and instead of taking two vehicles…"

She snorted. "Even the government makes people carpool these days. Can I see your badge?" After I fished it off my chest and held it for her inspection, she asked, "Garfield County, where is that?" Misty's expression kinda told me she weren't sure it was real.

"County seat is Panguich." Figured that name might ring a bell from her past.

"Oh." The light went on behind her eyes. "My grandparents used to live up near there."

I nodded. "Yes ma'am, the Richardsons."

"Someone else owns the ranch now." Setting the groceries by her feet, she asked another question. "This have something to do with them?"

Guess I weren't going to get invited inside. "No ma'am. I need to talk to you about your brother, Clay Young."

"I had a brother named Clay." Misty shoved her hands through her short brown hair. "Young wasn't his last name though. That was my dad's name. His dad was Wayne Beauchamps."

"He didn't ever take your daddy's name?" I leaned against the side of her car.

"No." She sounded darn sure. "Why are you asking about Clay? He's been dead for years."

That one sentence sent ice water down my spine. Somehow, I managed not to sound as completely terrified as I was. "How did he die?"

"Killed in some kind of fight, long, long time ago." She didn't seem at all saddened by her brother's passing. "Good riddance."

The information did nothing to settle my mind. "A fight." Caught the tremble in my own voice. Behind me, the gravel crunched. Sensed as Kabe came up to somewhere near the back bumper of the car.

As I tried to sort the jumble of my thoughts, Misty asked, "So why are you interested in Clay?"

Thrown as I was, I didn't really mind my words like I ought. "I think he might have known something about a murder down my way, back when he lived with your gran'parents." The control of the interview had swerved off course a bit.

"Who'd he kill?" She did not sound surprised.

I still hadn't quite gotten my wits back with me. "Excuse me?"

She crossed her arms over her chest. "Who'd that son-of-a-bitch kill?"

"You don't sound like you're a big fan of your brother." I wanted to get back to Clay's death, but couldn't quite manage the thought process.

"I'm not." She snorted.

"I'm looking into the murder of a little girl."

"Still not surprised." She stepped over and rested her butt on the hood. "Clay was a sicko. I complained about him to Mom." Something about the tone told me all I needed to know about what she'd complained about. "Dad drove long haul trucks and wasn't around much. I was like five when Clay started in on me; touching and worse shit. Mom didn't want to believe me, kept saying I exaggerated." She looked over at Kabe and that made me glance back too. His face had gone all wide-eyed and slack. "Don't look so shocked, I've talked through it so many times in therapy and survivor groups that it doesn't hold the same kinda pain it used to. Mom never believed me. He was maybe twelve when it started…who wants to think your little boy is abusing your baby girl." She kept rattling on, confirming that Clay was the likeliest suspect I had. "Then, when he was fourteen, he got caught *playing doctor* with a neighbor girl. She was eight. Rather than have the dad blow his head off, mom shipped him off to my grandparents. Never saw him again."

Figured this might be my chance to steer it back to Clay's death. "After he went to Utah?"

"Wasn't sorry to see him go." She didn't answer my question, but gave me some more information on her not-so-favorite sibling. "I could finally have pets again. I had two kittens. He put one in a plastic bag and smothered it. The other he hung from a tree. Kept teasing me that I'd be next. Total sicko."

"He had a car, in Utah." Again, tried to get the interview back on track. "State records show you ended up with it."

"Yeah." Nodding, she set her hands on the car, on either side of her legs. "They found it in a ditch near him. They figured he'd been drinking, got into a fight and then wrecked."

"Oh." About all I could manage with that news.

"So they impounded it. Mom had to go down and take care of things. Brought the car back with her. My dad fixed it up and gave it to me when I went off to college."

Jumped in with both feet. "So the accident killed your brother."

"No." She looked at me like she thought I hadn't been listening to her all this time. "He died after a fight."

"He was in a fight and there was a car wreck and he died."

"What?"

"The night he wrecked his car, he died."

"Oh hell no." Like she swatted a fly, she brushed her hand through the air. "Creep was around for years after that. Mom kept sending him money and never stopped defending him. Even after three rape convictions."

Once more, the rug had been pulled right out from under me and left me flat. "Rape?" And I was so happy it happened this time round. All that tension I'd been holding for days felt like it was uncoiling all my muscles at once.

"Yeah. Clay was a real winner." She snorted again. "First time was in Colorado. He went to live there with his dad. They pled him to statutory because he was eighteen and she was sixteen. She was pretty slow, you know, so nobody was certain what really happened."

This interested me. At sixteen, she seemed a bit old for someone with Clay's proclivities…but then again if she was a bit slow, that still equaled low risk. "What about the others?" If he had a history of rape that meant I might find his DNA in some database somewhere.

"After he got out, he moved to Salt Lake with a cousin." Misty told me this all pretty matter-of-fact, like she'd run it through her mind enough to take the sharp edges off. "Caught him for another iffy one because the girl was supposedly his girlfriend, but he was twenty-four, I think, and she was fifteen. The next one, not so iffy." She banged the side of her car and smirked. "Her thirteen year old sister. He got her drunk and then took advantage of her."

If he was in my state's databases I'd track him down. "In Utah?"

"Yeah." She nodded. "They sent the bastard to prison. In Draper, I think. He was killed in a fight with his cellmate there."

Still wondered why I hadn't found Clay in any record. "When did he stop using Young?"

Misty shrugged. "I didn't think he ever used it."

"Your gran'parents registered him at school under Young."

"My grandparents hated his dad." I got another shrug. "Maybe they didn't want to hear Beauchamps being used."

Something didn't jibe with a couple things I'd only half heard because fear had clogged up my ears. "So Clay came back here after he was in the car accident in Utah?"

"No." She corrected my not so accurate memory. "Mom took the car back because he'd been drinking when he wrecked." She crossed her arms over her chest. "He decided, though, to go live with his dad."

"Did he ever talk to you about the car accident?" Wanted to know what might have been said that might not go down so good for my dad and brother.

"Not to me." A look of distaste screwed up her otherwise soft features. "I never really talked to him after he left. If he called and I answered, I usually hung up on him. He talked to Mom, but she never told me what they talked about."

"Okay." I wanted to find out the details to clear my kin. "What year was he killed?"

"Sometime in the nineties. I didn't go to his funeral."

"Do you know how it happened?" I prodded.

"Some fight in prison with his cellmate." Sounded like she neither knew nor cared exactly how it happened. Her next sentence confirmed that. "I was beyond giving a shit about Clay by then."

"Did you ever talk with your brother about what was going on in Panguitch, maybe a few weeks before his accident?"

"Hell no." Her hands went to her hips and she rocked back a bit. "Like I said, I didn't talk to him, *at all*. Didn't even want to hear his voice."

"Did your mom ever mention anything that Clay might have done while he lived with your gran'parents?"

"If she started talking about Clay," got the sense just how much Misty hated her brother, "I just walked away. He was out of my life and I was fine with that."

"Is your mom around?" Thought that I might be able get a bit more from their mother. "I couldn't find a good phone or address for her."

"'Cause she's dead." She didn't sound sad.

I mumbled out a platitude. "I'm sorry."

"Don't worry about it." Seemed like a lot of Misty's life hadn't gone well. "Cancer. Ten years ago. I've worked through it by now." Misty stood up and then reached down for a bag.

I guess this interview was over. "Anything else you can tell me about your brother?"

"No, sorry I couldn't be more help." She fumbled with trying to get more than one bag off the ground.

Stepped in and handed a few up to her. "You've been great. I appreciate your honesty." I'd have shook her hand before she walked away, but they was all full. Instead, I turned around to find Kabe grinning at me. I couldn't help but echo it right back. I almost yelled, "They didn't kill him."

"I know." He stepped in and grabbed my arm. "I heard."

Then he used that grip to pull me into a big, celebratory hug.

Right then, I couldn't have cared who saw. I was just so darn happy. When I could do more than just grin like a fool, I stepped back and laughed. "Let's hit the road. I'll make some calls."

We stopped at a place called Fanci Freez for lunch. Hamburger for me, that came with a slice of ham, Kabe ordered a couple of corn dogs, still sizzling from the fryer, and we shared an order of tater-tots, which they called gems, dipped in fry-sauce. 'Course, I could have eaten three day old road-kill and been satisfied, that's how high I was flying right then.

First person I called, my mouth full of burger, was my Lieutenant. Let him know what I found out. He went ahead and pulled Clay's rap sheet and told me he'd call me back in a few. Now that we had his real last name and could reason out his year of birth, it weren't too hard to lay hold of. Second call was to my dad. I don't know whether he was relieved or pissed. Think he might almost rather have sent Clay to meet his maker. Knew he likely wasn't going to keep that attitude. But you go through your whole life not really knowing whether, but thinking you might, have taken a life, well it was probably going to take him a bit of time to process it. Then I left a message for Sam, since he didn't answer his phone.

Maybe ten minutes after I hung up with Pa, Lowell called me back with Clay's social so I could run it with my on-board computer. We finished up and hit the road. I punched in the info as we pulled out of town. My radio might have been out of range, but the satellite data uplink worked just fine. Kept one eye on the road and another on the data. Clay Beauchamps, in all his unrepentant glory, scrolled across the screen. Young didn't show as one of his aliases. Since he'd never been arrested in Panguitch, and that's the only place he used it, the name wouldn't have been linked to him. Beyond the three big convictions his sister told me about, he'd been picked up on a variety of minor sexual type violations, groping and the like, but never charged. That meant, to my officer mind, that there were a ton of crimes at all levels in between that never got reported.

Kabe, strapped into the passenger seat, leaned against the side window completely zonked out to the world. I didn't know how he could sleep with me darn near whooping and hollering right next to him.

I don't think the world could get any more perfect right then.

CHAPTER 33

Walked out the front of the station and set my Stetson on my head. Yesterday's good news kept a bounce in my step. Across the lot, an old man wearing a set of prison stripes hoed the gravel patch between the parking area and the road. There weren't much reason to have a real fancy garden or nothing, since, in any direction you looked, scrub and chaparral stretched for miles. We did like it to look cleaned up a bit though. I headed over to where a uniformed corrections officer leaned against the grill of somebody's truck. Least it weren't mine. Touched the brim of my hat in greeting, "Morning, Dell." The officer jerked his chin back at me in an acknowledgment of sorts. He wasn't who I was there to see.

Took a few steps closer to the man I sought. "Hey, Karl, how are you doing today?" I'd waited for this particular moment to come and talk to Karl. Wanted him out and away from the rest of the zoo. I could have pulled him into one of interview rooms we shared with the attached county jail, but I figured I might get more out of him if he didn't feel quite as set upon.

Karl hacked at the base of a weed. "Just fine, deputy, just fine."

Tried to keep my body loose, easy, not intimidating. 'Least wise, not any more intimidating than a big guy wearing a weapon was bound to be. See, I'd come in this morning to a set of faxed over records from the State Prison in Draper, the ones for Clayton Beauchamp. They'd had the name of his cellmate in there. The one who'd killed Clay. A lifer named Karl Rife. "Got some time to talk?" Darn well knew the answer to it, but I wanted Karl to feel like he had *some* choice in the matter. We kept him here on a contract with the state. Mostly, 'cause of his age, for his own protection.

"I ain't got nothing but time." He turned his head to grin up at me…both of us kinda in on the joke.

Offered out a wrapped piece of chocolate. "Candy bar?" Mounds, Karl's favorite from what the guards said. I'd gotten one from the vending machine before I came out. Real treats like that, prisoners didn't get them much. Expensive, brand name sweets weren't stocked in the prison store.

Karl leaned on his hoe and gave me a squinty-eyed once over. "Now that, that sounds like someone wants information." All the suspicion of a guy who'd spent the better part of his life behind bars rolled out with that sentence. 'Course, he still reached out and took the candy.

I shrugged. "Maybe I do."

"What could an old guy like me tell you?" Karl unwrapped that candy like it held the most precious substance on the planet. "I ain't got nothing but memories left." That came out kinda mumbled…you know, what with that candy bar right up under his nose and him just breathing in the scent of it.

I left him to it. Sure enough I meant it as a bribe; something to shake his tongue loose. Convict code said you didn't give the monkeys like me what they wanted. But every man has a price. That price often varied by what information you might be looking for and how long a man had been behind bars. After he'd nibbled off a few bites, I prodded him, just a little. "And that's what I need, some memories outta that gray head of yours."

"Not much nobody can do to me now." Nobody likes snitches in lockup. Not the guards. Not the other inmates. "What can I do you for?" Karl'd been around long enough that most folks just ignored him anyway.

"You had a cellmate, years ago, guy named Clay. Remember him?"

He made me wait while he finished off the first of the pair of sweets in the package. Then he carefully wrapped up the other half and tucked it into the patch pocket on the front of his shirt. Ol' timer like Karl would know to parcel out his pleasure 'cause he weren't likely to get more any time soon. "I suspect you know the answer to that, deputy."

"I reckon I do some." Brutal, bloody, twenty-five up close and personal stab wounds to Clay's chest and sternum, made by a sharpened up bit of rusty metal pulled from the side of a bunk. Took the man out while he was sawing logs in his bed. Then Karl climbed back into his own blankets and slept like nothing happened. "You ain't never told no one why you did it." Nobody'd ever really figured it out. Karl hadn't talked much. Not that the officers had a hard time figuring it out: two men, locked cell, one dead, other one had to have done it.

"Didn't much matter." Karl shrugged. "Clay was just as dead and I was still in prison for life."

"Well, yeah, that's a fact. But you weren't known as the violent type." Karl, for being a lifer, was easy going and quiet. A few scrapes here and there to make sure folks knew not to push him around, but that equaled the one big shot o' violence for his entire tenure under the state's watch. None at all since he'd been transferred to us. "Looked at your record." Hadn't had cause to before now. I didn't work the jail side of the facility and wouldn't never unless we had a riot or something. "You went up for felony murder." Karl had the unfortunate luck to hook up as the getaway driver for two other idjits. "Pled out, rolled on the guys you robbed that store with and avoided the death penalty." They'd shot up the place and killed three people. The rule of law is: someone dies while you're committing a crime, everyone involved, whether they pulled the trigger or not, goes up on a murder charge.

"Well, I weren't none too bright sometimes in my choice of friends."

"Model prisoner up until that day." I fudged a little, nobody's ever clean all the time. But Karl had never really been a problem. Just one big spike when he took out Clay. "Model prisoner since that time."

Karl went back to messing with the weeds. "Nobody'd rubbed me wrong before then."

I pushed my Stetson back on my head. "Clay rubbed you wrong?"

"What do you think?" He gave me a sideways glare.

Figured I deserved that. "So, Karl, what do you remember about Clay?"

He chuckled. "I remember I didn't like him much." A bitter sound.

"Well, he was in your cell for two years before you took matters into your own hands." Stuck my hands under my pits. "What happened?"

"Realized I weren't gonna get out never anyways, worst they could do was put me in solitary a while. Didn't figure they'd up and kill me for taking out the trash."

"Why was he trash?" Karl shrugged and kept raking without answering my question. "I think I know why he was trash. I think he killed someone."

"Clay went up for raping two gals." He didn't look up as he said it. "Never got charged with killing no one."

"Yeah," I acknowledged. "But I'm thinking, two years, little cell, maybe he got a little comfortable and told you some things." Going after info from a con is like tossing a baited hook into the water, knowing there's fish under the surface, but not so sure if any one of 'em is going to bite. "Some things that made you think that weren't all he'd done."

Karl stood up, leaned on the rake and stared off into the mountains. "Know what I miss?"

There it was. This information equaled special. And special came with a bigger price tag than a candy bar. "Don't know."

"Funeral Potatoes and a steak."

"Steak and Funeral Potatoes?" Local dish, one of those things that the Relief Society showed up with whenever there was a tragedy that demanded food. Potatoes, lots of cream, chicken soup and cheese with crushed up corn-flakes on top; there ain't a kid in Utah that hadn't eaten their share of it.

"Yeah." He gave me a smirk. "I ain't had neither in twenty-odd years."

"You know." Uncrossed my arms and grinned back. "I might be able to rustle up a steak sandwich maybe, probably have to have it with fries and fry-sauce though."

"You wouldn't lie to me 'bout that?" There ain't a con who ain't been conned by the cops.

I never promised anything I didn't have intention following through with. "What would that gain me, Karl?"

He thought for a while. I had a reputation for shooting straight, not giving anyone any more hassle than they deserved. Still, suspicious, he asked, "What does a steak sandwich get you?"

"I want to know what Clay told you." No reason to lie to him. "You cain't be tried again for it. They cain't use it against you."

He nodded, although it didn't seem I'd settled the distrust that he lived with every day behind bars. "What does that get you?"

"I think I know what he may have told you and I *need* to know if I'm right." I had to know. Needed to be able to tell Pa and Sam that they might not have done what was right, but they'd at least done it to the right pervert.

He licked his lips and narrowed his eyes. "About what?"

This time I hesitated. You didn't want cons in your head, even ones as tame as Karl. "About my sister." Had to be rumor running through the guards by now. Small station attached to a smallish county jail—we all kinda knew each other's business. If the guards knew it, soon enough the inmates would too.

"And what if what why I killed him had nothing to do with him telling me nothing?"

I reassured him. "Then you still get your steak sandwich, Karl."

A sly grin spread across his face. "Might be a nicer place to eat it though."

I pointed at his chest. "Now you're pushing your luck."

"Deputy, if I were going to run off on anyone," he swung his stare over to consider Dell, "it'd be that idjit when he starts dozing off."

"True." I almost laughed. "All right, Karl, let me see what I can do."

As I walked into the station, I fished my cell of my hip and dialed the local private campground. They hadn't barely opened up for the season and I think Payton's RV was the only one there right then. They had a couple little cabins, off in a corner, with picnic tables. Could keep us out of the sight of most folks. Thought I ought to clear if the owners would be okay with it before I even asked if the warden would let me take Karl for a drive. Got a hesitant sure after I promised them it wouldn't be more than half an hour.

Then it took some arranging to be allowed to take Karl off site. Since he was pretty much a trustee, it had more to do with me not being a corrections officer than the jail being worried about him going. That straightened out, I picked up the phone again and called Kabe.

When he picked up, I jumped in with, "Hey. I'm going to call in an order at the diner." Didn't really want to involve Kabe in all of this, but another officer might shut Karl down. "Can you swing by and pick it up for me?" And I'd either need to send someone on a burger run or have Karl sit handcuffed in my vehicle while I went inside. I chose the least of a bad set of options.

"I guess." He didn't sound thrilled. "Can't you get off and pick it up yourself?"

"I'm kinda tied up with a project." I kept my voice low so no one else around me would hear. "You want something?"

Kabe was silent for a bit, before he answered, "Sure, turkey, avocado and sprouts on wheat."

"Avocado and sprouts?" I couldn't think of anything worse to put on a turkey sandwich.

"Bite me, dude." At least he laughed as he said it.

"When I see you." I split my cards fair but not all that honest, then I got serious again. "All right, look, swing by in about fifteen and grab the grub. There'll be three meals there. Bring 'em over to the RV campground over at the edge of town."

"Why?" Kabe sounded a might confused.

I explained without really getting into the details. "I'm taking someone out there to talk."

"Kinda wide open for a threesome." He kept with the teasing.

"Put a sock in it." I ordered. "I'll see you in a bit." Said that a little more soft. Once I hung up with him, I called Jane over at the café and placed the order telling her I'd come by after work and pay for it all. Jane knew me well enough to be okay with that arrangement. Then I headed over to the jail side to get this whole shebang started. The signing Karl out, making sure he weren't carrying nothing and getting him into handcuffs and into my vehicle took a bit. Let Karl just sit in the back and drink in the sights while I drove. He seemed content with that situation, didn't even ask where we were headed. I guess that anyplace that didn't have bars equaled fine by him.

Pulled off the highway into the drive of the empty campground. Drove to the back end of the lot and parked my vehicle so that it blocked any view that folks out on the highway might have of us. Didn't want anyone to be calling up the station and complaining about the guy in jail stripes sitting at a picnic table.

Not long after I got Karl out of the vehicle and shackled his leg to the metal post of the table, Kabe pulled in. He must have seen my patrol car, not like he could miss it. As I took Karl's cuffs off, Kabe clambered out of his truck. He held up a plastic bag holding some take out boxes. "I'm guessing one of these two heart-attacks belongs to you?" Fishing the first carton out, Kabe glanced at the top. "Double steak sandwich and fries, not one of Joe's favorites so yours?" He slid the box with Jane's blue scrawl indicating the contents over towards Karl. Noticed he kept a decent distance between himself and the old man wearing prison stripes. Then, a sour look crossing his face, Kabe handed me a yellow wrapped burger. "Cheeseburger, double pickle, hold the lettuce and tomato. What does Doc Snow say about your cholesterol?" He snipped. "At least you didn't order fries."

I rolled my eyes and huffed out, "Yes, mom."

Karl belted out a laugh. "My Lord, it's true."

Both Kabe and I turned to him. "What you on about, Karl?" I asked. Don't know what sparked his amusement.

"There's been talk among some of the guards that you'd found yourself a punk." He used the prison slang for a mouthy young man. Kabe shook his head and scowled 'cause he knew what the term meant. "I'd never have guessed you for a dick hound." And there was one for me being gay. Worked corrections long enough to have a handle on the vocabulary. That piece said, Karl looked up at Kabe. "Word on the block says you were a convict. Were you solid?"

Kabe grimaced. "I kept my head down and my debts paid." One way of saying, he tried to just get the heck out without creating any waves.

I hadn't wanted him to stick around. Bring the food and buzz off. "You don't have to hang around." Tried to put a wedge in the conversation.

Popping his carton open, Karl ignored me and asked Kabe, "How long? Where?"

"Two years." Kabe swung his leg over the bench on the opposite side of the table. He opened up his sandwich box and added, "Lompoc."

Karl leaned over his foam box like it held the most precious substance on earth and took a deep breath. I bet he hadn't smelled anything that good in years. Almost absently, he muttered, "Easy street."

Kabe chuckled around his next bite. "Hard enough to make me not want to go back."

"Smart punk." Karl gave him a big smile.

I realized, then, that having Kabe here probably set Karl more at ease than I could ever manage. "So, Karl." I unwrapped my cheeseburger. "Can I pick your brain?"

After a deep huff, Karl brought his sandwich up to his mouth. He didn't take a bite. He just savored the scent of the meat. "What you want to know, deputy?" He pulled a little piece of the steak out from the bread and nibbled it.

Let him have that small pleasure while I took a bite of my own lunch. Once he took a few bites like that, I prompted. "Talk to me about Clay."

"Gimpy?" My eyebrows shot up and Karl must have taken note. "Clay was in a fight when he was young. Always limped around so we called him Gimpy." He laughed at the old joke. "What's there to know?"

"Well," I thought a second, "start with, why'd you kill him?"

He shrugged. "I thought it was better that he not be out in the world."

"Why?" An honor code existed among cons. Certain offenses rated the death penalty. A few of those sins might have happened outside of prison walls and carried the stink in with them.

"I had, have, two daughters." Karl made me wait while he ate a bit more, before adding. "I ain't never given my family nothing but grief." Another slow, small bite. Man didn't wolf his food down, he savored it. "Figured I could make sure one less monster roamed the streets."

Most cons wouldn't consider murderers, thieves and gang-bangers monsters. "How old were your daughters?" A rapist didn't qualify as that either. Took a special breed of awful for that designation.

"When I went up or when I killed Clay?" Guess he saw the answer on my face. "They were married, on their own. My eldest had a daughter of her own then. She sent me pictures. Never brought 'em to see me, but my girls sent birthday and Christmas cards. Pictures of their babies. They turned out all right despite having me for a dad."

Kabe just sat across from me and ate. I think he might have

been sorry he stayed, but not quite sure how to get up and leave. Instead, he shifted and looked at me like he wanted to know what he should do. I didn't want to disturb Karl's train of thought so I moved my hand over the top of the table, telling him not to budge. Then I flashed a quick smile to put him at ease some. Kabe gave me a nod to tell me he got what I meant.

Jumped back into the reason I'd brought Karl out here. "And what about having your girls made you think Clay was trash?" Karl was the one who made the connection.

Karl sneered. "You mean other than he couldn't get anyone to give it to him, so he took it?" Rapists weren't looked on highly behind bars.

If Karl had an issue with Clay's crime, he'd likely have gone after him right off. Cons all knew who was in for what before new meat even had their cell assignments. "You lived with him for two years and the rape thing weren't bad enough," I pointed out.

"Right that." Karl nodded, set his sandwich down, picked up a fry and swept it through the fry-sauce. That he brought up to his mouth and licked a bit of the mayo-ketchup mixture off the salted fry. The way his face dropped into a mask of sheer ecstasy, it looked like the angels sang in his ears. If you don't know what heaven fry-sauce is then you ain't grown up in Utah. He shoved the fry in his mouth and chewed awhile.

"Look, deputy, Clay never came out and said, 'I did this.'" I didn't hear any lie in Karl's voice. I think he was being as straight with me as knew how. "In fact, he was always full of excuses, how girls led him on, so nothing ever was his fault." Karl grabbed another fry, swept it through sauce, and shoved that one in his mouth. I had to wait while a few more got treated the same way. Almost angry, Karl started back into his story. "He told me about this girl he 'dated.'" The word came out all nasty and sarcastic. Rapists sometimes called their attacks *dates*. "Said he took her for a ride every so often in this red sports car he had." Karl couldn't keep the disgust out of his voice. "And after a few years of that story, I started to put two and two together in my head. And I didn't like what it all added up to."

When he went quiet for too long, just eating and not talking, I prodded, "Which was?"

"By 'dated,' Clay meant the same way he 'dated' the gals who got him sent up." Karl got all thoughtful then, his voice dropping low and quiet enough that I had to lean in a bit to hear him. "There were enough things he said, too, that made me kinda think that girl didn't survive her 'date' with Clay."

I didn't want to hear it, but I knew I had to hear it. "Like what?" Had to make certain we was talking about Rosalie and not some other poor girl who got in Clay's way.

Karl ate some more…now he just chewed and swallowed, like there weren't no joy in the taste of that food. "Well, when he first got bunked with me, he knew I'd gone up for murder." Within hours of being processed into Draper, Clay would have had the low down on who to know, who to stay away from and who the corrections department gave him for a cellmate. "So he kept on me about how it felt to kill someone." Karl set the sandwich down and licked his fingers before he continued. "Now when he realized I weren't the trigger man, he said, and I remember his words, 'Never mind, you got to do it up close and personal to understand how it feels anyway.'" Karl huffed and picked at his fries. "Realized then that he weren't looking for my tales, he was looking for a buddy to swap his with." That got delivered with a grimace. "And when he talked about the girl and that red car of his, it was all about how he took her up to see this lake." Karl looked up at me, straight into my eyes. "And I don't know how to tell you, deputy, but I know, by the way he said certain things, that he left her up there and that's how he knew what death was like 'up close and personal.'"

That equaled a lot of detail without being so specific it made me suspicious that Karl lead me on. "You remember all that from one telling?"

"No." Karl pulled another slice of steak out from between the bread, shredded it and then put it between his teeth. "He talked about her all the time, like she was his special one, the others weren't special." Before I could ask what he meant, Karl explained, "He'd, once in a blue moon, say something about one of them."

"Lot's of men kill women they're with," I reminded him. Unfortunate, but true, gals were more likely to die at the hands of someone who supposedly loved them. "You never killed a one of those bucks." He'd have served time with dozens of guys like that.

Karl kept shredding and chewing down the little bits. "When he first started talking about how cute she was, with blonde braids and little dress, you know, I'm thinking she was probably 'round the age of the other girls." Guess Karl meant the ones Clay was convicted of having his way with; teenagers, which, by prison standards were considered fair game. "And then the more he talked over the years, I started understanding that he weren't just a rape-o." Every offense has a nick-name behind bars. "Clay should have been in the special cages with the other short-eyed sons-a-bitches." Karl growled that last out with a bucket load of hate.

Heard Kabe suck in his breath and I think I did too. Pedophiles, in prison, had a lot of nick-names. Short-eyes, from the way I heard tell, was 'cause they looked closer to the ground for their preference. "Like what did he say?" That breed of pervert got segregated from other prisoners for their own protection. Being labeled short-eyes, a molester, was a prisoner imposed death sentence to be carried out by anyone in stripes who got close enough to shank 'em. "What made you think that that one was a child?"

"He'd talk about seeing her riding her bike around this little po-dunk town he lived with his gran'parents in." Karl almost laughed. "Didn't think much of that 'cause other things I'd heard from him made me think he was in high school at that time." That got a shrug. "Then, one day he slipped and mentioned helping her fix her training wheel when it fell off. Tried to catch himself and say, 'I meant her little sister's,' or something." Karl sounded like that realization burdened him more than he ever wanted. Had to wonder what other things Clay told him about the girl that churned all sour in Karl's head after that. "But I knew the first way he said it was the truth."

I figured, from what I'd heard already, Clay's *special one* had been my sister, Rosy. "What details did he tell you?" The more I had, though, the more certain I could be.

"Truth, Deputy, it ain't what details he told me, it's what details he told me I still remember all this time later." That Karl did laugh at. He took a few more bites of sandwich, ate a few more fries before he huffed and started talking again. "All right, from what I can put together. He gave this little blonde girl, who he'd been friendly with before, he gave her a ride home from school, or maybe primary." Back in those days, little kids had church school once a week after school: Mormon Primary. "He knew her family, I think. Anyway, she got in his car and he took her for a ride and they had a date up by this lake. Like I said, he never said nothing direct about killing her, but just how he talked about how he left her, he described her almost like she was sleeping. This perfect blonde angel in her little yellow dress with the red stripe up the front." There weren't nothing in the file about that dress. "Don't know why I even remember that little bit." He shook his head. "I knew she was dead the way he talked about her."

The yellow dress with the red stripe, there weren't no way for Karl to have heard that from anyone but Clay. Karl wasn't local, born and bred up north in Salt Flats. His file, the prison jacket, said he had a brother in Montana. His daughters lived in California and Oregon. Normally, the system, when they contract out a prisoner, tries to stash them somewhere near family, but Karl didn't have none close. I guess we'd just had the space. And I figure, well, Karl could have mined a bunch of information from those cycling through the county jail system or the guards. That'd be a heck of a lot of effort that he weren't sure would ever pay off. If he made it up, well, he'd have sold me a lot more bull in minor details.

Plus, what nailed it in my head, he'd killed Clay years before

Karl and I ever crossed paths. I couldn't ever get a conviction off information that sketchy, but it settled my mind and I could close the case pretty solid.

'Course, it also spelled out a lock-tight motive for what Karl had done. "Clay was going to get released." Spoke more to myself to straighten it all out in my head. His daughters wrote him, sent him pictures of their little girls. Clay, being his cellmate would have had access to names and addresses…and a reason to maybe drop on over and make friends. "And 'cause you had a little gran'daughter out there…"

Kabe must've figured that out too, 'cause I heard him hiss, "Shit."

Karl gave him a smile and me an answer. "I couldn't do much for my girls, but I could keep that pervert, one who knew me, away from my own flesh and blood."

CHAPTER 34

Kabe'd taken off to the big store in Cedar after our lunch with Karl. Me, I let the man finish his food and just sit in the sun that probably felt a whole lot warmer without the jail looming behind him. When I figured I'd stretched the outing as long as I could without getting myself in hot water, I rousted Karl and loaded him in the vehicle. Got back to the station, signed Karl back into the jail and headed to my desk. Didn't see the sheriff or my lieutenant around nowhere, but I'd already given them the most important news: that my kin didn't kill Clay.

Still, I had to wrap this all up, neat and tidy. That meant filling out and filing my final reports. The first sheets were your standard forms. Then it was on to the narrative, working with the five W's plus an H rule: Who, What, When, Where, Why and How. Although, most times How came before Why in the report. Took me a good two hours to connect all the dots of information and make sure it read logically to my conclusion. If Clay still walked the earth, I'd have to use it to convince the District Attorney to prosecute. Here though, it was more about making certain we had enough evidence to button the case up as solved. Lord knows I'd never win any awards for storytelling, but I laid it all out clear enough. When I was all done, I made a copy for the file and one each for my superiors. Those I put on their desks for the morning.

Tomorrow I weren't going to be at the station. In fact, I planned to be busier than a fire-bug on the Fourth of July. Dropped by the diner to pay my tab and then headed to my folks place. Figured Dad and Sam should get a rundown of the major happenings. I'd also need to tell my momma that I knew who took her baby girl away from her and that whatever justice Heavenly Father saw fit to give out was being done as Clay had been killed by Karl.

Pulled up to house and parked in my usual spot at the side

of the road. Lacy and Tina's cars were parked behind my folks' Ford. Didn't see sign of Jim's car nowhere, and was thankful for that. It's really kinda hard to realize you just don't like one of your brothers. 'Cause if he weren't kin, I'd just not deal with him. I didn't have no choice here though. Got out of my vehicle and headed round back. Figured everyone would be in the kitchen anyhow. I was wrong.

My daddy puttered around the back of the lot. He didn't seem to have any particular project going on, so maybe he just had to escape the gaggle of females in his house.

"Hey, Dad," I called out a greeting.

He looked up and glared. "Hay is for horses."

Tried again. "How you doing?"

"Fair to middl'n." Dad stood up and slapped his hands on his thighs.

Waited until I got up close to him before I said, "Well, you'll be glad to know I figured out who did it, who killed Rosalie."

Crossing his arms over his chest, Dad rocked back on his heels. "And I told you I know who did it."

"All right," I conceded that he'd always believed it, "I have enough info that tells me you beat the snot outta the right guy."

"I never had no doubts," he grumbled. Guess he didn't like that I questioned him.

"Well now it's certain." I pushed my Stetson back on my head. "Maybe it'll help Sam."

Dad snorted, "The only thing that can help Sam is Sam." He bent down and picked up a small branch then he chucked it on the wood pile next to the shed. "Unless he decides he's had enough, 'till he hits bottom, he ain't going to give that sin up."

Knew my daddy was right, but I hated to just not try. "Maybe we could talk to him or something?"

That earned me a bitter laugh, "Lord, ain't that rich?"

"What?" I didn't like the tone he kept at all.

Dad turned to me, his face kinda sour. "You got the biggest sin of us all and you're going to talk him outta his?" His tone echoed with sarcasm and hurt and a lot of other emotions I'm sure he weren't used to feeling.

I was fair certain he knew the difference between Sam's drinking and my sexuality...one being an addiction, the other who I was. "Dad," I snapped. Mostly, 'cause I knew that tone. Striking out at someone else because his thoughts inside just couldn't be mastered.

He waved me off and wandered towards the side of the house. "I should have been more, I don't know, more forceful with you." Kept talking as he walked. "Not let your momma baby you so much. Maybe, maybe this wouldn't have happened then."

Followed him, 'cause I didn't have much choice. "What wouldn't have happened?"

"You wouldn't be all with that boy." He pointed off in the general direction of my place. "You know with these thoughts in your head and acting that way."

I had to work to keep the snot tone outta my voice. "What way?" Unfortunately, I kinda already had an inkling of what way he meant.

"All funny." That didn't clarify his thoughts none.

"Dad." Well, if he wouldn't say it, I would. "It's not like I walk around wearing dresses or nothing. I like hunting. I climb mountains for fun. You brought me up just fine. I just don't like women...not in that way."

"I should have been more strict." He shrugged. "Made you man up." His voice lacked conviction though. I think he just recited some things that'd hit his ears these last few days.

"How, Dad?" I actually laughed. "You taught me to ride a dirt bike, catch a football and shoot a rifle. Took me out to get my first deer when I was all of twelve. Camping. Fishing." I remembered near every one of those times as some of the best memories of growing up. "All of it. Lord, in high school, remember what they called me: *Pounding Peterson*? 'Cause I'd just pound the other guy into the ground when I tackled." Dad came to every game. "You made me a man. I am a man."

Dad rested his hands on the split rail of the fence and leaned into his palms. "I shouldn't have let you be alone so long." That came out even less sure than the last crazy thing he'd said. "We should have pushed, your momma and me. There were all those girls that liked you." He huffed. "We should have pushed."

"Know what, Dad, if'n I'd let you push me like that, you'd have two miserable people on your conscience." I came up beside him, turned and rested my butt against the rail. "I couldn't have never been with any of them, not like a husband should be." I'd met a few gay LDS men who'd tried to pretend they weren't who they were. "And any gal with half a brain would have felt that lie in her bones." At least with me, I couldn't never have made it work. "Maybe, I might have been able to keep it going long enough to get some kid outta it." Some of the men managed to have a family. All told me how big of a train wreck the whole thing had been. "But I can tell you that would have been a miserable experience for everyone concerned." Took my hat off and spun it through my fingers. "And I know it wouldn't have been thoughts of gals keeping it up."

"I don't need to hear that filth." He spat.

"It ain't filth and you need to hear it," I came back at him just as hard. "'Cause you gotta understand that this is as much a part of me, a part that cain't change, like my blonde hair or my blue eyes. It's just what I am."

"It's a choice, that's what the church says." Scripture actually didn't say one way or t'other. The Profit and the Apostles of the church, that was a different story.

Hard to fight against their words, 'cause Mormons are taught from birth that what comes out of the mouth of those thirteen men is the word of God delivered direct. "Know what, yeah, it's not a choice." All I could do is give him the truth and hoped it help settle my daddy's mind. "Unless you mean it's a choice for me not to live a lie."

He went silent for a bit. Just stood there and kneaded the rail with his worn hands. Finally, all quiet, he asked, "Know what hurts me the most? Hurts your momma?"

"What?" I didn't want to hear it, but I knew if we were going to get past this, I had to let him say his piece.

He stood up straight and looked me dead in the eye. "We deserved better."

I wasn't quite sure I'd heard him right. "'Scuse me?"

"I deserved better!" He pointed first at his chest then over at the house. "She deserved better! We deserved to hear it from you long ago, not the night we got back into town." His face went hard. "Not after its all blown up so big that there's a hundred acres of burnt ground around you."

"I didn't want you to," I dropped my eyes, "I didn't want you to worry."

Felt Dad step in close. "Lord, Joey, you think I didn't kinda suspect?" He near whispered that out. "I mean, I tried to tell myself I was just reading more into things than I ought, but…"

"You trying to tell me you knew?" I sounded bitter to my own ears.

"I didn't know." He said that with conviction. "I'd have some suspicions and then I'd just talk myself out of them." After a minute or two he added, "Joe, you're past thirty. You ain't never married. Heck, you ain't never had a girlfriend. You think we didn't start wondering?"

I wondered how many other folks I knew had been like that. "Dad, I'm sorry." Wasn't sorry for who I was. Was darn sorry they'd gotten dropped in the middle of a boiling pot.

"It hurts." He sounded hurt; wounded in his soul. "It hurts that you thought you couldn't trust us with knowing. I ain't settled in my heart or my soul about this, but I would've thought my son would've, I don't know, understood I wouldn't walk away from him."

"I didn't know how to, Dad," I repeated, "I didn't know how," 'cause I wasn't sure what else to say.

He put his hand on my shoulder and squeezed. "We'd have come home for you. I've heard from folks what happened. We'd have come."

"I couldn't ask you to." What I had done, how it all came about with the town finding out, was my own fault. I had to deal with it like a man should, on his own two feet. "I couldn't. You were needed. You had to help them set up that church there. It was your calling."

He offered up a sad ol' smile. "My family is my calling."

"Dad, it wasn't your cross to bear right then." Frankly, if my folks had been around to see the actual fire rain down, I weren't so sure I could have withstood it. I'd have been too busy trying to protect them, I'd probably have messed things up even worse. "I had to face it on my own."

"Joe. Oh, Lord, Joe." He let go of my shoulder and then ran his hand over the top of my head, mussing my short crop of hair, just like he'd done when I was a boy. "You are the strongest person I know."

I don't know where he got that idea. "I'm not strong."

"You're stronger than you know. Look around you. When everything is falling apart, there you are. My boy, Joe. Just takes control and everyone turns to you and you tell them what to do. Whenever I see somebody having a problem or there's a crisis… you're in the middle of it. Keeping folks calm."

"That's my job, Dad," I reminded him.

He held his finger up in the air like he lectured me, "It's your job because you found something right for you to do," as he started walking on back to the house again.

Weren't much I could do again but follow. "That's one way of looking at it."

When I caught up to him, he put his hand back on my shoulder. "I tell you, there ain't nobody people rely on, like they rely on you."

I had to slow down to walk at his pace. "I guess." I shrugged. I know it seemed strange, how my dad could sit on opposite ends of the fence like that, but that's how he always had been. Heck, that's how a lot of old men were: crotchety, opinionated and somehow able to make it all square in their heads.

"Look, Joe. I don't understand." Dad shook his head. "And I ain't goin' to lie to you and say this thing you got with that boy don't hurt me deep." One thing I could say about my daddy was he ain't never been nothing but honest with me. Wished I could say the same about myself with him. That, though, was water under the bridge at this point. "I don't half know how to deal with it…with the comments and the looks that I get just being your daddy. It's so heavy on me." He stopped at the back stoop. "And then I start pondering it and, Lord, what you must be going through. It must be a real deep part of you for you to tolerate that."

Didn't think he fished for reassurance, but I gave it to him anyway, "It is, Dad, since I could remember."

We didn't head inside just yet, 'cause I guess he had more to say that was meant for my ears and no one else's. "Even when you were little?"

"I always kinda knew." I might not have been honest with him before, but I could start right then. "Even before I realized what I knew."

"I don't know. I don't know as I'll ever understand it." He studied the toes of his shoes while he talked. "What I do know is, you're my boy. I love Sam, even though I don't approve of a lot of how he's lived his life, leaving the church and all. And honestly, that new wife of his, yeah, I told your momma that the reason he's still working game trails in the middle of nowhere Alaska is to keep as far away from her as he can." Sam retired from the game wardens in Montana and then took the same job in even more remote lands.

I chuckled, "That's going to be easy when that divorce gets final."

Seeming not all that surprised, Dad looked up, "He's divorcing her?"

"Other way around." Kinda twirled my hat around in the air to make the point.

"Oh." Dad nodded like he understood. "I could imagine Sam ain't an easy man to live with." I figured he probably was a bear to live with. Dad's heavy sigh called my attention back to him. "That's my biggest regret about that night. We shouldn't have involved him. I go to bed every night asking Heavenly Father to forgive me for doing that to Sam."

"It's out now." Forgiveness weren't mine to grant, but I could offer a little bit of hope. "Open wounds heal better."

Dad fell silent for a while, but didn't make a move to go in the house. By the expression on his face, it looked like he might be trying to sort a few more things out in his head. After a bit, he started with, "That guy you're with…"

"Kabe?" Reminded him of my boy's name.

"Yeah, him." Dad stuck his hands in his pockets. "Nice enough fellow, I guess." The complement sounded a bit forced, but I'd take it for now.

"Better than Sam's third wife?" I teased to break the tension between us.

"Boy," Dad snorted, "you could have brought home some sort of Hari Krishna gal who shaved her head and hit up folks on the corner for nickels and it would be better than that minx." There was no love lost between my folks and Sam's third wife, or his second one for that matter. Dad switched back to his first topic, "I mean, your guy, he's young. I worry about that. I worry about a lot more than that, but that's hard, Lacy says there's ten years between you."

I shrugged again. "We manage." What else could I say to that?

"Look, Joe, I'm not happy, not going to pretend I am, because I respect you enough to be honest with you."

You don't know how much a word can affect you, 'till you've

heard it said. My daddy saying he respected me, puffed out my chest more than I could ever imagine. There were problems, but we was gonna get over 'em. "Thanks, Dad."

'Course his next words took a little bit wind outta my sails. "I don't like what it's going to do to the few years your momma has left with us." Figured though, we best air it all out in his way. You had to let my dad walk himself into a corral, 'cause he'd just fight you on principal if you tried to push or pull. "But you're my son. I love you. More than that, I trust you." This conversation was one I don't think neither of us ever planned on having. "You're the one who's stood by us, here. All the rest of them, I know they love us, but they chose to live lives out and away from our little slice of Utah. If I need help with the plumbing or your momma needs a ride into Cedar to see a doctor, you're the one who's here. I don't even have to ask, you just offer."

"I'm your son," I reminded him that I knew my duty. "That's what I'm supposed to do."

"But, it's not what you have to do," he chided. "You don't ever take it like it's an obligation. You're happy to do it."

"I am." I was. "You're my folks."

"And I know, I know none of you want this." Both of us knew he talked about what was going on with my momma. My being gay and her being sick had to be the two largest bulls in the herd. "I don't want it, your momma don't want it, but that's what's been decided for her. And if I asked any one of them, your brothers and sisters, they'd step up. You were the one who stepped up before I had to ask. Stood up to your brothers and sisters and said, 'No, you're gonna stay here, among your friends and in your house and I'm gonna take care of you.'"

Felt my face go slack. "How did you know?" We'd all agreed none of us were going to tell my folks we'd had that talk.

"Oh, your brother's wife Jen." His face went sour. "I swear that woman should be writing plays, she likes drama so much."

Lord, of course it was her. "Daddy, you ain't s'posed to talk ill about folks like that." Didn't know what else to say since I'd been caught flat footed learning Jen had spouted off.

"Don't you lecture me in scripture, boy." He took my Stetson outta my hand and dumped it back on my head. He had to reach up to do it. "And it ain't talking ill if'n it's the truth. Your brothers and sisters they don't just jump in and do what's right. I have always known that my boy, Joey, would do by me and his momma without me ever having to ask. And I don't know how to deal with this part of you I don't understand." He slapped my shoulder. "I do know I respect the hell out of what I do understand."

My daddy almost never used strong language. "Really?" Sorta made his words mean just a bit more.

"Yep." He grinned. "I even respected you when I thought you were going to slap the cuffs on me. Haul me off 'cause you thought I'd gone and killed somebody."

Looked at him suspicious. "You respected me for that?" He had to be pulling my leg pretty fierce.

"Well, I'd have been angrier than a bear in a trap," he admitted, "but I always tried to make sure y'all knew your duty to man and God. You'd have hated yourself. You'd have done it though, 'cause you know what the law says you got to do. That takes someone with a heck of a lot of backbone." He snorted, "Maybe I did do you right growing up after all." Another pat on my shoulder and dad stepped over to open the door. "Let's go on inside an' let them all pretend they ain't been listening."

CHAPTER 35

When we walked on into the kitchen, everyone seemed real busy at doing not much of anything. 'Cept my momma. She sat at the table peeling potatoes. "What have you boys been talking about outside?" If my sisters had asked, I'd have called them out on a lie. Mom, yeah, she wouldn't eavesdrop like that. If my daddy and I needed to have a private word, then the men should get their space to do so. She'd expect the same thing outta any of us.

Took my Stetson off as I cleared the door. "Not much, Mom." Tina reached out and took the hat from me and then hung it the off a knob end on the back of a chair.

"Trying to figure out what you're making for dinner," my dad grumbled.

Lacy turned away from the stove and pointed at the ice-box. "Dinner is sandwiches in the fridge."

Tina went back to washing dishes. "Every burner is taken up for cooking for tomorrow." She would have had a bird's eye view on our little chat…hoped she hadn't heard most of it.

"Oh, that reminds me." Snapped my fingers up near my head. "I got to go throw the briskets in the smoker."

The front door banged, someone either coming in or going out, as Lacy asked, "Making brisket?" She grabbed a set of potholders and went to pick up a big ol' pot on the stove.

"Let me." Stepped in and took 'em from her. The pot was filled with hot water and macaroni. Hefted it up off the stove. "Yeah, I got like five racks of ribs to bar-b-q too." As I talked, she directed me over to the sink and grabbed a strainer to hold to the top. Tina backed outta the way of a potential third degree burn. "Kabe bought close to ten pounds of chicken thighs." Managed to drain the macaroni without getting more than a steamed up face. "I don't know what he's doing with that."

Kabe, followed close behind by June, teased me as he walked into the kitchen, "I hear my name being used in vain."

Wiped the little sheen of water off my face. "What the heck you doing here?"

"We were shopping." June raised up a couple fistfuls of plastic grocery bags.

For his part, Kabe rattled half a dozen of those cheap tin roasting pans against his leg. "Lacy sent June and I to pick up a bunch of these tins at the Dollar Tree down in Cedar City." He pointed to June's set of bags. "We also hit the super store for napkins and plates. I needed a butt load of butter that I forgot when I picked up things the other day." Sliding the tins onto the top of the fridge, the only kinda open space in the kitchen, he added, "And I had to pick her up from our place since she was raiding our pantry when you called me to bring lunch." Kabe turned, shoved his hands in his pockets and leaned back against the fridge. "Dude, why did we have ten boxes of lime Jell-o?" From that, I guessed some of the contents of those bags came from our house. "Canned fruit, nasty, still I understand. But, Jell-o?"

"I don't know." I kept a good two years' worth of supplies in there. Mostly dried beans, powdered milk and the like, but I had a few odd bits of things I'd picked up. "In case you want salad at the end times." I didn't even remember that I had Jell-o. Not something I'd have bought myself. Likely, it'd been given to me and I'd shoved it to the back of a shelf behind tinned meat and twenty pound bags of rice.

He rolled his eyes. "The only resemblance lime Jell-o has to salad is the color."

"We might not kill you for being gay." Tina smacked him on the arm with a spoon. "But that's verging on blasphemy."

Mom smiled up at him, "You will love my salad when you try it, Babe."

The whole room went silent, like the cabinets themselves sucked in their breath. I think it dawned on my momma that she'd called him babe and not Kabe, 'cause her eyes seemed to skitter back and forth while her mouth tightened up. I glanced at Kabe. He looked at me. If my face wore half the panic of his, we were all dead. Then he smiled.

All sly he stepped over to the table, set his elbow on the top and rested his chin on the back of his hand. "If you made it, darling, I'm sure I will." He purred, sounding queerer than a three-dollar bill right then.

Nobody breathed and then June started to snicker. My mom put her face in her hands. I could hear the shame, tinged with relief that Kabe'd turned her misstep into a joke in her own quiet laughter. I leaned over and swatted the back of his head. "How dare you call my momma, *darling*." I kept the tease in my tone though, playing through the joke to ease her embarrassment. "You're gonna make my daddy fight you for her honor and then I'm gonna have to fight him."

Dad took a swig of water from a glass he'd gotten himself. "Then everybody's going to be dead and that's gonna make for not much of a party." Managed to keep a deadpan face as he said it.

The domino of giggles that started rolled into guffaws and flooded the kitchen 'till none of us could hardly suck down air.

That's when Kabe's phone went off. I'd never really listened to his ring-tone. I maybe should have. This song parody started that, well, I think that if I could have shrunk myself down to an ant and crawled outta there, I would have. A lot of beat box rhythms and words that made it perfectly clear that Kabe hailed from San Francisco. He pulled the phone outta his pocket so quick he almost fumbled it on the floor. Took him a couple of swipes to stop the off color music from flooding the room.

"Kabe," he huffed into the phone once he got it to his ear. His face dropped into this serious mask. "Yeah. I'm sitting down," he lied. I did not like how he said that. Had no clue who he jawed with, but the tone made my balls want to dig foxholes in my belly. "What?" Disbelief crept into his tone. "Wait!" Kabe pulled the phone away from his ear and tapped the face with one finger. "Okay, everyone be quiet." As my family tried to hush themselves, he held the phone out between us and spoke into the air, "Say that again so Joe can hear."

Figured the phone was on speaker and was proved right when I heard Mr. Bulger's voice, "I said, you are a free man, Kabe Varghese!" He crowed. "The judge granted our motion!"

I didn't even think on it. I just grabbed Kabe up in this big ol' bear hug and spun him around. "You don't know how good that sounds!" I think we were both laughing like we'd done gone 'round the bend.

"I can imagine, gentlemen," Mr. Bulger belted out a laugh. "I can imagine."

Daddy looked at us like we'd lost our minds. "What are you two on about?"

My momma just steepled her fingers under her nose. It couldn't hide the smile that threatened to split her face in two. I could still see her lips fluttering in an unspoken prayer.

"Kabe's record." My own voice almost broke with how happy I was: for him and me. "They've got his probation taken away. No more checking in. No more worrying."

Kabe bounced in my grip. "Thanks." His own words were choked with the joy of it all. "Oh God, thanks." June came 'round and smashed us all in a three way bear hug. Kabe managed to spit out. "We'll get the last of the money to you as soon as we get the bill."

"Sounds fine." The connection crackled. "Now, I don't want to see you again, young man," His his lawyer chided. "Repeat business in my line of work, it ain't so good."

"Thanks so much." He held the phone up near our faces as June let us go.

"You're welcome." Mr. Bulger sounded pleased. My guess, he didn't often get to give out good news. "I'd say have a good evening, but I'm sure you will. Good-bye and enjoy your freedom." The line clicked dead.

"Somebody going to tell me what that was all about?" My daddy's face had gone cross.

"Walt." Mom smiled up at him. "When we went to Salt Lake, that was what the boys were doing. In court." I knew it seemed odd that my momma might forget Kabe's name, but remember all of that. But that's how it was with my gran'daddy too. You never really knew what was gonna stick and what wouldn't. And heck, she might remember it today and not tomorrow. Tempered my joy just a bit thinking on that. "We were going to make a cake for all the April babies, but I guess we'll have to add a *Congratulations* on it as well."

Kabe untangled himself from my arm around his middle. "Okay." He grinned. "But only if it says Congratulations, Babe. 'Cause I like that name."

That's when my momma threw a small potato at his head. Missed him. Hit me. And we all started laughing again. Worked it outta our systems as the gals went back to cooking. Dad got himself a sandwich while Kabe and June sorted things into what they needed at the house and what we had to pack over to the Social Hall tomorrow. When Mom went to get some towels outta the linen closet, I followed her. "Mom, can I have a word with you?"

"Of course, Joseph." She stopped and smiled back at me.

"Let's sit down." I walked over to the couch, sat down and waited until she joined me. "I have some news for you."

"You found him?" I didn't think she'd have to guess much at what news I might have for her these days.

"Yep." I nodded. "I'm pretty certain who did it."

"Is there going to be a trial?" A taint of panic crept into her voice. "I don't know as I could manage a trial."

Quick, I reassured her, "No, Mom." That was the one blessing outta this all, she'd be saved having to relive Rosy's death in front of a courtroom of people. "He was in prison for something else and another inmate killed him."

She put her hand over top of mine. "How do you know it was this man, then?"

"'Cause of things he said to his cell mate." I weren't about to give her all the gruesome details, thin as they were. Wouldn't help her mind to know any of that. "It ain't a hundred percent, but I'd be darn surprised if he ain't a match on DNA." Since he'd died in custody, the state performed a detailed autopsy. They also kept blood and tissue samples in case there might be later inquiries into prisoner deaths. I'd faxed over a request to the Medical Examiner in Salt Lake to pull it and whatever they might get from the evidence outta Rosy's file that I sent over for processing. Take a few months, but hopefully they'd be able to confirm it for me.

Mom didn't speak for a long time. Just sat there with her hand wrapped around mine. "What was his name?"

"Clay Beauchamps." She looked at me funny, like the name should mean something to her. "You knew him as Clay Young."

Saw the light dawn in her eyes. "He went to school with Sam and Tucker."

"Yep," I confirmed. "I've talked to his sister and the guy who killed him. I've read his file. That boy weren't never right."

"Did he hurt someone else?" Both my tone and, well, just the facts of Rosy's death might lead her to wonder.

I fibbed a bit. "Not like he hurt Rosalie." Weren't completely untruthful since he hadn't killed any other girls—as far as we knew. "But he ain't gonna hurt nobody else ever again."

"I knew you'd figure it out." She squeezed my hand. "I knew my Joey would do that for me." Then she let go and patted my arm. "Can you give me some time?"

"Sure, Mom." I stood up. "You need anything?"

"Hand me that picture of Rosy off the wall." Hustled over, took it off the wall and over to her. "Thank you. I just want to spend a little time with her memory." She traced the outline of Rose's face under the glass. "Let Lacy and Tina know to come talk to me when they've got the potatoes on the stove. I'd like to tell them, if that's all right?"

"Of course it is, Mom." I bent down and kissed her forehead. "I'll let the girls know." Then I left her there with whatever filled her thoughts. I don't think I'd ever tell her full on what happened. Since he hadn't killed Clay, I figured it was my daddy's piece to say if'n he wanted her to know what he, her brother, father and son had gone and done.

That was his debt to reconcile with God.

CHAPTER 36

Kabe walked in while I was basting the ribs with sauce, trying to get them done before we had to head out to the family reunion. "Okay. Ta Da." I half turned around to see him holding an oblong package wrapped in brown paper. "Your birthday present." The darn thing was near as long as his whole torso and almost wider than his shoulders.

I scowled over my shoulder, but kept to tending the meat. "I'm too old for birthday presents." Tried to just give the ribs an even coat. I always started with a dry rub, but finished them off with just enough sauce to keep the meat moist. Smoking, grilling and barbecuing are as much of a religion out this way as the LDS church. You got to do it right, or you just don't do it at all. "I don't need nothing." Whatever he was making bubbled on the top of the stove. The whole house smelled like a spice rack.

"See." He came all the way into the kitchen and set the present on the table. "That's just what Nadia said you'd say. But, screw you, you're never too old. And I got you one. Picked it up yesterday when I went down to Cedar and then forgot it in my truck last night."

I pushed the pans with the ribs on 'em back into the oven. "I don't need a birthday present." Then I shut the oven door and stood up all the way. I think I had half a cow in there.

He echoed my scowl from a moment ago. "This ultra frugal thing you got going on," he slung one arm across his chest, cocked his hip out and pointed at my nose, "so not going to keep me from surprising you."

Had to admit, I was a little embarrassed. "Ain't quite my birthday yet." I weren't used to getting presents from anyone but my family. "You could have saved it." And not really even then.

"Okay, honestly." Kabe rolled his eyes. "Where the hell am I going to hide this around here?" He flipped his free hand around in a circle indicating the big open area that made up the living space and kitchen. "It'll get broken if I keep it in my truck until your actual birthday." He dropped both hands on the tabletop and pounded out a drum roll. "So fucking open it."

After I stuck the basting brush in the cup with barbeque sauce, I stepped on over. "What's in it?"

"Sheesh." I got a snort. "For someone who doesn't need any presents you sound pretty anxious to know."

I rolled my eyes and then ripped it open. A large photo. He'd had it framed by what looked like reclaimed barn wood…so weather-worn it bore almost a silver sheen between the knots and burls. A gray-green mat took that earthy look one step further. In the photo, a swarthy man with long dark hair and not quite a beard and mustache sat on a piece of playground equipment made out of pier posts. He wore a loose garment like some of those Arab men I saw in the news; light colored, like a shirt that went down past your knees. You could see a city street through the fence at the back of the shot. About ten kids, different ages and races, gathered 'round him like they listened to him talk. One of them, a lanky, not quite teen, straddled a bicycle and held a surfboard under his arm. I recognized that wild black hair and eyes the color of the trees.

I tapped that place on the picture. "That's you."

"Yep." He offered me up one of his magical smiles.

Picked it up and walked into the great room with it. Then I held it up to get a better look. "What's it meant to be?" Sun was a lot stronger in there.

"Dude." Kabe laughed. "Don't tell me you don't recognize the Jesus with the Children scene." Like I'd shocked him or something, he slapped his chest with his hand. "I mean, I'm hardly religious and I know that one."

Soon as he said it, I saw what he meant. But that brought up another question. "Why?"

He held up a single finger. "One, I thought you might get a kick out of it." Instead of ticking off a second he pointed to the wall where the stairs went up. I had a print of Jesus on the Mount hung there. "Two, can we please replace that drug-store poster? Not slamming your taste, but seriously, how about some original art in this house?"

"So, you were in this one and decided to give it to me?" I couldn't help but frown a bit, trying to puzzle it through my head. "You had your grams send it out to you?" Not the why he'd chose something religious, but that he'd owned something religious.

"Actually, the photographer is a family friend." He jammed his hands in his pockets and kinda shuffled his feet. "I appeared in three of the series. A local church commissioned him to do a bunch of these iconic scenes, but set in San Francisco locales." I'd seen paintings with similar subjects, but most weren't half as nice as this. "Anyways, I emailed him and asked for a print, told him to choose the one he thought was best of me." When I didn't say nothing, Kabe prodded, "You don't like it."

"No, I like it." I smiled. "I like it a lot. It's just taking me a bit to wrap my head around this all." I passed it on over to him. "Here, you go hang it up and I'm going to get the brisket outta the smoker. We need to head over soon."

He held the picture out at arms length and repeated. "You don't like it."

"I more than like it," I insisted as I passed. Added a swat to his butt and a kiss to the side of his head. "I especially like that you thought through that all and gave me something that personal." Kept talking as I headed into the kitchen. "I just ain't used to people doing things like that for me." I upped the volume of my voice so's he could hear me. "Tonight, when we ain't so rushed, I'm going to take some time to really admire it," I promised.

Kabe'd grabbed a few more of those roasting tins for me when he'd gone to the store. Big ol' ones like you'd cook a turkey in. Lucky for me he had the foresight to buy 'em. Brought in the brisket and sliced it up. Had Kabe separate the ribs. Filled up a good four tins that way. Another tin went for his chicken dish and we had a massive bowl of rice as well. He let me taste a bit of what he cooked. I expected the flavor of curry, but that weren't it. "What is that?" Not as spicy as I expected: it tasted richer, smoother, creamier.

"Chicken Makhani." When I looked at him funny he gave me the English name. "Butter Chicken." Of course that didn't explain nothin' other than why he'd needed the butter. "My *dadaji* taught me how to make it." He folded the foil over the top and then stacked the chicken on top of a similarly covered pan of brisket. "You ready to go?"

"Let's make like trees," I switched it up just to mess with him, "and split."

Kabe huffed as he picked up the stack. "You are such a dork."

Took us a little bit to load up my truck. Not the carrying out of the food, but more of the arranging things in the back so nothing would spill on the drive into town. I ducked back in the house and changed into a short sleeve western shirt…since I'd almost upended the two tins of ribs and dumped sauce all down my other shirt. Had to listen to Kabe tease me about being a slob the whole trip. Not that it was a long way. The Panguitch Social Hall was on Center, just off Main in the central section of town. Been built in the 1890's with walls three bricks thick and a curved roof. It'd burned some in the 20's when the town still had dirt roads. Folks rallied round it and rebuilt the building rather than lose a community mainstay.

We parked along the west side and I got a couple tins of meat to carry in. As I stepped in the front door, a gray carpeted hallway lead off into the interior. From the back, a couple of voices carried towards me.

"Why are we doing this here," Jen's voice was the first that I could make out, "when we could have had the Ward hall at the church for free?"

"Because," Lacy answered her, "I wanted everyone to feel comfortable."

"And why should we make *him* feel comfortable?" Trust Jen to stir up trouble.

Tina snapped back, "Which him are you talking about, 'cause I can think of several people?"

All high and mighty, Jen poured out her poison, "You know who I mean."

"This is about Mom and Dad." Lacy didn't let anger rise, but I'd known her long enough to know she sounded pissed. "Not about you, Jen. He's one of their sons, he's my brother."

"Well, if you want my opinion," Jen snipped.

Tina shut her down. "No, I don't really."

That's about when I stepped into the kitchen. Kabe rode hard on my heels. "Hey, ladies," kept my voice as even as I could manage. "We got ribs, brisket and chicken." Most folks didn't cook back there, but they had places to keep food warm or cold, depending on what you needed.

"Joe." Jen put on a coyote's smile. "How are you doing? We were just talking about you."

"Doing fine, bitch." Kabe jumped in before I could answer. "Your voice carries half way down the highway."

I didn't think anyone's eyes could bug that far out of the sockets without falling on the floor. Jen sputtered, "Well, I never." After that, her jaw kept working but no words came out. After a few seconds of that, she tossed the towel she'd been holding onto the counter and stormed out of the room.

Under his breath, Kabe hissed, "Yeah, right."

Dropped the trays with the meat on a counter. "Would you not do that?" They didn't bang as much as I wished. "She's my brother's wife. I have to play nice with her."

Tina lifted the corner on the tin of chicken Kabe set in front of her. "Not like she plays nice with any of us," she muttered as she drank in the smell of it.

I didn't answer that. I knew Tina was right, still, I couldn't go down that road of awful…'cause, with how black my thoughts were, it would just sink me down to Jen's level. "She's going to fire off her mouth 'cause that's how she is, but there ain't no sense in loading her gun for her." Kabe's cussing at Jen just gave her more reason to call us perverts.

Kabe grumbled, but left it at that. Then we were too busy to even think about Jen's problems. Cousins I hadn't seen in ages started to come on in. First good hour was a lot of holding babies and catching up on things. I did notice that a fair share of folks kinda kept away from me and Kabe.

So be it.

Once the food was all laid out I found a spot along the wall, and settled myself in with a plate of more food than I'd probably actually eat. Most everybody local'd brought some sort of covered dish, salad or dessert. Kabe got all bent out of shape that what he thought of as salad hadn't made an appearance. He'd picked through it all and found a few things he deemed acceptable 'cause they weren't mixed in with noodles, cheese or thick sauce. Sam came over and plunked his butt down in a chair next to mine. Kabe ambled over just a hair after. Between the three of us, that pretty much established our section as the corral for the black sheep.

Kabe dropped down heavy in his chair. "Oh my God, your brother is such a BAT." He growled.

"A what?" Sam and I said it at the exact same moment.

"A BAT—Bay Area Tool." He jerked his chin to indicate Jim across the room. Wondered what got Kabe started. "Trying so hard to look hip, clued in, sound relevant, but really he has no clue." Well, I guess for the area chinos, button down shirt and loafers set Jim apart from most folks. Kabe leaned forward so he could take a bite of rib over the plate set on his knees. "He won't even eat the ribs you made." He growled around the mouthful.

"Good." Sam tore into his with gusto. "More for the rest of us."

"His loss, I guess." I certainly wouldn't want to live in a head filled with that much hate.

Kabe licked his fingers. "Like he could catch gay from the food."

That made Sam laugh, "Even if you could." He held up a bone that was picked clean. "For these ribs, I'd risk it."

After that I steered our conversation towards nicer subjects like mountain climbing and hunting. Had to give Sam the rundown on how Kabe and I met. Payton's family joined us for a while. Basically, we managed to enjoy ourselves without stepping on nobody else's toes. If they were inclined to socialize with me, they could. Those that didn't want to could avoid us. Everybody got to just keep the reunion peaceful and happy.

'Course, some folks just cain't leave be. I looked up and found Jim standing over me. "That's disgusting." He hissed. "Sitting like that in public, touching."

I don't know why he couldn't leave me to my life and go on his own way. "What?" I asked it like I was already bored with talking to him. "That my knee's bumping Kabe's or that my elbow is brushing Sam's shoulder?"

"You know." Sam kinda leaned closer up against me. "I'm your brother, so that's just buckets full of wrong." Every since they were kids, Sam couldn't resist yanking Jim's chain.

"You know what I mean." Jim sneered.

"Put a sock in it, Jim," I shot back. "You had to walk all the way across the room to say something nasty." Pointed out that he'd felt compelled to come over to us. We hadn't shoved nothing under his nose. "Ain't you got better ways to occupy your time?"

"James Henry Peterson." We all jumped, 'cause none of us noticed my momma come up on us. "Get off your brother's back." She may have been older and slower, but Mom's voice was still strong.

James turned to her. "Mom." I think I caught resentment, embarrassment and a little edge of holier-than-thou roiling across his features. "How can you tolerate this?"

"He's family." Her tone cut him sharp as she reminded him of what we'd been taught to believe. "Your brother, and that's all that should matter." Family had always come in only second to Heavenly Father himself. "So if you have nothing nice to say, then don't speak."

"I can't believe what you've done." James couldn't go without a parting shot. "How you've twisted everything."

All right, if he needed to believe that to make his world sit right, the heck with him. "Know what, Jim, been nice talking to you." Wanted to get up and slug him for pulling that bucket of angry out in front of momma, but it wouldn't do no good for anyone. Instead, I ignored him and smiled at Mom. "Made Kabe try your salad."

"Yeah." Kabe pushed about the little bits of shredded carrots embedded in layers of lime and orange Jell-o with a pretzel crusted bottom. "It was great." He shaded the truth, 'cause I knew he'd had about half a bite and then looked at me funny when he tried it.

Mom beamed. "See, I told you you'd like it."

James, I guess figuring he weren't going to get any more traction on his hate, stomped back across the room. He joined a knot of other folks who kept giving us sideways glares. Luckily, Mom seemed oblivious to that. We talked a bit more before she got called over to see one of her great-gran'babies doing something everyone thought of as cute.

Once she stepped away, Kabe huffed, "It'd serve him right if one of his kids turned out to be flaming." Yeah, we all needed to process that bit of nastiness.

Sam set his picked clean plate on a chair next to him and crossed his arms over his chest. "Serve him right if all his kids turned out to be gay."

"I wouldn't wish that." Kabe gave me a funny look so I explained, "I wouldn't want to curse those poor kids with having to deal with an uptight jerk of a father." Grabbed Kabe's plate, put it 'top of mine and stood. "I need some air, right now, I think." Jim may have left, but the thick cloud of hate he'd poured on still lingered.

Kabe jumped up. "Here, I'll go with you."

Figured a walk around the block would clear my head some, make me not want to blow someone else's off right then. I might have put my arm around Kabe, while we walked over towards

Main, 'cept, well, Jim's attitude was far more common than I really liked to believe. Most folks wouldn't say nothing, but a good share might. Still, comforted me to know that my folks, Momma especially, while not easy with the whole arrangement, they loved me enough to ride it through.

Kabe waited until we'd turned the corner onto Main before observing, "Your brother's a douche-bag."

Knew exactly which one he meant. "Yep," I agreed. Couldn't help the smile on my face. "And then some." Sometimes you just got to laugh at things you cain't change. We'd just passed the café and I was about to say something more, when I recognized three of four people walking towards us. Stopped and stuck my thumbs in my front pockets. "Afternoon, Sheriff. Lieutenant." I greeted them when they got a bit closer. "Connie." I'd met Sheriff Simple's wife on more than one occasion.

"We're all off the clock, Joe. Myron's fine." Myron held out his hand and I took the shake. Then he indicated the woman I didn't know. "Have you met Melissa, Jared's wife?" He nodded at me. "This is Joe Peterson, one of my deputies."

"Pleasure's all mine." We shook hands too. "Where you all headed?"

Connie pointed just behind me. "We were on our way over to the café just to get a bite."

"You're welcome to join us," Melissa added.

"No, we just ate." I'd given my boss an invitation to the reunion. "Why don't you come back with us?" I waved off to my right, off in the general direction of the social hall. "We got enough food to feed an army."

Connie slid her arm through her husband's. "We didn't think we should impose."

"Yeah, no." I smiled. We were doing that whole back country dance of manners. "It's no imposition." You got a party going you invite anyone who wanders by. Then they're supposed to make some excuses. That way everyone can be polite, but all knowing that the hospitality was offered and accepted in the right fashion. "My folks would be offended if you don't come over for a bit." That they would. "Half the county's here."

"Dude," Kabe leaned against the building, his hands jammed into his pockets, and teased, "you're related to half the county." Okay, I did have a lot of third and fourth cousins around, but he exaggerated as much as I had.

"Shut up." Then I realized that the Lieutenant, or his wife, ain't never met Kabe. "And pardon my manners, this here's Kabe."

"Nice to meet you." Lt. Lowell echoed his wife's words. Then he shrugged. "I did want to discuss something with you." He held his hand out indicating the direction we'd just come from. "I guess sooner rather than later works."

We all started walking back towards the hall. "What?"

The sheriff fell into step right next to me. "Got the final report from your doctor." His wife came up next to him and he put his arm around her shoulder. "You're all done with treatment." Made me kinda remember that I couldn't ever do that with Kabe around here. "We had a long talk yesterday with a couple of the county supervisors." Figured the *we* meant him and the lieutenant. "We're gonna take you off patrol."

I darn near tripped over my own feet. "You're firing me?" That was the only thing I could think of.

Myron belted out a big laugh. "Oh, heck no, Joe." He slapped me between my shoulder blades as if to knock some sense back in me. "If we was gonna fire you we'd call you into my office and do it private." He shook his head and kept walking. "You explain it, Jared, 'cause I'm putting my foot in my mouth."

"I told you I was going to bring this department into the modern era." Lowell switched places with the sheriff. "Part of that is we need someone who just focuses in on investigation." His face was serious. "We don't have enough bodies or big cases to make that your only assignment, but I've been reviewing some of the matters you've handled. You've got the knack and I want to put that knack to good use."

Kabe, at my other shoulder mumbled, "I don't get it."

I guessed what the lieutenant was hinting at. "I think he wants to offer me a detective assignment." The man's nod confirmed it.

"That's like a promotion?" Kabe still sounded a little confused and a might suspicious.

It wasn't a promotion, "Not, really."

"It's a prestigious assignment." The sheriff explained it over his shoulder. His next words were for me. "We ain't gonna take you off patrol entirely, but we get something big and messy come through the doors, then it's your job to focus on that. That work for you?"

"I'm floored, sir." I really was. "I didn't think Lt. Lowell liked me all that much."

Lowell scowled. "It ain't about liking or not liking someone, it's about using the resources of the department in the best way possible." Then he laid out a few more specifics. "It's gonna come with a little bump in pay and your hours may get a bit wonky. If we need you on scene at midnight one place and then six am that morning at another…that's what you're signing up for."

"Great." I couldn't hardly believe what they was saying. "Why wouldn't I do it?" I'd been done worried that somehow, once my disability was over, I might be out of a job. This though, sealed that I was still in good with the department.

"Work that way a few months and you can tell me."

Not sure I liked the sound of that. By then we'd made it back to the door of the Social Hall. I ushered them in and spent a bit doing rounds of introductions. Looked around for Kabe and saw him playing peek-a-boo with one of my gran'nieces. Brought a big ol' grin to my face to see him with my family like that. I'd never thought on having anybody to share my life with. And even on the few times I'd dared imagine it, I never really hoped I could make them a true part of my world. That scene right there, made me realize it just might be doable.

Walked on over to him and put my hand on his shoulder. He

looked up and flashed me one of those soul shattering smiles of his. Life might not be perfect, but it was right fine. I had my family and I had him.

Mostly, I had him. And that meant all the world to me.

About the Author

James Buchanan, lawyer by day and the author of the beloved Taking the Odds Series, the Deputy Joe Novels as well as many stand alone books, lives in a 100 year old Craftsman Home in Pasadena with SexyGuy, two demon spawn and a herd of adopted animals. Between trying cases, raising kids and writing books, James has spoken and read at conferences such as Saints & Sinners, the Popular Culture Association and the CARAS Alternate Sexualities Conference. James' Hard Fall (Honorable Mention 2010) and All or Nothing (Finalist 2011) were both honored by the National Leather Association-International's Pauline Réage Novel Awards, recognizing positive portrayals of the Leather Lifestyle in fiction.

In the midst of midlife crisis, James bought and learned to ride a Harley—it went with the big, extended-cab pickup in the driveway. A member of CorpGoth since 1993, James has been known to wear leather frock coats to court. If you don't find James at the computer working on the next book, you probably won't find the bike in the garage.

You can find information about James' latest works and upcoming projects at http://www.James-Buchanan.com

TRADEMARKS ACKNOWLEDGMENT

The author acknowledges the trademark status and trademark owners of the following wordmarks mentioned in this work of fiction:

Barbies: Mattel Inc.

Charger: Daimler Chrysler Group LLC

Chevy Cavalier: General Motors

Deseret Industries: Intellectual Reserve, Inc

Dollar Tree: Dollar Tree, Inc.

Explorer: Ford Motor Company

Fiat: Chrysler Group LLC

Hallmark: Crown Media

Honda: The Honda Motor Company

Jell-o: Kraft Foods Global Brands LLC

MG: MG Motor UK Ltd.

Mounds: Hershey's

Outback: OS Asset, Inc.

Polaroids: Eastman Kodak Company

Porsche: Dr. Ing. h.c. F. Porsche AG

Stetson: John B. Stetson Company

Taurus: Ford Motor Company

Toyota: Toyota Motor Company

VW Van: Volkswagen of America, Inc.

Zeus Electrosex Torpedo Plugs: ZeusElectrosex.com

Lightning Source UK Ltd.
Milton Keynes UK
UKOW05f1915290713

214580UK00001B/102/P